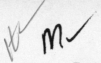

Praise for *Still Missing*

"An astonishingly well-crafted debut novel . . . will have you spellbound from the first page until long after you close the book."

—Karin Slaughter, *New York Times* bestselling author of *Broken*

"*Still Missing* runs deeper than the chills it delivers, the surprises it holds and the resilience of its main character. Ms. Stevens makes Annie a strong, smart woman who won't stop fighting to regain her sanity and equilibrium. She can't come back until she knows why she was taken away."

—Janet Maslin, *The New York Times*

"Crackling with suspense, this debut thriller stars Annie O'Sullivan, a young Realtor who recounts her year-long ordeal as a captive of a rapist she calls simply 'The Freak.' Her imprisonment, escape, and fraught reentry into ordinary life will have you glued to the page."

—*People* magazine

"This debut novel has the power to shock and awe with its explosively frightening premise about a woman who is kidnapped by a stranger and held against her will for more than a year. . . . This is one scary novel with a new twist on the classic kidnap and conspiracy story. *Still Missing* by Vancouver Island native and resident Chevy Stevens is sure to rock lovers of the thriller genre."

—*USA Today*

"*Still Missing* isn't just a gripping mystery about a woman's abduction, it's a story about her hard-fought return—to self, to independence, to life. Frank, fierce, and sometimes even funny, this is a dark tale pinpricked with light—and told by an unforgettable heroine."

—Gillian Flynn, *New York Times* bestselling author of *Sharp Objects* and *Dark Places*

"Grim and unsettling, *Still Missing* is a fast-paced read that is utterly absorbing."

—Kathy Reichs, *New York Times* bestselling author of *206 Bones*

"Stevens's impressive debut, a thriller set on Vancouver Island, pulsates with suspense that gets a power boost from the jaw-dropping but credible closing twist . . . [an] enthralling plot."

—*Publishers Weekly* (starred review)

"Chevy Stevens's *Still Missing* is a compelling, unputdownable thrill ride of a debut. The twists are so treacherous and unexpected, you'll need a neck brace by the time you finish."

—Linda Castillo, *New York Times* bestselling author of *Breaking Silence*

"Stevens's blistering debut follows a kidnap victim from her abduction to her escape—and the even more horrifying nightmare that follows. . . . A grueling, gripping demonstration of melodrama's darker side."
— *Kirkus Reviews* (starred review)

"Author praise of this highly touted debut includes comparisons to Karin Slaughter and Lisa Gardner, and those authors' fans will like this thriller. While this may be a stretch, the 'what-would-I-do' aspect of the reading experience may make this a match for some Jodi Picoult readers as well. Highly recommended." — *Library Journal* (starred review)

"This may be Stevens's debut novel, but it sure doesn't read like a first book. In fact, it's a knockout, a psychological thriller that pulls no punches and has a title that couldn't be more apt. Relentless and disturbing, Stevens's dark, mesmerizing character study follows a twisted path from victimhood toward self-empowerment. Sure to leave readers looking over their shoulders for a smiling stranger." — *Booklist* (starred review)

"Engrossing, terrifying, and ultimately full of girl-kick-ass, *Still Missing* will suck you in from page one."
—Chelsea Cain, *New York Times* bestselling author of *The Night Season*

"Simply terrifying." —Erica Spindler, *New York Times* bestselling author of *Bone Cold*

"Carefully and claustrophobically, Stevens crafts a double narrative of a woman's abduction and escape, and her attempts to recover and reclaim herself after the brutal ordeal. . . . With a gutsy but very human heroine, this book will abduct your reading time late into the night."
—*RT Book Reviews*

"At each turn of the page, you'll find yourself clutching the book with white knuckles and struggling to comprehend the sickening and terror-filled moments as this realistic and horrifying tale unfolds. A book that I truly couldn't put down, *Still Missing* is a frightening story that will leave a lasting effect." —*Suspense Magazine*

"A dazzling debut from Vancouver Island's Chevy Stevens. *Still Missing* brilliantly captures the terror of a kidnapped woman trapped in a cabin in the woods—and the puzzling aftermath of her escape." —*Chatelaine* magazine

"Chevy Stevens's novel is the most unnerving novel I've read since Thomas Harris's *The Silence of the Lambs*. . . . The conclusion is totally shocking and numbing. By far the best debut I've read this year and I'd be very surprised to read anything that tops it." —*Alfred Hitchcock Mystery Magazine*

STILL MISSING

CHEVY STEVENS

St. Martin's Griffin
New York

STILL MISSING. Copyright © 2010 by René Unischewski. All rights reserved. Printed in the United States of America. For information, address St. Martin's Press, 175 Fifth Avenue, New York, N.Y. 10010.

www.stmartins.com

The Library of Congress has cataloged the hardcover edition as follows:

Stevens, Chevy.
    Still missing / Chevy Stevens.—1st ed.
        p. cm.
    ISBN 978-0-312-59567-8
    1. Self-realization in women—Fiction.   2. Abduction—Fiction.
3. Women—Identity—Fiction.   4. British Columbia—Fiction.
5. Psychological fiction.   I. Title.
    PR9199.4.S739S75 2010
    813'.6—dc22

                                                2009047037

ISBN 978-0-312-57357-7 (trade paperback)

20 19 18 17 16 15 14 13 12 11 10

For my mother, who gave me an imagination

SESSION ONE

You know, Doc, you're not the first shrink I've seen since I got back. The one my family doctor recommended right after I came home was a real prize. The guy actually tried to act like he didn't know who I was, but that was a pile of crap—you'd have to be deaf and blind not to. Hell, it seems like every time I turn around another asshole with a camera is jumping out of the bushes. But before all this shit went down? Most of the world had never heard of Vancouver Island, let alone Clayton Falls. Now mention the island to someone and I'm willing to bet the first thing out of their mouth will be, "Isn't that where that lady Realtor was abducted?"

Even the guy's office was a turnoff—black leather couches, plastic plants, glass and chrome desk. Way to make your patients feel comfortable, buddy. And of course everything was perfectly lined up on the desk. His teeth were the only damn thing crooked in his office, and if you ask me, there's something a little strange about a guy who needs to line up everything on his desk but doesn't get his teeth fixed.

Right away he asked me about my mom, and then he actually tried to make me draw the color of my feelings with crayons and a sketch pad. When I said he must be kidding, he told me I was resisting my feelings and needed to "embrace the process." Well, screw him and his process. I only lasted two sessions. Spent most of the time wondering if I should kill him or myself.

So it's taken me until December—four months since I got home—to even try this therapy stuff again. I'd almost resigned myself to just staying screwed up, but the idea of living the rest of my life feeling this way . . . Your writing on your Web site was sort of funny, for a shrink, and you looked kind—nice teeth, by the way. Even better, you don't have a bunch of letters that mean God only knows what after your name. I don't want the biggest and the best. That just means a bigger ego and an even bigger bill. I don't even mind driving an hour and a half to get here. Gets me out of Clayton Falls, and so far I haven't found any reporters hiding in my backseat.

But don't get me wrong, just because you look like someone's grandmother—you should be knitting, not taking notes—doesn't mean I like being here. And telling me to call you Nadine? Not sure what that's all about, but let me guess. I have your first name, so now I'm supposed to feel like we're buddies and it's okay for me to tell you stuff I don't want to remember, let alone talk about? Sorry, I'm not paying you to be my friend, so if it's all the same to you I'll just stick with Doc.

And while we're getting shit straight here, let's lay down some ground rules before we start this joyride. If we're going to do this, it's going to be done my way. That means no questions from you. Not even one sneaky little "How did you feel when . . ." I'll tell the story from the beginning, and when I'm interested in hearing what *you* have to say, I'll let you know.

Oh, and in case you were wondering? No, I wasn't always such a bitch.

I dozed in bed a little longer than usual that first Sunday morning in August while my golden retriever, Emma, snored in my ear. I didn't get many moments to indulge. I was working my ass off that month going after a waterfront condo development. For Clayton Falls, a hundred-unit complex is a big deal, and it was down to me and another Realtor. I didn't know who my competition was, but the developer had called me on Friday to tell me they were impressed with my presentation and would let me know in a few days. I was so close to the big time I could already taste the champagne. I'd actually only tried the stuff once at a wedding and ended up switching it for a beer—nothing says class like a girl in a satin bridesmaid dress swilling beer out of the bottle—but I was convinced this deal would transform me into a sophisticated businesswoman. Sort of a water-into-wine thing. Or in this case, beer into champagne.

After a week of rain it was finally sunny, and warm enough for me to wear my favorite suit. It was pale yellow and made from the softest material. I loved how it made my eyes look hazel instead of a boring brown. I generally avoid skirts because at only a hiccup over five feet I look like a midget in them, but something about the cut of this one made my legs look longer. I even decided to wear heels. I'd just had my hair trimmed so it swung against my jawline perfectly, and after a last-minute inspection in my hall mirror for any gray hairs— I was only thirty-two last year, but with black hair those suckers show up fast—I gave myself a whistle, kissed Emma good-bye (some people touch wood, I touch dog), and headed out.

The only thing I had to do that day was host an open house. It would've been nice to have the day off, but the owners were anxious to sell. They were a nice German couple and the wife baked me Bavarian chocolate cake, so I didn't mind spending a few hours to keep them happy.

My boyfriend, Luke, was coming over for dinner after he was done working at his Italian restaurant. He'd had a late shift the night before, so I sent him a can't-wait-to-see-you-later e-mail. Well, first I tried to send him one of those e-mail card things he was always sending me, but all the choices were cutesy—kissing bunnies, kissing frogs, kissing squirrels—so I settled on a simple e-mail. He knew I was more of a show than tell kind of girl, but lately I'd been so focused on the waterfront deal I hadn't shown the poor guy much of anything, and God knows he deserved better. Not that he ever complained, even when I had to cancel at the last minute a couple of times.

My cell phone rang while I was struggling to shove the last open house sign into my trunk without getting dirt on my suit. On the off chance it was the developer, I grabbed the phone out of my purse.

"Are you at home?" *Hi to you too, Mom.*

"I'm just leaving for the open house—"

"So you're still doing that today? Val mentioned she hadn't seen many of your signs lately."

"You were talking to Aunt Val?" Every couple of months

Mom had a fight with her sister and was "never speaking to her again."

"First she invites me to lunch like she didn't just completely insult me last week, but two can play that game, then before we've even ordered she just has to tell me your cousin sold a waterfront listing. Can you believe Val's flying over to Vancouver tomorrow just to go shopping with her for new clothes on Robson Street? *Designer* clothes." Nice one, Aunt Val. I struggled not to laugh.

"Good for Tamara, but she looks great in anything." I hadn't actually seen my cousin in person since she'd moved to the mainland right after high school, but Aunt Val was always e-mailing just-look-what-my-amazing-kids-are-up-to-now photos.

"I told Val you have some nice things too. You're just . . . conservative."

"Mom, I have *lots* of nice clothes, but I—"

I stopped myself. She was baiting me, and Mom isn't the catch-and-release type. Last thing I wanted to do was spend ten minutes debating appropriate business attire with a woman who wears four-inch heels and a dress to get the mail. Sure as hell wasn't any point. Mom may be small, barely five feet, but I was the one always falling short.

"Before I forget," I said, "can you drop off my cappuccino maker later?"

She was quiet for a moment, then said, "You want it *today*?"

"That's why I asked, Mom."

"Because I *just* invited some of the ladies in the park over for coffee tomorrow. Your timing is perfect, as usual."

"Oh, crap, sorry, Mom, but Luke's coming over and I want to make him a cappuccino with breakfast. I thought you were going to buy one, you just wanted to try mine?"

"We were, but your stepdad and I are a little behind right now. I'll just have to call the girls this afternoon and explain."

Great, now I felt like a jerk.

"Don't worry about it, I'll get it next week or something."

"Thanks, Annie Bear." Now I was Annie Bear.

"You're welcome, but I still need it—" She hung up.

I groaned and shoved the phone back in my purse. The woman never let me finish a goddamn sentence if it wasn't something she wanted to hear.

At the corner gas station, I stopped to grab a coffee and a couple of magazines. My mom loves trashy magazines, but I only buy them to give me something to do if no one comes in to an open house. One of them had a picture of some poor missing woman on the cover. I looked at her smiling face and thought: She used to be just a girl living her life, and now everyone thinks they know all about her.

The open house was a little slow. I guess most people were taking advantage of the good weather—like I should have been. About ten minutes before it ended I started packing up my stuff. When I went outside to put some flyers in my trunk, a newer tan-colored van pulled in and parked right behind my car. An older guy, maybe mid-forties, walked toward me with a smile on his face.

"Shoot, you're packing up. Serves me right—saving the best for last. Would it be a huge inconvenience if I had a quick look around?"

For a second I considered telling him it was too late. A part of me just wanted to go home, and I still had to get some stuff from the grocery store, but as I hesitated he put his hands on his hips, stepped back a couple of feet, and surveyed the front of the house.

"Wow!"

I looked him over. His khakis were perfectly pressed, and I liked that. Fluffing my clothes in the dryer is my version of ironing. His running shoes were glaringly white, and he was wearing a baseball hat with the logo of a local golf course on the brim. His lightweight beige coat sported the same logo over his heart. If he belonged to the club, he had money behind him. Open houses usually attract neighbors or people out on Sunday drives, but when I glanced at his van I could see our real estate magazine sitting on the dash. What the hell, a few more minutes wouldn't kill me.

I gave him a big smile and said, "Of course I don't mind, that's what I'm here for. My name's Annie O'Sullivan."

I held out my hand, and as he came toward me to shake it, he stumbled on the flagstone path. To stop himself from falling to his knees, he braced his hands on the ground, ass up. I reached for him but he jumped to his feet in seconds, laughing and brushing the dirt from his hands.

"Oh, my God—I'm so sorry. Are you okay?"

Large blue eyes set in an open face were bright with amusement. Laugh lines radiated from the corners, leaked into flushed cheeks, and were commas to a wide grin of straight white teeth. It was one of the most genuine smiles I'd seen in a long time, and a face you just had to smile back at.

He bowed theatrically and said, "I certainly know how to make an entrance, don't I? Allow me to introduce myself, I'm David."

I dropped into a quick curtsy and said, "Nice to make your acquaintance, David."

We both laughed, and he said, "I really do appreciate this, and I promise I won't take up too much of your time."

"Don't worry about it—look around as long as you want."

"That's very kind of you, but I'm sure you can't wait to go and enjoy the weather. I'll make it quick."

Man, was it ever nice to meet a prospective buyer who treated a Realtor with consideration. Usually they act like they're doing us a favor.

I took him inside and chatted him up about the house, which was your typical West Coast style with vaulted ceilings, cedar siding, and a killer ocean view. He made such enthusiastic comments as he trailed behind me, it was like I was seeing the house for the first time too, and I found myself eager to point out features.

"The ad said the house is only two years old but it didn't mention the builder," he said.

"They're a local firm, Corbett Construction. It's still under warranty for a couple more years—which goes with the house, of course."

"That's great, you can never be too careful with some of these builders. You just can't trust people these days."

"When did you say you wanted to move by?"

"I didn't, but I'm flexible. When I find what I'm looking for I'll know." I glanced back at him and he smiled.

"If you need a mortgage broker, I can give you some names."

"Thanks, but I'll be buying with cash." Better and better. "Does it have a fenced backyard?" he said. "I have a dog."

"Oh, I love dogs—what kind?"

"A golden retriever, purebred, and he needs a lot of room to move around."

"I totally understand, I have a golden too, and she's a handful if she doesn't get enough exercise." I opened the sliding glass door to show him the cedar fencing. "So what's your dog's name?"

In the second that I waited for him to answer, I realized he was too close behind me. Something hard pressed into my lower back.

I tried to turn around, but he grabbed a handful of my hair and yanked my head back so fast and so painfully I thought a piece of my scalp would tear off. My heart slammed against my rib cage, and blood roared in my head. I willed my legs to kick out, run—to do something, anything—but I couldn't make them move.

"Yes, Annie, that's a gun, so please listen carefully. I'm going to let go of your hair and you're going to remain calm while we take a walk out to my van. And I want you to keep that pretty smile on your face while we do that, okay?"

"I—I can't—" *I can't breathe.*

Voice low and calm against my ear, he said, "Take a deep breath, Annie."

I sucked in a lungful.

"Let it out nice and easy."

I exhaled slowly.

"Again." The room came back into focus.

"Good girl." He released my hair.

Everything seemed to be happening in slow motion. I could feel the gun grinding into my spine as he used it to push me forward. He urged me out the front door and down the steps, humming a little melody. While we walked to his van, he whispered into my ear.

"Relax, Annie. Just pay attention to what I tell you and we won't have any problems. Don't forget to keep smiling." As we moved farther from the house I looked around—somebody had to be seeing this—but no one was in sight. I'd never noticed how many trees surrounded the house or that both of the neighboring homes faced away.

"I'm so glad the sun came out for us. It's a lovely day for a drive, don't you agree?"

He's got a gun and he's talking about *the weather*?

"Annie, I asked you a question."

"Yes."

"Yes what, Annie?"

"It's a nice day for a drive." Like two neighbors having a conversation over the fence. I kept thinking, this guy can't be doing this in broad daylight. It's an open house, for God's sake, I have a sign at the end of the driveway, and a car is going to pull up any minute.

We were at the van.

"Open the door, Annie." I didn't move. He pressed the gun to my lower back. I opened the door.

"Now get in." The gun pressed harder. I got in and he closed the door.

As he began to walk away, I yanked the door handle and pushed the automatic lock repeatedly, but something was wrong. I rammed my shoulder into the door. *Open, GODDAMMIT!*

He crossed in front of the van.

I pounded the locks, the power window button, tugged at the handle. His door opened and I turned around. In his hand was a keyless entry remote.

He held it up and smiled.

As he backed down the driveway and I watched the house get smaller, I couldn't believe what was happening. He wasn't real. None of this was real. At the end of the driveway he paused for a second, checking for traffic. My lawn sign advertising the open house was missing. I glanced into the back of the van and there it was, along with the two I'd placed at the end of the street.

Then it hit me. This wasn't random. He must have read the ad and checked out the street.

He chose me.

"So, how did the open house go?"

Fine, until he came along.

Could I pull the keys out of the ignition? Or at least press the unlock button on the remote and throw myself out the door before he grabbed me? I slowly reached out with my left hand, keeping it low—

His hand landed on my shoulder, and his fingers curled over my collarbone.

"I'm trying to ask about your day, Annie. You're not usually so rude."

I stared at him.

"The open house?"

"It was . . . it was slow."

"You must have been happy when I came by, then!"

He gave me that smile I'd found so genuine. As he waited for me to respond, his smile began to droop and his grip tightened.

"Yes, yes, it was nice to see someone."

The smile was back. He rubbed me on the shoulder where his hand had been, then cupped my cheek.

"Just try to relax and enjoy the sun, you look so stressed out lately." When he faced the road again, he gripped the steering wheel with one hand and rested the other on my thigh. "You're going to like it there."

"Where? Where are you taking me?"

He began to hum.

After a while he turned down a little side road and parked. I had no idea where we were. He shut off the van, turned to me, and smiled like we were on a date.

"Not much longer now."

He got out, walked around the front of the van, then opened my door. I hesitated for a second. He cleared his throat and raised his eyebrows. I got out.

He put an arm around my shoulders, the gun in his other hand, and we walked toward the back of the van.

He inhaled deeply. "Mmmm, smell that air. Incredible."

Everything was so quiet, that hot summer afternoon kind of quiet when you can hear a dragonfly buzzing ten feet from you. We passed a huge huckleberry bush close to the van, its berries almost ripe. I started bawling and shaking so hard I could barely walk. He lowered his hand off my shoulder to grasp the upper part of my arm, holding me up. We were still walking, but I couldn't feel my legs.

He let me go for a moment, tucked the gun into his waistband, and opened up the van's back doors. I turned to run, but he grabbed the back of my hair, spun me around to face him, and pulled me up by my hair until my toes grazed the ground. I tried to kick him in the legs, but he was a good foot taller and easily held me away from him. The pain was excruciating. All I could do was kick at the air and pound my fists on his arm. I screamed as loud as I could.

He slapped his free hand over my mouth and said, "Now, why did you go do something silly like that?"

I clung to the arm that held me in the air and tried to hoist my body up, to take away the pressure from my scalp.

"Let's try this again. I'm going to let you go, and you're going to get inside and lie down on your stomach."

He lowered his arm slowly until my feet touched the ground. One of my high heels had fallen off when I tried to kick him, so I was off balance and stumbled backward. The van's bumper hit the back of my knees, and I landed on my ass in the van. A gray blanket was spread out on the floor. I sat there and stared out at him, shaking so hard my teeth chattered. The sun was bright behind his head, turning his face dark and outlining him in light.

He pushed me hard on the shoulders, pressed me onto my back, and said, "Roll over."

"Wait—can we just talk for a minute?" He smiled at me like I was a puppy chewing on his shoelaces. "Why are you doing this?" I said. "Do you want money? If we go back and get my purse, I can give you my PIN number for my bank card—there's a few thousand in my account. And my credit cards, they have really high limits." He continued to smile at me.

"If we just talk, I know we can work something out. I can—"

"I don't need your money, Annie." He reached for the gun. "I didn't want to have to use this, but—"

"Stop!" I threw my hands out in front of me. "I'm sorry, I didn't mean anything by it, I just don't know what you want. Is it . . . is it sex? Is that what you want?"

"What did I ask you to do?"

"You . . . asked me to roll over."

He raised an eyebrow.

"That's it? You just want me to roll over? What are you going to do to me if I roll over?"

"I've asked you nicely two times now." His hand caressed the gun.

I rolled over.

"I don't understand why you're doing this." My voice cracked. Damn. I had to stay calm. "Have we met before?"

He was behind me, one hand on the middle of my back, pinning me down.

"I'm sorry if I did something to offend you, David. I really am. Just tell me how I can make it up to you, okay? There has to be some way. . . ."

I shut up and listened. I could hear small sounds behind me, could tell he was doing something back there, preparing for something. I waited for the click of the gun being cocked. My body shook with terror. Was this it for me? My life was going to end with me facedown in the back of a van? I felt a needle stab into the back of my thigh. I flinched and tried to reach back to touch it. Fire crawled up my leg.

Before we wrap this session up, Doc, I think it's only fair I fill you in on something—if I'm going to climb aboard the no-bullshit train, I should ride it to the end of the line. When I said I was screwed up, I actually meant royally fucked. The I-sleep-in-my-closet-every-night kind of fucked.

It was tricky as hell when I first got home and was staying in my old bedroom at my mom's, slipped out in the morning so no one knew. Now that I'm back in my old place, some shit is easier since I can control all the variables. But I won't set foot in a building unless I know where the exits are. It's a damn good thing you're on the ground floor. I wouldn't be sitting here if your office was any higher than I can jump.

Night . . . well, night's the worst. I can't have any people around. What if they unlocked a door? What if they left a window open? If I wasn't already waltzing with crazy, then running around checking everything while trying not to let anybody see what I'm doing would guarantee me a dance.

When I first got home, I thought if I could just find one person who felt the same as me . . . Dumbass that I am, I looked for a support group. Turns out there's no such thing as SAAMA, no Some Asshole Abducted Me Anonymous, online or off. Anyway, the whole concept of anonymity is bullshit when you've been on magazine covers, front pages, and talk shows. Even if I did track down a group, I'm willing to bet one of its wonderfully sympathetic members would be cashing in on my shit as soon as she walked out the door. Sell my pain to some tabloid and get herself a cruise or a plasma TV.

Not to mention, I hate talking to strangers about this stuff, especially reporters, who get it ass-backward often as not. But you'd be surprised how much some of the magazines and TV shows are willing to pay for an interview. I didn't want the money but they keep offering it, and hell, I need it. It's not like I could keep doing real estate. What good is a Realtor who's scared to be alone with a strange man?

Sometimes I go back to the day I was abducted—replaying my actions up until the open house scene by scene, like a never-ending horror movie where you can't stop the girl from answering the door or walking into the deserted building— and I remember the cover of that magazine in the store. So weird to think that now some other woman is looking at my picture, thinking she knows all about me.

SESSION TWO

On my way here today an ambulance came screaming up behind me—guy had to be doing over a hundred. Just about gave me a heart attack. I hate sirens. If they're not scaring the crap out of me, which isn't exactly hard to do these days—hell, Chihuahuas are probably more stable—they're sending me into family-flashback mode. I'd rather have the heart attack.

And before you start salivating over what possible hidden issue my ambulance hostility could be pointing to, thinking you're going to have me shrink-wrapped in no time, chill. We've just started digging through my crap. Hope you brought a big shovel.

When I was twelve my dad picked up my older sister, Daisy, from the arena where she had skating practice—this was during Mom's French cuisine stage and she was making French onion soup while we waited. Most of my childhood memories are wrapped in the aroma and flavors of whatever country's food she was into at the time, and my ability to eat certain foods depends on the memory. I can't eat French onion soup, can't even smell the stuff.

As sirens passed by our house that night, I turned the volume up on my show to drown them out. Later, I found out the sirens were for Daisy and my dad.

On their way home Dad stopped at the corner store, and then, as they pulled out into the intersection, a drunk driver ran the red and hit them head-on. Asshole crumpled up our station wagon like a used Kleenex. I spent years wondering if they'd still be alive if I hadn't begged my dad to pick up ice cream for dessert. Only thing that made it possible to move on was thinking their deaths were the worst thing that could ever happen in my life. Wrong.

After the injection into my leg and before I passed out, I remember two things: the scratchy blanket against my face and the faint scent of perfume.

Waking up, I wondered why I didn't feel my dog beside me. Then I opened my eyes and saw a white pillowcase. Mine were yellow.

I sat up so fast I almost blacked out. My head spun and I wanted to throw up. With my eyes wide open and my ears straining to hear every sound, I scanned my surroundings. I was in a log cabin, six hundred square feet or so, and I could see most of it from the bed. He wasn't there. My relief only lasted a few seconds. If he wasn't here, where was he?

I could see part of a kitchen area. In front of me was a woodstove and to its left, a door. I thought it was night but I wasn't sure. The two windows on the right side of the bed had shutters on them or were boarded up. A couple of ceiling lights were on and another was mounted to the wall by the bed. My first impulse was to run to the kitchen to look for some kind of weapon. But whatever he'd injected me with hadn't worn off. My legs turned to jelly, and I nailed the floor.

I lay there for a few minutes, then crawled, then pulled myself up. Most of the drawers and cupboards—even the fridge—had padlocks on them. Leaning heavily on the counter, I rifled through the one drawer I could open but couldn't find anything more lethal than a tea towel. I took a few deep breaths and tried to come up with some clue as to where I was.

My watch was missing and there were no clocks or windows, so I couldn't even guess at the time of day. I had no idea how far away from home I was, because I had no idea how long I'd been unconscious. My head felt like someone was squeezing it in a vise. I made my way to the farthest corner in between the bed and the wall, put my back into it as far as I could, and stared at the door.

I crouched in the corner of that cabin for what seemed like hours. I felt cold all over and couldn't stop shaking.

Was Luke pulling into my driveway, calling my cell, paging me? What if he thought I was working late again and forgot to cancel, so he just went home? Had they found my car? What if I'd been gone for hours and nobody had even started looking for me? Had anybody even called the cops? And what about my dog? I imagined Emma all alone in my house, hungry, wanting her walk, and whimpering.

The crime shows I've watched on TV cycled through my mind. *CSI*—the one set in Las Vegas—was my favorite. Grissom would've just gone to the house where I was abducted and by taking close-ups inside and analyzing a speck of dirt outside he'd know exactly what happened and where I was. I wondered if Clayton Falls even had a CSI unit. The only time I ever saw the Royal Canadian Mounted Police on TV was when they rode their horses in a parade or busted another marijuana grow-op.

Every second The Freak—that's what I called him in my mind—left me alone, I imagined more and more brutal deaths. Who would tell my mom when they found my mangled body? What if my body was never found?

I still remember her screams when the phone call came about the accident, and from then on it was rare to see her without a glass of vodka. I only recall a few times when I saw her outright drunk, though. Generally she was just "blurry." She's still beautiful, but she seems, to me anyway, like a once-vibrant painting whose colors have bled into one another.

I replayed what might be the last conversation we'd ever have, an argument about a cappuccino machine. Why didn't I just give her the damn thing? I was so pissed at her, and now I'd do anything to have that moment back.

My legs were cramped from holding one position too long. Time to get up and explore the cabin.

It looked old, like those fire ranger cabins you see up in the mountains, but it had been customized. The Freak had thought of everything. There were no springs in the bed. It was only two soft mattresses made from some kind of foam, lying on a solid wood frame. A large wooden wardrobe stood on the right side of the bed. It had a keyhole, but when I tried to pull on the doors they wouldn't budge. The woodstove and its rock hearth were behind a padlocked screen. The drawers and all the cupboards were made of some kind of metal, finished to look like wood. I couldn't even kick my way in.

There was no crawl space or attic and the cabin door was steel. I tried to turn the handle, but it was locked from the outside. I felt along its edges for brackets, hinges, anything that could be undone, but there was nothing. I pressed my ear to the ground, but not one sliver of light came through the bottom, and when I ran my fingers along the base I couldn't feel any cool air. There had to be one hell of a weather strip around that thing.

When I rapped on the window shutters they sounded like metal, and I couldn't see any locks or hinges on them. I felt all around the logs for signs of rot, but they were in good shape. Under the windowsill in the bathroom, I felt coolness on my fingers in one spot. I managed to remove a few pieces of insulation, then pressed my eye to the pencil-sized hole. I could see a blur of hazy green and figured it was early evening. I stuffed the insulation back in and made sure there were no remnants anywhere on the floor.

At first the bathroom with its older white tub and toilet seemed standard, but then I realized there was no mirror, and when I tried to lift up the lid on the toilet tank it wouldn't move. A steel rod ran through the fabric hoops of a pink shower curtain with little roses all over it. I gave the rod a good tug, but it was bolted in place. The bathroom had a door on it. No lock.

An island in the middle of the kitchen had two barstools bolted to the floor on either side of it. The appliances were stainless steel—those aren't cheap—and they looked brand-new. The white of the double enamel sinks and countertops sparkled and the air smelled of bleach.

When I tried one of the burners on what appeared to be a gas or propane stove, all I heard was a clicking sound. He must have disconnected the gas. I wondered if I could get any pieces of the stove apart, but I couldn't lift up the burners, and when I looked inside the oven I discovered the racks had been taken out. The drawer underneath the oven was padlocked.

There was no way I could protect myself, and no way out. I needed to prepare for the worst, but I didn't even know what the worst might be.

I realized I was shaking again. I took a few deep breaths and tried to focus on the facts. He wasn't there and I was still alive. Somebody had to find me soon. I walked to the sink and put my head under the tap for some water. Before I'd even taken a mouthful I heard a key in the lock—or at least what I thought was the lock. My heart lurched as the door slowly opened.

His baseball cap was off, revealing wavy blond hair and a face devoid of all expression. I studied his features. How had he made me like him? His bottom lip was fuller than the top, giving him a slight pout, but other than that all I saw was vacant blue eyes and a nice-looking face but not the kind of face you'd notice at first glance, let alone remember.

He stood there as his eyes landed on me and his whole face broke into a smile. Now I was looking at a completely different man. And I got it. He was the kind of guy who could choose whether he was noticed or not.

"Good, you're up! I was beginning to think I'd given you too much."

With a bounce in his step, he walked toward me. I ran back to the farthest corner of the cabin, by the bed, and, crouching, pressed myself into it. He stopped abruptly.

"Why are you hiding in the corner?"

"Where the hell am I?"

"I realize you probably aren't feeling a hundred percent, but there's no swearing here." He walked to the sink.

"I was looking forward to our first meal together, but you slept past dinnertime, I'm afraid." He took a huge key chain out of his pocket, unlocked one of the cupboards, and picked up a glass. "Hope you're not too hungry." He ran the water for a while, then filled the glass. He shut the tap off and turned to face me, his back against the counter.

"I can't break the dinnertime rule, but I'm willing to bend things a little today." He held the glass out. "Your mouth must be so dry."

Sandpaper was smoother than my throat right now, but I wasn't taking anything from him. He jiggled the glass. "Can't beat cold mountain water."

He waited a couple of seconds, an eyebrow raised in question, then shrugged and turned slightly to dump the water in the sink. He rinsed the glass out, then held it up and rapped his knuckle on it. "Isn't it amazing how real this plastic looks? Things aren't always as they seem, are they?"

He carefully dried it and put it back in the cupboard, which he locked. Then, with a sigh, he sat down on one of the barstools at the island and stretched his hands over his head.

"Wow, does it ever feel good to finally relax." Relax? I'd hate to see what he did for excitement. "How's your leg? Sore from the needle?"

"Why am I here?"

"Ah. She speaks." He rested his elbows on the island and steepled his fingers under his chin. "That's a great question, Annie. To put it simply, you're a very lucky girl."

"I don't consider being abducted and drugged lucky."

"You don't think it's possible that people can sometimes come to realize what they thought was a bad event in their life was actually an extremely good event, if they knew the alternative?"

"Anything would be a better alternative than this."

"Anything, Annie? Even if the alternative to spending some time with a nice guy like me was getting into an accident when you drove away from the open house—say, with a young mother coming home from the grocery store—and killing a whole family? Or maybe just one of the children, her favorite?" My mind flashed to Mom sobbing Daisy's name at the funeral. Was this creep from Clayton Falls?

"No answer?"

"That's not a fair comparison. You don't know what might have happened to me."

"See, there's where you're wrong. I do. I know exactly what happens to women like you."

This was good, I should keep him talking. If I could figure out what made him tick, I could figure out how to get away from him.

"Women like me? Did you know someone like me before?"

"Have you had a chance to look around yet?" He glanced around the cabin with a smile. "I think it turned out rather well."

"If some other girl hurt you, then I'm truly sorry—I am—but it's not fair to punish me, I've never done anything to you."

"You think this is punishment?" His eyes widened in surprise.

"You can't abduct someone and take them to . . . wherever. You just can't do that."

He smiled. "I hate to point out the obvious, but I just did. Look, how about I solve some of the mystery for you. We're on a mountain, in a cabin I handpicked for us. I've taken care of every detail so you'll be safe here." The guy fucking abducted me and he's telling me I'm *safe*?

"It took a little longer than I wanted—but while I was preparing, I got to know you better. Time well spent, I think."

"Got to—I've never even met you. Is David your real name?"

"Don't you think David is a nice name?" It was my father's name, but I wasn't about to tell him that.

I tried to speak in a calm, pleasant voice. "David's a great name, but I think you've got me confused with some other girl, so how about you just let me go, okay?"

He slowly shook his head. "I'm not the one who's confused, Annie. In fact, I've never been more sure of anything in my life."

He pulled the key chain out of his pocket again, unlocked a cupboard in the kitchen, grabbed a big box labeled "Annie" on the side, and brought it over to the bed. He pulled flyers out of the box, all from houses I'd sold. He even had some of my newspaper ads. He held one up. It was the ad for the open house.

"This one's my favorite. The address matches up perfectly with the date of the first time I saw you."

And then he handed me a stack of photos.

There I was, walking Emma in the morning, going into

my office, getting a coffee at the corner store. In one photo my hair was longer—I didn't even have the shirt I was wearing in it anymore. Had he swiped the photo from my house? No way he could have gotten past Emma, he must have stolen it from my office. He took the photos out of my hands, stretched out on the bed propped on one elbow, and spread them out.

"You're very photogenic."

"How long have you been stalking me?"

"I wouldn't call it *stalking*. Observing, maybe. I certainly haven't deluded myself into thinking you're in love with me, if that's what you're wondering."

"I'm sure you're a really nice guy, but I already have a boyfriend. I'm sorry if I unintentionally did something that confused you, but I don't feel the same way you do. Maybe we can be friends—"

He smiled kindly at me. "You're making me repeat myself here. I'm not confused. I know women like you don't get romantic feelings for men like me—women like you don't even see me."

"I see you, I just think you deserve someone who—"

"Someone who what? Is willing to settle? Maybe a tubby librarian? That's the best I can expect, right?"

"That's *not* what I meant. I'm sure you have lots to offer—"

"I'm not the problem. Women like to say they want someone who's always there for them—a lover, a friend, an equal. But once they have it, they'll throw it all away for the first man who treats them like a piece of garbage, and no matter what he does to them, they'll just keep coming back for more."

"Some women are like that, but lots aren't. My boyfriend is my equal and I love him."

"Luke?" His eyebrows shot up. "You think *Luke* is your equal?" He gave a small laugh and shook his head. "He would have been disposed of as soon as a real man came along. You were already growing bored."

"How do you know Luke's name? And why are you using past tense? Did you do something to him?"

"Luke's fine. What he's going through now is nothing compared to what you'd have put him through. You didn't respect him. Not that I blame you—you could have done so much better." He laughed. "Oh, wait, you just did."

"Well, I respect you, because I know you're a special guy who doesn't really want to do this, and if you just let me go, we—"

"Please don't patronize me, Annie."

"Then what is it you want? You still haven't told me why I'm here."

He began to sing, "Tiiiime is on *my* side," then hummed the next few bars of the Rolling Stones song.

"You want time? Time with me? Time to talk?" *Time to rape me, time to kill me?*

He just smiled.

When something doesn't work, you try something else. I got up, left the safety of my corner, and stood next to him.

"Listen, David—or whatever your name is—you have to let me go." He swung his legs over the side of the bed and sat on the edge, facing me. I leaned over right in his face.

"People are going to be looking for me—lots of people. It would be a hell of a lot better for you if you let me go now." I pointed my finger at him. "I don't want to be part of your sick game. This is *crazy*. You have to see—"

His hand shot out and grabbed my face so hard it felt like all my teeth were ground together. Inch by inch, he pulled me close. I lost my balance and was practically in his lap. The only thing holding me up was his hand on my jaw.

Voice vibrating with rage, he said, "Don't ever talk to me like that again, understand?" He forced my face up and down, tightening his grip with each down. My jaw felt like it was coming apart.

He let go.

"Look around, do you think something like this was easy to create? Do you think I just snapped my fingers and it all came together?"

Gripping the front of my suit jacket, he pulled me over him and pressed me back on the bed. The veins in his forehead had popped out and his face was flushed. Lying partly on top of me, he gripped my jaw again and squeezed. His eyes stared down at me, glittering. They were going to be the last thing I saw before I died. Everything was turning black—

Then all the anger left his face. He let go and kissed my jawline, where his fingers had been digging in seconds ago.

"Now, why did you go and make me do that? I'm trying here, Annie, I really am, but my patience has limits." He stroked my hair and smiled.

I lay there in silence.

He left the bed. I heard water running in the bathroom. With my photos spread around me, I stared at the ceiling. My jaw throbbed. Tears trickled out of the corners of my eyes, but I didn't even wipe them away.

SESSION THREE

Inoticed you don't have a bunch of Christmas junk in here, just the cedar wreath on the front door. Good thing, considering they say the holidays have the highest suicide rates and most of your patients are probably already teetering on the edge.

Hell, if anyone can understand why people go off the deep end around this time of year, it's me. Christmas sucked when I was a kid. It was hard seeing all my friends get shit I could only look at in store windows and catalogs. But the year before I was abducted? Now, that was a good year. Blew a fortune on gaudy ornaments and sparkly lights. Of course, I couldn't make up my mind on any one theme, so by the time I was done every room looked like a different float in some weird-ass Christmas parade.

Luke and I went on long winter walks complete with snowball fights, strung popcorn and cranberries to hang on the tree, drank hot chocolate laced with rum, and sang tipsy, off-key Christmas carols to each other. It was a goddamn made-for-TV movie special.

This year I could give a rat's ass about the holidays. Then again, there doesn't seem to be much of anything I care about. Like when I used your bathroom before our session today and caught sight of myself in the mirror. Before all this crap happened I couldn't walk by a store window without glancing at my reflection. Now when I look in a mirror I see a stranger. That woman's eyes look like dried-out mud and her hair lies limp on her shoulders. I should get a haircut, but even thinking about it wears me out.

Worse, I've become one of *them*—the whiny, depressing people who have no problem telling you exactly how shitty their end of the stick is. All delivered in a tone of voice that makes it clear they not only got the wrong end, you got the one that was supposed to be theirs. Hell, probably the exact tone I'm using right now. I want to say something about how pretty all the stores look lit up or how friendly everyone is this time of year, and they do, and they are, but I just can't seem to stop spewing bitter words.

Sleeping in my closet last night probably didn't help my attitude or the dark circles under my eyes. I started off on my bed—tossed and turned until it looked like a war zone—but I just couldn't feel safe. So I crawled into the closet and curled up on the floor, with Emma just outside the door. Poor dog thinks she's guarding me.

When The Freak came out of the bathroom he shook his finger at me, smiled, and said, "I don't forget the time that easily."

Humming some melody—I couldn't tell you what it was,

but if I ever hear it again I'll puke—he pulled me up from the bed, spun me around, and dipped me over his knee. One minute he's trying to break my jaw, the next he's goddamned Fred Astaire. With a laugh, he pulled me back up and led me to the bathroom.

Tea-light candles flickered on the counter, and the air was filled with the scent of burning wax and flowers. Steam drifted over the bathtub and rose petals floated on the water's surface.

"Time to get undressed."

"I don't want to." It came out in a whisper.

"It's *time*." He stared steadily at me.

I took off my clothes.

He folded them neatly and took them out of the room. My face burned. One arm was across my breasts, one hand over my crotch. He pulled them away and motioned me into the bathtub. When I hesitated, his face flushed and he stepped closer.

I got in the bath.

With that monster key ring he unlocked one of the cabinets and pulled out a razor—a straight-edge razor.

He lifted up my right leg and rested my heel on the edge of the tub, then slowly ran his hand up and down my calf and thigh. It was the first time I noticed his hands. There wasn't a single hair on them, and his fingertips were smooth, like they'd been burned. Terror roared through my body. What kind of person burns off his fingertips?

I couldn't stop staring at the razor, watching it move closer to my leg. I couldn't even cry.

"Your legs are so strong—like a dancer's. My mother was a dancer." He turned toward me but I was focused on the blade. "Annie, I'm talking to—" He sat back on his heels. "You're scared of the razor?"

I nodded.

He held it up so the light could reflect on it. "The new ones just don't cut as close." He shrugged and gave me a smile. Then he leaned back in and started shaving my calf. "If you remain open to this experience, you'll discover a lot about yourself. Knowing someone has life-and-death power over you can be the most erotic experience of your life." He stared hard at me. "But you already know how freeing death can be, don't you, Annie?" When I didn't answer, he looked back and forth between the razor and me.

"I—I don't know what you mean?"

"Surely you haven't forgotten all about Daisy."

I stared at him.

"What were you, again? Twelve, wasn't it? And she was sixteen? To lose someone you love so young . . ." He shook his head. "Things like that can really change a person."

"How do you know about Daisy?"

"Your father, now, he died on the way to the hospital, isn't that right? And Daisy, how did she die again?" He knew. The bastard knew.

I found out *how* at her funeral, when I overheard my aunt explaining to someone why Mom hadn't wanted her beautiful daughter to have an open casket. For months after that, my sister came to me in dreams, holding her bleeding face in her hands and begging me to help her. For months I woke up screaming.

"Why are you doing this?" I said.

"Shaving your legs? Don't you find it relaxing?"

"That's not what I meant."

"Talking about Daisy? It's good to talk about these things, Annie."

Another this-can't-be-happening wave rolled over me. I

can't be lying in a warm bath with some freak shaving my legs while he's telling me I need to get my feelings out. In what world does this shit happen?

"Stand up and put your foot on the side of the tub, Annie."

"I'm sorry, we can talk more. *Please* don't make me do that—"

His face went blank. I'd seen that look before.

I stood up and put my foot on the side of the tub.

Shivering in the cool air, I watched rose-scented steam roll off my body. I hate the smell of roses, always have. But The Freak?

He started to hum.

I wanted to push him away. I wanted to knee him in the face. But my eyes were riveted on the razor's shiny blade. He wasn't physically hurting me, just a little with his fingernails when he gripped my butt to hold me in place, but the terror was huge, a massive thing tearing into my chest.

Years ago I went to a doctor, an old guy I'd only been to once before. This time he had to do a Pap smear, and I still remember lying on my back with his head between my legs. He was a weekend pilot, and photos of airplanes were all over his office. As he jammed a cold instrument up me, he said, "Think about planes." And that's what I did while The Freak shaved me. I thought about planes.

When he was done and had rinsed me off, he led me out of the tub and gently toweled me off. Then he unlocked the cabinet, took out a big bottle of lotion, and started rubbing it on my body.

"Feels good, doesn't it?"

My skin crawled. His hands were everywhere, sliding around, rubbing the lotion in.

"Please stop. *Please*—"

"Now, why would I do that?" he said, and smiled. He took his time at it and didn't miss a spot.

When he was done he left me standing there on the stupid pink fuzzy bath mat, feeling like a greased-up pig and smelling like fucking roses. I didn't have to wait long before he came back with a handful of clothes.

He made me put on tiny white lace panties—not a G-string or thong, just regular panties—and a matching strapless bra. In my size. He stood back, gave me the once-over, and clapped his hands together, congratulating himself on a job well done. Then he handed me a dress—a virginal white thing I probably would have liked in a former life. Hell, it was a nice dress, felt expensive. It looked like that famous dress of Marilyn Monroe's but not so risqué, the good-girl version.

"Spin."

When I didn't move, he raised an eyebrow and made a circular motion in the air with his finger.

The dress floated around me as I twirled. He nodded his head in approval, then held his hand up for me to stop.

After he led me out of the bathroom, I saw that he'd cleared away all my pictures and the box was nowhere in sight. Candles were arranged on the floor, the lights were turned down low, and there it was, looking enormous: the bed. Ready and waiting.

I had to find a way to get through to him. Buy some time until somebody found me. Somebody would find me.

"If we waited, just until we know each other a little better," I said, "it would be more special."

"Relax, Annie, there's nothing to be scared of."

Mr. Rogers telling you it's a beautiful day to kill everyone in the neighborhood.

He turned me around and began to unzip the white dress. I was crying now. Not sobs, just stupid hiccupping whimpers. As he lowered the zipper all the way down my back, he kissed my neck. I shivered. He laughed.

He let my dress fall to the floor. While he undid my bra, I tried to pull away from him, but he held me firm with one arm around my waist. With his other hand he reached around and cupped my breast. Tears wet my face. When one dropped on his hand he turned me around to face him.

He brought his hand to his lips and covered the moist spot with his mouth. He held it there for a second, then gave a smile and said, "Salty."

"*Stop*. Please, just stop. I'm scared."

He spun me around and sat me down on the side of the bed. He never looked into my eyes once—he just stared at my body. A bead of sweat rolled down his face, dripped off his chin, and landed on my thigh. It burned into my skin, and I wanted desperately to brush it off, but I was scared to move. He knelt on the floor and started to kiss me.

He tasted like sour old coffee.

I squirmed and tried to pull away, but he just ground his lips harder against mine.

He finally left my mouth alone. Grateful, I gulped a lungful of air but it caught in my throat when he stood up and started taking his clothes off.

He wasn't a bulky guy but his muscles were well defined, like a runner's, and his body was completely hairless. His smooth skin gleamed in the candlelight. He stared at me like he was waiting for me to say something, but all I could do was stare back, shaking violently. His dick started to go soft.

He grabbed me around my knees and flipped me back onto the bed. As he forced my legs apart with his knee, he trapped one of my arms between our bodies and gripped the other above my head with his left hand, his elbow digging into my bicep.

I tried to twist away, bucking my hips, but he pinned my thigh down with his shin. His free hand began to tug at my panties.

My mind frantically scrambled over everything I'd ever learned about rapists. Something about power, they needed power, but there were different kinds, some of them needed different things. I couldn't remember. Why couldn't I remember? If I couldn't get him to stop, could I at least get him to wear a condom?

"Stop! I have a—" His chest pushed my fist into my solar plexus. I gasped out, "A disease. A sexual disease. You'll get sick if you—"

He tore my panties off. I started to buck wildly. He smiled.

Almost out of breath, I stopped struggling and gulped at the air. I had to think, had to focus, had to find a way—

His smile began to fade.

Then I got it. The more I reacted, the more he liked it. I forced my body to stop shaking. I stopped crying. I stopped moving. I thought about planes. It didn't take him long to notice.

He pressed down so hard with his elbow I thought my arm would break, but I didn't make a sound. He spread my legs wider and tried to force himself into me but he was soft. I noticed there was a mole on his shoulder with a lone hair sticking out.

He gritted his teeth, clenched his jaw, and grunted out, "Say my name." I didn't. There was no way I was going to call this freak by my father's name. He could control my body, but I wasn't going to let him control my words.

"Tell me what you feel."

I continued to stare at him.

He turned my face to the side. "Don't look at me."

He tried to force himself inside me again. I thought of that one mole hair. Everything on his body was shaved clean except that one mole. I passed by terror, arrived at hysteria, and started to giggle. He was going to kill me, but I couldn't stop. Giggles became laughter.

His body froze on top of me. I was still looking away, facing the opposite wall. His free hand shot out and clamped over my mouth. He turned my face back so I was looking at him, my lips mashed into my teeth. He ground his hand down harder. I tasted salt.

"Bitch!" he screamed, spraying me with spit. Then his face changed again. All life was gone. He leapt off the bed, blew out all the candles, and stalked into the bathroom. Soon I heard the shower.

I ran to the front door and tried the handle. It was locked. The shower shut off, my heart started to pound again, and I raced back to the bed. With my face turned to the wall, I sucked on my bleeding lip and cried. Tears and blood mingled. The bed sagged as he lay down beside me.

He sighed. "God, I love this place. It's so quiet—I put in extra insulation. You can't even hear the crickets."

"Please take me home. I won't tell anyone. I swear. *Please.*"

"I have the best dreams here."

He snuggled up to my side, folded his leg over mine, and held my hands until he fell asleep. I lay there with this naked freak cuddling me and wished the bed would open up and swallow me whole. My arm hurt, my face hurt, my heart hurt. I cried myself to sleep.

We still have some time left, but I'm finished. And, yes, I remember we're missing next week's session because of Christmas. Just as well—I need a break from this crap. To tell you about it, I have to go back there. Denial is a whole lot easier. Well, at least I can fool myself into thinking it is . . . for about half a second. Avoiding this shit is like closing a door on a raging river. Little trickles of water start coming through the cracks, and next thing you know, the door blows off. Now that I'm letting some of the water through, will the door come crashing in? If I unleash everything that's inside me, will I go floating down the river with it? Well, for now I think I'm going to go home and have a hot shower. And after that, I'll probably have another one.

SESSION FOUR

How was your Christmas, Doc? Hope Santa brought you something good. Dealing with a head case like me every week should've guaranteed you a spot on his "nice" list. Me? Well, despite my best intentions to avoid any form of holiday merriment or good cheer, it came knocking on my door. Literally. Some Boy Scouts came by selling Christmas trees, and maybe I was inspired by your wreath—or hell, maybe just by their being brave enough to knock on the only door with no Christmas lights—but somehow I ended up buying one. Always was a sucker for guys in uniform.

Problem was Mom had gotten rid of all my decorations, and every time I thought about going into a store . . . well, even if people didn't still stare at me like I have an elf growing out of my ass, I'd pretty much rather dance barefoot on broken ornaments than go into a store this time of year. Got so tired of looking at the damn tree sitting sad and naked in the corner that I dragged it down to the shelter in town. Figured someone might as well enjoy it.

Hell, there wasn't anything to put under it anyway. I told my friends and family I didn't want any presents, and I didn't go to any Christmas parties. I consider that my gift to the general public. No need to bring everyone else down. Compared to last year, this holiday's a raging success.

The morning after The Freak tried to rape me he made me shower with him. He washed me off like a child and didn't miss an inch. Then he made me wash him—all of him.

I had to stand facing the wall with my back to him when he shaved his body. I lusted after the razor. I wanted to slice his dick off. This time he didn't shave me. "Shaving is for bath time," he said. After we got out, he brought me some clothes.

"What did you do with my suit?"

"Don't worry, you never have to go into the office again."

He smiled. Today's choice was sexy underwear again, in bridal white, and a shift dress in a country pattern with little pink hearts on a cream-colored background. Something I never would have picked out—way too sweet and cute for me. After he gave me some flimsy slippers to wear, he sat me down on the stool while he made breakfast—porridge with dried blueberries. While I ate, he sat across from me and explained all my new rules. Actually, first he explained how truly screwed I was.

"We're miles away from any human being, so even if you did escape you'd never last outside longer than a couple of days. And if you're worried about how we'll survive, there's no need. I've taken care of everything. We'll live off the land, and the only time you have to be alone is when I go hunting or into town for supplies." I perked up—into town meant a vehicle.

"You'll never be able to find the van and even if you did, I've ensured you won't be able to start it."

"How long do you plan on keeping me here? You're going to run out of money eventually."

His smile grew.

"I don't deserve this, my family doesn't deserve this. Just tell me what I have to do so you'll let me go. I'll do it—I swear—whatever it is."

"I've tried to play women's games before, with some unfortunate results, but I won't make that mistake again."

"The perfume smell in the back of the van, on the blanket . . . is there another woman? Did you—"

"Don't you understand what a fantastic gift this is? This is your *redemption*, Annie."

"I don't understand *any* of this. None of it makes sense. Why are you doing this to me?"

He shrugged. "An opportunity arose and there you were. Sometimes good things happen to good people."

"This isn't a *good* thing. This is wrong." I glared at him. "You can't just take me away from every—"

"What exactly did I take you away from? Your boyfriend? We've already discussed him. Your mother? In general I find people rather tedious, but watching you two have lunch? People reveal so much through their body language. Your only real relationship is with your dog."

"I have a *life*."

"No, you merely existed. But I'm giving you a second chance and I suggest you pay attention—there won't be a third. Every morning after breakfast we'll have exercise time, then a shower. We had one before breakfast today, but there'll be no deviations from the schedule in the future."

He walked over to the wardrobe and unlocked it.

"I'll be choosing your clothes for the day." He held up a couple of dresses cut like the one I was wearing, one with navy hearts on a powder-blue background and the other just solid pale pink. My hatred for pink was escalating. Stacks of what was probably the same dress in various colors filled the top shelf. He reached back in and pulled out a lavender wool cardigan. "Winters can be cold up here."

Several sets of the same outfit he was wearing, beige shirt and pants, lined the lower shelf. And to the side I spotted a couple of beige sweaters. He noticed the direction of my gaze, smiled, then said, "You're the only color I need," and rolled right on.

"After you're dressed, I'll go outside and do my chores— yours are inside. You'll wash the dishes, make the bed, and do the laundry." He took a plate out of the cupboard and slammed it against the counter. "Incredible, isn't it? Made by the same company as the glass." Next he pulled out a pot and swung it through the air like a baseball bat. "Light as a feather, and in one piece too. I don't know how they do it." He shook his head.

"I'll spray down all the surfaces myself." He unlocked the cupboard under the sink and brought out a bottle of household cleaner. I noticed it was biodegradable but didn't recognize the brand.

"The cleaning fluid will be locked up at all times and you'll never be allowed to handle hot water or any utensils I feel are unsafe. After you're done with your cleaning duties, I expect you to finish your personal grooming. Your fingernails, which are a mess, must be perfect, and I'll file them for you. Your feet should be soft and your toenails painted. Women should have long hair, so I'll rub conditioner in yours to help it grow faster. You won't be wearing any makeup.

"Our day will start at seven A.M., lunch is at twelve sharp, and afternoons will be spent studying any books I require you to learn. I'll inspect your chores at five, dinner will be at seven, and after dinner you'll clean up again and then read to me. After reading hour, I'll bathe you, then it's lights out at ten o'clock."

He showed me a small pocket watch with a timer on it, like a stopwatch, that he kept on a key chain in his front pocket. No other clocks were in the cabin, so I never knew what time it was unless he told me.

"You'll be allowed to relieve yourself four times a day. These breaks will be supervised, and the bathroom door will be left open. In fact . . ." He glanced at the watch. "It's your first bathroom break now." I took the long way around the kitchen, putting as much space between him and me as possible. "Annie. Don't forget to leave the door open."

After I'd been there a couple of days he was outside when I decided to sneak in a pee. He came back in just after I'd flushed the toilet, so it was still running. I stood by the bed, trying to look like I was straightening it up. I thought maybe he wouldn't hear the toilet, but just as he started to turn on the kitchen tap and fill up a cup he paused, cocked his head, then went into the bathroom. Within seconds he stomped toward me, his face red and lips twisted into a snarl. I cringed in the corner, then tried to dart past him, but he grabbed my hair.

He dragged me to the bathroom and made me kneel in front of the toilet. Then he lifted the lid and shoved my head down, smashing my forehead into the toilet seat. He yanked my head back up by my hair while he reached around with his free arm and filled the cup with toilet water. He crouched behind me, forced my head to tilt back, then brought the cup to my mouth.

I struggled to move my face away, but he pressed the cup so hard against my lips I thought he'd break it. Some of the water went into my mouth and some up my nose. Before I could spit it out, he clamped his hand over my mouth, and I had to swallow it.

Afterward he made me brush my teeth twenty times—he counted out loud—then forced my mouth open wide so he could inspect my teeth. Next I had to rinse my mouth out with salt and warm water ten times. For the finale, he took some soap and water and scrubbed around my lips until I thought at least two layers of skin had been rubbed off. I never tried that again.

Feels like I'm never going to break free of all his screwy rules, Doc. And man, were they ever screwy. It doesn't matter that I know they're total bullshit. They're locked in and I'm locked down. On top of his rules, my psyche has added a few of its own—any little personality quirk I had before has been blown up twenty times and now I'm some weird hybrid of freakdom.

I take the same route to get here and stop at the same coffee shop. I hang my coat on the same hook in your office every session and sit in the same spot. You should see my routine before I go to bed—doors locked, all the blinds down, every window locked. Then I have a bath and shave my legs—left leg first, then the right, armpits last.

Once I'm done with the bath I apply lotion all over, and before finally going to bed I check the doors and windows again, put cans in front of the door, and double-check that the alarm is set—the cans are in case the alarm fails—then finally I make sure the knife is under the bed and the pepper spray on the night table.

A lot of nights when I try to sleep in my bed, all I do is lie there listening to every little sound, so I get up and crawl into the closet, dragging a blanket—I crawl in case anyone's peeking through the windows. Then I tuck myself in and arrange the shoes so they're in front of me.

Last time, you said my routines were probably providing me with a sense of security—and yes, I've noticed the casual something-to-think-about's and have-you-considered's you've started sliding in there once in a while. As long as you don't start asking a bunch of questions, we'll be okay. But I swear to God, if you ever ask how I'm feeling, you'll be talking to my back as I cruise right out of here for good.

So, this routines thing? At first I thought you were totally off base, but I've been giving it some brain time, and I guess my bedtime ritual does make me feel safe—which is ironic, to say the least. I mean, the whole time I was up there I was never safe. It was like riding a roller coaster through hell with the devil at the control switch, but the routine was the one damn thing I could count on to stay the same.

Each day I push myself a little further, and some shit has been easier to shake than other shit, but certain things? No way. Last night I drank a gallon of tea and spent almost an hour on the toilet, at least it felt like an hour, trying to force myself to pee at an unscheduled time. Almost got a dribble—had this oh-my-God-I'm-going-to-pee moment—but then my bladder seized up again. All that experiment produced was another sleepless night.

On that note, I've had enough for today. I have to go home and pee, and no, I don't want to use your bathroom. I'd just be sitting in there, thinking about you in here, wondering if you're wondering whether I was able to pee or not. No, thanks.

SESSION FIVE

On the way over here today I stopped at the coffee shop on the corner of your street. Looks dingy on the outside but has killer java, just about makes the drive into the city worth it. I'm not sure what you have in that mug of yours—for all I know it's scotch—but I took a chance and got you a tea. There should be some perks to having to end your day with me.

By the way, I like the chunky silver jewelry you're always wearing. Matches your hair and kind of gives you a chic grandma feel. The kind who might still have sex and like it. Don't worry, I'm not hinting for details—I know shrinks don't like to talk about their lives and I'm way too self-absorbed these days to listen, anyway.

Maybe I like your jewelry because it reminds me of my real dad, which fits with that whole self-absorbed thing. Not that he wore a bunch of the stuff, but he did have this one claddagh ring of his father's. My dad's parents were straight from

Ireland, came over and opened a jewelry store. The ring was the only thing he got when they were killed in a fire soon after my parents were married—bank took everything else. I asked Mom for the ring after the accident, she said it was lost.

I like to think if my dad were alive he'd have tried everything in his power to rescue me, but I don't really know how he'd have handled it. He was a pretty laid-back guy, and in my mind he'll always be forty years old, wearing his nice fuzzy sweaters and khakis. Only times I remember him getting excited were when he told me about a new shipment of books at the library where he worked.

I thought about him sometimes on the mountain, even wondered if he was watching over me. Then I'd get pissed off. If he was my guardian angel, like I told myself growing up, why the hell didn't he make it stop?

On my second night, The Freak tenderly washed my back in the bath. "Let me know if you want more hot water." He squeezed the cloth and let the rose-scented water trickle over my shoulders and back.

"You're quiet tonight." He nuzzled the wet hair at the nape of my neck. Then he took a strand into his mouth and sucked on it. I ached to thrust my shoulder up into his face and break his nose. Instead, I stared at the bathtub wall and counted how many seconds it took for a bead of water to fall. "Did you know every woman has a unique flavor to her hair? Yours tastes like nutmeg and cloves."

I shuddered.

"I knew the water wasn't warm enough." He ran the hot water for a minute. "I can tell just by looking at a woman how she'll taste. Some men are fooled by the color. It would be easy to think your mother with her young face and blond hair would taste clean and fresh, but I've learned to look deeper for the truth." He moved in front of me and began to gently wash my leg. I continued to focus on the wall. He was just trying to mess with me—I couldn't let him see it was working.

"She is a beautiful woman, though. Makes me wonder how many of your boyfriends wanted to have sex with her. If, when they were making love to you, they thought about her."

My stomach flipped. Over the years I got used to my boyfriends ogling my mom. When they weren't busy shoving in one of her dinners they were staring at her full mouth. One guy actually told me my mom looked like a hotter, grown-up version of Tinker Bell. Even Luke stumbled over his words sometimes when she was around.

Seventeen seconds, eighteen . . . that bead was *slow*.

"I doubt any of them could see, as I could, that she'd taste like a green apple, the kind you think is ripe until you take a bite. And your friend Christina, with her long blond hair always pinned up, always businesslike. There's more to her than meets the eye." I lost track of the bead of water.

"Yes, I know about Christina. She's a Realtor too, isn't she? Quite a successful one, I understand. I wonder why you surround yourself with people you envy."

I wanted to tell him I wasn't jealous, I was proud of Christina—we'd been best friends since high school. She taught me everything I know about real estate. Hell, she taught me everything I know about a lot of things, but I kept my mouth shut. This guy would use anything I said to screw with me.

"Does she remind you of Daisy? Daisy was cotton candy, but Christina, mmmm . . . Christina. Bet you she tastes like imported pears." My eyes met his. He began soaping my feet. I was sick of being played with.

"How did your mother taste?" I said.

The hand on my foot stilled and tightened. "My mother? Is that what you think this is all about?" He laughed as he plunged my foot underwater, then he got the razor from the cupboard.

This time when his hand gripped my leg I began to count the lines in the tiled wall. When the cold blade of the razor slid down my calf, I lost count and started again. When he made me stand up, so he could shave everything, I divided the tiles by the number of cracks in the grout. When his hands spread lotion on me, he hummed a song and I counted drips of wax down the sides of the candles.

I took inventory of whatever I looked at. I'd multiply and divide the numbers. If another thought or a feeling crept into my mind, I kicked it out and started again from the top.

While he tried to rape me for the second time, I didn't move, didn't cry, just stared at the bedroom wall. If I didn't react, he couldn't get it up. Help had to be on the way, I just had to tough it out until it showed up. So no matter what he did to me, I counted or thought about planes while I lay there like a rag doll. He gripped my face and looked right in my eyes and kept trying to force his limp penis into me. I counted the blood vessels in his eyes. His dick got softer. He yelled at me to call him by his name. When I didn't, he pounded his fist into the pillow right next to my ear, screaming, "You stupid, stupid bitch!" with each blow.

The pounding stopped. His breathing slowed. On his way to the bathroom he started to hum.

While he showered, I clutched the pillow over my face and shouted into it. *You sick fuck! You limp-dicked asshole! You picked the wrong girl to mess with.* Sobs went into the pillow next. The second I heard the shower shut off I flipped the pillow over, placed it back under my head dry side up, and turned my face to the wall.

Unfortunately, failure didn't discourage him. Each time it started with the same routine, bath time—which was when he liked to talk the most—followed by shaving, a lotion rub-down, then the dress. I felt like a Broadway performer: same stage, setting, lighting, and costume night after night. The only thing that changed was his increasing frustration and what he did about it.

After his third failed attempt, he slapped me twice in the face so hard I bit my tongue. This time there was no satisfaction, bitter or otherwise. I muffled my sobs with the pillow, sucked on my bloody tongue, and dreaded the end of his shower.

The fourth night he punched me twice in the stomach—my breath whooshed out of me, and the pain shocked me as much as it hurt—and once in the jaw. That pain was excruciating. The room dimmed. I prayed for everything to go completely black. It didn't. I stopped crying into the pillow.

The fifth night he flipped me over, knelt on my hands, and ground my face into the mattress so hard I couldn't breathe. My chest burned. He did this three times, always stopping right before I passed out.

Most nights ended with him getting up, his face expressionless, and then I'd hear the shower run for a while. After he got back into bed, he'd cuddle me and talk about something trivial—how natives cured meat, what constellations he saw on his nightly patrol, which fruits he liked or disliked.

But one night he lay down beside me and said, "I wonder how Christina is. She's so calm and self-possessed, isn't she? I wonder what it would take for a woman like her to lose control."

I struggled to catch my breath as he wove his fingers through my stiff hands and softly rubbed his thumb against mine.

As he snored beside me the idea of his hands anywhere on Christina, or of her feeling one second of the terror I was feeling, tore at my insides. I couldn't let that happen. My current plan wasn't working, unless my goal was to get myself, and possibly Christina, killed. It was taking too long for me to be found, and he wasn't going to turn to me one day and say, "This doesn't seem to be working out, so I'm going to take you home now." I might have gambled longer with my own life, but not Christina's.

I was going to have to help him rape me.

Understanding his behavior was critical. I dredged up everything I'd ever read about rapists, every TV show I'd ever seen about them—*Law & Order: SVU*, *Criminal Minds*, a couple of A&E specials—mostly focusing on what rapists like and under what circumstances they kill their victims.

I remembered that some rapists need to think the victims enjoy what they're doing to them. Maybe The Freak was able to delude himself into thinking I was actually turned on, but still couldn't get it up because on some level a little voice of doubt was creeping in on him. Right now it was making him impotent. If it got louder, I'd be dead.

The next night in the bath, I said, "You're very gentle." He stared at me hard and I made myself look into his eyes.

"Really?"

"Most men, you know, are kind of rough, but you have a nice touch."

He smiled.

"I'm sorry I've been difficult, I just wasn't sure, you know, at first, but I've been thinking maybe . . . maybe it's not too late for me to start a new life." How much should I hesitate? If I was too positive he'd never buy it.

"Difficult?"

"I mean, it will take a while for me to get used to everything and all, but I'm beginning to see that maybe I could like it up here. With you."

"You think so, do you?" He dragged out each syllable.

Forcing myself to make eye contact again, I tried to convey as much sincerity as possible.

"Yes, I do. You understand a lot of things most men don't."

"Oh, I definitely understand a lot of things most men don't." His face broke out in his award-winning smile. Bingo.

When he rubbed lotion on me, I said, "I really like that scent." His smile grew even bigger.

After I put on the dress, I twirled for him and said, "It's exactly what I would have picked out."

Back on the bed I moaned for him and kissed him back, but cautiously, as though I were awakening to his touch. His pants sped up and I counted the seconds between them like contractions. Inside, I died.

With his breathing heavy and his face flushed, he lay on top of me. Worried he would lose his erection—and then lose control—I reached down and fondled him before things could turn ugly. It had to be done.

Deep inside myself I curled into a ball and hid from my own words as I whispered, "I've waited for this moment."

His arms tensed and his face turned dark with rage. He clamped his hand down on my throat. His hand tightened as I clawed uselessly at it.

"I could kill you at any second, and you talk like a whore? You should be terrified. You should be begging. You should be fighting for your life. *Don't you get it?*"

He finally released my throat, but my relief was interrupted by a blow to my stomach. He pounded my body with his fists, against my breasts, face, crotch. I struggled, but his fists were everywhere at once. The blows rained down until I couldn't feel them anymore. I had passed out.

It's strange, Doc, when The Freak called me a whore and beat me, I felt pain but no sense of outrage, because I *wanted* him to hurt me. Even while my body struggled against him, my mind cheered him on. I *deserved* the pain. How could I say those things? How could I touch him like that?

I did a lot of things on the mountain, a lot of things I didn't want to do and a lot of things I didn't want to believe I was capable of doing. But that time? When I wonder how I became the zombie I am now, how I could have gotten so lost, it always traces back to that moment—the moment I put my soul on the shelf to make room for the devil.

SESSION SIX

Yesterday, I sat in a church for a while. Not to pray—I'm not religious—but just to sit in the quiet. Before the abduction I'd probably passed that church a thousand times without noticing it. We're not exactly a churchgoing family, my mom and stepdad were usually too busy sleeping their "religion" off on a Sunday morning. But I've gone a couple of times over the last few months. It's an old church and smells like a museum—in a good way, a survived-lots-of-shit-and-still-standing kind of way. Something about the stained-glass windows works for me too. If I were to get all deep on you, I could say the idea of all those broken pieces being made into something so damn pretty appeals to me. Good thing I'm not that profound.

The church is usually empty, thank you, God, but even if there is someone else inside, nobody ever talks to me or even looks at me. Not that I would make eye contact.

When I first came to after The Freak beat me unconscious, my whole body hurt, and it took a long time for me to lift my head enough to look around. Waves of nausea passed through me. The right side of my chest burned every time I took a breath. One eye was closed up pretty good and the other one made things fuzzy, but I could see outlines. He was nowhere in sight. Either he was sleeping on the floor or he was outside. I lay still.

The bathroom was calling, but I didn't know if I could move that far, plus I dreaded his catching me going for an unscheduled pee. I must have passed out again, because I don't remember anything until I woke from a dream in which I was running on the beach with Luke and our dogs. When I remembered where I really was, I cried.

My bladder burned—if I waited much longer I was going to pee in the bed. God only knew which offense would piss him off the most. There was no way I was putting that dress back on, so I crawled naked to the bathroom. Every few seconds I paused, waited for the black dots in my vision to go away, then crawled another few inches, whimpering the whole time. He would have loved it.

Petrified to use the toilet in case he came in, I squatted over the drain in the bathtub. Leaning my head on the side wall, I tried to breathe in the perfect amount of air that wouldn't hurt and prayed I didn't die in there. Eventually I crawled back into bed and passed out again.

My head ached, but it was a distant throbbing, like background noise. I still didn't know where The Freak was, and terrifying images of his abducting Christina raged through my mind. I prayed that my attempts to manipulate him hadn't just sent him straight to her.

I wasn't sure how long I'd been slipping in and out of consciousness, but I thought it had been at least a day. When I got back some strength, I made my way to the door. It was still locked. Shit. I hung my head under the tap, washed the stickiness I assumed was blood off my face, and drank my fill. As soon as the cold water hit my stomach, I clung to the sink and puked.

When I was finally able to move without getting dizzy, I searched the place again. My fingers explored every crack and bolt. Standing on the kitchen counter, I kicked the shutter so hard I thought I'd torn the muscles in my leg. My feet didn't even leave a mark. I was hurt bad and couldn't remember the last time I'd had any food, but I still would've taken my chances on the mountain, except there was no way out of the damn cabin.

To keep track of how many days I'd been missing, I pulled the bed away from the wall and pressed my fingernail into the wood until it left faint marks. If there was light through the little hole in the bathroom wall, I figured it was morning, and if it was still dark I waited until it brightened up, then made another mark. Two marks since he'd left me alone. To keep myself on some sort of schedule resembling The Freak's, I peed when I couldn't hold it any longer, and then only in the bathtub with my ears peeled for any sound. Too scared to have a shower or bath in case he came home and caught me, I avoided both, and whenever the hunger pangs got too bad, I filled myself up with water. I pictured everyone back home at candlelight vigils and imagined all my friends holding meetings, or handing out flyers with my smiling face on them. My mom must have been going crazy. I could see her at home, crying, probably looking beautiful—tragedy agreed with her. Neighbors would be bringing over casseroles, Aunt Val would be fielding calls, and my stepdad would be holding her hand, telling her it was going to be all right. I wished I had someone telling me that. Why hadn't anybody found me? Had they given up? I'd never heard of anyone going missing and being found weeks later. Unless the missing person was a corpse.

Maybe Luke was on TV pleading for my return. Or would the cops question him? Wasn't it always the boyfriend they suspected first? They were probably wasting time on him when they should be looking for The Freak.

I worried about Emma and who was taking care of her. Were they feeding her the right food for her sensitive tummy? Were they walking her? Mostly I just wondered if she thought I'd abandoned her, and that always made me cry.

To comfort myself I played memories of Luke, Emma, and Christina like home movies in my head: pause, rewind, and repeat. One of my favorites of Christina was the two of us on our candy bender. She came over to play Scrabble last Halloween and we decided to break open one of the bags I'd bought for trick-or-treaters. One bag turned to two, then three and four. We were both so stoned on sugar our Scrabble game just dissolved into a mess of dirty words and hysterical laughter. Then we ran out of candy for the kids, so we had to turn off all the lights. We hid in the dark and listened to fireworks, giggling our asses off.

But then my thoughts always turned to The Freak and what he might be doing to her now. I'd imagine her at the office, maybe working late, and then I pictured The Freak waiting outside in the van. My powerlessness enraged me.

———

As another day went by and I put a new mark on the wall, I stopped feeling any cravings for food, but the feeling that The Freak was coming back continued. And if I wanted to survive, I needed to be ready. My previous attempt at seduction had nearly gotten me killed, so I had to figure out why he flipped out when I pretended to be turned on.

Was he a sadist? No, he wasn't sexually aroused by beating me. He was reenacting something. This guy had a pattern. It started with the bath—maybe his version of foreplay?—and then it got rough later. What the hell was his deal?

He said women don't want nice guys, we all want to be treated like garbage, and then, when I was too overt in my attempts at seduction, it enraged him and he called me a whore, said I should be fighting him. He must think a "nice" woman secretly wants an aggressive man who's rough with her and overpowers her, but in his mind only a "whore" would actually show she likes it—a nice woman would resist. So he probably didn't feel like a real man unless I *was* scared of him.

He was trying to please me—with fear and pain. And the more I didn't react, the more he thought he had to hurt me. Holy shit. He was a rapist who thought every woman had a rape fantasy. At last I knew what he wanted—I had to struggle and show him my pain and fear.

If there'd been anything in my stomach to vomit up, I would have. Somehow, the thought of allowing him to see my real feelings was worse than pretending I liked being raped.

On my fourth day alone it became harder to distinguish my dreams from my reality as I slept more and woke less. There were times I'm sure I was hallucinating, because I was wide awake yet I could hear Luke's voice and smell his cologne, but when I opened my eyes there was nothing but those damn cabin walls.

I realized I was so weak I might forget my plan, so I created a rhyme to help myself remember. I chanted it over and over as I slipped in and out of sleep.

The Freak is insane, he needs fear and pain. The Freak is insane, he needs fear and pain.

By the fifth day, I began to be afraid he wouldn't come back before I starved to death. I spent most of the day on the bed or sitting with my back to the corner, waiting for the door to open and chanting my rhyme, but I kept nodding off. I think it was early evening but I was so weak it felt later. Then the lock on the door clicked and he walked in.

I was actually glad to see him—I wouldn't starve. I was especially glad to see he was alone, then I wondered if Christina was unconscious and tied up in the van.

He closed the door and stood staring at me. His image swam in front of me.

The Freak is insane, he needs fear and pain. . . .

Body and voice trembling, I said, "Thank God, I've been so scared. I—I thought I was going to die here all alone."

His eyebrows rose. "Would you rather die here with company?"

"No!" As I shook my head, the room spun. "I don't want *anyone* to die. I've been doing thinking . . ." My food-deprived brain struggled to remember words. "Doing *some* thinking about . . . things. Things I want to tell you, but I need to know . . ." My chest tightened. "Christina, is Christina okay?"

He sauntered over to one of the barstools, sat down, and rested his chin in his hand. "Don't you care how I am?"

"Yes, yes, of course, I just thought—just wanted to know . . ." The Freak blurred and came into focus, then blurred again. "I messed up. Messed up bad. Last time."

His eyes narrowed and he nodded.

"But I have a plan. See—"

"You have a plan?" He sat up straighter. What the hell was I saying?

I dug my fingernails into my hand. The room came back into focus.

"For how we can make things work."

"Interesting, but I've been doing a little thinking myself. It's become clear I have to make some decisions and I don't think you're going to like the options."

Time to roll the dice. I slowly got to my feet. The room began to spin again. I braced my hand on the wall, closed my eyes, took some deep breaths. When I opened my eyes back up, The Freak was staring at me. No expression.

Hand clutching my stomach, I staggered over to sit on the stool next to him.

"I guess I can understand that. You've gone to a lot of trouble and I've been a lot of trouble, right?" Eyelids at half-mast, he nodded his head slowly.

"The thing is, the last time we tried . . . some of the things I said? That wasn't really me. I just thought that's what you wanted, what would make you happy."

He still wasn't showing much expression, but he was look-ing intently into my eyes. The best liars stick close to the truth. I took another deep breath.

"I was *really* scared, of you and of the feelings you were bringing up in me, but I didn't know . . ." He lifted his chin from his hand and sat up straight. I was going to have to talk faster.

"I get it now, I just have to be honest with you, with *myself*, and I'm ready to do that." I prayed for the strength to say the next words. "So I'd like to try again. Please give me another chance, *please*." I waited through a long pause, then braced myself as he got up from the stool.

"Perhaps I should give this a little more time, Annie. I wouldn't want to make a hasty decision." He stood before me with his arms out and his head cocked to the side.

"How about a hug?" His smile didn't reach his eyes. I was being tested. I stepped into his arms and put mine around him. "Christina is fine," he said. "We spent a delightful afternoon looking at houses. She sure knows her real estate."

I finally exhaled.

"I can feel your heart beating against me." He squeezed me harder. Then he released me and said, "Let's get some food in you." He left the cabin but came back moments later carrying a brown paper bag.

"Lentil soup, freshly made at my favorite deli, and some organic apple juice. The protein and sugars will help."

After The Freak warmed up the fragrant soup, he brought a steaming bowl and a glass of juice over to me. My frantic hands reached for the soup, but he sat down beside me and placed the bowl on the table in front of him. Tears came to my eyes.

"Please, I have to eat, I'm so hungry."

In a kind voice he said, "I know."

He brought a spoonful up to his mouth and blew on it. I watched in agony as he took a sip. He nodded his head once, then dipped the spoon back in the bowl. He blew on it again, but this time brought the spoon toward my mouth. As soon as I reached for it, he paused and shook his head. I placed my hand back in my lap.

The Freak slowly spoon-fed me the soup, blowing on every mouthful first and stopping once in a while to feed me sips of the apple juice. When half of the soup and juice was gone he said, "That's probably all your stomach can handle right now. Feel better?"

I nodded.

"Good." He glanced at his watch and smiled. "Time for your bath."

This time when he led me out of the bathroom to the bed and began unzipping my dress from behind, I knew what to do.

"Please don't touch me—I don't want to do this."

With his chin digging into my shoulder, he nuzzled my earlobe. "I can feel you shaking. What are you scared of?"

"You—I'm scared of you. You're strong and you're going to hurt me." My dress fell to the floor and he moved in front of me. In the candlelight, his eyes glowed. He stood before me and traced his middle finger around my neck.

The finger traveled down to right above my pubic bone and paused.

My skin crawled.

"Describe your fear to me." His voice lingered over the word "fear."

"My knees—they feel weak. I feel sick in my stomach. I can't breathe. My heart, it feels . . . it feels like it's going to burst."

With his hands pressed into my shoulders, he walked me backward until the edge of the mattress hit the back of my knees, then shoved me hard, so that I fell onto the bed. I watched as he ripped off his clothes.

I crawled across the bed, but he dragged me back by my ankle. Then he was on me, tearing my panties and bra off. It all happened so fast. He was hard, then he was inside me. I screamed. He smiled. I gritted my teeth, squeezed my eyes shut, counted his thrusts—struggling when he faltered—and prayed.

LetitbeoverLetitbeoverLetitbeover

When he finally came, I wanted to pour bleach on my crotch and scrub with boiling water until I bled, but I couldn't even get up to wash. When I asked, he said, "That's not necessary, just rest."

In his postcoital afterglow, he lay there stroking my hair and said, "I'll take some chicken breasts out of the freezer tomorrow." He pulled me close against him and nuzzled my neck. "We can make chow mein together, okay?" He cuddled me until he fell asleep.

His wetness was still between my legs, but I didn't cry. When I thought of Luke a sob almost broke free, but I bit the inside of my cheek, hard. I whispered, "I'm sorry," into the dark.

I've watched shows about women who stay married for years to guys who keep beating the crap out of them—worse, they don't just stay, they try desperately to make the guy happy, which of course never works—and I'd want to be sympathetic, want to understand, but I just never got it, Doc. Seemed pretty simple to me. Pack your shit and tell the jerk good-bye, preferably with a boot to his ass. Oh, yeah, I thought I was one tough cookie. Well, all it took was five days of being left alone for this cookie to crumble. Five stinking days, and I was ready to do *whatever* he wanted. And now I get to be paraded around as a heroine. Heroes dive into burning build-ings and save children. Heroes die for the cause. I'm not a hero, I'm a coward.

I have to do another interview tonight, look at some perky blonde with her Chiclet smile who's going to ask, "How did you feel up there, were you scared?" No shit, Sherlock. They're no better than him—just sadists with a bigger paycheck.

Interesting that hardly anyone asks how I feel now, not that I'd tell them. I just wonder why nobody cares much about the after—just about the story. Guess they figure it stops there.

I wish.

SESSION SEVEN

Hard to believe it's already the third week of January, isn't it, Doc? I'm just glad all the Christmas and New Year's hoopla is finally out of the way, which reminds me, did I ever tell you about Christmas with The Freak? You know, I don't think I ever did get around to sharing his not-so-good word on all things red and green. Well, one day he sat me down and told me it was December but we wouldn't be celebrating Christmas, because it was just one more way society tries to control people.

It didn't stop there. I got to listen to an endless rant about the evils of Christmas and how society has taken a myth and blown it up into a money grab. The last thing in the world I'd wanted to do was celebrate *anything* with The Freak, but by the time he was done talking about every shitty aspect of the holiday I would've helped the Grinch steal Christmas myself. Actually, *that's* what the jerk did. He stole Christmas from me. Along with a lot of other stuff, of course. You know, like pride, self-esteem, joy, security, the ability to sleep in a bed, but hey, who's complaining?

Well, at least I tried with the tree. . . . Maybe next year will be different. Like you told me, I need to allow for the possibility I won't always feel the way I do now, and it's important to take note of small signs of progress, no matter how insignificant they may seem. Today when I stepped out onto my front porch I caught the scent of snow in the air and for a couple of seconds I felt excited. We haven't had any snow yet this year, and as soon as there was even an inch out there Emma and I used to tear around in it. She's so damn funny to watch. She runs, slides, pounces, digs, and eats it. Always wished I knew what she was thinking. Probably, *Bunnies, bunnies, got to get the bunnies.* Sometimes I'd toss a handful of treats into the snow so she'd actually find something.

Afterward I'd have a hot bath, make a cup of tea, snuggle up by the fire with a book, and watch Emma's feet twitch as she reenacted the fun in her dreams. All those memories came back, and I felt good. Like I had something to look forward to.

The good feeling left as soon as I remembered last Christmas, though—trust me, spending an entire winter inside a place with shuttered windows takes "cabin fever" to a whole new level. And then, by the middle of January last year, I was four months pregnant.

On the mountain, I lived for the moments when I got to read—The Freak had good taste—and I didn't even mind reading out loud to him. While those pages were turning, I was somewhere else. And so was he. Sometimes he kept his eyes closed, or he'd lean toward me with his chin in his hand

and his eyes glowing, and other times, during intense scenes, he paced around the room. If he liked something, he'd place his hand over his heart and say, "Read it again."

He always asked me what I thought about what we'd read, but at first I was hesitant to express any ideas and tried to paraphrase his opinions. Until the time he slapped the book out of my hand and said, "Come on, Annie, use that pretty head of yours and tell me what *you* think."

We were reading *The Prince of Tides*—he liked to mix up the classics with contemporary novels, and they usually featured screwed-up families—and it was the scene where the mother cooks up dog food for the dad.

"I was glad she screwed him over like that," I said. "He deserved it. He was an asshole."

The second the words were out of my mouth, I panicked. Was he going to think I was talking about him? And "asshole" wasn't exactly ladylike. But he just nodded his head thoughtfully and said, "Yes, he didn't appreciate his family at all, did he?"

When we read *Of Mice and Men*, he asked if I felt sorry for "poor dumb Lennie," and when I told him I did, he said, "Well, isn't that interesting. Is it because the girl was a slut? I think you were more bothered about the poor puppy he killed. Would Lennie be so deserving of your sympathy if she were a nice girl?"

"It would be the same either way. He was messed up—he didn't mean to."

He smiled and said, "So it's okay to kill someone as long as you don't mean to? I'll have to remember that."

"That's not what I—"

He broke into laughter and held up a hand, while my cheeks burned.

The Freak was careful with the books—I was never allowed to place them facedown when they were open or dogear a page. One day when I was watching him carefully stack some books back on the shelf, I said, "You must have read a lot as a kid." His back stiffened and he slowly caressed the binding of the book he was holding.

"When I was allowed." Allowed? A strange way to put it, but before I could decide whether I should ask about it, he said, "Did you?"

"All the time—one of the bonuses of having a dad who worked at the library."

"You were lucky." He gave the books a final pat and left the cabin.

When he paced around, ranting about a character or plot twist, he was so articulate and passionate I'd get caught up in it and reveal more thoughts of my own. He encouraged me to explain and defend my opinions but never flipped out, even when I contradicted him, and over time I began to relax during our literary debates. Of course, when reading time ended, so did the only moments I didn't dread, the only activity I enjoyed, the only thing I did that made me feel like a human being, like myself.

Every night I lay in bed imagining The Freak's sperm crawling up inside me and willing my eggs to hide. Since I'd been on the pill when he took me, I hoped my body was messed up and I'd be rescued before I could get pregnant. But I also thought I'd get my period right after the first missed pill, and that didn't happen until about a week after he was finally able to rape me.

One morning we were in the shower, doing the routine,

me facing the wall as he stood behind me washing my legs, up and down and between them. Then he stopped abruptly. When I turned around, he was just standing there looking at the cloth. There was blood on it, and when I looked down at myself, I saw blood on my inner thigh. His jaw clenched and his face reddened. I knew that look.

"I'm sorry—I didn't know." I cringed against the wall.

He threw the cloth at me, got out of the shower, and stood silent on the bath mat, glaring at my crotch. The curtain was half open and water dripped onto the floor. I thought for sure he'd flip out over that, but he reached back in, moved the showerhead so the water hit me, and turned the tap to cold—I mean suck-the-wind-out-of-you cold.

"Wash yourself off."

I tried not to scream, the water was so cold. He picked up the cloth from the shower floor and threw it at me.

"I told you to wash yourself off."

When I thought I was done, with the cloth in hand, I said, "What do you want me to do with this?"

He motioned for me to give it to him, examined it, and handed it back.

"Do it again."

When there was nothing left on the cloth, and I was practically blue, he let me get out.

"Don't move," he said. I wondered if my shivers counted as movement. The Freak left the room for a couple of minutes and came back with a scrap of material.

"Use this." He threw it at me.

I said, "Do you have any tampons or anything?"

He put his face close to mine and slowly said, "A real woman would be pregnant by now." I didn't know what to say, and his voice rose. "What have you done?"

"There's no way I could—"

"If you don't do your job, I'll find someone who will."

While he watched, I got dressed and put the stupid rag in my underwear. My fingers were so numb I couldn't get the row of buttons done up on the dress, and as I fumbled with them, he shook his head and said, "You're pathetic."

My period went on for six days, and every morning he waited outside my cold shower until I handed him the cloth with no blood on it. The entire bathtub had to be wiped down with cleaning fluid before he'd have his shower. He made me put the used rags in a bag, which he took outside and told me he burned. We skipped bath time too, which was fine by me—it was six days he didn't lay a hand on me.

During the afternoons he made me study books on how to get pregnant. I still remember the title of one, *The Fastest Way to Get Pregnant Naturally.* Yeah, that was The Freak, because, you know, abducting a woman, locking her in a cabin, and raping her is *real* natural.

As soon as I stopped bleeding, he was trying to knock me up again. I prayed my body would know his sperm was sick and reject it, or all the stress and fear would make it hard for me to conceive. No such luck.

About three weeks later, I knew my period was due and hoped every twinge in my belly was cramps. Every time I went to the bathroom, I prayed to see blood in my underwear. After four weeks, I knew. Judging by my little wall calendar, I figured I'd gotten pregnant around the middle of September, about two weeks after my period ended.

I hoped to hide it from The Freak, but one morning I woke to the sensation of his hand caressing my belly.

"I know you're awake. You don't have to get up right away today." He nuzzled my shoulder. "Look at me, Annie." I turned to face him. "Good morning," he said with a smile, then looked down at his hand on my belly.

"My mother, Juliet, the woman who raised me, wasn't my biological mother, she adopted me when I was five. The whore who gave birth to me was supposedly too young to raise a child." His voice was tight. "She wasn't too young to spread her legs for whoever my father was." He shook his head and in a softer voice said, "But then Juliet changed my life. She lost her own son when he was only a year and still nursing. She had so much love to give. . . . It was she who taught me family is everything. And you, Annie, losing half your family so soon, I know you've always wanted one of your own—I'm glad I'm the man you chose."

Chose? Not quite how I'd put it. Even before The Freak abducted me, I wasn't sure how I felt about having kids. I'd been pretty happy living the independent career woman's life and I never was the type to walk into a roomful of kids and go, "Wow, I gotta get me one of these." But here I was, knocked up, brewing some demon child. And here he was, talking about his mother, giving me a chance to get inside his head and learn more about him. Part of me was scared to rock the boat, but I had to think long-term gain.

"You said her name *was* Juliet. Did your mom pass away?"

The smile left his face. He rolled over and stared up at the ceiling.

"She was taken from me when I was just eighteen." I waited for him to elaborate, but he looked lost in thought.

I said, "She sounds like she was someone very special. It's nice you were so close. My mom never abandoned me, like your real one did, but the doctors kept giving her drugs after the accident, so she was pretty messed up. I had to go live with my uncle and aunt for a while. I know what it feels like to be alone."

His eyes flicked to me, then away. "What was it like, living with these relatives? Were they kind to you?"

I did some therapy in my twenties to deal with my feelings about the accident and to work through my issues with Mom—fat lot of good that did me—but no matter how many times I told the story, it never got easier. I hadn't even discussed those feelings with Luke.

"My aunt is my mom's sister, they're always trying to one-up each other, but she was nice enough, I guess. My cousins were older and pretty much ignored me. But I didn't care."

"Didn't you? I bet you cared a lot." There was no mockery in his voice. "Wasn't there any other family you could stay with?"

"Dad's family is all dead and Mom just has her sister." She actually had an older stepbrother too, but he was in jail for robbery and Mom sure as hell didn't consider him family. "It was hard, but now that I'm older I try to understand what my mom must have been going through. Back then, people didn't go to counseling or grief support groups. The doctors gave out pills."

"She sent you away."

"It wasn't that bad." But I remembered my cousins' whispers and the way my uncle and aunt would stop talking when I came into the room. If Mom was a blurred version of herself, my aunt was hard edges and crisp lines on the same canvas. Both were blond and small-framed, all the women in my family are blond except me, but Aunt Val's lips were just a little thinner, her nose longer, and her eyes narrower. And where Mom was all emotion, good or bad, Aunt Val was calm, cool, collected. Not a lot of comforting hugs there.

"And then your mom sold your house, didn't she? Half your family is gone and so is your home?"

"How do you know—"

"If you want to get to know someone, *really* get to know them, there are many ways. As there were many ways your mother could have dealt with the situation."

"She had to sell it, Dad didn't have any life insurance." Six months after the accident Mom finally came and got me, and that's when I found out my home no longer existed.

"Perhaps, but it couldn't have been easy moving when so much had already changed. And into such a small house?"

"It was just the two of us. We didn't need a lot of space."

We moved to a cramped two-bedroom rental in the worst part of Clayton Falls, with a view of the pulp mill. The pill bottles had been replaced with vodka bottles. Mom's pink silk robes were now nylon and her Estée Lauder White Linen perfume was a knockoff version. We may have been tight on money, but she still managed to scrape up enough for her French cigarettes—Mom thinks anything French is elegant— and her not-so-elegant vodka. Popov isn't Smirnoff.

Not only had she sold our house, she'd also sold all Dad's things. Of course she kept Daisy's trophies and her costumes, which hung in Mom's closet.

"But it wasn't just the two of you for very long, was it?"

"She was going through a lot of stuff. It's hard for a single mother. There weren't a lot of options back then."

"So she thought she'd found a real man to take care of her this time around." He smiled.

I stared at him for a second. "She worked . . . after the accident."

As a secretary with a small construction firm, but mostly she just worked hard at looking good. She never left the house without a fully made-up face, and she was usually half cut when she was applying the stuff, so it wasn't uncommon to see her eyes smudged or her cheeks too bright. Somehow it worked for her, in a broken-down-doll sort of way, and men looked at her like they wanted to rescue her from the big bad world. Her recently widowed status didn't stop her from smiling back.

Four months later I had my new stepdad, Mr. Big Shot Wannabe. The sales guy for the firm, he drove a Caddy, smoked cigars, even wore cowboy boots—which might make sense if he was from Texas, or even Alberta, but I don't think he's ever left the island. I suppose he's rough-around-the-edges handsome in an aging Tom Selleck way. Mom quit her job right after they got married. Guess she thought he was a sure thing.

"What did you think of your new father?"

"He's okay. He seems to really love her."

"So your mother had a new life, but where did you fit in?"

"Wayne tried."

I wanted at least some of the closeness with him I'd had with my father, but Wayne and I didn't have anything to talk about. The only things he read were girlie magazines or flyers for get-rich-quick schemes. Then I learned I could make him laugh. As soon as I realized he thought I was funny, I turned into a total goof around him, doing anything I could to crack him up. But if he did, Mom would get pissed off and say something like, "Stop it, Wayne, you're just encouraging her." So he stopped. Hurt, I'd make fun of him whenever I could, just being an all-around smart-ass. Eventually we just ignored each other.

The Freak was staring at me intently, and I realized that my attempts at learning more about him had served only to further his knowledge of me. Time to get things back on track.

"What about your father?" I said. "You haven't mentioned him."

"Father? That man was never a father to me. And he wasn't good enough for her either, but she didn't want to see it." His voice rose. "He was a traveling *salesman*, for God's sake, a fat *hairy* salesman, who . . ."

He swallowed a couple of times, then said, "I had to set her free."

It wasn't just his words that sent the shiver up my spine, it was the flatness of his voice when he said them. I wanted to know more, but my instincts told me to back away. It didn't matter. Whatever storm was stirring in him had passed.

He leapt out of bed with a smile, stretched, and after a sigh of contentment said, "Enough talk. We should be celebrating the beginnings of our own family." He stared hard at me, then nodded. "Stay there." He threw on his clothes and coat and disappeared outside. When he opened the door, the smell of rotting leaves and wet dirt drifted over to the bed—the scent of a dying summer.

When he came back in, his skin was flushed and his eyes glittered. One hand was behind his back. He sat next to me, then brought his hand out. His fist was closed.

"Sometimes we have to go through difficult times in life," he said. "But they're just a test, and if we stay strong, we're eventually rewarded." His eyes met mine. "Open your hand, Annie." Maintaining eye contact, he pressed something small and cool into my palm. I was scared to look at it.

"I gave this to someone long ago, but she didn't deserve it." My palm itched. He raised his eyebrows. "Don't you want to see?" I slowly looked down at my hand, and in it a fine gold chain glistened. His finger reached out and touched the tiny gold heart that lay at the center. "Beautiful, isn't it?" I wanted to throw the necklace as far away from me as I could.

I said, "Yes, yes, it is, thank you."

He took it out of my hand. "Sit up, so I can put it on you." My skin crawled as the chain tickled against me.

I wanted to ask what happened to the girl who owned the necklace, but I was scared he might tell me.

SESSION EIGHT

All righty, Doc, I'm seriously starting to question my attitude—yeah, yeah, I knew I had one. But now it's really beginning to get in the way of things. You know, things like my life. See, I may not have always been Little Mary Sunshine before all this went down, with some damn good reasons—dead sister, dead dad, drunken mom, dumbass stepdad—but at least I tried not to take my shit out on the *entire* world. Now? Man, there doesn't seem to be anybody who doesn't piss me off. You, the reporters, the cops, the mailman, a rock in the middle of the road. Actually, I'd probably be okay with the rock. And I mean, I used to *like* people. Hell, you could even say I was a goddamn people *person*. But these days?

Take my friends. They call or try to visit, they still invite me to stuff, but right away I start thinking they're just hoping to get the inside scoop on how the investigation is going, or the offers are just your we-really-should-invite-the-poor-girl kind of thing. Then, when I say no, they probably sit around and talk about me

And see, that's a spiteful, childish thing for me to even *think*, let alone say, because I should be grateful people care enough to try, right?

Thing is, there's not much going on in my life I want to share, and I'm out of touch with half the shit they're discussing. I'm behind on movies, world events, trends, and technology. So if I do run into someone I know during one of my brief forays into the outside world, I ask them about their lives, and they look relieved and blather on about a work crisis or a new boyfriend or a trip they're taking. I tell myself it's almost comforting to hear that even though *my* life is fucked, people are getting up and going about their lives every morning. One day I could be bitching about my work too.

But after we say our good-byes and I watch them walk away, back to their nice normal lives, I just start feeling all pissed off again. I hate them for not being in pain like me, hate them for being able to enjoy themselves. Hate myself for feeling that way.

I've even managed to alienate Christina, although she didn't go down without a fight. When I first moved back to my house she busted her ass setting up the place, gathering furniture, hooking up the utilities. She even stocked the fridge. Her take-charge attitude used to be one of the things I liked most about her. Hell, in the past, I was more than happy to let Christina run my life. But when she started marching around my house with her feng shui book in hand, looking for things to rearrange so I'd attract healing energy, bringing me lists of shrinks' phone numbers—this was before you—and pamphlets on retreats for rape victims, I got more argumentative and she just got more aggressive.

Then she started in on her let's-talk-about-it kick, bringing over bottles of wine and her tarot cards. She'd do a spread, then read key phrases from the book like, "You have struggled greatly on your own. It's time to share your burden with those closest to you." In case I didn't get the point, each statement was followed by eye contact and a pause. I was dealing with these visits, if not actually enjoying them, but when she set the cards down one day and said, "You're *never* going to get over this if you don't start talking about it," I lost it.

"Your life must really suck if you need to get off on my shit, Christina."

She got such a hurt look on her face. I mumbled an apology, but she left not long after.

The last time we talked, months ago, we arranged a time for her to bring over some of her old clothes—I tried to get out of it but she wouldn't take no for an answer, insisted they'd cheer me up. An hour before she was supposed to arrive, my guts were twisted into knots of anger and resentment. I paged her and canceled, then went for a three-hour drive. I came home to a big box of clothes on my front doorstep, which I promptly stuck down in the basement.

When she phoned the next day I didn't answer, but she left a message, sounding giddy and excited, asking if I got the clothes and saying she couldn't wait to see them on me. I called back and thanked her voice mail, but I've never returned any of her messages since.

What the hell is wrong with me? Why am I so fucking mad at everyone?

One night, I'm sure I heard The Freak say some name. It wasn't loud enough for me to make out, but I could tell it wasn't mine. I wasn't stupid enough to ask about it, but I wondered.

He was pretty basic in the sex department. Thank God. I guess as far as freaks go I got an okay one. Look, I'm not complimenting him. I just mean he wasn't ramming me up the ass or making me give him blow jobs—he probably knew I'd try to bite his dick off. I had my role down pat. I knew just where to touch, how to touch, what to say, and how to say it. I did whatever it took to get it over with fast and I got damn good at it.

Physically it made things easier to help him along, but emotionally one more part of me gave up and slipped away.

As soon as The Freak knew I was pregnant, he no longer seemed to care about doing it every single night, but the baths never stopped. Sometimes he'd just rest his head on my chest and talk to me until he fell asleep. His voice mellow, he'd give me his theories on everything from dust to vomit. But he was mostly fixated on love and society, like he'd say our society is all about acquiring and keeping—not that it had stopped him from acquiring and keeping me.

The idea of my genes mixing with his to create something made me sick. The last thing I wanted was to be connected to him in any way, and when we lay in bed at night I willed my body to miscarry. Every negative thought I could dream up, I aimed at this monster growing inside me and visualized it being expelled from my body. My sleep usually ended in cold sweats after nightmares about hideous fetuses tearing my insides apart.

All that winter, my head was filled with images of giving

birth up there with The Freak by my side. When he made me read aloud from one book about childbirth at home, I had to force every word out of my throat. In the past, if I saw a delivery on TV I covered my eyes, because I couldn't stand looking at some poor woman screaming while this *thing* was being ripped from her body. Always thought if I ever gave birth I'd be on lots of drugs, with a husband murmuring encouragement while I zoned out.

The Freak's good mood over my pregnancy only lasted a couple of months. Then one day he was pleased with the way my nails looked, but the next he was ordering me to do them all over again. One minute peeing at two o'clock was okay, the next I was jerked off the toilet and told to wait until three. For a pregnant woman who already had a small bladder, it was excruciating.

In the morning, I'd put on what he picked out for me to wear, then halfway through the day he'd make me go change. If there was even a minuscule fleck on the dishes when he inspected them, he made me do them over again. Once I refused to scrub the bathroom, insisting it was clean, and earned myself a backhand across the face and a wall-to-wall scrubbing of the cabin floor. I learned to keep the perfect amount of submissive shame in my expression, forced myself to look down, and curled my shoulders like a beaten dog.

Toward the end of January, we'd just finished breakfast one morning and I was cleaning up. The Freak watched me for a while and then said, "I'm taking a trip," like he was telling me he was going to carry out the garbage.

"For how long? Where? You can't leave me alone up here—"

"I make the rules, Annie." His face was impassive.

"You could take me with you. You can tie me up in the van or something? Please?"

He shook his head. "You're safer here."

The Freak took some food out of the cupboards, mostly vitamin drinks and protein powder you mix with water, and left those on the counter. No utensils.

Usually I wasn't allowed near the woodstove, but he unlocked it and took the screen away. Then he stacked up a ton of wood inside the house and lit a fire for me. I didn't have an axe, or newspaper, or anything to light a new fire with, so I'd have to make damn sure I never let that one go out.

He hadn't left for a few months, so I figured we must be running short of supplies and he was going into town to stock up. I had no idea where he kept the food, and anything he brought in was in ziplock bags so I could never identify a store, but I assumed he had a deep freeze and a cellar or shed outside. I hoped supplies were the reason behind his trip. Was he going to go see Christina again? What if he found another woman he liked better and forgot about me? How long does it take to starve to death? I was more scared of being left alone up there than I was of him.

A girl disappeared from Clayton Falls a couple of years before I did, and I used to worry about finding her body in the woods when I was walking Emma. Now I wondered if the world was full of girls like me. Their families had moved on. They weren't front-page news anymore. They were locked up in some cabin or dungeon with their very own freak, still waiting to be rescued.

When I made another mark on the wall, I tried not to think about how long I'd already been there. I tried to believe as each day went by I was getting closer to being found. The longer I stayed alive, the more time I was giving them to find me. I thought about what would happen if I was rescued while I was pregnant. I was close to five months, and I was pretty sure that was too late for an abortion, but I didn't think I could have gone through with one no matter how I felt about the baby. I wondered how my family and Luke would feel about my being pregnant. I couldn't see Luke cuddling my rapist's child in his arms and welcoming it into his life. I was having a hard enough time seeing myself doing that.

You'd think I would have liked it when The Freak was gone, but every day I was more anxious. Waiting for the door to open, praying for the door to open. I hated him, but I couldn't wait to see him. I was completely dependent on him.

Not knowing how long he was going to be, I rationed out the food he'd left. He wasn't there to tell me what time to eat, so I tried to follow my body's rhythm, but I was hungry all the time. I know a lot of pregnant women feel sick in the beginning, but I never felt nauseous, just sleepy and famished.

All my life I'd preferred to be outside as much as possible—I went swimming every night in the summer and skied every weekend in the winter. But there I was, staring at four walls. I constantly paced back and forth on one side of the cabin. Years ago I saw a bear in a zoo who kept running along the fence, one end to the other. He'd worn a deep groove in the ground. I remember wondering if he'd rather be dead than live a life like that.

When I wasn't pacing, I leaned on the walls and wondered what was on the other side, or sat in the bathroom with an eye pressed to my hole in the wall. If the sun was out, the hole made a small spot of light on the back of the bathroom door, and I spent hours watching it inch its way down until it disappeared.

Without him there were no novels, so I made up cinematic fantasies. I visualized my mom at home praying I was okay, talking to the police, pleading for my return on TV. I could see Christina and Luke combing the woods for me every weekend with Emma trying to pick up my scent. Best of all, I saw Luke breaking down the cabin door and lifting me up in his arms.

I imagined that Mom had even quit drinking and started a mom's search-and-rescue group like you see those mothers of missing children doing. I dreamed up an epiphany for her— realizing how she'd treated me my whole life, she wanted to make it all up to me. Once I was rescued, we'd be closer because of all this.

I never thought I'd miss Wayne's dumbass jokes and the way he sometimes ruffles my hair like I'm still twelve. But now I made bargains with God and promised that if I could just go home I'd listen to a thousand of his lame business ideas.

I spent a lot of time touching my stomach and wondering what the baby looked like. Some of the books showed pictures of the fetus at various stages and I thought every one of them was gross. I was pretty sure my baby would look good, but with The Freak as a father what kind of child would it be?

The Freak returned after five endless days.

"Sit down on the bed, Annie," he said the minute he came in. "We need to talk." I sat with my back to the wall and he sat beside me, holding my hand.

"I went back to Clayton Falls, and I really wish I didn't

have to tell you this. . . ." He shook his head back and forth, slowly. "But all the searches have been called off."

No!

His thumb rubbed slow circles on my hand. "Are you okay, Annie? I'm sure that was quite the blow."

I nodded.

"I have to admit, I was surprised to see your house on the market so soon, but I suppose they feel it's time to move on." Anger displaced shock at the thought of my house for sale— a Victorian three-story I fell in love with as soon as I saw its gorgeous stained-glass windows, nine-foot ceilings, and original hardwood floors. Could Mom do that? She'd never liked the house, thought it too old and drafty. Had Wayne helped her pound the FOR SALE sign into the front yard? He was probably happy to be rid of his smart-ass stepdaughter.

"How did you find out?"

"It doesn't matter how, it matters that I care enough to tell you. I learned something else while I was there." He paused. I knew he was waiting for my line, and I didn't want to play into his hands. But I had to know, which meant I had to ask.

"What else?" *How are you going to hurt me next, you bastard?*

"Something extremely interesting about Luke. . . ."

This time I forced myself to remain silent. He broke after a couple of beats.

"It would seem he's already grown tired of waiting for you."

"I don't believe you. Luke *loves* me—"

"Well, when I saw him walking with his arm around that lovely blond woman, and he leaned down to whisper in her ear, I don't think he was telling her how much he loved *you*, Annie."

"You're lying, he wouldn't—"

"He wouldn't what? Can you honestly tell me you *never* wondered if sweet Luke was just too good to be true? He's *weak*, Annie."

Mind reeling, I stared at the far wall.

The Freak nodded. "But you're starting to see it now. What I saved you from."

Was it possible Luke could already be dating someone else? There was one blond hostess, I couldn't remember her name but I'd thought she had a crush on him. He told me I was being silly.

The day before I was abducted, Luke hadn't sounded enthusiastic when I invited him over for dinner the next night. He was at the restaurant, and I figured he was just busy—or maybe thought I might have to cancel again. Had there been another woman even back then? No, there couldn't have been. Luke never once told me he was unhappy, and he didn't have a cheating cell in his body.

The Freak turned my chin so I was forced to make eye contact. "I'm the only one you have left, Annie."

He was just lying. All of this was his latest, best move in his sick game. He loved nothing more than to shake me up. Other people cared about me, lots of people. So I hadn't been a perfect girlfriend, especially right before I was abducted, but Luke wasn't going to replace me just like that. And Christina loved me—she'd been my best friend forever, I knew she wouldn't forget about me. Maybe Mom and I didn't always see eye to eye—she and Daisy always got along better—but she'd be devastated that I was missing. Selling my house didn't mean anything, if it was true. It was probably for reward money.

But, what if The Freak wasn't lying? What if they really weren't looking for me anymore? What if they'd all moved on? Luke might have a new girlfriend, one who didn't work all the time. Mom could be signing a deal on my house right now, Emma could have forgotten all about me too. Was she with Luke and this blonde? Everybody was going forward with their lives and I was going to be trapped with a crazy sadist-rapist forever.

The Freak made it seem so real, and what evidence did I have to prove any different? Nobody had found me, had they? I wanted to argue with him and convince him that other people loved me, but when I opened my mouth, nothing came out. Instead I remembered the dog pound.

I used to help out there—mostly just cleaning out kennels and taking dogs for walks. Some of the dogs had been abused and bit anyone who came near them. There were others that wouldn't let themselves give or receive affection no matter what, and some that became completely submissive and peed if you so much as raised your voice. Then there were the ones that had given up and just sat in their cages, staring at the wall when possible new owners came in.

This one dog, Bubbles, an ugly little thing with a skin condition, was there for ages, but as soon as anyone new came in he pranced up to the front of the cage like he was the most beautiful creature in the world. Always hopeful. I wanted to take him home, but I was living in an apartment at the time. Eventually I had to quit because of work, so I never got to see whether anybody adopted him. Now I was the dumb dog waiting for someone to take me home. I hoped they put Bubbles to sleep before he finally figured out no one was coming for him.

SESSION NINE

I stopped to get some gas on the way home from our last session, and up by the register, the shelves were loaded with bags of candy. I was never allowed anything like that on the mountain, and for so long I missed things, stupid little day-to-day things, then as time passed I stopped missing them, because I couldn't remember what I liked anymore. Standing there, looking at the candies, I *remembered* I liked them and rage boiled up inside me.

The girl behind the counter said, "Is that all?" And I heard myself say, "No," and then my hands were scooping bags and bags of candy off the shelves—sours, jujubes, wine gums, jelly snakes, anything. People were standing behind me, watching a crazy woman grab at candy like it was Halloween, but I didn't give a shit.

In my car I ripped open the little bags and started stuffing my mouth full of candies. I was crying—didn't know or care why—and I ate so many that I threw up when I got home and my tongue was covered with little sores. But I ate more—a whole lot more—and fast, like I was afraid someone was going to stop me any second. I wanted to be that girl who used to like candy so bad, Doc. So bad.

I sat at my kitchen table—wrappers and empty bags all around me—and couldn't stop crying. I had a sugar headache. I was going to throw up again. But I was crying because the candies didn't taste like I remembered. *Nothing* tastes like I remember.

The Freak never did tell me why he'd gone back to Clayton Falls or what he did there other than spy on my so-called loved ones, but the first night after his return he sure was in a good mood. Nothing puts a skip in a freak's step like telling a girl no one gives a shit about her. While he made dinner he whistled and danced around in the kitchen like he was on a cooking show.

When I glared at him, he just smiled and took a bow.

If he'd made it to Clayton Falls and back in five days, I couldn't be that far away or that far north, unless he just parked the van and flew somewhere. Regardless, none of it seemed to matter anymore. Whether I was five or five hundred miles from my home, the distance was insurmountable. When I thought of my house I'd loved so much, friends and family, search parties that weren't searching, all I felt was a giant blanket of fatigue wrapping itself around me and pulling me down. *Just sleep. Sleep it all away.*

I might have felt like that indefinitely, but two weeks after The Freak came home, around the middle of February, when I was about five months along, I felt the baby move. It was the strangest sensation, like I'd swallowed a butterfly, and in that moment the baby stopped being something evil, stopped being something of *his*. It was mine and I didn't have to share it.

After that, I liked being pregnant. Each week, as I grew and rounded out, I was amazed that my body was creating a life. I didn't feel dead inside, I felt alive. Even The Freak's recharged obsession with my body didn't change my feelings about being pregnant. He'd make me stand in front of him while he ran his hands all over my stomach and breasts. During one of these "examinations," which I'd spend counting knotholes in the ceiling, he said, "You don't know how lucky you are to have your child born away from today's society, Annie. All human beings do is destroy—they rip apart nature, love, and families, with war, with governments, with greed. But here I've created a pure world, a *safe* world, for us to raise our child in."

As I listened to him, I thought about the drunk driver killing my dad and sister. I thought about the doctors loading Mom up with pills, the Realtors I knew who'd do anything to get a deal, my friends and family who were moving on, cops who must have their heads stuck up their asses or I'd have been found by now.

I hated that I was even considering the opinion of a freak. But if somebody is telling you the sky is green, even though you know it's blue, and they act like the sky is green and they keep saying it's green day in, day out, like they really *believe* it, eventually you could start wondering if maybe you're nuts for thinking it's blue.

I often wondered, *Why me?* Why, of all the girls he could have taken, did he pick a Realtor, a career woman? Not exactly mountain wife material. Not that I'd have wished this on anyone, but wouldn't he want someone he knew would be weak? Someone he knew it wouldn't take much to fuck with? But then I realized he did know. He knew all along.

I thought I'd worked past my childhood, past my family, past my pain, but when you've rolled around in manure long enough, there's no getting away from the stench. You can buy every damn type of soap out there and scrub your skin until you're raw, but then one day you're out walking around and a fly lands on you. Then another one, then another— because they *know*. They know that underneath that fresh-scrubbed skin you're just manure. Nothing but shit. You can clean it up all you want, but the flies always know where to land.

That winter The Freak put me on a reward system. If he was happy with me he gave me things—one extra slice of meat at dinner or one extra pee break. If I folded the laundry perfectly, I was allowed a little bit of sugar in my tea. After one of his trips into town, he said I'd been a good girl and gave me an apple.

So much had been taken away that when he gave me anything, even something as mundane as an apple, it became huge. I ate it with my eyes closed, and in my mind I was sitting under a tree in the summer—I could almost feel the sun on my legs.

He still punished me if I did something wrong, but he hadn't hit me for a long time, and sometimes I wished he would. Being hit was a physical act that made me feel defiant. But the mind shit? That really did a number on me, and as the months passed, the voices of my loved ones faded to whispers and their faces blurred. Little by little, day by day, the sky became green.

He still continued with the rapes after I started to show, but they were different somehow, more like he was now the one acting a role. Once in a while he'd even turn gentle, loving, then catch himself and blush, as though it were the niceness that was wrong.

A couple of times he simply stopped and rested beside me with his hand on my belly, then he'd ask me questions: What did it feel like to be pregnant? Could I feel the baby moving? If he wasn't in the mood for sex I'd still have to put on the dress, and we'd usually lie in bed with his head on my chest.

One night the weight of his head on my breasts triggered a nurturing sensation, and I started daydreaming about the baby. Without thinking I started singing, "Hush little baby, don't you cry," out loud. I stopped as soon as I realized what I was doing. He shifted his head so it rested on my shoulder, then looked me in the eye.

"My mother used to sing that to me. Did your mother ever sing to you, Annie?"

"Not that I remember."

My mind searched for ways to keep the conversation going. I wanted to know more about him, but it wasn't like I could just come out and say, "So how did you turn into such a freak?"

"Your mom must have been an interesting person," I said, hoping I wasn't stepping onto a land mine, but he didn't say anything. "Do you want me to sing you something special? I don't know many songs, but I could try. I took lessons when I was a kid."

"Not right now. I want to hear more about your childhood."

Shit. Could I get him to tell me revealing stuff by talking about my crap?

"Mom wasn't really the sing-you-to-sleep type," I said.

"And these lessons, were they your idea?"

"That was all Mom."

My whole childhood was spent trying something new, singing lessons, piano lessons, and of course figure skating. Daisy was into skating from the time she was little, but I didn't last long. I spent more time with my ass on the ice than in the air. Mom tried me in ballet, too, but that ended when I spun into another little girl and just about broke her nose.

Even the accident didn't stop my mom. If anything, her golden child's death increased her need to make me good at *something*. Well, what I got good at was sabotage. It's amazing how many ways you can break instruments or ruin sequined costumes.

"What kind of lessons did you want to take?"

"I was into art, painting and drawing, stuff like that, but Mom wasn't."

"So if she wasn't, then you couldn't be?" His eyebrows rose. "Doesn't sound like she was very fair, or much fun."

"When we were younger, before Daisy died, she could be fun. Like every Christmas we made huge gingerbread houses, and she'd play dress-up with us all the time. Sometimes she'd build forts in the middle of the living room with Daisy and me, then we'd stay up late watching scary movies."

"Did *you* like the scary movies?"

"I liked being with Daisy and her. . . . They just had a different sense of humor. Mom's really into pranks and stuff, like one Halloween she poured ketchup all over the floor by my bed so when I woke up and stepped in it I'd think it was blood. She and Daisy laughed about it for days." I still hate ketchup.

"But you didn't think it was so funny, did you?"

I shrugged. The Freak began to look bored and shifted his weight like he was going to get up. Shit. I had to start showing him some real feelings if I wanted him to connect with me.

"It made me cry. Mom still likes to tell everyone how she fooled me. She gets off on stuff like that, fooling people. She even used to trick-or-treat with us."

"Interesting. And why do you think your mother likes to 'fool people,' as you say?"

"Who knows, but she's damn good at it. It's how she gets most of her makeup and clothes—she has every saleswoman in and out of town wrapped around her finger."

It didn't take many bottles of knockoff perfume before Mom went hunting for a sucker behind a department-store cosmetics counter. Saleswomen not only gave the pretty grieving widow makeovers but plenty of free samples as well, especially when Mom was so good about talking up the products to any woman who happened by.

That's not all she was good at. She may have small hands but Mom has sharp eyes, and those hands of hers are fast. The top of her dresser was littered with half-used cologne, potions, and lotions she'd gotten bored with after plucking them off a counter when a saleslady's back was turned. Sometimes she actually bought stuff, but she generally returned it at the same store in a different town. I finally said something, but she told me that with all the sales she was helping the women make, she considered the occasional bottle her commission.

Once Mom realized how easy it was to steal perfume she

moved on to clothes and lingerie. Good stuff too, from boutiques. When I got older I refused to go with her. I'm pretty sure she still does it, I don't ask, but the woman is better dressed than most fashion models.

"Sometimes I think she liked me better as a kid," I said. The Freak's eyes burned into mine. I'd touched a nerve.

With our eyes locked, I said, "Maybe I was more fun for her when I was little, or maybe it's because I started getting my own opinions and actually challenged her. Whatever the reason, I'm pretty sure she's disappointed I grew up."

The Freak cleared his throat, then paused and shook his head. He wanted to say something, he just needed a little nudge. In my gentlest voice I said, "Did you ever feel like that when you were a kid?"

He rolled onto his back and stared up at the ceiling, his head still resting on my arm. "My mother didn't want me to grow up."

"Maybe all moms feel sad when their kids grow up."

"No, it was . . . it wasn't that."

I thought of his total lack of body hair and his obsessive shaving. I forced myself to curl my arm around under his head and rest my hand on his forehead. He flinched in surprise, then glanced at me, but he didn't pull away.

I said, "So her first child died . . ." His body tensed against my side. I lifted my palm to stroke his hair so he'd relax, but, unsure of his response, slowly dropped it back down on his curls and just pressed my leg against his so he'd feel its warmth. "Do you think it had something to do with that? Did you feel like you had to live up to him? You know, like you were a replacement?" His eyes darkened as he turned slightly away. I had to stop him from shutting down.

"You asked me about Daisy before, and I didn't want to

talk about it because it's still pretty hard for me. She was great, I mean she was my big sister and I'm sure sometimes she got annoyed with me, but I thought she was perfect. Mom did too. After the accident I'd catch her staring at me, or she'd walk by and touch my hair, and just in the way she did it, I knew she was thinking about Daisy."

He faced me again. "Did she ever say anything?"

"Not really. At least, nothing I could point to. But you don't have to hear the words to know. She'd never admit it, but I'm pretty sure she wishes I was the one who went through the windshield. And I can't even blame her for it—for a long time I wished it too. Daisy was the better one. When I was a kid I thought that was why God wanted her."

I don't know what the hell happened, it was probably just the stupid hormones, but I started to cry. That was the first time I'd admitted those feelings to *anyone*. He opened his mouth and took a breath like he was about to say something. But he didn't, he just closed it, gave my leg a pat, and stared back up at the ceiling.

What was he afraid of? How was I going to get him to trust me and open up? So far, all I'd been able to do was put myself through emotional hell by dredging up this shit. I'd heard some kids feel loyalty to their abusers. Was that what was holding him back?

"I probably shouldn't even be telling you this stuff," I said. "My mom did so much for me over the years that I feel like if I say anything bad about her I'm betraying her." His head cocked toward me. "But I guess parents are humans who make mistakes too." My mind worked to call up every forgive-your-parent self-help platitude I'd ever read. "I keep telling myself it's okay to talk about these things, I can still love my mom and not always like everything she does."

"My mother was a wonderful woman." He paused. I waited. "We had dress-up time too."

Now things were getting interesting.

"I was only five, but I still remember the day she came to see me at my foster home. The idiot she was married to was there too but he barely looked at me. She was wearing this white sundress, and when she hugged me she smelled clean, not like the fat pig who was my foster mother. She told me to be a good boy and she was going to come back and get me, and she did. Her husband was away on another of his trips, so it was just us, and when we got home—I'd never seen such a clean house—she gave me a bath."

I tried not to show any emotion in my voice when I spoke. "That must have been nice. . . ."

"I'd never had one like it, there were candles and it smelled good. When she washed my hair and back, her hands were so gentle. She let the dirty water drain away, then she added more and got in with me, to wash me better. When she kissed my bruises, her lips felt soft, like velvet. And she said she was taking the pain out through my skin and into her." He glanced at me, and I don't know how I pulled it off, but I nodded as though what he'd just told me was the most natural thing in the world.

"She told me I could sleep in her bed because she didn't want me to be scared. I'd never felt another human being's skin against mine—no one had ever even held me before—and I could feel her heart beating." He patted his chest. "She liked to touch my hair, like how your mom touched yours, and she said it reminded her of her son's." My hand resting on his curls itched and I fought the urge to pull away.

"She couldn't have any more children, and she said she'd waited a long time to find a boy like me. She cried that first night. . . . I promised I'd be a good boy." He grew quiet again.

"You mentioned playing dress-up together. . . . You mean like cowboys and Indians?" It took him a long time to answer. When he did, I wished he hadn't.

"After our bath every night. . . ." Oh, *shit*. "I slept in her bed, it made her feel safer, but on the nights when he was coming back from a trip, we'd have our bath earlier and then I'd help her get dressed." His voice flattened. "For him."

"That must have made you feel kind of abandoned. You get to have her all to yourself, then as soon as he's home you're shoved to the side."

"She had to do that, he was her husband." He turned his face back to me and in a firm voice said, "But I was special to her. She said I was her little man."

Got it.

"*Of course* she thought you were special—she picked you, right?"

He smiled. "Just like I picked you."

Later, when he climbed into bed beside me and laid his head on my chest, I realized I felt bad for him. I did. It was the first time I'd felt something other than disgust, fear, or hatred for him, and it scared me more than anything.

The guy *abducted* me, Doc, raped me, hit me, I shouldn't have given a shit about his pain, but when he told me that stuff about his mother—and I knew there had to be even more—I felt *bad* he had a fucked-up mom who fucked him up. I felt bad he'd been in an abusive foster home, bad that his new dad didn't seem to give a shit about him. Was it because my family's warped? Is that why I felt his pain, because I have it too? All I know is I hate it, Doc, I hate that I felt one ounce of compassion for that freak. I hate that I'm even telling you this shit.

Most people assume the guy had me at gunpoint the whole time, and I don't tell them any different. How could I ever explain? How can I tell them that when he told me about places in the world like the Rock of Gibraltar, where all those monkeys are, I found him interesting and articulate? And that sometimes when he rubbed my feet, they were so damn swollen, I *liked* it. Or that he could be so enthusiastic and funny during book-reading time, or when he was cooking—he had this one stupid dance he did every time he flipped an egg and he'd talk in different accents—I'd see the guy who first stopped at the open house. How could I ever tell anyone he made me *laugh*?

I was always so proud, proud of my strength. I've always been a no-man-is-ever-going-to-change-me girl, but he did. He did change me. I felt like I still had a little flame inside that was me. Like the pilot light on a gas fireplace, flickering in the background, but I worried that it would blow out one day. I *still* worry it's going to blow out one day.

There are all these books that say we create our own destiny and what we believe is what we manifest. You're supposed to walk around with this perpetual bubble over your head thinking happy thoughts and then everything is going to be sunshine and roses. Nope, sorry, don't think so. You can be as happy as you've ever been in your life, and shit is still going to happen.

But it doesn't just *happen*. It knocks you sideways and crushes you into the ground, because you were stupid enough to believe in sunshine and roses.

SESSION TEN

Man, did I ever have a big moment last night, Doc. I was asleep—in my bed, which should make you happy—but then I needed to pee, so I stumbled to the bathroom. On my way back I realized what I'd done, and damn if that didn't wake me right up—of course I got so excited, I couldn't sleep for the rest of the night.

It was just an old habit, going in the middle of the night, but that's good because it means my old routines are coming back, right? And maybe it means *I'm* coming back. Don't worry, I remember what you said about learning to accept that I'll never be the exact same person I was before the abduction. But still, it's *something*.

Maybe it worked because I'd been asleep and didn't have a chance to think about it first. I've always liked that expression, "Dance like no one's watching." Say you're at home alone and a funky song comes on the radio, you might start grooving to it a little, feeling good, finding the beat, really getting into it.

Your legs are going every which way, your hands are in the air, and you're shaking some serious ass. But as soon as you're out in public somewhere you start thinking everyone is watching you, judging you. You go, Is my ass jiggling too much? Am I in rhythm? Are they laughing at me? Then you stop dancing.

Every single day up on the mountain, I was being tested. If he was happy, I got extra privileges. If I didn't do something fast enough or perfect enough, which wasn't often because I was damn careful, I got slapped or privileges were taken away.

While The Freak was busy evaluating my behavior, I was analyzing his. Even after our talk about his mother I couldn't get a handle on what might set him off, and each situation was a clue to be collected and filed in my memory. Interpreting his needs and wants became my full-time job, so I studied every nuance of his expression, every inflection in his speech.

Years of living with a mother whose sobriety I'd learned to judge by the exact droop of her eyelids had honed my skills, but I'd also learned in mom-school that it's like trying to predict the actions of a tiger—you never know whether you're about to be a playmate or a meal. *Everything* depended on his mood. Sometimes I could make a mistake and he barely reacted, then I'd commit a lesser offense and he'd totally lose it.

Around March, when I was about six months pregnant, he walked in after one of his hunting trips and said, "I need your help outside."

Outside? As in *outdoors*? I stared at him, looking for any sign that he was joking or planned on killing me out there, but his face showed no emotion.

He threw one of his coats and a pair of rubber boots at me. "Put these on."

Before I even had the zipper done up on the coat, he grabbed my arm and pulled me out the door.

The smell of fresh air hit me in the face like I'd walked into a wall, and my chest tightened up with the surprise of it. I tried to check out my surroundings as he led me over to a deer carcass about twenty feet from the cabin, but it was a sunny day and the brightness of the snow made my eyes water. All I could tell was that we were in a clearing.

My whole body stung from the cold. The snow only covered the foot part of my boots, but I wasn't used to being outside and my legs were bare. My eyes started to adjust to the light, but before I could register much of anything, he pushed me to my knees beside the deer's head. Blood still oozed from a hole behind its ear and a slit across its throat that had turned the snow around it pink. I tried to look away, but The Freak turned my face toward the carcass.

"Pay attention. I want you to kneel at the rear of the deer, and after we roll him onto his back, you'll hold his back legs apart while I gut him. Understand?"

I understood what he wanted me to do, I just didn't understand why he was asking—he never had before. Maybe he just wanted me to see what he could do, or more precisely, what he could do to *me*.

But I nodded and, avoiding the deer's glazed eyes, I moved to crouch in the snow at its hind end and grabbed its stiff back legs. The Freak, smiling and humming, knelt at its head, and we rolled it onto its back.

Even though I knew it was already dead, it bothered me to see the deer look so helpless and undignified on its back with its legs held spread-eagle. I'd never seen a dead animal up close before. Perhaps sensing my distress, the baby moved restlessly.

My stomach heaved as I watched the tip of The Freak's knife slice into the skin at the deer's groin like it was butter. My nose caught the metallic scent of blood as he circled the deer's privates, then slit all along down its stomach. I was struck with an image of his slicing into me with that same serene expression on his face. My body jerked, and he gave me a look.

I whispered, "Sorry," gritted my teeth against the cold, and forced my muscles still. He went back to his humming and slicing.

While he was distracted, I looked around the clearing. A big stand of fir trees surrounded us, their branches weighted down with snow. Footsteps, drag marks, and what looked like the odd drop of blood disappeared around the side of the cabin. The air smelled clean, moist, and the snow crunched under my feet. I've skied on some mountains across Canada, and snow smells different in other areas, drier somehow, and it even feels different. The modest amount of snow and the lay of the land, along with the scent, had me hopeful I was still on the island or at least somewhere on the coast.

The Freak talked to me while he sliced. "It's better for us to eat food off the land, food that's pure and hasn't been touched by humans. When I went into town I bought some new books, so you can learn how to cure meats and can foods. Eventually we'll be completely self-sufficient, and I'll never have to leave you alone."

Not high on my wish list, but I have to say I was excited at the idea of doing something, anything, new.

When he finished slicing the whole deer open, and its stomach sack bulged out, he looked up from the carcass and said, "Have you ever killed, Annie?" As if a knife in his hand wasn't threatening enough, he has to start *talking* about killing?

"I've never been hunting."

"Answer the question, Annie." We stared at each other over the deer.

"No, I've never killed."

Holding the knife by the very tip of its handle, he swung it back and forth like a pendulum. With every upswing, he repeated, "Never? Never? Never?"

"Never—"

"Liar!" He tossed the knife up, grabbed the handle as it fell, and plunged it into the deer's neck to the hilt. Startled, I lost my grip and fell onto my back in the snow. He didn't say a word as I struggled to sit up. When I was back in a crouched position, I quickly grabbed the deer's legs and braced for him to flip out because I'd fallen, but he just stared at me. Then his gaze dropped to the slit in the deer's stomach, moved to my belly, and met my eyes again. I started babbling.

"I hit a cat with my car when I was a teenager. I didn't mean to, but I was coming home late and I was really tired, and then I heard this thunk, and I saw it spin up in the air. I saw it land and go into the woods, and I pulled over." The Freak kept staring at me and the words kept pouring out.

"I walked in the woods looking for it, and I was crying and calling, 'Kitty, Kitty,' but it was gone. I went home and told my stepdad, and he came with me back to the spot with flashlights and we looked for like an hour, but we couldn't find it. He told me it was probably fine and had run home. But in the morning, I looked under my car and there was all this blood and fur on my axle."

"I'm impressed," he said with a big smile. "I didn't think you had it in you."

"I don't! It was an accident—"

"No, I don't think so. I think you saw his eyes reflect in the headlights and for a moment you wondered what it would feel like. And suddenly you just *hated* that cat, and then you floored the accelerator. I think the thud when you connected, when you knew you'd hit it, made you feel powerful, made you—"

"NO! No, of course not. I felt terrible—I *still* feel terrible."

"Would you still feel terrible if the cat was a killer? He was probably out hunting, you realize—have you seen a cat torture its prey? What if the cat was diseased and homeless with no one to love it? Would that make it better, Annie? What if you could tell by looking at it that its owners were abusing it, not giving it enough food, kicking it?" His voice rose. *"Maybe you did him a goddamn favor, did you ever think about that?"*

It almost seemed like he wanted my approval of something he'd done. Did he want to confess or just fuck with my head? The latter seemed more likely, so I'm not sure which of us was more surprised when I finally spoke.

"Have you ever . . . have you ever killed a person?"

He reached out and gently caressed the handle of the knife.

"A brave question."

"I'm sorry, I've just never met anyone who's . . . you know. I've read a lot of books and watched TV and movies, but it's not like talking to a real person who's done it." It was easy to sound genuinely interested—I've always been fascinated with psychology, especially abnormal psychology. Murderers definitely fit that category.

"And if you did talk to, as you say, 'a real person who's done it,' what would you ask?"

"I . . . I would want to know why. But maybe sometimes they don't know, or don't even understand it themselves?"

It must have been the right answer, because he nodded decisively and said, "Killing is a funny thing. Humans make all these rules about when they consider it to be okay." He gave a quick laugh. "Self-defense? No problem. You find a doctor to say you're insane, and that's okay. A woman kills her husband, but she has PMS? If you have a good enough lawyer, that's okay too."

With his head tilted up at me, he rocked back and forth on his heels in the snow. "What if you knew how things were going to turn out and you could stop it? What if you could see something, something no one else could?"

"Like what?"

"It's a shame you didn't find the cat, Annie. Death is simply an extension of life. And if you witness death, the opening of a new dimension, you become aware of how unnecessary it is to limit yourself in this one."

He still hadn't actually admitted to killing anyone, and I wondered if I should leave it alone for now, but knowing when to pull back has never been one of my strengths.

"So what does it feel like? To kill someone?"

His head cocked to the side and his brows rose. "Planning on killing someone, are we?" Before I could deny it, he continued, but not in the direction I expected. "My mother died of cancer. Ovarian cancer. She rotted from the inside out, and at the end I could smell her dying." He paused for a second, his eyes flat and dead. I was trying to think what to ask next when he said, "I was only eighteen when she got sick— her husband had died a couple of years before—but I didn't mind looking after her. I knew how to take care of her better than anyone. But she wouldn't stop crying for him. Even though I'd told her he left and that he hadn't cared about her, not like I did, all she wanted was for me to find him. After everything I'd done for her. . . . I saw what he did to her. Saw it with my own eyes, but she cried for him."

"I don't understand, you said he died. What do you mean you told her he left?"

"He'd be gone for months, *months*, and we'd be fine. And then he'd come home, and I always knew when he was coming, because I helped her put on the dress for him, and she'd wear makeup. I told her I didn't like it, but she said *he* liked it. He wouldn't even let me eat with them. I know she wanted to feed me, but he made her wait until he was done. I was nothing more to him than a stray dog his wife had brought home from the pound. Later, after dinner, they went into the bedroom and closed the door, but one night, when I was around seven, they didn't close it all the way. And I saw . . . she was crying. His hands . . ." His voice drifted off and he stared at nothing.

"Was your dad hitting her?"

I'd noticed before that when he talked about his mom his voice would flatten, and when he answered this time it sounded almost robotic.

"I was gentle . . . I was always gentle when I touched her. I didn't make her cry. It wasn't right."

"He was hurting her?"

Staring hard at the center of my chest, his eyes vacant, he shook his head back and forth and repeated, "It wasn't right."

He caressed the base of his neck. "She saw me . . . in the mirror. She saw me." The flesh around his fingers reddened as he tightened his grip on his throat for a second, then he pulled his hand down to rub at his thigh like he was trying to wipe something off his palm.

In a raspy voice he said, "Then she *smiled*." The Freak's mouth lifted up into a beatific smile, then widened until it was almost a grimace. He held it so long it had to be painful. My heart lurched in my chest.

Finally meeting my eyes, he said, "After that she always left the door open. For *years* she left the door open."

His voice flattened again. "When I was fifteen she started shaving me too, so I was smooth all over like her, and if I held her too hard in the night she got mad. Sometimes when I had dreams, the sheets . . . she made me burn them. She was changing."

Careful to keep my voice tender and soft, I said, "Changing?"

"I came home early from school one day. There were sounds from the bedroom. I thought he was on a trip. So I went to the door." He was rubbing at his chest now, like he was having a hard time getting air.

"He was behind her. And another man, a stranger. . . . I left before she could see me. Waited outside, under the porch—"

He stopped abruptly and after a few beats I said, "Under the porch?"

"With my books. That's where I hid them. I was only allowed to read inside if he was home. When he was gone she said they interfered with our time. If she caught me with one, she ripped the pages out." Now I knew why he was so careful with books.

"An hour later when the men passed over me, I could still smell her on them. They were going for a beer. She was inside—*humming.*" He shook his head. "She shouldn't have let them do those things to her. She was sick. She couldn't see it was wrong. She needed my help."

"So did you? Help her?"

"I had to save her, to save us, before she changed so much I couldn't help her anymore, you see?"

I saw. I nodded.

Satisfied, he continued. "A week later when she was at the store, I asked him to take me for a drive so I could show him an old mine up in the woods." He stared down at the knife in the deer's neck. "When she got home I told her he'd packed all his belongings and left, he'd found someone else. She cried, but I took care of her, just like in the beginning, but this time it was even better because I didn't have to share her. Then she got sick and I did everything for her that she liked, everything she asked. Everything. So when she got sicker and asked me to kill her she thought I would just do it. But I didn't want to. I couldn't. She begged, she said I wasn't a real man, that a real man could have done it. She said *he* would have done it, but I just couldn't."

While he'd been talking the sun had disappeared and it began to snow—a light dusting of white frosted us and the deer. One of The Freak's blond waves had fallen over his forehead in a curl, and his eyelashes spiked together and sparkled. I wasn't sure if it was from the snow or tears, but he looked angelic.

My thighs ached from holding a crouched position for too long, but there was no way I was asking him if I could stretch. My body may have been motionless, but my mind reeled.

He shook his head, then looked up from the knife.

"So to answer your question, Annie, it can feel great. But we'd better get a move on, or some wild animal is going to smell the fresh blood and come hunting us." His tone of voice was now cheerful.

For a minute I didn't get what question he was talking about. Then I remembered. I'd asked him what it felt like to kill someone.

While I continued to hold the deer's legs, he reached into the slit and gently rolled the stomach sack, about the size of a beach ball, out onto the snow. It was still attached at one end, by something that looked like an umbilical cord, from under the rib cage. He pulled his knife out of the neck—it stuck for a second, then released with a pop. Then he reached back in with the knife and cut out what looked like the deer's heart and organs. He dropped them near the sack like they were garbage. The smell of raw meat churned up bile at the back of my throat, but I choked it down.

He said, "Stay here," and disappeared into a large shed at the side of the cabin. He returned in seconds carrying a small chain saw and some rope. My breath caught in my chest when he knelt at the deer's head. The pristine silence of winter wilderness was shattered by the sound of the saw cutting through the deer's neck. I wanted to look away but I couldn't. He put the saw down, picked up the knife, and walked to the rear of the deer. I flinched as he reached toward me, which made him laugh, but he was only taking the legs from me. Then he used his knife to slice a hole through the ankle, right behind the Achilles tendon on both legs, and threaded the rope through.

We dragged the carcass to the shed, each holding one of its front legs. I glanced back. The deer's body had left a trail of blood behind us and a bloody indentation in the snow. I'll never forget the sight of that poor deer's head, heart, and guts lying out in the cold.

The shed was solid metal—no wild animals welcome—and a big freezer stood against one wall inside. Some sort of machinery that I think was a generator hummed noisily at the back, beside it a pump that must have been for the well. Six big red barrels labeled DIESEL lined the opposite wall. Next to them was a propane tank. I didn't see any firewood, so I figured it was stored somewhere else. The air smelled like a mixture of oil, gas, and deer blood.

He threw the rope attached to the deer's back legs up over a crossbeam in the ceiling, then we both pulled on it until the carcass was hung. Would my body be hanging up there one day?

I thought that was the end of it, but he started to sharpen the knife on a stone, and I began to tremble violently. Meeting my eyes, he scraped the knife back and forth in a rhythmic motion with a smile playing about his lips. After a minute or so, he held it up.

"What do you think? Sharp enough?"

"For . . . for what?"

He began to walk toward me. I threw my hands in front of my belly. Awkward in the rubber boots, I stumbled backward.

He stopped, and with a confused expression said, "What's wrong with you? We have to skin it." He cut around each ankle, then took a leg. "Don't just stand there, grab the other one." We rolled the hide down—he had to use his knife to nick at the tissue once in a while to help it along, but mostly just down the legs, and when we reached the main part, it peeled off like dead skin after a sunburn.

When it was off, he rolled it up and put it in the freezer. Then he made me stand outside where he could see me while he collected the saw, put it back in the shed, and locked it up. I asked him what he was going to do with the innards and its head—he said he'd deal with them later.

Back inside, he noticed I was shivering and told me to sit by the fire to warm up. Our talk didn't seem to have upset him. I considered asking if he'd killed anyone else, but my stomach clenched at the thought of hearing his answer. Instead I said, "Can I wash off, please?"

"Is it time for your bath?"

"No, but I—"

"Then you know the answer."

The rest of that day I wore deer blood. It made my skin crawl, but I tried not to think about it, I tried not to think about anything—not blood, dead deer, or murdered fathers. I just focused on the fire and watched the flames dance.

Later that night, as he drifted off to sleep, he said, "I like cats." He *liked* cats? The murdering sadistic fuck *liked cats*? A hysterical giggle fought to come out my throat, but I clamped my hand over my mouth in the dark.

SESSION ELEVEN

Got to tell you, Doc, I feel like I'm doing pretty good these days. Yesterday afternoon I wanted to just crawl back into bed, but I grabbed Emma's leash and took her down to the waterfront for a walk. As opposed to up in the woods for one of our usual jaunts designed to guarantee we won't see a soul.

Instead, we were kind of social. Well, Emma was—she has a weakness for smaller dogs, has to stop and smooch all of them. She's hit or miss with the big ones, but show her a poodle and she's in puppy make-out heaven. I'd managed to avoid most human interactions by staring off into the distance, or at the dogs, or at my feet while jerking on her leash to hurry her by, but when she insisted on visiting with a cocker spaniel, I stopped and actually shot the breeze with the owners, an elderly couple. It was standard dog-owner drivel: What's his name? Timber? And how old? But damn,

Doc, a couple of weeks ago I'd rather have pushed them into the sea than communicate with them on any level.

When I first came back, I had to stay at my mom's place for a while because my house was rented out, and man, was I relieved they hadn't sold it—just another lie The Freak fed me. Fortunately I was so paranoid about ever losing my house that I'd just taken the entire commission from a house sale and placed it in a separate account so I'd have a year's worth of mortgage payments banked. The mortgage company just kept taking their payments out, month after month, and I suppose when my bank account was drained they'd have foreclosed.

I asked Mom where my things were, and she said, "We had to sell it all, Annie. How do you think we came up with the money for your search? Most of the donations went for your reward. We had to use all the rental money too." She sure wasn't kidding—they sold *everything*. I keep expecting to see some chick walking around in my leather coat.

My car was a lease, and once the cops processed it, it went straight back to the dealership. Now I'm driving that piece of shit out there until I figure out what I want to do—a fancy car doesn't seem that important anymore.

I had a lot of savings, but all my bills were on direct withdraw, so I don't have much left. My office gave Mom my paychecks from some deals that closed after I was abducted. She tried to cash them so they could add to the reward money, which has now gone to charity, but they wouldn't let her so she had to deposit them into my account—good thing, or my whole life would've folded.

A few days ago I was cuddling with Emma on the couch when my phone rang. I wasn't in the mood to talk to anyone, but I saw Mom's number on the call display and knew if I didn't answer, she'd just keep calling.

"How's my Annie Bear today?"

"Fine." I wanted to tell her I was tired because the night before—the fifth night in a row I slept in my bed—a branch scratched against my window, and I spent the rest of the night in my closet, wondering if I was ever going to feel safe again.

"Listen, I have some great news—Wayne has come up with an *amazing* business idea. I can't tell you any details until it's finalized, but he's on to something *big*."

You'd think eventually they'd realize the guy just doesn't have the Midas touch. I almost feel sorry for Wayne sometimes. He's not a bad man or even stupid, he's just one of those guys who really wants to be something, but instead of putting the pedal to the metal and driving forward, he's too busy trying to figure out the quickest route there and just ends up going in circles.

When I was a kid he took me with him a couple of times when he went to pitch a new investment idea. I was embarrassed for him—he stood right in people's faces as he was speaking, and when they tried to lean away, he talked louder. For the first few days after a meeting he'd walk around the house all happy, checking his phone messages a million times, and he and Mom would stay up drinking and toasting themselves. Nothing ever came through.

Once in a while he did something that made me think he might not be a total loser. Like when I was fifteen there was a concert I really wanted to go to, and I spent a whole weekend collecting bottles around town. On Monday—the day the tickets had to be bought—I turned them in but I didn't even have close to the amount I needed. I locked myself in my room and cried. After I finally surfaced, I found an envelope under my door with Wayne's handwriting on the front and a ticket inside. When I tried to thank him, he just flushed and said, "Don't worry about it."

As soon as I started making good money in real estate I tried to help them out—new tires, new computer, new fridge, even just cash for bills and groceries. In the beginning it felt good to give them a hand, but then I realized it was like throwing money down a hole—a hole that drained right into the next dumbass business scheme. After I bought my house I couldn't afford to help as much, so I sat them down and explained how they could set up a budget. Mom just stared at me like I was speaking a foreign language. They must be getting by somehow, because their lifestyle sure hasn't changed.

Mom noticed my lack of enthusiasm on the phone and broke into my thoughts. "You haven't said anything."

"Sorry, I hope it works out for him."

"I have a good feeling about this one."

"That's what you said last time."

She was silent for a moment, then said, "I really don't appreciate your negative attitude, Annie. After everything that man did for you while you were missing—after everything we *both* did—the least you could do is show a little more interest."

"I'm sorry. I'm just not in a very good mood right now."

"Maybe if you left your house once in a while instead of moping around all day, you'd be more pleasant to talk to."

"Not likely. Whenever I do try to leave, some dickhead reporter is jumping all over me, not to mention Hollywood agents with their bullshit offers."

"They're just trying to make a living, Annie. If it wasn't for those reporters you hate so much paying you for interviews, you wouldn't have anything to live on yourself, would you?"

Leave it to Mom to make me feel like I was the asshole. Especially when she was right—the vultures *were* funding my living expenses now that my savings were almost gone. But I still couldn't get used to the process, or seeing myself in print and on-screen. Mom saved every newspaper clipping from every interview—finally her chance to have a scrapbook for me—and taped every show. She gave me copies, but I watched only two of them and shoved the rest in a drawer.

"Your fifteen minutes are almost over, Annie. What are you going to do for money then? How are you going to keep your house?"

"I'll figure something out."

"Like what?"

"Something, Mom, I'll think of something." What *was* I going to do? My stomach twisted into knots.

"You know, an agent isn't such a bad idea. They might be able to get you some up-front money."

"You mean get themselves some money. One I talked to wanted me to sign away all my rights—if I'd listened to him the movie people could've done *whatever* they wanted."

"So talk to a producer yourself, then."

"I don't want to talk to *any* of them, Mom. Why is that so hard to understand?"

"Jesus, Annie, I just asked a simple question, you don't have to take my head off."

"Sorry." I took a deep breath. "Maybe I do need to get out more. We better talk about something else before I totally lose it." I forced a laugh. "So how's your garden doing?"

Two things Mom loves talking about—gardening and cooking. They're also two things that take a lot of TLC, always a lot easier for my mom to lavish on food and plants than on me.

When I was a kid, I actually remember being jealous of her roses—the way she talked to them, touched them, checked on them all the time, and was so proud when one of them won a ribbon at the local fair. It was bad enough I had a sister who was a prizewinner, not to mention a cousin, but how the hell do you compete with *roses*? Sometimes I wondered if it was because she could follow recipes or shape plants and everything turned out the way she wanted—unlike most things in life, especially kids.

She did try to teach me to cook, though, and I wanted to learn—but my lack of any cooking ability was only exceeded by my lack of a green thumb. Hell, I couldn't even keep a hanging basket alive before the mountain. That all changed there, when spring hit around the middle of April and The Freak started letting me outside to plant a garden.

I was around seven months pregnant the first time, and my eyes felt like they were going to explode with spring's light and beauty. When I took that first breath of clean mountain air—all I'd smelled in months was wood smoke and cedar walls—my nostrils tingled with the scent of fir trees in the sun, wildflowers, and the moss-covered earth at my feet. I wanted to lie down and grind my face into it. Hell, I wanted to *eat* it.

If I was farther north or off the island, I figured there'd still be snow, but it was warming up and everything was lush and green in every shade you could imagine—sage, emerald, pine, moss—the air even smelled green. I couldn't tell if it was comforting to know that I was probably close to home or if that made it worse.

He didn't let me go very far from the cabin the first time but he couldn't stop my eyes from exploring. The trees encircling us were so dense I couldn't see if there were any other mountains around. A few grassy spots showed through the moss carpeting of the clearing, but it was mostly just moss and rock. Must have been hard to drill a septic tank up here, not to mention a well, but I figured we were probably pulling from the river. At the forest's edge I saw some stumps, so they'd logged up here in the past. I couldn't see a road, but there had to be an access point close by.

The river was on the right side of the cabin—where the raised garden beds were—and down a bit of a hill. It was a beautiful jade color, and judging by some areas where the current calmed down and the water turned such a dark green it was almost black, it had some deep swimming holes.

From the outside, the cabin looked cute with its shutters and window planter boxes. Two rocking chairs rested side by side on the covered front porch. Maybe a husband and wife had built the cabin together years ago. I wondered about this woman who liked window planter boxes and brought soil in for a garden. I wondered how she'd feel about who was living in the cabin now.

I went into labor while I was gardening. He'd been letting me out—supervised, of course—to water and weed around the vegetables, which were looking great, and I could have spent all day working in the garden. I didn't even care when he decided I hadn't done something right and made me do it all over again, since that just meant I could stay out longer. The sensation of digging into cool dirt—which I could still feel through the gloves he made me wear to protect my perfect nails—and the scent of freshly turned earth sure beat being locked in the cabin with him.

I was intrigued by the idea that the tiny seeds I'd planted were growing into carrots, tomatoes, beans, while I was growing my own seed in my belly. Technically it was partly his seed, but I didn't let myself think about that. I was getting good at not thinking about stuff.

The one thing I could never seem to shut out was my ache for simple, affectionate touch. I never knew how essential it was to my well-being until I didn't have Emma to snuggle, Luke to cuddle, or even one of my mom's rare hugs. Affection from Mom always seemed an afterthought on her part, unless it was given as a reward, which always left me feeling manipulated and angry at myself for wanting her warmth so much.

The only time my mom's touches were given freely was when I was sick and she dragged me everywhere, talking to doctors and pharmacists about each symptom in embarrassing detail, her arm around my shoulder and her small hands pressing against my forehead. I never said anything, I liked it too much. She even slept with me when I was ill, and to this day the scent of Vicks VapoRub reminds me of the warm weight of her small body next to me, which felt reassuring and solid.

Whenever The Freak walked by he'd grab me for a hug, pat my stomach, or run his hand along my back, and he still cuddled me every night. In the beginning his touch disgusted me, but as the months passed I became disconnected enough that sometimes I was able to hug back and feel nothing. Other times, the ache for touch was so strong I'd find myself leaning into his embrace with my eyes shut tight, pretending it was someone I loved, and hating myself for it.

I wondered why his skin didn't reek of the rot in his soul. Sometimes I'd catch the clean fragrance of the laundry detergent we used—a natural biodegradable brand—on his clothes, and for a few minutes after the shower I could smell the faint scent of soap on his hands and skin, but it would fade quickly. Even when he'd been working, I couldn't smell the outside world on him—fresh air, grass, pitch, fir needles, anything— let alone sweat. Even scent particles didn't want to touch him.

Water had to be brought up from the river in a bucket for the garden every day, but I didn't mind because it was a chance to run my hands through its cool currents and splash my face. It was almost the middle of June, and I figured I had to be close to nine months, but I was so huge I sometimes wondered if I was past due—I didn't know exactly when I got pregnant, so it was hard to calculate. On this particular day I dragged a big bucket of water up the hill and began to lift it up to pour over the plants, but it was warm out and I'd been working pretty hard, so sweat dripped into my eyes. I set the bucket down to catch my breath.

As I massaged my back with one hand, a cramp crawled across my belly. I ignored it at first and tried to lift the bucket back up. The pain hit again, worse this time. Knowing he'd be pissed if I didn't finish my chores, I took a deep breath and watered the rest of the garden bed.

When I was done I found him on the porch fixing a board and said, "It's time." We went back inside, but not before he checked to make sure the watering was finished. Soon as we walked into the cabin, I felt a whooshing inside me, a weird sensation of something letting go, and then warm fluid poured down my legs, onto the floor.

The Freak had read all those books with me, so he knew what was going to happen, but he looked horrified and froze at the entrance to the cabin. I stood in a puddle with stuff dripping down my legs and waited for him to snap out of it. But as the blood drained from his face, I realized I might be waiting awhile. Even though I was scared to death, I had to calm him down. I needed his help.

"It's totally normal—my body's supposed to do that—everything will be okay." He started pacing, partway into the cabin, then out, then in again. I had to get him to focus.

"May I have a bath?" Baths help with menstrual cramps, and I figured I had time—the contractions didn't seem that close together. He just stopped and stared at me wild-eyed.

"Is it okay? I think it would help." Still mute, he raced to the bathroom and ran a bath for me. I was getting the feeling he would have agreed to anything at that point.

"Don't make it too hot, I don't know if heat would be good for the baby." Once the tub was full, I eased my huge body into the warm water.

The Freak leaned against the counter in the bathroom, his eyes darting all over the place, looking at everything but me. His hands clenched and unclenched as if they were grasping at the air. This control freak stood trembling, tongue-tied, like a teenager on his first date.

In a gentle, even tone of voice I said, "I need you to move the bedding off the bed and put some towels down, okay?"

He raced out of the room, then I heard him moving around

by the bed. To calm myself down, I tried to remember every-thing I'd read in the books and concentrated on my breath-ing instead of the fact that I was about to give birth in a cabin with no one but a freaked-out Freak to help me. The beads of water on the side of the bathtub became my focal point, and I counted the seconds it took them to drip down. When the water was lukewarm, almost cool, and the contractions were closer together, I called him—he'd been hiding out in the other room.

With his help I got out of the tub and dried off. The con-tractions were hitting hard and fast by this point and I had to lean on him so I didn't fall. When we walked back into the room, I stumbled and gripped his arm while white-hot pain wrenched my belly. The cabin was cold, and goose bumps broke out on my skin.

"Why don't you get a fire going while I get myself onto the bed?"

After I settled myself down and put a pillow behind my shoulders, I don't remember too much other than a lot of pain—most women get the option of drugs, and trust me, I'd have gone with that option. The Freak was like a sitcom hus-band, pacing around and wringing his hands and putting them over his ears every time I screamed—which was often. While I writhed around on the bed, chewing on the fucking pillow, he was in the corner at one point with his whole head tucked between his knees. He even left the cabin for a while, but I started screaming "HELP ME!" so loud he came back.

All the books said to start bearing down when I could feel I was close, but hell, everything in my body was telling me to push. I propped my back against the wall and pressed into it so hard I must have had welts from the logs on my back. With my hands on my knees, I spread my legs, gritted my teeth, and pushed. When I could breathe, I ordered him around. The more in control I was, the more he seemed to calm down—control being a loose term, considering I was covered in sweat and screaming out every order in between pushes.

A lot of the actual birth is hazy, but I think I was in labor for a few hours—a lucky first-timer, and one of the few things on the mountain I had to be thankful for. I do remember that when I made him stay between my legs and help the baby out, his face was pale and covered with sweat, and I wondered what the hell he was sweating about since I was doing all the work. I didn't give a flying fuck about his feelings or mine—I just wanted this thing out of me.

When the baby finally came through, it hurt like a son of a bitch but it felt *so good* at the same time. Through eyes blurry from sweat dripping into them, I glimpsed The Freak holding the baby away from him in the air like he did with my rags. Shit, he didn't know what to do next. And the baby hadn't cried yet.

"You have to clean the face off and lay the baby on my stomach."

I closed my eyes and let my head loll to the side.

The tiniest of whimpers turned into really loud wails, and my eyes flew open. God, it was such an incredible sound. It was the first live creature I'd heard other than him in ten months, and I started crying. When I lifted my arms up, he handed the baby to me quickly, as though relieved to be free of the responsibility.

A girl. I hadn't even thought to ask. A slimy, bloody, wet, wrinkly girl. I'd never seen anything more beautiful.

"Hi, sweetie, welcome to the world," I said. "I love you," I whispered against her little forehead, then softly kissed it.

I glanced up and he was staring down at us. He didn't look scared anymore, he looked pissed off. Then he turned and left the cabin.

As soon as he left I passed the afterbirth. I tried to wriggle farther up the bed to get away from the wetness, but I was already near the wall, and when I tried to inch sideways, every movement hurt. So I lay there in an exhausted sticky mess with the baby on my belly. The cord needed to be cut. If he didn't come back soon, I was going to have to try to bite it off.

While I waited, I checked her over and counted all her toes and fingers. She was so small and delicate, and although her hair was ridiculously soft and silky, it was as dark as mine. Once in a while she whimpered, but when I rubbed my thumb on her cheek, she quieted.

He came back after about five minutes, and as he came toward me I was glad to see he didn't look pissed off anymore, just disinterested. Then I looked away from his face and realized he was holding his hunting knife.

Disinterest turned to horror when he saw the mess the afterbirth had made between my legs.

"I have to cut the cord," I said. But he stood frozen.

I slowly reached out with my free hand, and just as slowly, he handed me the knife.

I shifted the baby, then tore a strip off the sheet and tied it around the cord before cutting it. As soon as I did, she mewled, and the sound snapped The Freak out of his trance. His hand lashed out and bent my wrist back until the knife dropped on the bed.

"I was going to give it back!"

He picked it up and leaned toward me. I gripped the baby and tried to wriggle up the bed. He paused. I paused. Maintaining eye contact, he slowly wiped the knife off on the corner of a towel. He held the knife up to the light, nodded, then headed into the kitchen.

He helped me roll over and put fresh bedding under me. While he cleaned away the medical supplies, I tried to put my nipple to her mouth, but she wouldn't take it. I tried again, same result. Tears prickled in my eyes, and I swallowed hard. Remembering that the books said it took them a while sometimes, I tried again. This time when I pressed my nipple into her mouth a bit of watery-looking yellow liquid came out. Her little rosebud mouth opened and she finally latched on.

With a sigh of relief, I looked up just as The Freak came back to the bed carrying a cup of water and a baby blanket. Focused on the task, he didn't look at me until he'd set the cup on the side table. When he did glance over, his eyes went straight to the baby nursing from my exposed breast. His face flushed and he quickly averted his gaze. Staring at the wall, he tossed the blanket to me and said, "Cover yourself."

I draped the blanket over my shoulder and baby just as she made a loud slurping sound.

He took a couple of steps back, then spun around and headed into the bathroom. Soon I heard the shower running. It ran for a very long time.

He was quiet when he came back. He stood at the bottom of the bed and stared at me for a few minutes. I'd learned not to make eye contact with him when he was in one of his moods, so I pretended to be dozing, but I could still make him out through my eyelashes. I had seen his pissed-off look, his I'm-going-to-hurt-you look, and I'd seen him tune out completely, but this was different. It was thoughtful.

My arms tightened around my daughter.

SESSION TWELVE

I'm in a weird-ass mood today, Doc. Wired up, mind all over the place, looking for answers, reasons, something solid to cling to, something *real*, but just when I think I've got it figured out and neatly filed under fixed instead of fucked, turns out I'm still shattered, scattered, and battered. But you probably already knew that, didn't you?

At least your office feels real. Real wood shelves, real wood desk, real native masks on the wall. And in here I can be real because I know you can't tell people about me, but I wonder if when you sit around with your shrink friends, talking about whatever it is you guys talk about, you want to just blurt it out. . . . No, forget I said that, you look like the type that went into the profession because you genuinely want to help people.

You might not be able to help me. That makes me sad, but not for me. It makes me sad for you. It must be frustrating for a shrink to have a patient who's beyond fixing. That first shrink I saw when I got back to Clayton Falls told me no one is a lost cause, but I think that's bullshit. I think people can be so crushed, so broken, that they'll never be anything more than a fragment of a whole person.

I wonder when it happened to The Freak. What the defining moment was—the moment when someone stepped down with the heel of their shoe and crushed both of our lives. Was it when his real mother left him? Would he still have been repairable if he'd had a nice foster family? Would he never have killed anyone or abducted me if his adoptive mom hadn't been such a freak herself? Did it happen in the womb? Did he ever even have a chance? Did I?

There was The Freak side of him, the guy who abducted me, beat me, raped me, played sadistic games with me, terrified me. But sometimes when he was thoughtful or happy or excited, when his face lit up, I saw the guy he *could* have been. Maybe that guy would have had a family and taught his child to ride bikes and made balloon animals for her, you know? Hell, maybe he'd have been a doctor and saved people's lives.

After I had my daughter, I even felt maternal toward him sometimes, and in those fleeting moments when I did see his other side, I wanted to coax it out. I wanted to help him. I wanted to *fix* him. But then I'd remember. He was a little boy standing in front of a hayfield holding a match, and he didn't need an excuse to drop it.

Right after the baby was born The Freak tossed me some cloth diapers, a couple of sleepers, a few blankets, and for a week barely spoke to me unless he was telling me to do something—he only let me rest in bed for one day. My first day up I got dizzy doing the dishes and he let me sit down for a few minutes, but then he made me wash them all over again because the water had grown cold. The next time I just leaned on the counter and closed my eyes until the feeling passed.

He never touched the baby, but when I changed or bathed her, he hovered and picked that moment to ask me to do something for him. If I was folding her laundry, he'd make me finish his first. Once, when I was about to nurse her while our dinner was simmering, he made me put her down and serve him. The only time he left us alone was when I nursed her. Not knowing exactly what was pissing him off, I picked her up and soothed her if she made so much as a peep, but his eyes only turned darker and his jaw clenched. He reminded me of a viper waiting to strike, and as I comforted my child, my insides hummed with anxiety.

When she was a couple of days old, he still hadn't mentioned anything about naming her, so I asked him if I could.

He glanced at her in my arms and said, "No," but later I whispered a secret name into her tiny ear. It was the only thing I could give her.

I couldn't stop thinking about the way he'd handled his jealousy and resentment of his adopted father. So when he was in the cabin I made sure I looked indifferent to the baby and only met her basic needs—luckily, she was a content and happy baby who never fussed much. But as soon as he went outside for his chores, I'd take her out of the blanket and look at every inch of her, amazed she came out of my body.

Considering the circumstances of her conception, I was surprised how much I was capable of loving my daughter. With my fingertips I traced her veins, marveling that my blood flowed through her, and she never squirmed. Her little ear was perfect for singing lullabies into, and sometimes I just buried my nose in her neck and inhaled the scent of her, fresh and sweet—the purest thing I'd ever smelled. Behind her pudgy left knee she had a tiny birthmark, a coffee-colored half-moon that I loved to kiss. Every delicate inch of her made my heart shiver with the overwhelming urge to protect her. The intensity of my feelings terrified me, and my anxiety grew with my love.

We still had bath time every night, but she wasn't allowed in the water with me and The Freak never touched my breasts. After the bath, I nursed her on the bed while he cleaned the bathroom. When she was finished I laid her down in a little bed he'd put at the foot of ours—it was just a wicker basket with some blankets in it, like a dog bed, but it didn't seem to bother her.

I remembered a couple of my friends who had kids complaining about how they never got any sleep in the beginning, and I didn't either. Not because of the baby—she only woke up once a night—but because I was so terrified of what he'd do if she woke him up that I lay there listening to every faint sigh or the tiniest hitch in her breathing. I became adept at slithering to the bottom of the bed at the first signs of her waking so he wouldn't feel my weight leave the mattress, and like a dog nursing a puppy I'd hang my breast over the side, lift her up slightly, and feed her. If he moved or made any sound, I lay perfectly still with my heart pounding and wondered if she could feel it pulse through my breast. As soon as his breath evened out, I'd slither back up.

At bedtime, after she was down, he examined me and tenderly put cream on my privates, pausing to make soothing sounds if I flinched, his face sympathetic. He said we had to wait six weeks before we could "make love" again. When he'd raped me it was a hell of a lot more painful but somehow less disturbing. Sometimes I actually forced myself not to react if it hurt when he spread the cream, so he'd keep going. Pain was normal.

When she was a little over a week old I was cooking and needed two hands, so I was about to go put her down in her basket, but he stood in front of me and said, "I'll take her." My eyes moved back and forth between him and the safety of her bed—I'd been so close—but I didn't dare refuse him. After I gently placed her in his arms, he strolled away with her, and my heart climbed into my throat. He sat on the end of the bed.

She began to whimper, and I dropped what I was doing to stand in front of him.

"I'm sorry she disturbed you—I'll put her in her bed."

"We're just fine here." He bounced her up and down in his arms, and as he gazed down at her he said, "She knows I'm her father and she's going to be a good girl for me, isn't she?" She quieted and he smiled.

I turned back to the stove, but my hands were shaking so badly I could barely stir the pot—every once in a while I twisted around to grab some spices so I could keep an eye on things.

At first he just stared down at her, but then he unrolled the blanket and took off her sleeper so she was lying on his lap in only her diaper. I was terrified she might start bawling, but she just wiggled her arms and legs around in the cool air. He looked her over, grabbed her arm, then slowly bent it backward. Even though he wasn't doing it hard, my body tensed as I waited for her cries to fill the air, but she was quiet. He did the same with her other arm and legs—it was like he'd never seen a baby before.

His expression was calm, more curious than anything, and he was gentle when he wiped a bit of drool off her chin, even smiled, but the urge to go over and rip her out of his arms was powerful. Only fear of the consequences overrode it. Finally dinner was done, so I walked over on shaky legs, put out my arms for him to hand her to me, and said, "Your plate is ready."

It took him a second to give her to me, and as he passed her through the air a look crossed his face that I'd never seen before. He let go. For a heartbeat she was in the air, and then she dropped. I leapt forward and caught her just before she would have hit the floor. With my heart hammering my chest so hard it hurt, I clutched her against me. He smiled and got up to eat his dinner, humming a tune under his breath.

In the middle of taking a bite, he paused and said, "Her name is Juliet." I nodded, but no way was I naming her after his crazy mom. In my head I called her by her secret name, and other than you, I've never told anyone what he named her.

After that he picked her up sometimes, usually when I was doing something, like folding the laundry or cleaning. He always sat on the bed with her, rolled her onto her stomach, and then bent her arms and legs back. She never whimpered, so I don't think he was hurting her, but I still wanted to run over and grab her—only the knowledge that he might hurt her to punish me held my feet fast. Eventually he'd put her back in her basket, but once he just left her on the edge of the bed like a toy he'd grown bored with. My body broke out in a cold sweat every time he went near her.

When I worked in the garden he let me take her outside with me, nestled in a little blanket tied around my neck. I loved being out there with her, seeing the vegetables I planted grow, smelling earth warmed by the sun, or just rubbing my hands over the down on my baby's head. Saying I found some happiness up there feels wrong, because it's like saying it was okay—it was *never* okay. But when I had my baby I did feel happy at least some of the time every day.

The Freak never let me outdoors unless he was working out there as well, but he usually had something going on, chopping wood, weatherproofing the shutters, staining some of the logs, so I made it out often. He wanted me to repaint the rocking chairs from the porch, and I took them down to the river with me to work on while I enjoyed the sun with my daughter.

If he was pleased with me, he let me just sit by the river when my chores were done. Those were good days, days when I wished I had a sketch pad to capture the contrast of my baby's milky-white skin against the emerald-green grass, or the way she scrunched up her face when an ant crawled over her. Images of fireweed in bloom, sunlight dancing on the river, and the reflection of fir trees on its surface made my hands itch to paint. I thought if I could just get all that beauty on paper I'd have a way to remember there was still an outside world to return to when things got bad in the cabin, but when I asked The Freak for a sketch pad he said no.

Because it was warm, he had me doing laundry in the river every couple of days—he was big on conserving water. The stupid baths he made me take every night used up a ton of water, but I never said anything. Hell, I liked the way river water and sun made the clothes smell. A rope strung from an apple tree someone must have planted years ago to a corner of the cabin served as our clothesline. That was The Freak and me, a regular pioneer couple.

I first noticed the mallard duck floating around the edge of the river, where the water slowed down, before I had the baby. Sometimes other ducks were with him, but usually he was alone. If The Freak wasn't looking in my direction, I stopped what I was doing and admired the duck. The first couple of times I went down to the river to wash clothes or just to sit, the duck flew off as soon as he spotted me. But when my baby was a week old I sat on a rock to rinse out some blankets and enjoy the feel of cool water on my hands, and the duck just moved to the opposite side of the river and paddled around, pecking at the water, catching bugs.

The Freak came down and handed me some bread. The gesture surprised me, but I was happy to be allowed to feed the duck.

Over the next few days I coaxed the duck closer and closer with the bread. Soon he was taking it out of my hand. I wondered if he ever flew over my house. He was a reminder of life beyond my narrow existence, and I couldn't wait to get down to the river to see him every day, but I was careful not to let my excitement show. Practiced indifference was becoming second nature—I'd learned the hard way that letting The Freak know I liked something was the quickest way to end it.

He never let us out of his sight or running distance, but he usually left us alone down at the river. Sometimes I was even able to tune out his presence enough to convince myself I was just relaxing by the river on a typical summer day, smiling at my daughter's growing awareness of the world. Before she was born, I'd wondered if she'd be able to sense the evil around her, but she was the happiest baby I'd ever been near.

My eyes had stopped searching the clearing for avenues of escape. I wouldn't be able to move fast carrying her, and I knew my fears of what he might do if he caught us were probably tame compared to the reality.

When my daughter was two weeks old, The Freak came down to the river and crouched near me. As soon as the duck saw him it backed away from my hand and swam into the middle of the pool. The Freak tried to tempt him closer with bread, but the duck ignored him, and a flush crept up The Freak's neck. My breath trapped in my throat, I prayed the duck would take it, but he didn't, and finally The Freak dropped the bread and headed back up to the cabin, saying he had to get something ready for dinner. The duck came right back.

I heard a sickeningly loud explosion as his beautiful head blew up in front of me. Feathers floated in the air—landing on me, on the baby, on the river's surface. Through the ringing in my ears, I heard screams and realized they were mine. I jumped up from my crouch and spun around. The Freak stood on the porch with a rifle in his hand. With my hands clamped over my mouth to hold in the screams, I stared at him.

"Bring it inside."

My mouth struggled to form words. "Why did you—" But I was asking the air. He'd already left the porch.

With my baby's wails expressing my own feelings, I waded into the river and grabbed what was left of the duck. Its head was practically gone and its poor bloody body was upside down, floating downstream.

Later that day I learned how to pluck feathers off a duck. I'll never forget the smell. Tears welled up and spilled over the whole time, and no matter how often he told me to stop crying, and God knows I tried, sobs kept breaking free. With every feather I pulled out of that duck's body, my guilt mounted. If I hadn't tamed him, he'd still be alive.

When it was time to sit down and eat our roast duck dinner, I froze. The Freak sat opposite me, and between us, arranged on a big platter, was my duck. I had given in to demand after demand, but watching him carve up my symbol of freedom, I hated him like never before. My hand couldn't lift the fork to my mouth. It didn't take him long to notice.

"Eat your dinner, Annie."

The only movement was tears down my face. It was bad enough I was the reason it was dead—I couldn't *eat* it. The Freak grabbed a handful of meat, strode over to me, pried my mouth open, and shoved it in. While I gagged and choked—drowning in duck—he screamed at me.

"Chew it!"

His other hand held the back of my head so I couldn't pull away, and once he'd shoved my mouth full, he clamped his other hand over my lips. I ate my duck. I had to.

The Freak went back to eating his. I was mesmerized by the flashing metal of his fork and knife as he carefully cut the duck into small pieces on his plate. Aware of my attention, he slowly brought the fork to his mouth and delicately took a piece off with his teeth. His lips closed around it, his eyelashes fluttered down, and he gave a sigh of pleasure. As he leisurely chewed, he opened his eyes to stare at me. Finally he swallowed.

Then he smiled.

That night was the first time I couldn't look at my daughter while she nursed. She was drinking the duck, drinking my beautiful duck, and I wondered if she could taste my pain.

Last night it was damn hard to stay out of the closet, Doc. My room was so dark, pitch-dark, and I kept thinking that something was reaching for me, but when I turned on the flashlight I keep by my bed, there was nothing. I tried sleeping with a candle, but that just made creepy flickering shadows on the wall. I turned on all the lights, but then I was wide awake. Which only made it that much easier to hear every creak in my house, and it's an old house—lots of creaks. So the good news is I never slept in the closet last night, Doc; bad news is there sure are some crappy late-night TV shows.

It did give me time to think about fear and all that stuff you told me on how PTSD manifests in different ways, but I still can't tell you exactly why sleeping in the closet makes me feel safer. All I know is, something about the bed just feels so exposed. There are so many ways I could be gotten to—from my feet, left side, right side, or even from above— too much empty space pressing in on me.

The more painful the stuff I tell you, the more I want to— need to—sleep in the closet. You asked what it is I'm trying to keep away from me, and maybe this is a good time to go into the granddaddy of all my lingering side effects—this paranoid itch that won't go away no matter how much I scratch.

I just can't seem to shake the overwhelming feeling I'm

still not safe. And I know it's whacked, because the cops have been totally cool about keeping me up to date on the investigation, especially this one cop, Gary—man, the poor guy probably wishes he'd never given me his cell number—and they'd have told me if I was still in danger. They bloody well *have* to. That's their whole deal—protect the people and all that crap. So what the fuck?

Please don't give me any of the It's-just-PTSD-natural-after-your-experience garbage. Look, I get that I came home with major hang-ups and fear and shit. Like I said, I thought about everything you told me—even did some research on the Internet. Hell, I was *hoping* that was all it was, but there's something different about this. Feels too real.

That's where you come in, Doc. You have to help me get rid of this obsession that I'm still not safe. That *someone* or *something* is out to get me. Don't worry, I'm not expecting some instant shrink just-add-bullshit porridge answer. Give it some thought. Maybe I'll have it all figured out in a couple of weeks when you're back from your holiday—wouldn't it be nice if this shit was that easy.

Thanks for referring me to another shrink, but I'll wait for you to come back. For some strange reason, I have trust issues.

SESSION THIRTEEN

Nice to see you back, Doc. At least one of us is relaxed. Just giving you a hard time—I don't doubt for one minute you needed a break from all this doom and gloom. You do a good job of hiding it, but I know this stuff gets to you. Right from our first session I noticed whenever I talk about something intense, you rip off a corner of your notepad and roll it into a ball with your fingers. The faster you roll, the harder this shit's hitting you. We all give ourselves away somehow.

Like I said, I'm glad you had a nice time, but I'm a hell of a lot gladder you're back. Sure could have used you last week. And no, not just because of all that someone's-still-out-to-get-me crap I was talking about last time, although that vulture is still hovering in the background—something else happened. I saw my ex, in a grocery store, picking out apples with some girl. . . . God, the way he smiled at her *killed* me. And the way she tilted her head back—in her tight white turtleneck and designer jeans—laughing at something he'd said . . .

Before they spotted me and I had to see Luke's beautiful smile turn sympathetic, I ducked around the corner. Basket ditched in the middle of the store, I walked out, head down, and jumped in my car with my heart beating faster than a crack addict's. Trying not to squeal my tires in my desperation to get the hell out of there, I pulled around the back of the store, parked far away from any other cars, and with my head on the steering wheel, cried my eyes out.

She wasn't supposed to be there. He was mine. I should be the girl picking out apples with him. Eventually I drove home, but I couldn't stop crying and I never did get any groceries. Ended up eating hard cheese on stale crackers that night while I pictured them cuddling in bed on a Sunday morning, or him kissing her with his hands wrapped in that beautiful hair. Hell, by the time my mind was done with it they were pretty much engaged and naming their future children.

In those few seconds he looked so fucking *happy*, and I wanted to be the only woman who could make him smile like that. Just talking about it is making me feel all crazy inside. I know I'm supposed to want him to be okay, want what's best for him and all that, but man, oh, man—does it have to be someone like her? Miss Perfect Blonde, so clean in her white turtleneck I felt dirty just looking at her. I used to wear clothes like hers, used to *want* to wear clothes like that.

I wonder if this woman, this *stranger*, knows all about me. She's probably a nice person too—can't see him dating someone who isn't. Maybe she feels sorry for me. God, I hope not. I'm doing a damn good job of that on my own.

After The Freak killed the duck, a piece of me tore off and left a black hole in its place. Terror moved in and brought a giant hand gripping my heart and guts. Over the next couple of days whenever I watched him pick my daughter up, examine her, hell, even walk by her basket, the hand squeezed harder.

One morning she was fussing in her bed and I was about to pick her up when he beat me to it. A little cry escaped from the bundle in his arms; she was still wrapped in her blanket as he bounced her. He put his face close to hers and said, "Stop it." I held my breath, but she was quiet, and he smiled with pride. I knew it was the bouncing, not the words, that had calmed her, but I wasn't suicidal enough to set him straight.

"She listens well," he said. "But at this age their brains are sponges, easily poisoned by society. It's good she's here. Here she'll learn *real* values, values I'll instill in her, but most of all she'll learn respect."

Shit, how the hell was I going to deal with this?

"Sometimes kids, you know, they test their boundaries and she might not understand what you're trying to . . . teach her. But it won't mean she's bad or doesn't respect you, it's just what kids do."

"No, it's not what kids do—it's what parents allow them to do."

He didn't seem upset by the conversation, so I said, "Maybe it's good if a child has curiosity and tests authority? You told me the women you knew before always made bad decisions over men and their careers, but maybe they were just rebelling because they weren't allowed to think for themselves when they were younger."

Still calm, he said, "Is that what your mother did? Raised you to be free-thinking?" Sure, I was free to think exactly like her.

"No, but that's why I want to give my daughter a better

life. Don't you want your child to have a better life than you had?"

He stopped bouncing her. "What are you implying?"

Oh, shit.

"Nothing! I'm just concerned you might have some expectations that aren't—"

"Expectations? Yes, I have expectations, Annie. I expect my daughter to respect her father. I expect my daughter to grow up to be a lady—not some whore spreading her legs for any man who comes along. I don't think that's expecting too much, do you? Or are you trying to raise my daughter to be a whore?"

"That's not at all what I'm trying to say—"

"Do you know what happens to girls who grow up thinking they can do whatever they please? I worked in a logging camp for a while." The Freak was a *logger*? "And there was a female helicopter pilot. She said her father told her she could be whatever she wanted. He was a fool. When I met her, her boyfriend—one of the idiot loggers in camp—had just discarded her."

Well, he didn't seem to have a good opinion of loggers, so maybe he was a foreman or worked in the office.

"I listened to her talk about this Neanderthal and let her cry all her pathetic tears on my shoulder for six months. She started saying she wished she could find a nice man, so I asked her out, but she said she wasn't ready. So I waited. Then one day she told me she wanted to go for a walk. Alone. But I saw him leave the camp a few minutes later, and I followed him."

He bounced the baby faster and faster and she began to whimper. "They were in the woods on a blanket, and she was letting this man, this man she despised, this man who threw her away like garbage, do things to her. So I waited until he left and tried to talk to her, tried to tell her he was only going to hurt her again, but she told me to mind my own business and walked away from me. *Away from me!* After everything I'd done to try to protect her, she was going to go back to that man. I had to save her. She left me no choice." His arms tightened around the baby.

I stepped forward with my hands out.

"You're hurting her."

"*She hurt me.*" He jerked his head as the baby began to wail, then stared down at her like he didn't know how she got there. He shoved her into my arms, almost dropping her in the process, and stalked toward the door. With his hands gripping the frame, he said over his shoulder, "If she becomes one of them . . ." He shook his head. "I can't let that happen." Then he slammed the door behind him, leaving me to quiet the baby and wish I could break down and bawl myself.

He came back in after an hour with his face serene and made his way over to the baby basket. "I think if you take a look at what I've spared her from, Annie—the diseases, drugs, and pedophiles running rampant down there—and then ask yourself if you really want what's best for our daughter, or what you think is best for you . . ." He crouched over her and smiled down. "You'll realize it's time you put her life above your own." His smile disappeared as he looked up to stare hard at me. "Can you do that, Annie?" My eyes dropped to his hands resting on her tiny body—hands that had killed at least one person and done God only knows what to that helicopter pilot.

With my head bowed I said, "Yes, yes, I can."

For the rest of that day every nerve in my body screamed at me to run, and my legs ached from unreleased adrenaline coursing through them. My hands shook—I dropped dishes, clothes, soap, everything. The more frustrated he became, the more things I dropped, and the more my legs cramped. The smallest sound made me jump, and if he moved fast, my blood surged in my veins and I broke out in a sweat.

The next day he packed up a small bag with a change of clothes and took off without saying a word about where he was going. My relief was underscored by my terror that he'd finally had enough of us and wasn't going to come back. My frantic fingers searched the cabin top to bottom again, but there was no way out. He came back the next day, and I still didn't have a clue how I was going to get my child out of this hell.

Wherever he'd been, he brought back germs, and soon he started coughing and sneezing. True to form, he was a demanding patient. Not only did I have to care for the baby and do my chores, I now had to wipe his brow every five fucking seconds, keep the fire going, and bring him blankets hot from the dryer—his idea, not mine—while he languished in bed. I prayed he'd develop pneumonia and die.

He made me read to him until my throat became raspy. I wished I could just play poker with him like I used to with my stepdad. Wayne wasn't the wipe-your-brow kind of guy, which was just fine by me, but he did teach me to play cards when I was sick. At the first sign of a sniffle he'd whip out a pack and we'd go at it for hours. I loved the feel of cards in my hands, the numbers, the set order of them. Mostly I loved winning, and he had to teach me increasingly harder games so he could beat me once in a while.

By the second day coughs wracked The Freak's body, and I paused from my reading to say, "Do you have any medicine?"

As if I was threatening to pour something down his throat

right there and then, he grabbed my arm, dug his nails in, and said, "No! No medicine."

"It might help."

"Medicine is *poison*." Against my arm his hand burned with fever.

"Maybe if you went to town and found a doctor—"

"Doctors are even worse than medicine! Doctors are what killed my mother. If she'd just let me take care of her she'd have been fine, but they pumped their poisons into her and she got sicker and sicker. They *killed* her." Even through a stuffed-up nose his contempt infused every syllable.

After a few days he stopped coughing, but the baby began crying at night and waking up every couple of hours. When I reached my hand down to her she felt warm. I tried to comfort her as soon as she woke up, but once I wasn't fast enough and he threw a pillow at her bed.

Another time he wouldn't let me go to her, saying, "Keep reading, she just wants attention." I wanted to take care of my daughter, I wanted to keep us both alive. I kept reading.

Her wails grew louder. He ripped the book out of my hands. "Make her stop or I will."

My tone as calm and reassuring as I could make it, I lifted her out of her bed and said, "I think she might be getting sick too."

"She's fine. You just have to learn how to control her." He buried his head under the pillow. I had the insane urge to go over and press my whole body down on the pillow, but then his head popped up and he said, "Get me a fresh glass of water, and this time make it cold." I gave him a cheerful smile while inside another piece of me snapped off and spun away.

———

The next morning, earlier than usual, she woke me crying. I picked her up right away and tiptoed around, trying to calm her down, but it was too late. The Freak jumped out of bed and threw his clothes on while glaring at me.

"I'm sorry, but I think she's really sick."

He stalked outside. I lay back in bed and got ready to nurse her. It was one of my favorite things to do with her. I loved the way she stared up at me, one small hand resting on my breast, how her belly swelled up when she was full, how her little bottom fit my hand perfectly. Everything about her was so delicate—her hands with their little lines and tiny fingernails, her smooth cheeks, her silky dark eyelashes.

Usually after she was finished nursing I kissed every part of her, starting at her toes and her soft instep. Once I got up to her hands, I'd pretend to nibble her fingertips and work my way back down her arm. For the grand finale, I'd blow on her belly until she emitted happy little squeaks.

But today my normally happy baby was restless and edgy, and every time I tried to nurse her she moved her mouth away from my nipple. Her skin was hot to the touch and her cheeks were circles of red, like someone had drawn a clown's face on her. Her belly looked distended and I thought she might have gas, so I walked around with her, but she threw up all over my shoulder and finally just cried herself to sleep. I'd never felt so helpless in my life. I was terrified of what The Freak might do if I told him, but I had to get her some help.

"The baby's really sick, she needs a doctor," I said as soon as he came back inside.

He glanced at me. "Start breakfast."

During breakfast she started crying in her basket and I moved to get her, but he held his hand up and said, "Stop. Going to her only reinforces negative behavior. Finish your meal."

Her wails ripped the air apart, and as she inhaled between each lusty cry, I thought I heard a wet rattle in her chest.

"She's not doing well. Can we please get to a doctor? I know your mom died, but she had cancer—it wasn't the doctors that killed her. You can tie me up in the van and take her in." I hesitated for a second. "Or I'll wait here and you can just take her, okay?" Had I really said that? She'd be *alone* with him. But she'd get help.

He chewed slowly. Finally he paused, wiped his mouth on his napkin, took a sip of water, and said, "Doctors ask questions." Her wails reached heart-wrenching levels.

"I know, but you're smart—smarter than any doctor—you'll know what to say so they never suspect a thing."

"Exactly. I *am* smarter than a doctor, that's why I know she doesn't need one." He stomped toward her bed, with me right on his heels. His voice rose to compete with her cries as he said, "She just needs to learn some respect."

"Why don't you relax, and I'll quiet her?"

"I don't think so, Annie. Obviously you've been doing something wrong." As he picked her up from the basket, I gripped the fabric of my dress at my thighs to stop my hands from pounding on his back and prayed she'd calm down for him. But when he bounced her, the wails only grew frantic.

"Please just give her to me." I held my shaking hands out. "*Please.* She's scared."

One minute he was staring at me, his face burgundy with rage, and the next his hands were up and she was dropping. I managed to catch her, losing my balance and falling hard on my knees at the same time. Whether from surprise or finally fatigue, the baby gave an exhausted hiccup and was quiet in my arms. He knelt down, putting his face close to mine, so close I felt his breath against my face.

"You've turned my daughter against me. Not good, Annie. Not good at all."

My voice a shaky whisper, I said, "I would *never* do anything like that—she's just confused, because she's not well. She loves you. I know she loves you, I can tell." His head was cocked to the side. "When she hears your voice her eyes move in that direction. She doesn't do that for me when you're holding her." Total bullshit, but he *had* to buy it.

His eyes drilled into mine for an excruciating minute, then he clapped his hands and said, "Come on, our breakfast is getting cold." I placed her in her basket and followed him, my body tensed for her screams. Thankfully, she'd fallen asleep.

After breakfast he stretched his hands over his head and patted his stomach. I had to try again.

"Maybe if you let me look through the books I could find some herbs or plants that grow up here for medicine. That's natural, and you could look at the books too and check what's okay to give her."

He glanced at her bed and said, "She'll be fine."

But she wasn't. Over the next couple of days a fever raged through her. Her silky skin burned against my hands and I didn't have a clue what to do for her. Coughs left her gasping, and I put hot cloths on her chest in an attempt to loosen her congestion, but that just made her cry more, and cold cloths made her scream even louder. Nothing worked. She started waking up every hour at night, and I never went all the way to sleep—I lay half awake in a constant state of fear. Sometimes I heard her breath hiccup in her throat, and my heart froze until I heard her take another.

The Freak decided that if she cried during the day we had

to ignore her so she would learn self-control, but he usually only lasted maybe ten minutes before he stormed outside while screaming, "Deal with her!" I was quick to get her when she cried at night, but if he did wake up, he'd throw the pillow—at her, at me, or put it over his head. Sometimes he punched the bed.

So he could go back to sleep, I'd hide in the bathroom with her until she calmed down. One night, hoping the steam would help her breathing, I ran the shower, but I never found out whether it would have worked—he came tearing in, yelling at me to shut it off.

After a few of these nights, I was a zombie. On the fifth night she was sick, it felt like she was waking up every half hour and it was getting harder for me to stay awake in anticipation. I remember my eyelids feeling so heavy I just wanted to rest them for a second, but then I must have fallen asleep, because I woke up with a start. My first thought was how quiet the cabin was, and, glad she was finally resting, I let my eyelids drift closed. Then I realized I didn't feel The Freak next to me and I bolted up.

The cabin was dark. Even though it was summer, it had been cool the night before, so he'd had a small fire going, and from the glow of the embers I made out his shape at the foot of the bed. He was hunched over slightly, so I thought he was picking her up, but when he turned around, I realized he was holding her. Groggy, I reached out.

"I'm sorry, I didn't hear her cry."

He handed her to me, turned on the lamp, and started getting dressed. I didn't understand why. Was it already time to get up? Why hadn't he said anything? The baby lay quiet in my arms, and I pulled the blanket away from her face.

For the first time in days it wasn't twisted in discomfort and her cheeks weren't red or sweaty. But their paleness didn't seem right either, and her rosebud mouth was tinged blue. Even her eyelids were blue. The sounds of his dressing were muffled by my heart whooshing in my ears, and then everything grew quiet in my head.

When I laid my cool hand against her cheek, her cheek was colder. She didn't move. I brought my ear to her mouth, and my chest tightened as my own lungs fought for breath. I heard nothing. Felt nothing. Then I put my ear to her small chest, but the only sound was my own racing heart.

I pinched her tiny nose, blew into her little mouth, pushed on her chest. I was aware of mewling sounds in the room. My heart surged with joy—until I realized they were coming from me. In between CPR attempts, I pressed my ear to her mouth.

"Please, oh, please, just breathe. *God help me, please*."

It was too late. She was too cold.

I sat frozen at the foot of the bed and frantically tried to deny the fact that I was holding my dead daughter in my arms. The Freak stared down at us with an impassive face.

"*I told you she needed a doctor. I TOLD YOU!*" I screamed at him while pounding on his legs with one hand and clutching her to me with the other.

He slapped me across the face, then in a flat voice said, "Give me the baby, Annie."

I shook my head.

He gripped my throat with one hand and curled the other under her body. We stared at each other. The hand around my throat began to squeeze.

I let go.

He lifted her out of my arms and brought her to his chest, then stood up and walked toward the door.

I wanted to say something, anything, to make him stop, but I couldn't make my mouth form words. Finally I held her blanket up in the air, thrust it toward his retreating back, and choked out, *"Cold—she's cold."*

He stopped, then came back and stood in front of me. He took the blanket but just stared at it in his hand, his expression unreadable. I reached for my baby, eyes pleading. His gaze met mine and for a moment I thought I saw something cross his face, a slight hesitation, but in the next second his eyes darkened and his face grew hard. He brought the blanket up to cover her head.

I began to scream.

He was headed out the door. I leapt off the bed, but it was too late.

My fingernails clawed, desperately, uselessly, at the door. I kicked it and threw myself at it until I couldn't lift my bruised body off the floor. Finally, I lay with my cheek against the door and screamed her secret name until my throat was raw.

He was gone for about two days. I don't know how long I spent pressed against the door, screaming and begging for him to bring her back. I bloodied my fingers, destroyed every one of my nails scrabbling at the door without managing to make even a mark on it. Eventually I made my way back to the bed and cried until there were no tears left inside me.

In a pathetic bid to buy time against the pain, my mind tried to reason out what had happened and make sense of it, but all I could think was that it was my fault she died—I'd fallen asleep. Had she cried? I was so in tune with her every sound, surely I'd have heard her. Or was I just so exhausted I slept right through? It was my fault, all my fault, I should have woken up and checked on her during the night.

When he opened the door, I was sitting up in the bed with my back against the wall. I wouldn't have cared if he'd killed me right then. But when he strolled toward me I realized he was holding something in his arms and my heart lifted. *She was still alive!* He handed the bundle to me. It was her blanket, only her blanket.

I hurled myself at The Freak's chest and hammered on it. With every blow, I repeated, *"You sick fuck, you sick fuck, you sick fuck!"* He gripped the upper part of my arms, lifted me up, and held me away from him. Like a demented alley cat I clawed at the air.

"Where is she?" Spit flew from my mouth. "Tell me right now, you bastard. *What did you do with her?*"

He actually looked confused as he said, "But I brought you her—"

"You brought me a blanket. *A blanket?* You think that's going to replace my daughter? *You idiot!*" Hysterical giggles bubbled through my lips and turned to laughter.

He let go of my arms, my feet hit the floor with a thud, and I staggered forward. Before I was able to regain my balance, his arm cocked back and his fist slammed into my jaw. As the floor rushed toward me, the room turned black.

I woke up alone on the bed, where he must have placed me, my jaw throbbing. My baby's blanket was neatly folded on the pillow next to me.

To this day no one knows my baby's name—not even the cops. I've tried to say it out loud, just to myself, but it stays locked in my throat, in my heart.

When The Freak walked out that door with her body, he took everything left of me with her. She was only four weeks old when she died—or was killed. Four weeks. That's not enough time to have lived. She lived nine times longer in my belly than she did in the world.

I see pictures in magazines of kids the same age she would be now, and I wonder if she'd have looked like them. Would her hair still be dark? What color eyes would she have? Would she have grown up to be a happy or a serious person? I'll never know.

My clearest memory of that night is him sitting at the foot of the bed with her in his arms and I think, *Did he do it?* Then I think even if it wasn't intentional, he killed her by refusing to get any help for her. It's easier to hate him, easier to blame him. Otherwise I go over and over that night trying to remember how she was lying when I last placed her back in her bed. For a while I'll convince myself that she was on her back and it was my fault because she probably had pneumonia and drowned in mucus. Then I think, no, I must have placed her on her stomach, and I wonder if she smothered while I lay sleeping not five feet from her. I've heard that a woman is supposed to know when her child is in trouble. But I didn't feel *anything*. Why didn't I feel it, Doc?

SESSION FOURTEEN

Sorry I missed the last couple of sessions, but I really appreciate how understanding you were when I canceled, and I have to say, it sure surprised the shit out of me when you called last week to see how I was doing—didn't know shrinks ever did that. It was nice.

After our last session I needed to retreat for a while. Looks like I finally hit the depression stage—or actually, it hit me. And not with some gentle tap. Nope, that bitch hauled off and knocked me to the ground, then sat on me for good measure. I've never talked about my feelings around my baby's death before—cops just want the facts, and I refuse to discuss it at all with reporters. Most people know not to ask about her, I guess people still have some sensitivity, but once in a while a dumbass reporter steps over the line.

Sometimes I wonder if people don't ask because it doesn't occur to them that I might have loved her. When I'd just got back home and was staying at Mom's, I overheard her and

Aunt Val whispering in the kitchen one afternoon. Aunt Val mentioned something about my baby, then Mom said, "Yes, it's sad she died, but probably for the best in the end."

It was for the best? I wanted to storm in there and tell her how wrong she was, but I didn't even know where to begin. With the pillow clamped against my ears, I cried myself to sleep.

I feel like a hypocrite, letting everyone believe he killed her and I'm the innocent victim—all the while knowing it's my fault she died. And yes, you and I already talked about this on the phone, and I liked that article you e-mailed me about survivor's guilt. It made sense, but I still thought, *How nice for the people this applies to.* It doesn't matter how many books or articles I read, I've already tried and convicted myself for not protecting her.

I tried writing my baby a letter like you suggested, but when I got out my notepad and pen, I just sat at my kitchen table and stared at the blank page. After a few minutes, I looked out the window at my plum tree and watched the hummingbirds hover at their feeder, then I stared back at the page. All those thoughts I had about her being a monster when I was first pregnant ate at me—did she feel them in my womb? I tried to focus on my happy memories of life with her and not how she died, but my mind wouldn't cooperate, it just kept going over and over that night. Finally I got up and made myself a cup of tea. The goddamn notepad and pen are still sitting there. "I'm sorry," just doesn't seem to cover it.

———

For the first few days after our last session, I didn't do much but cry. It didn't even take anything in particular to set me off. Emma and I could be walking in the woods and the pain would hit me so hard I'd be doubled over with the sheer force of it. On one of our walks I heard what sounded like a baby crying, but when I whipped around on the trail, I saw it was a baby crow up in a fir tree. Next thing I knew I was lying in the middle of the trail, hands clawing into the dirt, sobbing into the earth, with Emma trying to shove her nose into my neck and wash my face.

As if I could outrun my pain, I sprinted for home, and the feel of my feet thudding against the earth felt right and solid. The jingle of Emma's collar as she ran in front of me brought back memories of us jogging together in the past, another thing I'd forgotten I enjoyed. Now I run every day. I run until my body is coated in sweat and my only thoughts are of my next breath.

Luke called a week after our last session—he used to leave messages asking me to give him a call if I felt like it, but I didn't return them. He stopped leaving the messages but he still called at least once every couple of weeks even though I never picked up the phone. It's been about a month since the last call, just before I saw him with that girl, and I didn't think he'd try again.

When the phone rang, I was down in my laundry room and I had to run around to find the cordless. As soon as I saw his number, my already racing heart hit overdrive, and I almost set the receiver back down in the cradle, but my finger was on the talk button and he was saying, "Hello?" before I realized what I'd done. Then I didn't realize I hadn't responded until he said, "Annie?"

"Hey."

"You answered. I didn't know if you would . . ." He paused and I knew I should say something, something that sounded friendly, something that said, *I'm glad you called.*

"I was doing laundry." Jesus, I might as well have told him I was in the bathroom.

"Did I interrupt?"

"No, I mean yeah, but it's okay. It can wait."

"I saw you a few weeks ago and I wanted to call then, but I didn't know if you'd want me to."

"You saw me?"

"You were just leaving the grocery store, I tried to catch up to you but you were moving too fast." My face burned. Shit, he *did* see me leave the store.

I waited for him to say something about the girl but when he didn't, I said, "Really? I didn't notice you. I just stopped to get something in a hurry, but the store didn't have it."

We were both silent for a few beats, and then he said, "So what are you doing these days? I keep expecting to see your signs in someone's yard." I fought the urge to be mean and say the last sign I ever had in someone's lawn was at the open house where I was abducted. I knew he hadn't meant to hurt.

"You might have a long wait."

"I miss driving by them—your four-leaf clovers always made me smile." I'd thought I was so clever when I put four-leaf clovers on my signs, business cards, and car door. My logo was, "Annie O'Sullivan has the luck of the Irish." Luck was my whole damn marketing campaign. Now, that's irony for you.

"Maybe one day—or maybe I'll do something else." Like throw myself off a bridge.

"You'll be successful whatever you do, but if you ever get back into it, you'll be right up there again in no time. You were so good at it."

Not as good as I'd wanted to be, not as good as my mom thought I should have been—the entire time I was in real estate she showed me the ads for every other Realtor in town and asked why I didn't get that listing. And I wasn't as good as Christina, who was one of the main reasons I got into real estate in the first place. After high school I had a series of shitty jobs—waitress, cashier, secretary—but then I got one I liked, working in the back room of a newspaper creating ad layouts. There wasn't any money in it, though, and by the time I was in my later twenties I was tired of being broke. Especially when Christina and Tamara made killer money, which Mom kept pointing out, and hell, I wanted to drive a nice car too.

"I've been seeing a shrink." Man, first the laundry, now my therapy—all I'd wanted to do was stop talking about real estate.

"That's great!" Yeah, now I can pee more during the day, I can actually eat when I'm hungry, and up until I had to talk about my dead daughter, I'd gotten that whole closet-sleeping thing down to a couple of times a week. Wasn't that *great*? But I choked back my bitter words—he was just trying to be nice, and who the hell was I kidding? I did need a shrink.

"You still there?" And then with a sigh he said, "Crap, I'm sorry, Annie. I'm saying all the wrong things, aren't I?"

"No, no, it's not you, it's just, well, you know . . . stuff. So how are things going at the restaurant?"

"We have a new menu. You should come in sometime? Customers seem to like it."

We talked for a while about the restaurant, but it felt like having one of our old conversations through a fun-house mirror—everything was distorted and neither of us knew which door was the safe one. I opened an unsafe one.

"Luke, I never said—and I know I should have before now—but I'm really sorry about the way I was to you when you first came to the hospital. It's just that—"

"Annie."

"The guy who took me, he'd told me things, and . . ."

"Annie—"

"I didn't find the truth out until later." When I kept refusing to see Luke, Mom wanted to know why. Then she told me not only did Luke not have a girlfriend, he actually held fund-raisers for searches at his restaurant with Christina right up until a week before I came home. Mom also told me the police questioned him for a few days, but he proved he was at the restaurant when I was abducted. She said that even after they let him go, a lot of people still treated him like he had something to do with it.

I remembered my reaction when The Freak told me Luke had moved on with another girl—while he'd actually been accused of hurting me and then kept trying and trying to find me. The least I could do was agree to see him.

I said, "But then I made such a mess of the visit."

"*Annie!* Sshhhhh, it's okay—you don't have to do this." But I did.

"And then when you saw me at Mom's . . ." I didn't even know how to begin to explain what happened there. Only out of the hospital for two weeks, I was napping in my old room at my mom's when I heard voices in the kitchen and stumbled out to ask her and Wayne to keep it down.

Mom's back was to me as she stood at the stove with a big pot of something in front of her and a man next to her. The man, whose back was also to me, bent down as she fed him something from a spoon. I began to back out of the room, but the floor squeaked. Luke turned around.

Distantly I heard Mom say, "Good, you're up just in time! Luke was just tasting some of my Spaghetti Surprise, and he wants the recipe for his restaurant. But I told him, if he wants it, he's going to have to name the dish after me." Her husky laugh filled the air already heavy with oregano, basil, tomato sauce, and tension.

Luke's honest face had been one of the things I'd loved about him, and now it paled with shock. He'd seen me in the hospital, and I'm sure he'd seen my photo in the paper, but I'd lost more weight and in Wayne's old tracksuit I probably looked even thinner than I was. My eyes were ringed by dark circles and I hadn't washed or brushed my hair in days. Of course, Luke looked even better than I remembered. His white T-shirt set off the tan on his forearms and the muscles in his chest. His dark hair, longer than when I was abducted and perfectly tousled, shone in the kitchen's bright lights.

"I brought you flowers, Annie." He waved a hand toward a vase on the counter full of roses. *Pink* roses.

"I put them in water for you, Annie Bear." Mom was looking at the roses, eyes narrowed—slightly, not enough for anyone else to see, but I know my mother. They had been measured against her own roses and found wanting.

I said, "Thanks, Luke. They're pretty."

For a few seconds that felt like hours, the only sound in the kitchen was the bubbling of the sauce on the stove, then Wayne swaggered in and thumped Luke on the shoulder.

"Luke! Great to see you, boy. You staying for dinner?"

Mom, Wayne, and I looked at Luke as a flush rose in his face. He looked at me and said, "If Annie—"

"Of course Annie wants you to stay," Wayne said. "Shit. Do the girl good to have some friends over." Before I could say anything one way or another, Wayne had his arm around

Luke's shoulders and was leading him out of the kitchen. "Let me get your opinion on something. . . ."

Mom and I were left staring at each other. "You could have warned me he was here, Mom."

"And when was I supposed to do that? You never leave your room." She wobbled slightly and braced a hand against the counter.

Now I saw it—Mom's face wasn't just glowing from the heat of the stove. Her eyelids drooped slightly and one—the right one, as always—drooped lower. My eyes found what they were looking for behind the container of pasta but within reach, a glass of what I knew would be vodka.

I'd noticed that Mom's predilection for "blurriness" seemed to have achieved new heights in my absence. After I'd been home for only a couple of days, I surfaced out of my bedroom when I smelled something burning. I discovered a batch of what I think were peanut butter cookies in the oven and Mom passed out in front of the TV, where they were replaying an interview with me—taken when I was just released and shouldn't have been talking to anyone. I had turned my face to the side so my hair fell like a curtain and shielded me from the camera. I turned the TV off.

Her pink robe—or, as she would say in a really bad French accent, her *peignoir*—gaped, revealing the skin of her neck and the upper swell of her small breasts. I noticed that her skin, always her pride and joy, although there weren't many parts of her body she didn't consider her pride and joy, had begun to turn crepey. In her hand she gripped a vodka bottle—my first sign things had changed; she used to at least mix the stuff. She must have just fallen asleep, because the cigarette between her full lips was still burning. The ash at the end was over an inch long, and while I stood there it quivered, fell, and landed on her exposed chest. Transfixed by the cigarette cherry glowing closer to her lips, I wondered if she'd even wake up when it began to burn her, but I gently removed it. Without touching her, I leaned over and blew the ash from her chest, then threw the cookies out and went back to bed. I figured her drinking would abate some once I'd been home for a while.

Now, standing in her kitchen, she spotted my eyes on the drink and moved to stand in front of it. Her eyes dared me to say anything.

"You're right. Sorry." It was just easier.

Not able to think of a graceful way to get out of it, I soon found myself helping bring dinner out to the table while trying to avoid Luke's eyes. His hands reached to take a hot bowl from me and I remembered those hands on me, then I remembered The Freak's hands on me, and I dropped the bowl. Luke's quick reflexes caught it right before it hit the table, but not before Mom noticed.

"You okay, Annie Bear?"

I nodded, but I was far from okay. I sat with Luke across from me and pushed the pasta around on my plate. I was all too aware of the clock above my head telling me I wasn't allowed to eat at this hour, and my empty stomach curled in on itself.

During dinner my stepdad was trying to tell Luke all about his latest business idea when Mom interrupted to ask Luke whether he noticed her use of fresh parsley in the garlic bread she'd baked herself. Oh, and did she mention the parsley was from her own garden? Wayne got another two sentences in, then paused to take a mouthful. Mom was off and running. She explained the finer points of creating the perfect spaghetti sauce, which seemed to involve her touching Luke's arm every twenty seconds and smiling up at him encouragingly when he asked questions.

After everyone else's plates were empty there was a pause in the conversation as they all focused in on my still-full plate. Then Wayne said, "Annie's doing much better." We all stared at him and I thought, *Compared to what?*

Luke said, "Lorraine, that was amazing, and you're right, ours at the restaurant doesn't even come close."

Mom tapped his arm and said, "I told you, didn't I? If you're nice to me I might show you a few of my tricks." Another throaty laugh.

"I'd be honored if you'd share your recipe with me, but right now I'd like a few minutes alone with Annie, if that's okay?" He turned to me, but the thought of being alone with Luke had frozen my blood in my veins and apparently my lips, because they couldn't seem to form the words, *No, it's not okay, it's really, really not okay.*

I wasn't the only one caught off guard. Mom's and Wayne's heads rose up in tandem like puppets on a string. Mom's hand had been resting on Luke's arm. She pulled it back like she'd been burned.

"I guess I'll just start cleaning up the kitchen, then." When no one moved to stop her, she pushed her chair back so fast it scraped the linoleum and she grabbed a couple of plates. Wayne got up to help, and after they were in the kitchen I heard him say something about giving the kids some privacy while he and my mom went outside for a smoke. Her muffled answer didn't sound happy, but soon I heard the kitchen door open and shut and both of their feet on the outside deck. For a quick second Mom peeked in the sliding glass door that opened from the dining area to the deck, but when I caught her she moved out of sight.

I continued to twirl my spaghetti with my fork. Then Luke bumped my foot under the table with his and cleared his throat. My fork dropped with a clang onto my plate, splashing tomato sauce on me and, worse, on his white shirt like a spray of blood.

I leapt up to grab a paper towel, but Luke leaned over and gripped both my arms.

"It's just spaghetti sauce." I stared down at his hands wrapped around my arms, then tried to pull away. He released them instantly. "Crap. I'm sorry, Annie."

I rubbed my hands up and down my arms.

"Can I not touch you at all?"

My eyes blinked desperately to hold back the tears, but one broke free when I saw the answering shimmer in his own eyes. I sat back down with a thump.

"I just can't. Not yet. . . ."

His eyes pleaded with me to explain it to him, to share my feelings as I always had, but I couldn't.

"I just want to help you through this, Annie—I feel so damn *useless*. Isn't there anything I can do for you?"

"*No!*" The word came out angry-sounding, *mean*-sounding, and his face flinched like I'd hit him. There was nothing he could do, nothing anyone could do. It was that very knowledge that made me hate him in that second, and hate myself for feeling that way in the next.

His lips curled into a rueful smile. He shook his head and said, "I'm a real dumbass, aren't I? I just thought if we talked, then I could understand—"

In my pain, I aimed to hurt. "You *can't* understand. You could *never* understand."

"No, you're right, I probably can't. But I want to try."

"I just want to be left alone." My words hung in the air between us like flies on the carcass of what used to be our relationship. With a nod of his head, he stood up. Inside I screamed, *I'm sorry. I take it back. I didn't mean it. Please stay.*

But he'd already opened the sliding glass door. He was thanking Mom for dinner, saying he had to get back to the restaurant and he'd be sure to get the recipe, sounding so polite. So polite. While I sat there red-faced in my shame, in my regret.

Then he was standing at the door and with his hand on the knob he turned and said, "I'm so sorry, Annie." The sincerity in his voice made me hurt deep inside, in places I'd thought were too full of pain to possibly feel any more, and I turned away, turned away from his beauty and kindness, and walked down the hall past him without even the grace to meet his eyes. From my bedroom, I heard the front door close and then I heard his truck pull away. Not even fast in anger like I would have, but slowly. Sadly.

Now, months later, he interrupted me on the phone and said, "Please stop, Annie. You don't owe anyone an apology, least of all me. I screwed up. I shouldn't have just showed up like that. I rushed you. I've kicked myself over and over for that. That's why I kept calling. I knew you'd be blaming yourself."

"I was so mean to you."

"You had every right to be—I was an insensitive prick. That's why I've tried to keep my distance, but maybe you're still not ready to talk to me? I won't be mad if you say so. Promise." That was always our thing—he'd say I love you, and

I, not quite willing to say it back even after a year, would say, *Promise?*

"I do want to talk to you, but I can't talk about what happened."

"You don't have to. What if I just call you once in a while, and if you feel like talking, pick up the phone and we'll yak about whatever you want. Does that work? I don't want to push, like before."

"That works. I mean, I'll try, I want to try. I'm getting a little tired of only talking to my shrink and Emma." His soft laugh broke the tension.

After that we chatted about Emma and Diesel, his black Lab, for a while. Finally he said, "Talk to you in a few, 'kay?"

"Don't feel like you have to call."

"I don't, and don't feel like you have to answer."

"I won't."

He called the next day and again earlier this week, Doc, and we just had brief casual conversations, mostly about the restaurant and our dogs, but I still don't know how I feel about it. I like it, but then sometimes I feel rage toward him. How can he still be so kind to me? I don't deserve it—the guy needs to give his head a shake. His very goodness makes me love him and hate him. I *want* to hate him. I'm like a wound barely sewn shut, and every time we talk the stitches break, the wound reopens, and I have to sew it back together.

On top of all that, his kindness makes me feel even stupider because my biggest fear in seeing him again is that he might try to touch me. Just *thinking* about it makes my armpits flood with sweat. And to react that way to Luke, of all men? Luke, who would remove spiders from the sink and carry them outside? It's beyond ridiculous. If I can't get my-self to the point where I can be comfortable around a person like Luke, then I'm royally screwed. Might as well pack up my crap and move right into the penthouse suite at Chez Crazy.

SESSION FIFTEEN

Thanks again for accepting that I didn't want to talk about the mountain last session, and it's been a hell of a week, so I'm still not sure if I'm ready to tackle it today—I'll see how I feel. My grief is a windstorm. Sometimes I can stand straight up in it, and when I'm angry, I can lean into it and dare it to blow me over. But other times I need to hunker down, tuck around myself, and let it pummel my back. Lately, I've been in hunker-down mode.

Hell, you probably need a break yourself—pretty damn depressing stuff, isn't it? I wish I could tell you happy stories, or make you smile at something witty I've said. When I leave here, I feel bad that you had to listen to all my crap—it makes me feel selfish. But not enough that I want to change. This shit *made* me selfish. I have a righteous sadness.

When I first came to you, I mentioned I had a couple of reasons for giving therapy another go, but I never told you what finally popped the I'm-doing-just-fine-on-my-own-thank-you-very-much bubble I'd been bouncing around in.

It happened in a grocery store—I only shop late at night and with a baseball hat on. I've considered Internet shopping, but God knows who they'd send to deliver the groceries, and I've had enough of reporters using any ruse to get inside my house. Anyway, a woman was bent down reaching for something on the bottom shelf. Nothing weird about that, except a few feet behind her sat her cart, unguarded, with a toddler in it.

I tried to just walk by, tried not to stare at the baby girl's little white teeth and rosy cheeks, but as I passed, one of her tiny arms waved out at me, and I stopped. Like metal to magnet, I was helpless to keep my feet from bringing me close or my hand from reaching out. I just wanted to touch that tiny hand for a second. That's all I needed, I told myself, just one second. But the baby's hand curved over my outstretched finger and she giggled as she squeezed it. Hearing her giggle, her mom said, "That's my girl, Samantha, Mommy will be there in a sec."

Samantha, her name was Samantha. It echoed in my head, and I wanted to tell this woman, who was kneeling down to choose jars of what I now saw was baby food, that I had a baby too, the most goddamn beautiful baby you ever saw. But then she'd ask how old my baby was, and I didn't want to say she was dead and see this woman's eyes turn to her daughter in relief and gratitude that it wasn't her child, then see in those eyes that she was sure—sure with a mother's necessary confidence—that nothing terrible was *ever* going to happen to *her* daughter.

When I tried to pull my finger away, Samantha squeezed tighter, and a tiny bubble of spit formed at her lips. My nostrils inhaled her scent—baby powder, diapers, and the faint sweet odor of milk. I wanted her. My hands ached to lift her out of the seat and into my arms, into my life.

With furtive glances down either end of the aisle—empty—my mind worked to calculate how many steps it would take me to escape. I knew only one cashier worked this late. *Easy breezy.* I stepped closer to the cart. With my heart whooshing in my ears, I noticed every one of the baby's fine blond hairs glimmering in the store's fluorescent lights and reached out with my free hand to finger one silken strand. My baby had dark hair. This wasn't my baby. My baby was gone.

I stepped back just as the mother rose to her feet in the aisle, noticed me, and began to walk back toward the cart.

"Hello?" she said with a tentative smile.

I wanted to say, *What were you thinking? Turning your back on your child like that. Don't you know what could happen? How many crazies are out there? How crazy I am?*

"What a happy baby," I said. "And so beautiful."

"She looks happy now, but you should have seen her an hour ago! It took me forever to get her to calm down." While she went on about her mom-stress, stress I would have traded my soul for, I wanted to call her an ungrateful bitch, tell her she should be glad for every cry out of her baby's mouth. Instead I stood paralyzed and gave an occasional smile or nod to the woman until she finally ran out of steam and wrapped it up by saying, "Do you have kids?"

I felt my head shake back and forth, felt my lips straighten out from the smile, even felt my throat vibrate with the words, "No. No kids."

My eyes must have revealed something, though, because she smiled kindly and said, "It'll happen."

I wanted to slap her, wanted to scream and rage. I wanted to cry. But I didn't. I just smiled, nodded my head, and wished her a pleasant evening as I left them there in the aisle.

That was when I realized I might not be doing such a good job of handling things on my own. I'd managed to shove that moment behind all my other moments of near-madness until I saw a notice in the paper yesterday that one of the girls I used to work with just gave birth to a boy. I sent a card, but I knew I didn't trust myself to be around that baby. Even picking out the card was agony. Not sure why I did it, other than as another pathetic attempt to prove to myself I can handle shit I very clearly can't.

"Wayne and I would like you to come for dinner tonight," Mom said when she called late Tuesday afternoon. "I'm making a roast."

"Damn, I just had an early dinner. Wish I'd known." I hadn't eaten, but I'd rather rake my body over hot coals—hell, I'd rather eat hot coals—than go over there and hear what I was fucking up on now. Only Mom could manage to make me feel like shit about feeling like shit. I was already in a bad mood because of this one asshole movie producer who keeps taping proposals to my front door—he actually stands there and tries to talk to me through the wood, raising the amount every few minutes like he's bidding at a goddamn auction. He's wasting his breath.

Years ago, I remember watching the movie *Titanic*. People stuffed with popcorn were commenting on their way out about the great special effects and how realistic it was, particularly the bodies bobbing in the sea. And me? I went to the bathroom to throw up, because people actually died like that—hundreds and hundreds of people—and it seemed wrong to sit there and eat candies and lick salty butter off your fingers and admire how authentic their deaths in the freezing water looked.

I sure as hell don't want people stuffing their faces while they rate my life for its entertainment value.

"I *tried* to call you earlier, but you didn't answer." Mom never says, "You weren't home," it's always, "You didn't answer," in an accusing tone as though I let the phone ring just to piss her off.

"Emma and I went for a walk."

"What's the point of having voice mail if you don't check it?"

"You're right—sorry. But I'm glad you called back, I wanted to ask you something. I went through my things last night looking for my pictures of Daisy and Dad but I couldn't find them."

Not that I'd ever had a lot of photos anyway. Most of them had been given to me by relatives, and the rest were held hostage by Mom in her scrapbooks and albums with vague promises of their coming to me "one day." I was especially pissed that Mom was holding on to one with just Dad, Daisy, and me—it was unusual to find a picture Mom wasn't in.

"I'm sure I dropped those off after you moved back to your place."

"Not that I remember, and I looked everywhere for them the other night. . . ." I waited for a couple of seconds, but she offered up no explanation for the missing pictures, and I knew she wouldn't unless I pressed harder. But there was something else I wanted to ask her, and I'd learned to choose my battles with Mom. Russian roulette was probably less risky.

"Mom, do you ever think about Dad and Daisy?"

An exasperated sigh hissed through the phone. "Of course I do. What a silly question. So how much did you eat? Those canned soups you live on aren't a meal. You're getting too thin."

"I'm trying to talk to you about something, Mom."

"We've already talked—"

"Actually, no, we haven't. I've always wanted to because I think about them all the time, especially when I was up there, but whenever I brought the subject up, you either changed it or you just talked about Daisy's skating and all her—"

"Why are you doing this? Are you trying to hurt me?"

"No! I just wanted . . . well, I thought . . . because I lost a daughter and you lost a daughter, I thought we could talk and maybe you'd have some insight on how to deal with it." Insight? What the hell was I thinking? The woman had never shown any insight deeper than an ounce of vodka.

"I don't think I can help, Annie. The child you had . . . It's just not the same thing."

My voice turned to steel as my pulse sped up. "And why's that?"

"You won't understand."

"No? Well, how about you explain to me why my daughter's death doesn't *compare* to your daughter's so I *understand*." Rage made my voice tremble, and my hand gripped the phone so tight it hurt.

"You're twisting my words. Of course what happened to your child was a tragedy, Annie, but you can't compare it with what happened to me."

"Don't you mean what happened to *Daisy*?"

"This is just like you, Annie—I call with an invitation to dinner and somehow you turn it into another of your attacks. Honestly, sometimes I think you just look for ways to make yourself miserable."

"If that was the case, I'd spend more time with you, *Mom*."

Her shocked gasp was followed by the loud click of her hanging up. Anger propelled me out the door with Emma, but after a half hour of hard running, my brief high from the exercise and saying no to Mom was snuffed out when I imagined the next phone call. The one where Wayne would tell me how much I'd hurt my mother, how she was just beside herself, how I really should apologize and try to understand her better—she's the only mother I'm going to have in this life and the poor woman's already been through so much. Meanwhile, I sit there thinking, *Why the hell doesn't she try to understand me? What about what I've been through?*

After my baby died on the mountain, I woke up staring at her folded blanket, and my breasts began to leak milk through the front of my dress as though they were weeping for her. Even my body hadn't accepted her death. When The Freak noticed me awake he came over, sat behind me on the bed, and rubbed my back.

"I have some ice for your face." He set an ice pack down near my head.

I ignored it and rolled over to face him, in a sitting position. "Where's my baby?"

He stared down at the floor.

"I'm sorry I yelled at you, but I didn't want her blanket, I want *her*." I slid over the side of the bed and knelt in front of him. "Please, I'm *begging* you. I'll do anything." He still hadn't looked at me, so I moved my face directly into his line of sight. "*Anything* you want, just tell me where you put her . . ." My mouth couldn't form the word *body*.

"You *caaan't* always get what you want—" He broke off and hummed the last few bars of the Rolling Stones song.

"If you have an ounce of compassion, you'll tell me—"

"*If I have an ounce of compassion?*" He leapt off the bed and, with his hands on his hips, paced back and forth. "Have I not proven to you over and over how compassionate I am? Have I not always been there for you? Am I not still here for you, even after you said those terrible things to me? I bring you her blanket so you can find some comfort and all you want is *her*? She *left* you, *Annie*. Don't you get it? She left you, but I stayed." My hands pressed frantically against my ears to shut out his terrible words, but he pulled them off and said, "She's gone, gone, gone, and knowing where she is won't help you one bit."

"But she was gone so fast, I just want to . . . I need . . ." *To say good-bye.*

"You don't need to know where she is, now or ever." He leaned closer. "You still have me and that's all that should matter. And right now it's time for you to make my dinner."

How was I going to do this? How was I going to get through the next—

"It's *time*, Annie."

I stared at him dumbfounded.

He snapped his finger and pointed to the kitchen. I'd only made it a few steps when he said, "You can have an extra piece of chocolate for dessert tonight."

————

The Freak never did tell me where my baby's body was, Doc, and I still don't know—the cops even brought in cadaver dogs, but they couldn't find her. I like to think he put her body in the river and she floated downstream peacefully. That's what I try to hold on to when I lie awake at night in the closet, thinking about her alone up on the mountain, or when I wake up screaming and covered in sweat after another nightmare about wild animals tearing into her with their teeth.

I have no way to honor my baby—no grave, no memorial. The local church wanted to put up a headstone for her, but I said no because I knew journalists and people obsessed with morbid crap would be out there taking pictures. I've made myself her cemetery. That's why it stung when Mom said I wanted to be miserable. A lot of truth to that.

When Luke called again the other night, I found myself laughing for a few seconds when I told him Emma had fallen in the water on our walk. I stopped myself right away, but it was out there, my *laugh* was out there. And I felt ashamed, like I'd let my baby down by feeling even one moment of care-free enjoyment. Her life was taken away and with it her chance to smile, laugh, or feel, so if I laugh and smile, then I'm betraying her.

I should be celebrating that I didn't sleep in the closet once last week—that talk we had about acknowledging when I'm feeling paranoid but not reacting to it might've had something to do with it. Even though I couldn't resist checking the front and back doors to make sure they were locked last night, I managed not to check all the windows by reminding myself that none of them had been opened after I'd inspected them during the day. It was the first night since I've been home that I've been able to skip part of my bedtime ritual.

The peeing thing has gotten better and better—the yoga tapes you gave me helped a ton with that. Most days I can go when I need to and without even having to do any of the breathing exercises or repeat my mantras.

Like I said, I should feel proud of my progress, and I am, but that just adds another layer of guilt. Healing feels a lot like leaving my daughter behind, and I already did that once.

SESSION SIXTEEN

Well, I thought about your suggestion, Doc, and I'm not sold. I know no one is *actually* trying to harm me, it's all in my head, so making a list of anyone who might want to seems goofy as all get-out. Tell you what I *will* do, though. The next time I'm feeling paranoid, I'll make a mental list, and when I can't think of a single name to put on it I'll feel like a dumbass, which beats feeling paranoid.

The blue scarf you're wearing looks great with your eyes, by the way. You're pretty stylish for an older woman, you know, with your black turtlenecks and long fitted skirts. A classy look—no, streamlined. Like you don't have time for bullshit, even when it comes to your clothes. I've always tended to dress conservatively, the exact opposite of Mom's style—Hollywood Housewife. But Christina, who was my personal shopping guru, had been trying to coax me out into the light before I was abducted.

Poor girl wasn't having much luck with me, though. I

generally avoided shopping, especially in the fancy stores she liked. My favorite suit was the result of an accidental walking-by-the-store-window-I-have-to-have-it moment. If there was an event I had to go to, I just headed over to Christina's house. She'd bounce around, ripping things out of her closet, draping me with scarves and necklaces, telling me how pretty I looked in this dress or that color. She loved doing it and I loved having someone decide for me.

She was really generous with her hand-me-downs, too—Christina got bored with clothes the week after she bought them—and a lot of my wardrobe was made up of her cast-offs. That's why I still can't figure out why I got so pissed at her for trying to give me clothes when I got back from the mountain.

When I found out Mom had gotten rid of all my clothes, I loaded up at the Goodwill. Man, you should have seen the look on Mom's face when she saw the oversized jogging suits and sweatpants I brought home. I didn't care what color anything was, it just had to be soft and warm-looking, the baggier the better.

Running around up there in all those girlie dresses The Freak liked made me feel so exposed. One thing you can say for the way I dress now: nobody's tempted to look underneath.

Luke called Sunday morning and asked if I wanted to get together and take the dogs for a walk. The first word out of my mouth was *No!* Before I could soften my reply with a reason—believable or otherwise—he launched into a rundown on something going on at the restaurant.

The thought of seeing him again terrified me. What if he

STILL MISSING · 181

tried to touch me and I pulled back again? I couldn't stand to see that hurt look in his eyes a third time. What if he didn't try to touch me? Would that mean he didn't care anymore? Now that I'd said no I wondered if he'd suggest a walk again—I wasn't sure if I'd feel any braver next time but I knew I didn't want him to stop asking. When I did finally drag my butt outside to take Emma for a walk I couldn't stop thinking about Luke and wondering what it would have been like if he was with me.

The next morning, instead of camouflaging myself with yet another shapeless jogging suit, I carried up from the basement the box of clothes Christina had dropped off on my doorstep months ago. I didn't realize until I checked out the faded jeans and sage-colored sweater in a mirror how long it had been since I'd looked in one.

It's not like I'd put on a slinky dress—the jeans were a relaxed fit and the sweater wasn't tight—but I couldn't remember the last time I chose something because I liked the color, or put on anything even hinting at curves. For a second, staring in the mirror at the stranger wearing Christina's clothes, I almost saw the shadow of the girl I used to be, and it freaked me out so much I wanted to tear off all the clothes. But Emma—anxious for her morning walk—whined at my heels, and I left them on. I don't care what she looks like, and she doesn't care what I look like.

Emma stayed at my mom's while I was missing—definitely not my first choice and it sure wouldn't have been Emma's. Later, I found out Luke and a couple of my friends offered to take her but my mom said no. When I asked her why she took Emma, she said, "What was I supposed to do with her? Can you imagine what people would've said if I'd given her away?"

Poor dog got so excited when she first saw me she started dribbling pee—she's never done that, even as a puppy—and shaking so hard I thought she was having a seizure. When I squatted down to hug her, she shoved her head into my chest and whined for the longest time, telling me all her woes. And she had a right to complain. For one thing, she was tied up to the Japanese maple tree in Mom's backyard, and Emma had never been tied up in her life. Mom said she'd been digging in her garden beds. No doubt—she probably thought she'd landed in dog hell and was trying to dig her way out.

Judging by Emma's long toenails, the last year of her life had mostly been spent tied to that tree. Her fur was matted and her beautiful glossy eyes were dull. On the porch I found a bag of food—the cheapest crap you could buy—and it smelled moldy.

This dog used to sleep with me every night and I walked her two, sometimes three times a day. She had every dog toy and treat ever manufactured, the softest bed in case she got too hot to sleep with me, and I planned my workdays so she never had to be alone for too long.

Furious at the way she'd been treated, I wanted to say something, but I'd just come back, and if being around people was like crawling uphill through mud, then talking to Mom was like crawling uphill wearing a heavy backpack. Besides, what could I have said? "Hey, Mom, next time I'm abducted you don't get my dog"?

After I finally got back to my place Emma preferred being outside, but it only took a couple of days for her to remember the good life and she's probably on my couch drooling all over the cushions right now. Her fur is back to shiny gold and her eyes are once again full of life. She's not the same dog as before, though. She stays a lot closer to me on walks than she used to, and if she does forge ahead, she comes back every few minutes to check on me.

I don't think Mom meant to hurt my dog, and if I accused her of cruelty she'd be shocked. She didn't raise her fist to Emma—not that I know of, anyway, but I doubt she would. But she didn't give her any love for a year, and as far as I'm concerned that's just as damaging as physical blows. Mom would never get that lack of affection is abuse.

After my baby died, I blocked out my grief by focusing on my hatred for The Freak as he forced me to continue with my daily routines like she'd never existed.

Late one morning after about a week of this, he went outside to chop wood in preparation for winter. I thought it was close to the end of July, but I wasn't sure. Time only counts when you have a purpose. Sometimes I forgot to make a mark on the wall, but it didn't matter—I knew I'd been there for almost a year, because when he opened the door I'd caught the scent of hot earth and warm fir trees, the same scents that filled the air on the day he took me.

While he cut wood, I was inside sewing some buttons on his shirt. I kept sneaking little glances at the baby's basket, but then I'd see her blanket hanging neatly over the side where he'd placed it and jab the needle into my finger instead of the fabric.

After about twenty minutes he came back inside and said, "I have a job for you."

The only other time he'd asked for my help was with the deer, and as he motioned for me to follow him outside, nerves made my legs go rubbery. Still gripping the shirt and with my hand holding the needle suspended in the air, I stared at him. His flushed face glowed with a fine sheen of sweat—I couldn't tell whether it was from anger or exertion, but his voice was neutral when he spoke.

"Come on, we don't have all day." While I followed him out to a pile of large fir rounds, he said over his shoulder, "Now, pay attention. Your job is to pick up the pieces as I split them and stack them over there." He pointed to a neat stack that came halfway up the side of the cabin.

Once in a while, when I was inside the cabin and he was outside, I heard the sound of a chain saw running, but I couldn't see any fresh stumps at the edge of our clearing or any drag marks. A wheelbarrow leaned against the pile where he was chopping, so I figured he must have felled a tree in the forest and wheeled the bigger blocks in to be split into smaller pieces.

The pile was only about twelve feet from the stack. Seemed to me it would be easier to either chop the tree up into smaller pieces where he'd cut it down, or at least wheel the bigger blocks right next to where they had to be stacked. Just like with the deer, something told me this was him showing off.

I hadn't been outside much since the baby died, and as I carried wood to the stack my eyes searched for any evidence of recently disturbed dirt. I didn't find any, but I was only able to give the river a quick glance before memories of my baby on her blanket in the sun overwhelmed me.

After we'd been working for about an hour, I deposited an armload in the stack and came to stand a couple of feet behind him until he finished swinging the axe and it was safe for me to pick up more. He'd taken his shirt off and his back glistened with sweat. He paused for a breather, his back to me and the axe resting on his shoulder.

"We can't let this distract us from our ultimate goal," he

said. "Nature has a plan." What the hell was he talking about? "But so do I." The shiny blade of the axe lifted high in the air. "It was better we found out early that she was weak."

Then I got it, and my frozen heart shattered in my chest. He continued chopping, emitting one little grunt with each downswing, talking in between strokes.

"The next one will be stronger."

Next one.

"It's not quite six weeks, but you're healed, so I'm going to let you get pregnant early. We'll start tonight."

I stood perfectly still, but a loud screaming began in my head. There were going to be more babies. It was never going to end.

The silver of the axe flashed in the bright sun as he lifted it over his shoulder for the next swing.

"No response, Annie?"

I was saved from having to answer when his axe got caught halfway through a piece of wood. He used his foot to pry the axe out, then leaned it against the woodpile to his right. With his foot braced on one side of the block, which shifted his body slightly away from the axe, he bent down and tried to break the split apart by hand.

Treading softly, I came up behind him on his right—the side angled away. I could have reached over and flicked one of the beads of sweat off his back. He grunted as his hands fought with the wood.

"Ouch!"

I held my breath as he brought his finger to his mouth and sucked at a sliver. If he turned, we'd be face-to-face.

He bent over again and resumed his struggle with the wood. Keeping my body directly behind him and facing the same direction, I focused my gaze on his back for the slightest sign he was about to turn, then reached for the axe. My hands caressed the warm smooth wood handle, still slick from his sweat, and curled over it in a tight grip. The weight of it felt right and solid as I lifted it up and brought it to rest on my shoulder.

His voice straining with effort, he said, "We'll have another one by spring."

I lifted the axe high.

I screamed, "*Shut up, shut up, SHUT UP!*" as I sank it into the back of his head.

It made the strangest sound, a wet thunk.

For a few seconds his body stayed bent, then he fell over facedown with both of his arms and the wood underneath him. He twitched a couple of times, then stilled.

Shaking with rage, I leaned over his body and yelled, "*Take that, you sick fuck!*"

The forest was quiet.

Leaving a red trail in his blond curls, blood rolled down the side of his head, hit the dry ground with a *plop, plop, plop,* made a rapidly spreading pool, and stopped plopping.

I waited for him to turn around and hit me, but as the seconds turned to minutes my heart rate settled down and I was able to take a few deep breaths. The cut hadn't split his head wide open or anything, but the blond hair around the axe head—embedded halfway into his skull—was a glistening mass of scarlet, and some of the hair seemed to have gone into the cut. A fly landed and crawled around in the wound, then two more landed.

Walking backward to the cabin on weak legs, I hugged my trembling body with my arms. My eyes were mesmerized by the axe handle reaching toward the sky and the crimson halo surrounding his head.

Safe inside the cabin, I ripped off my sweaty dress, then ran the shower until it was so hot it almost scalded my skin. Shaking violently, I sat down in the back of the tub, tucked my knees under my chin, and wrapped my arms tight around them to stop the muscle spasms. The water thundered down on my bowed head in a fiery baptism while I rocked myself and tried to comprehend what I'd done. My mind couldn't grasp that he was really dead. Someone like him should have taken a silver bullet, a cross, and a stake through the heart to die. What if he *wasn't* dead? I should have felt for a pulse. What if he was making his way back to the cabin right now? Despite the hot shower, I shivered.

Expecting him to jump out at me, I slowly opened the bathroom door and sent steam billowing out into the empty room. Slowly picked the dress off the floor and pulled it over my head. Slowly made my way to the cabin door. Slowly placed my ear against the cool metal. Silence.

I tested the knob, praying the door hadn't locked behind me. It turned. I opened the door just an inch and peeked through. His body was still in the exact same position in the middle of the clearing, but the sun had shifted and the handle of the axe cast a shadow like a sundial.

My legs tense in case I had to break into a run, I snuck up on him. Every couple of steps I paused and strained my eyes and ears for any sounds or the slightest movement. When I finally got up to him, his body looked awkward with his arms under him, and the position made him seem smaller.

Holding my breath, I reached around his neck, on the opposite side of the blood river, and checked for a pulse. He was dead.

I backed away slowly, then sat on the porch in one of the rocking chairs and tried to figure out my next step. Keeping beat with every creak of the chair, my mind repeated the words, *He's dead. He's dead. He's dead. He's dead. He's dead.*

In the hot summer afternoon the clearing was idyllic. The river, calm without spring's heavy rains, was a soft hum, and the occasional robin, swallow, or blue jay warbled. The only sign of violence was the buzz of the rapidly growing mass of flies that coated his wound and the pool of blood. His words tripped through my reverie: *Nature has a plan.*

I was free but I didn't feel free. As long as I could see him, he still existed. I had to do something with the body. But what?

The temptation to set the son of a bitch on fire was huge, but it was summer, the clearing was dry, and I didn't want to start a forest fire. Digging through the dry, compact ground to bury him would be next to impossible. But I couldn't just leave him there. Even though I'd confirmed he was well and truly dead, my mind refused to accept that he couldn't hurt me anymore.

The shed. I could lock him in the shed.

Back at his body, I tilted him slightly to the side and searched his front pockets for the keys. With my teeth clamped over the ring, I gripped both of his ankles—then dropped them quickly when I felt his warm skin. I don't know how long it takes a body to cool down, and he was lying in the sun, but it scared me enough that I checked his pulse a second time.

Grabbing hold of his ankles again and ignoring their warmth, I tried to drag him backward, but I was only able to move him enough that his body slid off the log round, and when it hit the ground, the axe handle in his head *wobbled*. I fought the bile rising in my throat, turned my back to him, and tried to pull him that way. I was only able to move him a foot before I had to stop and take a breath—my dress was already damp, and sweat dripped into my eyes. Even though the shed wasn't far away, it might as well have been on the other side of the clearing. Casting my eye around for an alternative, I spied the wheelbarrow.

I rolled it over to his body and braced myself for the sensation of his skin touching mine. With my eyes averted from the axe, I gripped him by his upper arms and managed to pull them out from under his body. Eyes still averted, I grasped him under the armpits and with my heels dug into the ground threw my whole body into trying to haul him up—I could only move him a few inches. I straddled his back and tried to pick him up from around the waist, but I was only able to get him up a foot before my arms began to shake from the exertion. The only way he was getting in that wheelbarrow was if he came back to life and climbed into it himself.

Wait. If I had something to roll his body onto, something that would slide across the ground, I might be able to drag him. The rug under the bed wasn't smooth enough. I hadn't noticed a tarp near the woodpile, but he had to have one somewhere, maybe in the shed.

After trying five keys on his monster key chain, I was able to open the padlock. It took a while because my hands were shaking like a burglar's on his first job.

I half expected to see the deer still hanging from the ceiling, but there was no sign of it, and on a shelf above the freezer I found an orange tarp. Unfolding it near his body, I considered how I was going to roll him over onto the tarp with the axe in his head.

Damn. It was going to have to come out.

With my hands wrapped around the handle, I closed my eyes and pulled, but it wouldn't budge. I tried a bit more force, and the sensation of flesh and bone resisting as they let go of their prize had me gagging. It had to be done fast. With my foot braced against the base of his neck, I shut my eyes tight, took a deep breath, and wrenched the axe out. I dropped it, bent over, and dry-heaved.

Once my stomach settled down, I knelt beside his body, on the opposite side of the blood, and rolled him onto the tarp. He fell onto his back, glassy blue eyes staring up at the sky, a smear of blood on the orange tarp arcing out from his head. His face had already paled and his mouth was slack.

With quick fingers I closed his eyelids—not out of respect for the dead but because I thought of all the times I'd had to force myself to look at them. Now, in a few seconds, I'd fixed it so I'd never have to see those eyes again.

My back to him, I grasped the edge of the tarp, leaned forward like an ox with a gruesome cargo, and pulled him over to the shed. Getting him over the lip of the doorway was tricky, because he kept sliding farther down the tarp. Eventually I had to drag it out again, move him up it, and fold the end over him like a napkin. Then with both ends in my hands I wiggled, dragged, shoved, and pulled him inside. At one point his hand fell out and touched my knee. I dropped the tarp, leapt backward, and hit my head on a post. It hurt like a son of a bitch, but I was too focused to pay the pounding any attention.

I stuffed his arm back in the tarp and tucked it all around him. I found some bungee cords, wound them tight around his legs and upper body. As I wrapped him up like a mummy I kept telling myself he couldn't hurt me anymore. Not one part of me believed it.

Dehydrated, sweat-soaked, head pounding, and aching all over from the physical exertion, I locked the shed and made my way back to the cabin for some water. Once I'd slaked my thirst, I lay on the bed clutching the keys and stared at his key-chain pocket watch. It was five o'clock—the first time I knew the hour myself in almost a year.

At first I didn't think, I just listened to the ticking of the second hand until the pounding headache calmed down, then I thought, *I'm free. I'm finally fucking free.* But why didn't I feel like I was? *I killed a man. I'm a murderer. I'm just like him.*

All I'd gotten rid of was a body.

During one of the first press conferences I held after I came home—I stupidly thought if I got it all over with at once, they might actually stop calling and lurking outside the trailer—a bald guy in the audience holding a Bible up in the air chanted, *"Thou shall not kill. You're going to hell. Thou shall not kill. You're going to hell!"* The crowd let out a collective gasp as he was dragged off by bystanders, then turned back to me. Camera bulbs flashed, and somebody shoved a microphone in my face.

"How would you respond to what he said, Annie?"

As I looked out at the crowd and the back of the bald-headed guy, who was still chanting, I thought, *I'm already in hell, asshole.*

I wish sometimes that I could talk to my mom about these things, Doc, about guilt and regret and shame, but as much as I have a talent for shouldering all the blame, Mom has one for ducking it. Which is one of the reasons I still haven't talked to her since our fight, not that she's tried either. That doesn't surprise me, but I thought for sure Wayne would have called by now.

Shit, I'm getting so damn lonely these days I might even have to give one of your meet-your-fears-head-on experiments the old college try. But it's just so stupid that I still feel like I'm in danger. The Freak is *dead*. I'm as safe as safe can be. Now, can someone please tell my psyche that?

SESSION SEVENTEEN

You know, Doc, all along, even while you were giving me techniques to work through my fears or explaining what might be causing them, I still told myself they'd eventually go away on their own—especially after I read up on all that grief stuff. Then this week some dickhead broke into my house.

I came back from my morning run to find my alarm blaring, cops parked in my driveway, the doorjamb on my back door kicked apart, and my bedroom window open. Judging by the broken branches on my shrubs, that's how the bastard got out. Nothing seemed to be missing and the cops said they couldn't do much unless I figured out if anything was gone. They also told me there's been a couple of B&E's in my neighborhood recently, but they didn't find any fingerprints at them either, like that was supposed to make me feel better.

After they all went home and my full-body shaking had subsided to occasional tremors, I headed to my bedroom to change. A thought stopped me in the hallway. *Why would you risk going in but not steal anything?* Something wasn't right.

I walked around my house slowly, trying to think like a burglar. Okay, bust open back door, race upstairs, then what? Run to the living room—nothing small visible, stereo equipment and TV are too big to grab fast, especially if you're on foot. Run down hallway to bedroom—search drawers for valuables?

I examined each one carefully. All were shut tight and my clothes were neatly folded. Everything still hung straight in the closet and the door was closed evenly—sometimes one side sticks. I stepped back and surveyed the bedroom. A hamper full of clothes I'd just taken out of the dryer was in the same place on the floor, the big T-shirt I sleep in still tossed across the foot of the bed. The bed.

Was that a slight indent near the edge? Did I sit there when I put my socks on? I came closer and inspected every inch of the bed. Examined every hair. Mine? Emma's? I brought my nose close to the duvet cover and sniffed the length of it. Was that the faint traces of cologne? I stood up again.

A stranger forced his way into my house, was in my *bedroom*, looking at my things, *touching* my things. My skin crawled.

I stripped my bed, grabbed my T-shirt, dumped everything in the wash with lots of bleach, and wiped down every surface of my house. After I boarded up the back door and the window—house looked like an army bunker by the time I was done—I grabbed the cordless phone and hid in the hall closet for the rest of the day.

Gary, the cop I was telling you about, called me later to make sure I was all right, which was nice of him considering he doesn't deal with robberies. He backed up what the other cops were saying, that it was most likely a random event and the guy raced in to grab what he could, then panicked and took the quickest exit out. When I argued with him, insisting it was a dumbass thing to do, he said criminals do a lot of stupid things when they're scared. He also suggested I call someone to stay with me or go to a friend's until my doorjamb was fixed.

I may have been scared to death, but no way was I going to my mom's. And friends? Well, even if I wasn't more paranoid than Howard Hughes, I'm not sure how many of those I have left these days. Luke is about the only one who still calls. When I first came back, everyone—friends, old coworkers, people I went to school with but haven't seen in years—was making such a fuss over me, I just couldn't handle it. But you know, people only try for so long, and if you keep shutting the door in their face they eventually go away.

Christina is about the only one I'd consider asking, but you know what happened there, or at least you know about as much as I know, because I still don't understand why I reacted so badly to her. She's probably just trying to be a good friend by leaving me alone now, but sometimes I wish she'd haul off and force me out into the light, bully me like she used to.

Of course, right away I thought about moving, but dammit, I love the house; if I ever sell, it won't be because of some asshole burglar. Not that I could, anyway. How the hell am I going to qualify for a mortgage? I thought about looking for work. I have a whole new set of skills, but I'd hate to see what kind of job they'd land me.

All of which leads me to the call I got from Luke when I got home from our last session.

"My bookkeeper up and quit on me, Annie. Any chance you could take over until I find someone else? It would be just part-time, and—"

"I don't need your help, Luke."

"Who said anything about you needing help? This is about me, I need *your* help—I can't make heads or tails of these books. I feel bad even asking, but you're the only person I know who's good with numbers. I can just bring the stuff to your house, you won't even have to go into the restaurant."

I think it was embarrassment that made me tell him okay, I could try it, before I realized what I'd just committed to. Later, it was a different story. *I'm not ready for this!* I almost called and canceled. But I took a few deep breaths, then told myself to just sleep on it. Of course the next morning is when my house got broken into. In the midst of all that drama and the ensuing panic attack, I forgot about my conversation with Luke. Then last night he left a message that he's going to come over this weekend with an accounting program to load on my computer. He sounded so damn relieved and grateful, I couldn't think of a way out. And I wasn't sure if I really wanted one.

I tell myself it's just a business thing on Luke's part, but I'm sure I'm not the only person who could do his bookkeeping— the phone book is full of names.

Last Monday night I had a cold that was threatening to escalate and was sitting at half-mast on the couch in faded blue flannel pajamas and hedgehog slippers, a box of Kleenex in my lap, the TV on but the sound down. A car door slammed at the end of my driveway. I held my breath for a second and listened. Footsteps on the gravel? I peeked out the window but couldn't see anything in the dark. I grabbed the poker from my fireplace.

Soft footsteps on the stairs, then silence.

Poker gripped tight, I peered through the peephole, but couldn't see anything.

Rustling sounds near the bottom of the door. Emma barked.

I yelled, "I know you're out there. You better tell me who you are RIGHT NOW!"

"Jesus Christ, Annie, I was just picking up your paper."

Mom.

I slid open the deadbolts—when the locksmith came to repair the doorjamb I had an extra one installed. Emma took one sniff of Mom and headed straight to my room, where she probably crawled under the bed. I felt like joining her.

"Mom, why didn't you call first?"

With a toss of her head that made her ponytail shimmy, she shoved my paper into my hand and headed back out. I grabbed her shoulders.

"Wait—I didn't mean you had to leave, but you scared the crap out of me. I was just . . . dozing off."

She turned around and with her big blue doll eyes staring at the wall over my shoulder she said, "Sorry."

Well, that threw me. Even though the "sorry" did have a slight edge to it, I can't remember the last time my mom apologized for anything.

Her gaze traveled down to my hedgehog slippers, and her eyebrows rose. My mom wears marabou-feathered high-heeled slippers, summer or winter, and before she could comment on mine I said, "Did you want to come in?"

As she stepped into the house to stand in the foyer, I noticed she was clutching a large brown paper bag to her chest with one hand. For a second I wondered if she'd brought some booze with her, but no, the package was flat and square. In her other hand she held a Tupperware container she now thrust toward me.

"Wayne dropped me off on his way into town—I made you some Annie Bear cookies."

Ah. Peanut butter cookies in the shape of a bear's paw with chocolate chips melted for the pads. When I was a kid she made them for me if I was sad or if she felt guilty about something, which wasn't often. She must have felt bad about our argument.

"That was really thoughtful, Mom. I've missed these." She didn't say anything, just stood there with her eyes darting around my house, then she wandered over to finger the dry leaves of the fern on my mantel.

Before she could critique my plant-mothering skills, I said, "I don't know if you want to be around me—I have a cold— but if you want to stay I could make us some tea."

"You're sick? Why didn't you say something?" She perked up like she'd just won the mother lottery. "When Wayne comes back, we'll drive you to my doctor's. Where's your phone? I'll call their office right now."

"I've had *enough* of doctors." Shit, I sounded like The Freak. "Look, if I decide I need one, I can drive myself, but it doesn't matter anyway, we're not going to get an appointment this late in the day."

"That's ridiculous—of course my doctor will see you." My whole life Mom has never thought she should have to wait for anything—not doctor's appointments, tables in restaurants, supermarket lines—and sure as shit she generally ends up with an appointment within the hour, the best table, and the store manager opening the next checkout for her.

"Mom, stop, I'm *fine*. There's nothing a doctor can do for a cold—" I held up my hand as she opened her mouth to interrupt. "But I promise if I get sicker I'll go." She sighed, set her purse and package down on my end table, and patted the couch.

"Why don't you lie down and I'll make you a hot lemon tea with honey."

Telling her I was capable of boiling my own water would just get me a look, so I collapsed on the couch.

"Sure, it's above the stove."

Once she'd brought me a steaming mug, a plate of Annie Bear cookies, and poured herself a healthy glass of the red wine I had in the kitchen, she sat at the end of the couch and spread my throw over the both of us.

She took a good long gulp of the wine, handed me the package, and said, "I found that photo album you were talking about, it must have gotten mixed up with our stuff somehow." Sure it did. But I let it go. She'd brought the pictures back and the hot tea was spreading a pleasant glow throughout my body and even my feet felt warm tucked against her leg.

As I started to flip through the album, Mom took out an envelope from her purse and handed it to me.

"You didn't have these photos, so I made you copies."

Surprised at the unexpected gesture, I focused on the first one. She and Daisy were at one of the ice rinks in town wearing matching outfits, matching ponytails, and matching skates. Daisy looked about fifteen, so it was probably taken just before the accident, and in the pink sparkly costume Mom looked about the same age. I'd forgotten she skated with Daisy sometimes when she was practicing.

"People used to tell me all the time that we could be sisters," she said. I wanted to say, *Really? I don't see it at all.*

"You were prettier."

"*Annie*, your sister was gorgeous." I looked at her face. Her eyes were shining and I knew she was pleased, but I also knew she agreed with me.

While she got up to get herself more wine, I flipped through the rest of the photos, and as she settled back down at my feet with a full glass—this time she brought the half-empty bottle with her and set it on the end table—I stopped at the last one, of Dad and her on their wedding day.

When I glanced over at her, she was staring into her glass. It may have just been a trick of the light, but her eyes looked moist.

"Your dress was beautiful." I looked down at its sweetheart neckline, at the long beaded veil in her blond hair. Then back up from the photo.

Leaning toward me, she said, "I made it from a pattern Val wanted for her own wedding dress one day. I told her she didn't have the chest for it." Mom laughed. "Can you believe she's *never* forgiven me? For that or for going out with your father." She shrugged. "Like it was *my* fault he liked me more."

This was news. "Aunt Val dated Dad?"

"They only went out a few times, but I suppose she thought they were something. She was just awful at the wedding, barely spoke to me. Did I tell you about our cake? It was three layers, and . . ."

While mom went step by step through their wedding feast, the details of which I'd heard a million times, I thought about Aunt Val. No wonder she was always trying to get back at

Mom. Might also explain her attitude toward Daisy and me. When we were kids she and Mom did the take-each-other's-kids-for-the-weekend thing, which Daisy and I dreaded. Aunt Val mostly ignored me, but I swear she actually hated Daisy, looking for any reason to make fun of her while Tamara and her brother giggled.

Our families didn't do a lot together after the accident. Wayne and Uncle Mark don't have much in common, or even like each other, so it was mostly just Aunt Val and Mom. When they did include us kids, my cousin Jason teased the hell out of me, but Tamara kept her distance—I thought she was stuck-up. Now I figure her mother was probably giving her the gears about me as much as mine was about her.

One afternoon after I moved into my house Mom and Aunt Val popped in from a shopping trip. Aunt Val glanced around, then asked me how I was enjoying real estate.

"It's good, I like the challenge."

"Yes, Tamara seems to really thrive on it too. She got the top sales award for her office this quarter, won a bottle of Dom Pérignon and a weekend trip to Whistler. Does your office ever do anything like that, Annie?" Nice dig, if not subtle. My office was large for Clayton Falls, but nowhere near the size of Tamara's downtown Vancouver firm—we'd be lucky to get a bottle of wine and a plastic plaque.

Before I could answer, Mom said, "Oh, she's still doing residential? Annie's getting a huge project, all waterfront units. Didn't you say it was going to be the largest building in Clayton Falls, Annie Bear?" I'd only been talking to a developer, hadn't even done a presentation yet, which Mom well knew, but she just enjoyed twisting the knife so much, I didn't have the heart to take it out of her hand.

I said, "It's a big one."

"I'm sure Tamara will get a project one day too, Val. Maybe Annie can give her some tips?" Mom smiled at Aunt Val, who looked like her tea had just turned to poison in her mouth.

Of course, Aunt Val rallied.

"That's a lovely offer, but right now Tamara is finding she can make more money selling houses and doesn't want to spend years marketing a project that may not even sell. But I'm sure Annie will be fabulous at it."

Mom's face turned so red I was actually worried for a minute, but she managed to force a smile and changed the subject. God only knows what those two were like growing up.

Mom never talks about her childhood much, but I know her dad split when she was pretty young and her mom remarried another deadbeat. Her older stepbrother, Dwight, is the one who's in prison. He robbed a bank when he was nineteen, just before Mom got married, served his sentence, and was released a month after the accident, then managed to get arrested a week later. Dumbass even shot a guard in the leg the last time. I've never met him and Mom refuses to talk about him. I made the mistake of asking if we could go see him once and she flipped out. "Don't you even *think* about going near that man." When I said, "But Tamara told me Aunt Val takes them, so why can't we—" that got me a slammed door.

After we moved into the shitty rental house, I came home from school one day to find Mom sitting on the couch, staring at a letter in her hands with a half-empty bottle of vodka beside her. It looked like she'd been crying.

I said, "What's wrong, Mom?" She just kept staring at the letter.

"Mom?"

Her voice was desperate. "I won't let it happen again. I won't."

A jolt of fear shot through me. "What—what won't you let happen?"

She held a lighter to the letter and dropped it in the ashtray. When it was gone she picked up the bottle and stumbled to her room. On the kitchen table I found an envelope with a prison as its return address. The envelope was gone by the morning, but she didn't leave the house for a week after that.

I tuned back in when Mom said, "You know, Luke's a lot like your father."

"You think? I guess in some ways. He's patient like Dad was, that's for sure. We've been talking a lot recently, I'm going to help him with his bookkeeping."

"Bookkeeping?" She said the word like I'd just announced I was going to become a prostitute. "You *hate* bookkeeping."

I shrugged. "I need to make some money."

"So you haven't talked to an agent or a producer?"

"I decided I don't want to make more money off what happened to me. It makes me sick that people, including me, have made any money off it at all. "

The first time I saw an old high school friend being interviewed on TV, I sat stunned on my couch while this girl I hadn't seen in a decade told the talk show host about the first time we tried pot, about the outdoor party where I got drunk and threw up in the backseat of a car belonging to a boy I had a major crush on, then read aloud from notes we supposedly passed each other in class. That wasn't even the worst of it— the guy I lost my virginity to sold his story to a major men's magazine. Jerk even gave them pictures of us from when we were together. One of them was of me in a bikini.

Mom said, "Annie, you *really* need to think about this. You don't have the luxury of time." Her face was concerned. "You never went to college or university. Sales is just about all you can do, but try selling anything now—all people see when they look at you is a rape victim. And bookkeeping for Luke? How long is that going to last?"

I remembered a call a few days back from a movie producer. Before I could hang up on her she said, "I know you must be sick of people bothering you, but I promise if you just take a few minutes to hear me out, and you still say no, I'll never call again." Something about her no-bullshit tone of voice connected with me, so I told her to go ahead.

She gave me her pitch on how I could set the record straight and my story could benefit women all over the world. Then she said, "What's holding you back? Maybe if you tell me what you're afraid of I can see what we could do."

"Sorry, you can talk, but sharing my reasons wasn't part of the bargain."

So she talked, and it was like she knew exactly what I was worried about and what I wanted to hear—she even told me I could have final script and actor approval. And she said the money could set me up for life.

I said, "It's still a no, but if anything changes, I'll call you first."

"I hope you do, but I hope you also understand that there's a time limit to this offer. . . ."

She was right, and Mom was right. If I waited much longer I was going to be a hell of a lot more than a day late and a dollar short. But I wasn't sure what was worse, going down in a ball of flames like Mom predicted, or actually taking her advice.

Mom looked away from the TV and took another slug of wine. I said, "Did you give a movie producer my number?"

She paused with her glass in midair and her forehead wrinkled. "Did someone call you?"

"Yeah, that's why I'm asking. My number's unlisted."

She shrugged. "Those people have ways."

"Don't talk to any of them, Mom. Please." We held eyes for a moment, then she let her head fall to rest on the back of my couch.

"I know I was hard on you girls, but it was only because I wanted more for you than I'd had." I waited for her to say more, but she just gestured to the TV with her hand holding the glass. "Do you remember when I let you and Daisy stay up late to watch that?" Now I realized she'd been staring at a preview for *Gone with the Wind*—one of her favorite movies.

"Sure. You stayed up with us and we all slept in the living room."

She smiled at the memory, but her face was sad. It turned thoughtful as she turned to look at me. "It's on in an hour. I could stay over tonight, if you're sick?"

"Oh, I don't know, I've been getting up around seven and going for a run, you—" She turned back to the TV. The sudden withdrawal of her attention hurt more than I care to admit. "Okay, sure, it might be nice to have some company, probably stupid to run feeling like this anyway."

She gave me a smile and patted my foot under the blanket. "Then I'll stay, Annie Bear." She dragged the cushions off the other couch and started building a bed in the middle of the living room floor. When she asked me where I kept my spare blankets, her cheeks pink with excitement, I figured what the hell. Beats another night lying awake in the hall closet thinking, *Why didn't the burglar take anything?*

Later that night, after Mom sent Wayne home when he stopped by to pick her up, after we'd eaten popcorn, Annie

Bear cookies, and ice cream while watching *Gone with the Wind*, Mom passed out with her small body pressed against my back and her knees tucked into the curve of mine. As her breath tickled my back and her arm lay over me, I stared at her tiny hand touching my skin and realized it was the first time I'd let anyone physically close to me since I came back from the mountain. I turned my face away so she wouldn't feel my tears against her arm.

Just thinking, Doc, every time I say something bad about Mom, I have this urge to list all her good qualities right after—my version of knocking on wood. And the thing is, Mom *isn't* all bad, but that's the problem. It would be easier if I could just hate her, because it's the rare times when she's loving that make the other times so much harder.

SESSION EIGHTEEN

On my way to your office I walked by a bulletin board, and a concert poster caught my eye. I was checking out the announcement, just about to take a sip of my coffee, when I noticed part of a different flyer underneath the poster. Something about it seemed familiar, so I pulled it out. And holy shit, Doc, it was a flyer with my face on it—*my* face— over the words *Missing Realtor*. I just kept staring, and until a drop landed on my hand, I wasn't even aware I was crying.

Maybe I should put up my own flyers: *Still Missing*. That smiling face belonged to the woman I used to be, not the woman I am now. Luke must have given them the photo—he snapped it on our first Christmas morning together. He'd just handed me a beautiful card and I was grinning up at him, all happy and shit. My hand shook like I was holding ice instead of warm coffee.

The flyer is stuffed in the garbage can outside your office

now, but I still have the urge to go back and pull it out. God knows what I'd do with it.

Now that the shock of seeing my picture's worn off, I really want to talk about what happened when I finally sat down and made a list of all the people in my life like you suggested. Yes, Fräulein Freud, I actually gave one of your ideas a whirl. Shit, I had to do something—couldn't keep sitting around freaking myself out over the break-in.

My internal scare-yourself-silly sound track goes a little something like this: *My car was in the driveway, so the burglar must have seen me leave with Emma. How long had he been watching the house? Days, week, months, still? What if it wasn't a burglar?*

Then I spend the next hour telling myself I'm an idiot—the cops are right, it was just a random event, a stupid burglar who got freaked by the alarm. But then the whispers start up again. *Someone's watching you right now. The second you relax he's going to get you. You can't trust anyone.*

Like I said, I had to do something.

Starting with the ones closest to me—Luke, Christina, Mom, Wayne, any family like Tamara, her brother Jason, Aunt Val, and her husband Mark—I made a column beside each one for any reasons they might want to hurt me, feeling like a complete idiot because of course there's nothing to put there.

Next I moved down the list to anyone else I might have pissed off—former clients, coworkers, ex-boyfriends. I've never been sued, the only Realtor who might've had an issue with me is the "mystery" Realtor competing against me for that project back when I was abducted, and although I've broken the odd heart, I never did anything deserving of revenge so long after the fact. Even wrote down the names of a couple of Luke's exes—one was still hung up on him when we started dating, but hell, she moved to Europe before I was even abducted. I put The Freak down too, then wrote "dead" by his name.

I sat at my table, staring at this ridiculous list with its got-a-listing-they-wanted, didn't-return-their-call, didn't-sell-their-house-fast-enough, kept-one-of-his-CDs notes in the column, and when I tried to imagine any of these people lurking outside my house or breaking in so they could "get" me, I shook my head at my craziness.

Of course it was just a burglar, probably some junkie teenager looking to buy his next fix, and he's not going to come back now that he knows I have an alarm.

Man, as silly as I felt making that list, I'm glad I did. Even got a good night's sleep in my bed that night. By the time Luke came over Saturday afternoon to set up that bookkeeping software, I was as ready as I was ever going to be.

Aiming for casual but not sloppy, I'd rummaged through the box of clothes from Christina and found some beige cargo pants and a periwinkle-blue T-shirt. Part of me wanted to throw on a jogging suit and mess up my house again, but when I looked in the mirror I didn't mind what I saw.

I still haven't gotten around to having my hair cut, so I just washed it and pulled it back. I've finally gained a bit of weight—never thought I'd think that was a good thing—and my face has filled out.

I debated putting on makeup—Mom brought me a bag of cosmetics in the hospital—but none of it was colors or brands I like. Anyway, even if I hadn't heard The Freak's voice telling me makeup is for whores, I couldn't bring myself to call that much attention to my face. I settled for moisturizer, light pink lip balm, and mascara. I probably didn't look as good as the old days but I'd definitely looked worse.

Luke, however, looked amazing when I answered his knock. He must have just come from work, because he wore black dress pants and a burnt-orange shirt that set off his warm olive skin and the amber flecks in his brown eyes.

Emma rolled over and wriggled at his feet. I answered his "Hi" with a barely audible one of my own, then stepped back so he could come in. We stood awkwardly in my foyer. He raised an arm as though he was going to touch me or pull me in for a hug, then let it drop. Considering my reaction the last two times he tried to touch me, I wasn't surprised.

He crouched down to pet Emma. "She's looking great, huh? I thought about bringing Diesel over but I didn't know if that'd be too much chaos."

I told the top of his head, "I'm not an invalid."

"Never said you were." Still crouched, he looked up and met my eyes with a smile. "So, should we have a look at this program? And by the way, you're looking great yourself."

I stared at him while my cheeks grew warm. A grin spread across his face. I twisted around so fast I almost tripped on Emma, and said, "Let's go down to my office."

The next hour whipped by as he showed me how to set up the program and we went through the system together. I enjoyed learning something new and was glad we had something to focus on besides each other—I was having a hard enough time adjusting to him sitting next to me. He was in the middle of explaining a section when I blurted out, "That time you noticed me leaving the store? I saw you with a girl. That's why I was in such a hurry."

"Annie, I—"

"And when you saw me in the hospital you were so fucking *kind*, with those flowers and that stuffed golden retriever, but I just couldn't deal—with you, with *anything*. After that I asked the nurses to tell you I was only allowed visits from family and the police. And I hate that I did that, it was so nice of you, you're *always* so nice, and I'm such a—"

"Annie, the day you were abducted . . . I was late for dinner."

Well, that was news.

"The restaurant got busy and I lost track of time—I didn't even call when your open house ended like I usually did, and when I finally called on my way to your house a half hour late and you didn't pick up, I just thought you were mad. And when your car wasn't there, I assumed you got stuck with your clients, so I went home to wait. It wasn't until you still hadn't returned my calls an hour later that I finally headed over to where you said you were doing the open house. . . ." He took a deep breath. "God, when I saw your car in the driveway, then all your things just lying there on the counter . . . I called your mom right away."

Turns out it was Mom who got the cops to take things seriously. She met Luke at the police station, convinced the desk sergeant I would never stand my boyfriend up, and was at the house when the cops found my purse in a closet, where I always put it for safekeeping. Since there weren't any signs of a struggle, Luke was their main suspect in the beginning.

"After a few weeks I started drinking at the restaurant almost every night after work."

"But you hardly ever—"

"I did *a lot* of dumb things then, things I never would have done. . . ."

I wondered what dumb things he was talking about, but he looked so awkward and red-faced I said, "Don't beat yourself up, you handled it better than I probably would have. Are you still drinking a lot?"

"After a few months I knew I was relying on the buzz, so I quit. By then most people thought you were dead. I didn't feel like you were, but everyone was acting like you'd never be found and a lot of the time I was angry at you. I knew it was irrational, but in a way I blamed you. I never told you this, but I didn't like you doing open houses—that's why I usually called you after. You were so friendly, men can take that the wrong way."

"But that was my *job*, Luke. You're friendly at the restaurant—"

"I'm a guy, though, and look, I had stuff I had to work out for myself. I went a little crazy."

Emma butted her head between us and broke the tension. We gave her a few strokes, then I asked her where her ball was and she took off.

"I went out with the girl you saw a couple of times, but I ended up talking about you and the case, so I knew I wasn't ready. What I'm trying to say, Annie, is that I'm just as confused as you—and that we've both changed. But I do know I still care about you, still like being with you. I just wish I could help you more. You used to tell me how safe you felt with me."

He gave a sad smile.

STILL MISSING · 213

"I did feel safe with you, but now no one can *make* me feel safe. I have to get there on my own."

He nodded. "I can understand that."

"Good, now can you help me understand this damn program of yours?"

He laughed.

About twenty minutes later we were done and just as I was debating whether to invite him to stay for dinner, he said he should get back to the restaurant. At the door he stepped toward me, hesitated for a second, then raised his eyebrows and—just slightly—his arms. I moved toward him and he folded me into a hug. For a minute I felt trapped and wanted to wrench free, but I buried my nose in his shirt and inhaled the aroma of his restaurant—oregano, baked bread, garlic. He smelled like long dinners with friends, like too much wine and laughter, like happiness.

Against my hair, he murmured, "It was really good to see you, Annie." I nodded and as we slowly pulled apart, I kept my eyes down until I'd blinked back the tears. Later, I wondered if he would have stayed for dinner if I'd asked, but my regret was balanced with relief over not having to hear him say no. I used to be so good at quick decisions, but ever since I killed The Freak I've lived in perpetual hesitation. I remember reading once that if you have a bird that's lived in a cage for a long time and you leave the cage door open, the bird won't leave right away. I never understood that before.

I'd fallen asleep on the bed, where I'd collapsed after killing The Freak, and the throbbing of my breasts woke me—my milk was still drying up. My first awareness was of the keys gripped in my hand. I'd held them so tight while I slept that they'd left marks in my skin. In my sleepy confusion over why I had the keys and fear that The Freak would catch me with them, I let go. The jingle they made falling onto the bed startled me out of my haze. He was dead. I'd killed him.

My bladder urged me to the bathroom, but I checked the watch and saw I had ten minutes to wait. When I tried to go anyway, my bladder froze. Ten minutes later, no problem.

On my way back to the bed, my leg brushed the baby's blanket on her basket. I picked it up and pressed my face into it, breathing in the last traces of her scent. My daughter was still out there—alone. I had to find her.

I pulled on a white dress and stuffed my bra with cloths dampened with cold water for breast pads. After grabbing some slippers, I headed back down to the river and searched its shores in either direction until trees or sheer cliffs blocked my path. From a distance, any pale boulders the size of a baby stopped my breath until I was close. A bundle of cloth snagged on a tree in the middle of the river had my knees wobbling until I waded out and realized it was nothing but rags. When I wasn't able to find any trace of her there, I examined the clearing inch by inch for any signs of disturbed earth but I couldn't find a thing.

I even dug my hands through the soft garden dirt surrounding the cabin—I wouldn't have put it past the sick bastard to bury her where we planted food—and crawled under the porch. Nothing. The only place I hadn't searched yet was the shed.

The summer sun had been beating down on the metal shed all morning, and as the door opened, the odor of his already decomposing body rushed toward me in a nauseating wave. I grabbed a gasoline-scented rag off the bench and held it against the bottom of my face. Then, concentrating on breathing through my mouth, I tiptoed past his body. Flies that had hitched a ride in with his corpse the day before hummed around the tarp, as loud as the generator.

With trembling hands I dug everything out of the freezer. She wasn't in there, and the shelves held nothing but lanterns, batteries, kerosene, and ropes. I found a trapdoor with stairs to a root cellar, its dank scent fresh compared to the stench of death above. All it contained was canned foods, household items, a first aid kit, some boxes, and in an old coffee can a roll of money with a pink hair elastic wrapped around it. I hoped the elastic didn't belong to another girl who'd been hurt. It wasn't a lot of money, so I figured he had more stashed elsewhere. His wallet still hadn't showed up, not in his pocket when I grabbed the keys or in any of the cupboards in the cabin, but I'd never seen him with one. One of the keys hadn't fit any locks yet and I hoped it was for the van, hidden somewhere, his wallet inside.

In a wooden crate I discovered a rifle, a handgun, and ammo. I stared down at them. I'd never really seen the gun he threatened me with the first day, only felt it in my back and saw the butt of it in his waistband. It looked small next to the rifle, but I hated them both. One had killed the duck and one had forced me into this hell. My hand moved for just a second to the spot on my lower back where it had been pressed. I closed the crate and shoved it behind some others.

Each time I opened a box I was afraid I might discover my baby's body shoved inside, something that needed to be stored away and neatly labeled "Practice." But the final box only held my yellow suit and all my photos and newspaper ads. When I opened it I caught a trace of my perfume and I pressed the soft material against my nose. I tried the blazer on over my dress but it felt wrong to wear it—like I'd put on a dead girl's clothes. I left the suit in the box and only took the photo of me I thought was from my office as I headed back up and out into the light.

The only area I hadn't searched was the surrounding forest, so after I drank some cold water, I stuffed an old packsack I'd found in the cellar with protein bars, the first aid kit, and a Thermos of water. I was about to head out when I spotted the photo on the counter next to my baby's blanket and one of her sleepers. I added them all to my packsack of treasures.

Soon after I stepped into the forest on the right side of the cabin, the steady rush of the river and the chirp of the birds that usually clustered in the clearing faded and the only sounds were my footsteps muffled by the blanket of fir needles covering the ground. I spent the rest of the afternoon climbing over and under dead logs, digging at every slight mound, and sniffing the air for any trace of rot. I never went into the woods any deeper than fifteen minutes from the cabin and worked my way toward the highest point of the clearing in a sweeping radius.

When I finally made it to the top, I discovered a narrow trail at the edge of the woods heading into the forest. Crowded with salal and lady ferns, it was a vague line discernible only by the odd faded machete mark on the tree trunks. Some of the trees, Douglas firs reaching higher than I could see, were a couple of feet around and their trunks were blanketed in moss, which meant it was a moist forest. I was probably still on Vancouver Island.

I looked back at the clearing one final time and prayed that if there was a heaven—and I've never wanted to believe more than in that moment—then my baby was with my dad and Daisy.

As I headed down the trail, I spotted a possible break in the tree line in the distance and after another five minutes I stepped out of the woods onto an old gravel road. Judging by the potholes and lack of tire tracks, it hadn't been used for a while. About ten feet down, the bank dipped in slightly on the right.

Moving toward it, I realized the dip was the start of a smaller road veering off the main one. The Freak would've had to hide the van close to the cabin, so I decided to follow it. Not much wider than a truck, it was covered in grass and if you were driving by you probably wouldn't even notice it. It curved around to run parallel to the main road, about twenty feet of trees between the two.

Farther down the road I came across a small white bone, and my feet stopped along with my heart. I scanned the ground inch by inch, then found a bone too large for my baby, and within a few feet I nearly stumbled on the skeleton of a deer.

I followed the road until it ended in a wall of dead broom bush and branches. At the bottom, a piece of metal glinted in the sun. With frantic hands I ripped the vegetation away. I was staring at the back of a van.

A quick search of the glove box turned up no wallet or registration papers, not even a map. Peering between the seats into the dim back of the van, I noticed some material wadded into a ball and reached for it. It was the gray blanket. The one he used to abduct me.

The sensation of the rough wool in my hand combined with the scent of the van was all too familiar. I dropped the blanket like it was on fire and flipped around in the seat.

Trying not to think about what had happened in the back, I focused on turning the key in the ignition. Nothing.

I held my breath. *Please start, please start* . . . and tried the key again. Nothing. My body dripped with sweat in the sweltering van and my legs stuck to the vinyl seats, where my dress had ridden up. With my forehead against the hot steering wheel I took a few calming breaths, then popped the hood. I spotted the disconnected battery cable right away, tightened it back up, and gave the engine another try. This time it came to life immediately and the radio began to blast country music. It had been so long since I'd heard music that I laughed. When the DJ came on I caught the words ". . . back to a commercial-free hour." But no clue to where I was, and when I tried to find another station, the knob just spun around.

I threw the van in reverse, backed down the little road, ran right over some saplings, and shot out onto the main road. It hadn't been graded for a while, so I took my time coming down the mountain. After about a half hour my tires hit pavement, and maybe twenty minutes later the road straightened out.

Eventually my nose caught the familiar scent of ocean air tinged with the sulfur from a pulp mill, and I came into a small town. Stopped at a red light, I noticed a coffee shop on my left. The smell of bacon drifted through my open window and I inhaled the aroma with longing. The Freak never let me have bacon, said it would make me fat.

My mouth filled with saliva as I watched an old guy sitting near the window pop a piece of bacon into his mouth, chew quickly, then shove another one in. I wanted bacon—a plateful, nothing else, just strips and strips of bacon—then I'd chew each piece slowly, savoring the salty yet slightly sweet juices every crunch released. A big bacon fuck-you to The Freak.

The old guy wiped his greasy hands on the shoulder of his shirt. The Freak whispered in my head, *You don't want to be a pig, do you, Annie?*

I looked away. Across the street was a cop shop.

SESSION NINETEEN

Hope you're feeling better this week, Doc. Guess I can't give you a hard time for canceling our last session, considering I was probably the one who gave you the cold. I'm feeling better myself, about a lot of things. For starters the cops called early this week to tell me they nabbed the guy who's been doing all the break-ins, and yep, it was just a teenager.

You'll also be happy to hear I haven't slept in the closet since I last saw you, and I've stopped having a bath at night. Now I can shave my legs in the shower and I don't even need to wash and condition my hair twice. I can pee over half the time without having to do any deep breathing and I eat when I need to. Sometimes I don't even hear The Freak's voice when I break one of his rules.

Only thing that keeps nagging at me is that stupid photo The Freak had of me—the older one. I hadn't thought about it once since I came home, too much other shit going on, but then after I mentioned it to you the other day I came across it in a little box where I keep the stuff I brought home from the mountain, during another of my many that-bastard-must-have-stolen-something searches of my house.

The real estate company where I worked had cubicles and I kept a corkboard above my desk with lots of photos pinned to it, so I figured *maybe* The Freak had snatched it from there. If he said he was looking for a house, he could have been in the office meeting with any of the Realtors. That might even have been when he first saw me, for all I know. But why would I have had one of just myself up in my office? And why am I driving myself nuts trying to figure it out? It's not like it matters anymore. Hell, sometimes I think my mind just looks for shit to obsess about. It's like trying to put a group of kids to bed—one worry finally drifts off, and another is out and running.

This week I was thinking about how in the past Christina and I would've gone over every minute of Luke's visit, analyzing it scene by scene, and I had a wave of missing her. Reminding myself how relieved I'd felt after I made my list, and how proud I'd been when I finally faced Luke, I dialed her cell before I could chicken out.

"Christina speaking."

"Hey, it's me."

"Annie! Hang on a sec—" I heard muffled sounds of Christina speaking to someone, then she came back on the line. "Sorry, Annie, hectic morning, but I'm *so* glad you called."

"Shit, it's tour day, isn't it? Want me to call later?"

"No way, lady—I'm not letting you off that easy. I've been waiting too long for you to pick up the phone." We both paused.

Not knowing how to explain my avoidance of her and everyone else, I said, "So . . . how have you been?"

"Me? Same old, same old."

"And Drew?"

"He's good . . . he's good. You know us, nothing ever changes. How are *you* doing?"

"Okay, I guess. . . ." I searched my mind for something interesting in my life I could share. "I'm doing some book-keeping for Luke."

"You guys are talking again?" Out came the fake Russian accent. "Vell, vell, vell, that's good news."

"It's not like *that*—it's just a business thing," I said, quicker than I meant to.

She gave her I-know-you're-full-of-shit laugh, then said, "If you say so. Hey, how's your mom doing? I saw her and Wayne downtown the other day and she was looking, ummm . . ."

"Pissed out of her mind? Seems to be the theme lately. But she did come over a couple of weeks ago to bring me back my photo album and some pictures of Dad and Daisy I'd never seen. That shocked the shit out of me."

"She thought she lost you—she's probably still trying to come to terms with it all."

"Yeah." I didn't feel like getting into it, so I said, "I was wondering what my house is worth these days."

"Why? You're not thinking of selling, are you?"

Not wanting to talk about the break-in, I said, "It's just not the same since Mom rented it out—doesn't even smell like me anymore."

"I think you should give it some time before you—" A voice said something to Christina in the background. "Darn, my clients just arrived out front. We're already late, so I've gotta run, but give me a call this evening, okay? I *really* want to talk to you."

During and after the phone call, I missed Christina more than ever, and I did think about calling her that night, but her sign-off told me she was gearing up for another of her this-is-what-you-should-do talks and I just couldn't deal with it. So when I heard the knock on my door Saturday afternoon and looked through the window to find Christina, who's always dressed to the nines, standing on my front porch wearing white overalls, a baseball cap, and a shit-eating grin, I didn't know what the hell to think. I opened the door and saw she was holding a couple of paintbrushes in one hand and a huge paint can in the other. She handed me a brush.

"Come on, now, let's see what we can do about this house of yours."

"I'm kind of tired today. If you'd called—" She blew right by, leaving me talking to my doorstep.

Over her shoulder she said, "Oh, please, like you *answer* your phone." She had me there. "Quit your whining and get your ass in gear, girl." She started pushing one end of my couch, and unless I wanted my hardwood floor damaged, I didn't have much choice but to join in moving all the crap out of my living room. I'd always wanted to paint the beige walls but I'd never gotten around to it. When I saw the gorgeous creamy yellow she'd chosen, I was hooked.

We painted for a couple of hours, then took a break and sat outside on my deck with a glass of red wine. Christina won't drink anything under twenty dollars a bottle and always brings her own stuff. The sun had just gone down, so I turned all my patio lanterns on. We sat in silence for a few minutes, watching Emma chew her rawhide bone, then Christina looked me straight in the eyes.

"So what happened between us?"

I played with the stem of my glass and shrugged. My face felt hot.

"I don't know. It's just . . ."

"Just what? I think if people are friends, they should be honest with each other. You're my best friend."

"I'm trying, I just need—"

"Did you follow up on any of my suggestions or did you block them out too? There's a book out now by a rape survivor you should read, it talks about how victims had to build up walls to survive, but then afterwards they can't—"

"It's *that*. The *pressure*. The endless, constant 'you shoulds.' I didn't want to talk about it, but you just couldn't let it go. When I tried to tell you I didn't want the clothes, you just steamrolled right over me. " I stopped to take a breath. Christina looked stunned.

"You were trying to help, I get that, but man, Christina, sometimes you just have to *back off*."

We were both quiet for a minute, then Christina said, "Maybe if you explained why you didn't want the clothes?"

"I *can't* explain, that's the problem, and if you want to help, then you just have to accept me the way I am. Stop trying to make me talk about shit, stop trying to fix me. If you can't do that, then we can't hang out."

I braced for fireworks, but Christina nodded a couple of times and said, "Okay, I'll try it your way. I need you in my life, Annie."

"Oh," I said. "Well, good. I mean, that's great, because I want you in my life too."

She smiled, then her face turned serious. "But there's something I have to tell you. A lot of things happened when you were away. . . . Everyone was so emotional and nobody knew how to handle it. And—"

I held up a hand. "Stop. We have to keep things light. It's the only way I can do this."

"But Annie—"

"No, no buts." I had a feeling she wanted to tell me she got the project—I drove by her signs in front of it the other day—but the last thing I wanted to do was talk about real estate. Besides, it made sense that she got it, and I was happy for her. Hell, I'd way rather it be her than whoever I was competing against.

She stared at me hard for a few seconds, then shook her head.

"All right, you win. But if you're not going to let me talk, then I'm going to make you paint some more."

With a groan I followed her back into the house, and we finished the rest of the living room.

After we said our good-byes on the porch and she was about to step into her BMW, she turned back.

"Annie, before, I was just being the same way with you as I've always been."

"I know. But *I'm* not the same."

She said, "None of us are," and shut her door.

The next afternoon I decided to go through a couple of boxes of my stuff I'd found in my mom's carport when I was borrowing some gardening tools. The first one was full of my real estate awards and plaques, which I put away in my office without hanging them. The second box, with all my old art supplies, drawings, and paintings, interested me much more.

Tucked into the pages of my sketchbook was a brochure for an art school I'd forgotten I wanted to go to. For once, a trip down memory lane wasn't lined with screaming ghosts, and the smell of charcoal pencils and oil paints made me smile.

I pulled out my sketch pad and the brochure, grabbed my pencils, poured myself a glass of Shiraz, and headed for my deck. For a while I just stared at a blank page. Emma was lying in one of the last rays of the setting sun, which made her coat glow and accentuated the shadows on her. With my pencil I followed the curve of her body on the paper, and then it started coming back to me. Reveling in the sensation of my hand brushing against crisp paper, I watched my simple lines create a form, then smudged some of them with my fingertips for shading. I kept working at it, changing the balance of light and dark, then stopped to gaze for a few seconds at a bird whistling in a tree near me. When I focused back on my paper I was startled—no, shocked. I'd glanced away from a drawing of a dog, but when I looked back I saw Emma. Right down to the little cowlick at the top of her tail.

I sat there enjoying my sketch for a few minutes, wishing I had someone to show it to, then my attention turned to the brochure. As I flipped through it I smiled at notes I'd made to myself. But my smile faded when I noticed I'd circled the tuition fee and put a big question mark beside it.

Mom got a small inheritance when my grandma died, but when I asked about using some of it for school, she said it was all gone. Whatever was left when she hooked up with Wayne no doubt disappeared before the ink was dry on the marriage license.

I thought about getting a part-time job to put myself

through art school, but Mom kept telling me artists don't make any money, so I wasn't sure what to do and I just started working. I figured once I'd saved up enough, I'd look into going to school, but it just never happened.

When Luke called last night I told him about my afternoon sketching. "That's great, Annie, you always liked art." He didn't ask about seeing my drawing, and I didn't ask if he wanted to.

Christina's come over a couple of times to help me paint the other walls in my house. She keeps it light, like I asked, but it feels strained in a way. Not tense, just odd. But the second I think about sharing anything that happened on the mountain, a massive wave of anxiety presses in on me. Right now all I can handle is gossip about Hollywood stars and people we used to work with. The last time I saw her she told me about this goofy cop who taught her self-defense class.

Took me right back to the ones I had to deal with when I first got off the mountain. Let's just say, since my expectations were based on TV reruns, I was hoping for Lennie Briscoe but I got Barney Fife.

I was happy to see a woman behind the front desk of the cop shop, but she didn't even glance up from her crossword. "Who you looking for?"

"A policeman, I guess."

"You guess?"

"No, I mean, yes, I want to see a policeman." What I really wanted was to leave, but she waved over some guy who was just coming out of the men's room and wiping his hands on the legs of his uniform.

"Constable Pepper will help you," she said.

It's a good thing his title wasn't sergeant, the guy already had enough to deal with. He was at least six feet tall and had a really big gut but was skinny everywhere else—his gun belt looked like it was losing the fight to hang on to his narrow hips.

He glanced at me, grabbed some files from the front desk, and said, "Come on."

He stopped to pour himself a cup of coffee from a beat-up coffeemaker—didn't offer me any—and dumped sugar and creamer into the mug. He motioned for me to follow him past a glass-walled office and three cops in the main area crowded around a table with a small portable TV, watching a game.

He pushed a stack of files to the side of his desk, set his coffee mug down, and waved me into the chair across from him. It took him a two-minute rummage through his drawer to find a pen that worked and another few were spent pulling out various forms and then shoving them back in. Finally he was settled with a working pen and a form in front of him.

"Your name, please?"

"Annie O'Sullivan."

He looked straight at me, his eyes searching every angle of my face, then he got up so fast he knocked over his coffee.

"Stay here—I have to get someone."

Leaving the coffee soaking into his papers, he went into the glass office and started talking to a short gray-haired guy I assumed was important because he had the only private office. Judging by his hands waving around, Pepper was pretty excited. When Pepper pointed to me, the older guy turned to look, and our eyes met. I already had that get-out-of-here-NOW feeling.

The cops near the television turned it down and looked back and forth between me and the office. When I glanced at the front desk, the woman there was watching me. I looked back at the office. The old guy picked up his phone and talked into it, pacing around as far as the cord would go. He hung up, pulled a file from a drawer behind him, then he and Pepper looked in the file, talked to each other, stared at me, looked at the file again. Subtle these guys were not.

Finally the old guy and Pepper—carrying the file—left the office. The old guy leaned down close to me with one hand resting on his knee and the other stuck out. He spoke slowly and enunciated every word carefully.

"Hello, my name is Sergeant Jablonski."

"Annie O'Sullivan." I shook his outstretched hand. It was cool and dry.

"Nice to meet you, Annie. We'd like to talk to you in private—if that's okay?" Why the hell was he dragging his words out? *English isn't my second language, dumbass.*

"I guess." I got to my feet.

Grabbing a couple of legal pads and pens off his desk, Pepper said, "We're just going to take you to one of our interview rooms." At least he was talking at a normal speed.

As we walked away from the desk, all the cops in the room stood still. Pepper and Jablonski moved to stand on either side of me, and Pepper tried to hold my arm, but I pulled it back. You'd think I was being escorted to the electric chair—I swear the phones even stopped ringing. Pepper managed to suck in his gut slightly and walked with his shoulders back and chest puffed out like he'd hunted me down all by himself.

It was definitely a small town. So far I'd seen only a few cops, and the cold concrete room they led me into was the size of your average bathroom. Just as we sat down across from each other at a metal table, Pepper got up to answer a knock on the door. The woman from the front desk handed him two coffees and tried to peer around him, but he stepped in front of her and shut the door. The older guy nodded to me.

"You want coffee? A pop?"

"No, thanks."

One of the walls had a large mirror on it. I hated the idea of someone I couldn't see watching my every move.

I pointed at the mirror. "Is anybody there?"

"Not at this time," Jablonski said. Did that mean there might be someone later?

I nodded toward the upper left corner. "What's the camera for?"

"We'll be audio- and videotaping the interview—it's standard procedure."

That was just as bad as the mirror. I shook my head. "You have to shut it off."

"You'll forget it's even there. Are you Annie O'Sullivan from Clayton Falls?"

I stared at the camera. Pepper cleared his throat. Jablonski repeated the question. The silence continued for another minute or so, then Jablonski made a quick slicing motion across his neck. Pepper left the room for a couple of minutes, and by the time he came back the little red light on the camera was off.

Jablonski said, "We have to leave the audio recorder on, we can't conduct an interview without it." I wondered if he was bullshitting—on the TV shows, sometimes they use one, sometimes they don't—but I let it go.

"Let's try this again. Are you Annie O'Sullivan from Clayton Falls?"

"Yes. Am I on Vancouver Island?"

"You don't know?"

"That's why I'm asking."

Jablonski said, "Yes, you're on the island." His slow, precise speech disappeared with the next question. "Why don't you start off by telling us where you've been?"

"I don't know, other than that it was a cabin. I don't know how I got there, because I was doing an open house, and a guy—"

"What guy?" Pepper said.

"Did you know this man?" Jablonski said.

As the two spoke—at the same time—I flashed to The Freak stepping out of the van and turning toward the house.

"He was a stranger. I was almost done with the open house, and I went outside to—"

"What was he driving?"

"A van." I saw The Freak smiling at me. Such a nice smile. My stomach clenched.

"What color was it? Do you remember the make and model? Had you seen this van before?"

"No." I started counting the blocks on the concrete wall behind them.

"You don't remember the make and model, or no you hadn't seen it before?"

"It's a Dodge, Caravan I think, tan and newer—that's all I know. The guy had the real estate paper. He'd been watching me, and he knew stuff—"

"He wasn't a past client, or maybe some guy you turned down in a bar one night or chatted with on the Internet?" Jablonski said.

"No, no, and no."

He raised his eyebrows. "So let me get this straight. You're trying to tell us this guy picked you out of thin air?"

"I'm not *trying* to tell you anything, I don't know why he picked me."

"We want to help you, Annie, but first we need the truth." He leaned back in his chair and crossed his arms over his chest.

My arm shot across the table and sent their stupid little pad of paper and coffees flying. I stood up, leaned over the table with both of my hands flat on it, and screamed into their shocked faces.

"*I AM telling the truth!*"

Pepper held out both of his hands. "Take it easy! You're getting all worked up here—"

I flipped the table over on its side. As they tried to get out of my way and scurry out the door, I yelled at their backs, "I'm not saying another damn word until you get me some *real* cops!"

After they left me alone in the room, I stared at the mess in shock—I'd even broken one of their mugs. I righted the table, picked up the notepad, and tried to wipe up the coffee with some of the paper. After a few minutes Pepper slunk in and grabbed the notepad off the table. One palm held out in front of him and the other clutching the notepad to his chest, he slowly backed out of the room.

"Just relax, we have some people coming in to talk to you."

The front of his pants was wet with coffee from when I'd knocked the table over. I was about to hand him the broken pieces of mug and apologize, but he was through the door in a flash.

I laughed for a couple of seconds, then put my forehead down on the table and cried.

SESSION TWENTY

Not sure if you saw the article in the paper this weekend, Doc, but they recovered some stolen goods from a shed on that teenager's property. Well, actually the parents' property. Anyway, I called the cop who handled my break-in, wondering if anything was mine, but he said everything was accounted for. Later I remembered something else the article said, that all the robberies occurred at night.

So why would a burglar, especially a teenage burglar, change his pattern just to break into my house? He had to have timed it perfectly to know exactly when I went for my run, but then he didn't take anything?

I started thinking about how The Freak timed his abduction of me, arriving at the end of the open house on a hot summer day when he knew things would be slow. The Freak, who said the cabin hadn't been easy to set up. The Freak, who might have needed help—

What if he had a partner?

He could have had a friend or, for all I know, a freaky brother who was pissed off that I killed him. I just assumed the person who broke into my house saw me leave. But what if he thought I was *home*? My car was in the driveway and it was pretty early. But why come for me after all this time?

By Monday I was so obsessed by the idea I decided to call Gary and ask him if there was any chance The Freak had some help. This crap is like cancer—if you don't get every last thread and cell of it then it'll grow back into an even bigger tumor. But his phone was off and when I called the station they said he was away until this weekend.

I was surprised he hadn't told me he was going away, since we generally talk a couple of times a week. He's always friendly when I call, never says anything stupid like, "What can I do for you?" Luckily, since I'm not always sure why I phone him. In the beginning it wasn't even a conscious choice. Everything in my world would feel like it was spinning out of control, and then the phone's in my hand. Sometimes I couldn't even speak—good thing there's caller ID. He'd wait a couple of seconds and if I was still quiet he'd start talking about the case until he ran out of new information. Then he'd tell me funny cop stories until I felt better and hung up, sometimes without even saying good-bye. One day he was reduced to describing the proper way to clean a gun before I finally let him go. Can't believe the guy kept answering.

Our conversations have been dialogue instead of mostly monologues for a few months now, but he never reveals anything personal, and something about him stops me from pressing. That's probably why he's away, something to do with his personal life. Guess cops have those too.

The cops I fired left me in that room by myself for a couple of hours, long enough for me to count every concrete block more than a few times, and I wondered whether they'd called my family and who was coming to talk to me. I took the packsack off and held it on my lap, stroking its rough fabric—somehow the motion was comforting. None of those meat-heads bothered to ask if I needed to use the ladies' room, and it's a good thing I was trained to hold it, because it never occurred to me to just get up and leave.

Eventually the door opened and a man and a woman walked in, both wearing serious expressions and dark suits—a very good suit in the man's case. His short hair, more salt than pepper, had me figuring him for early fifties, but his face looked more like he was in his forties. He was over six feet for sure, and the way he held his shoulders squared and his back straight told me he was proud of his height. He looked solid. Calm. If this guy had been on the *Titanic*, he'd have finished his coffee.

He met my gaze and walked toward me with a smooth, unhurried gait and his hand held out.

"Hello, Annie, I'm Staff Sergeant Kincade with the Clayton Falls Serious Crime Unit."

Nothing about this guy said Clayton Falls, and I had no idea what a staff sergeant was, but it clearly was a step up from Jablonski and his sidekick. His grip was strong, and as his hand slid out of my mine I felt calluses and for some reason was relieved.

The woman waiting just inside the doorway now walked briskly toward me. She was slightly plump with huge boobs, I'd say somewhere in her later fifties, but she carried her curves well in her skirt and blazer. Her hair was cut short and neat, and I was willing to bet she rinses out her pantyhose every night and always wears a full support bra.

She shook my hand, smiled, and with a hint of a Quebec accent said, "I'm Corporal Bouchard. It's really good to finally meet you, Annie."

They sat down across from me. The staff sergeant's eyes turned toward the doorway, where the old guy was trying to wrestle a third chair in.

"We'll take it from here," Kincade said. Jablonski paused in the doorway with the chair. "Some coffee would be great."

Kincade turned back toward me. I swallowed a smile, the closest I'd come to one since my baby died.

They had called me by my first name, like we were buddies, but they hadn't given me theirs.

"Can I have your business cards, please?" I said. The two looked at each other. The guy held eyes with me for a second, then slid his card across the table. She followed suit. His first name was Gary, and hers, Diane. Gary spoke first.

"So, Annie, like I said, we're both members of the Serious Crime Unit in Clayton Falls, and I was the lead investigator in your case." Fat lot of good that did me.

"You don't look like you're from Clayton Falls," I said.

One eyebrow rose. "Don't I?" When I didn't respond, he said, "A physician will be here shortly. He'll want to—"

"I don't need a doctor."

We held eyes for a moment. He launched into general questions like my birth date, address, job, things like that. The tension in my shoulders eased.

He started to lead into the day I was taken, then stopped.

"Do you mind if we turn the video recorder back on, Annie?"

"Yes, *Gary*." The way he kept using my first name reminded me of The Freak. "And I don't want anyone behind that mirror, either."

"I didn't mean to upset you." His chin down and his head tilted to the side, he looked up at me with blue-gray eyes. "But it would make my job a lot easier, Annie."

Nice manipulation. But seeing as how I had just done his job by finding my own way back, I wasn't inclined to help him out any further. They were both silent as they waited for me to agree, but I said nothing.

"Annie, what were you doing on August fourth of last year?" I couldn't remember the date I was taken.

"I don't know, *Gary*. If you're asking about the day I disappeared, I was doing an open house, it was a Sunday, and it was the first weekend of the month. I guess you'll have to figure it out from there yourself."

"Would you prefer I not use your first name?"

Caught off guard by his respectful tone of voice, I searched his face for signs he was messing with me. All I found was sincerity, which left me wondering if it was just a trick to gain my trust or whether he actually gave a shit.

"It's fine," I said.

"What's your mother's middle name, Annie?"

"She doesn't have one." Leaning across the table, I said in an exaggerated whisper, "Did I pass the test yet?"

I understood his need for verification, but shit, they had pictures, and I'm pretty sure I didn't look like a girl who'd just had a great year. I was skin and bones, with ratty hair and wearing a sweat-stained dress.

He finally got around to straight-out asking me what happened. I said The Freak grabbed me at the open house. I used his real name, though, or at least the one he'd given me. I was going to explain more, but Gary jumped back in.

"Where is he now?"

"He's dead." They both stared at me intently, but I wasn't

going any further until they answered some of *my* questions.

"Where's my family?"

"We called your mother, she'll be here tomorrow," Gary said.

I started to tear up at the thought of seeing my mom again, so I stared down at the packsack and counted the lines in its fabric. But why wasn't she here now? It had been hours since I walked into the joint. How much of a drive was it? It hadn't taken these guys that long.

"I want to know where I am."

"I'm sorry," Gary said. "I thought you knew you were in Port Northfield."

"Can you show me on a map?"

Gary nodded to Diane, who left the room. When she brought a map back, he pointed out a town northwest of Clayton Falls—about three-quarters of the way up the island and right on the West Coast. The roads to any of the towns off the beaten track were usually pretty rough, and you had to drive slowly. I calculated at least a four-hour drive from Clayton Falls.

"How did you guys get here so fast?"

"Helicopter," Gary said. Seeing that sucker fly in must have got this town all atwitter.

So I was right, I was never that far from home. I stared at Gary's finger resting on the dot for Port Northfield and blinked back my tears.

"How did you get here?" Gary asked.

"I drove."

"Where did you drive from?" His fingers tapped on the table.

"A cabin on a mountain."

"How long were you driving for, Annie?"

"About an hour."

He nodded and showed me a mountain on the map, near the dot for the town.

"Is this it? Green Mountain?" Somebody with no imagination named that one.

"I don't know. I was on it, not looking down on it."

He sent Diane to get a map of just the town. Gary and I sat there looking at each other until she returned, the only sound his foot tapping under the table. When she got back, Gary handed me a pen and asked me to draw the route I'd driven. I tried to rough it out the best I could.

"Can you take us to it?"

"There's no way I'm going back up there." I still had the keys to the van gripped in my hand and now I shoved them across the table to Gary.

"The van's parked across the street."

He sent Diane out with the keys. She must have given them to someone outside, because she was back in about two seconds. Something tickled at the back of my mind. If I was only about four hours away, Mom could have left right away and still been in Port Northfield that night.

"Why is it taking my mom so long to get here?"

"Your stepfather is working tonight and they can't leave until the morning." Gary stated it like a fact, so I took it like a fact, but I wondered why she didn't drive up by herself. Not to mention, since when did Wayne work at night? It was rare enough he even had a job. I figured Gary told them not to come until the next day so he could question me without them there.

Gary excused himself and left me alone in the room with Diane for a few minutes. I stared at the wall above her head.

"Your mother will be here soon. She was so happy to hear you've been found—she's missed you a lot." I hadn't been *found*—I'd found them.

When Gary returned, he said he'd sent some people to look for the cabin—one of the cops used to hunt in that area and thought he might know where it was. I still hadn't told them I killed The Freak or said anything about my baby, and at the thought of all the questions they might ask, my head hurt. I needed to be by myself. I needed to be away from these people.

"I don't want to answer any more questions."

Gary looked like he wanted to press on, but Diane said, "How about everyone gets a good night's sleep and then we can pick up in the morning? That okay with you, Annie?"

"Sure, whatever."

They booked a room in a motel for me and took the rooms on either side. Diane asked if I wanted her to stay with me but I shut that one down fast—there wasn't going to be any late-night girl bonding here. She also asked what I'd like to eat, but my stomach was in knots and I managed to decline politely. I didn't feel like turning the TV on and there wasn't a phone in the room, so I lay on the bed staring at the ceiling until it got dark and I turned off the light. When I was just about asleep, I felt the weight of the darkness pressing down on me, then I heard something—a door creak, a window *opening*? I leapt out of bed, but when I threw the lights on, there was nothing. I grabbed a flat pillow, a blanket, and the packsack and crawled into the closet, where I slept fitfully until I heard the maid roll her cart down the hallway in the morning.

A few minutes later Diane came knocking on my door, bright-eyed and bushy-tailed, bearing coffee and a muffin. She sat on the edge of the bed, talking too loud and giving me a headache, while I picked at the muffin. I didn't want to have a shower with her there, so I just splashed some water on my face and ran a brush through my hair for maybe two seconds.

She drove me back to the little concrete room at the cop shop, where Gary was already seated with a tray of coffees in Styrofoam cups. As Diane and I settled in, a young, pretty cop brought in a couple of pads of paper, blushing and sneaking peeks at Gary when she handed them over. He glanced at her as he thanked her, then focused his gaze on me. Disappointment radiated off her as she walked out. He was wearing another nice suit, dark blue with silver pinstripes, and a blue-gray shirt that set off his silver-streaked hair. I wondered if that was why he'd picked it.

Seeing me glare at the mirror, Gary said, "No one's in there and we'll only turn the camera back on if you tell us it's okay." Wishing I could see through it, I stared hard at the mirror and hugged the packsack to my chest.

"Would you feel more comfortable if you had a look for yourself?"

I was surprised by the offer. I looked at his face, decided he meant it so there was no point in checking, and shook my head.

He started by asking me to describe in as much detail as possible exactly how The Freak had abducted me. Whenever he asked a question he leaned back in his chair with both hands splayed on the table in front of him, and when it was my turn to answer, he leaned toward me with both arms flat on the table and his head cocked to the side.

I tried to find a pattern to his questions, but I just couldn't predict where he'd go next, didn't even understand the relevance of some. The hair on the back of my neck was damp with sweat.

Retelling that day and describing The Freak made my mouth dry and my heart lurch around in my chest, but I kept it together until Gary told me the cops who'd investigated the "crime scene" had found The Freak's body.

"He appears to have been hit with something in the head. Is that how he died, Annie?"

I looked back and forth between them, wishing I could read their minds. Gary didn't sound accusing, but I could feel the tension in the room.

I hadn't even thought about what some of my choices or actions might look like to someone who hadn't been there. The room seemed hot, Diane's perfume overwhelming in the small space. I wondered how Gary would feel if I puked all over his nice suit. I raised my eyes to his.

"I killed him."

Gary said, "I have to caution you at this time that you need not say anything further, and that anything you do say may be used as evidence against you in a court of law. You have the right to consult an attorney and to have one present during our questioning. If you can't afford one, we can provide some phone numbers for legal aid. Do you understand?"

The words sounded routine and I didn't think I was going to be in trouble, but I considered asking for a lawyer. The idea of delaying this process to talk to another suit made my head hurt.

"I get it."

"You don't want a lawyer?" He said it casually, but I knew he didn't want me to ask for one.

"No."

Gary made a note. "How did you do it?"

"I hit him in the back of the head with an axe." I swear my voice echoed, and even though it was hot as hell, my skin broke out in goose bumps. Gary's eyes burrowed into me like he was trying to read my thoughts, and I busied myself with ripping my Styrofoam cup into little pieces.

"Was he attacking you at the time?"

"No."

"Why did you kill him, Annie?"

I looked up and met his eyes. What a stupid fucking question.

"Maybe because he abducted me, beat me, raped me pretty much every night, and . . ." I stopped myself before I said anything about the baby.

"Would you feel more comfortable talking with just Constable Bouchard about this?" Gary's face was grave as he waited for me to answer.

Staring back at them, I wanted to smear Diane's sympathetic expression across her face. I knew I'd rather deal with Gary's tough, no-muss-no-fuss approach than get one more understanding look from her.

I shook my head and Gary made another note. Then he leaned in so close across the table I smelled cinnamon on his breath.

"When did you kill him?" His voice was quiet but it wasn't soft.

"A couple of days ago."

"Why didn't you leave right away?"

"I couldn't."

"Why not? Were you restrained?" Gary's fingers tapped on the table and his head was cocked.

"That's not what I meant." I wanted to get up and walk out the door, but the firmness in his voice had me nailed to my chair.

"So why couldn't you leave?"

"I was looking for something." Bile rose in my throat.

"What?"

My body grew even colder, and Gary's edges blurred in front of my eyes.

"We found a basket," he said. "And some baby clothes."

The stupid rickety ceiling fan creaked as it went around and around, and I wondered for a minute whether it would crash down on my head. There were no windows, and I couldn't get a deep breath of air.

"Is there a baby, Annie?"

My head pounded. I *would not* cry.

"Is there a baby, Annie?" Gary wouldn't shut the fuck up.

"No."

"*Was* there a baby, Annie?" His voice was gentle.

"Yes."

"Where's the baby now?"

"She . . . my baby. Died."

"I'm very sorry to hear that, Annie." His voice was still gentle, soft and low. Sounded like he meant it. "That's a terrible thing. How did your baby die?" He was the first person to express condolences. The first person to say it mattered that she'd died. I looked at all the little ripped-up pieces of Styrofoam on the table. Someone answered him, but I didn't feel like it was me.

"He just . . . I don't know."

I clung to the calm in Gary's voice as he said, very gently, "Where's her body, Annie?"

The strange voice answered again. "When I woke up, he

had her. She was dead. I don't know where he took her, he wouldn't tell me. I looked everywhere. *Everywhere.* You guys have to look, okay? Please, can you find her, can you—" My voice broke, and I shut up.

Gary's shoulders stiffened, his face flushed under his tan as his jaw tightened, and his hands balled into fists on the table like he wanted to punch someone. At first I thought he was mad at me, but then I realized he was furious at The Freak. Diane's eyes were shiny in the fluorescent light. All the walls closed in. My body was drenched in sweat, and sobs tried to come out of my throat but I couldn't breathe and they piled up, strangling me. When I tried to stand, the room tilted, so I dropped the packsack and gripped the back of the chair, but it started to slide. My ears rang.

Diane rushed to my side and lowered me slowly until I was lying on the floor, halfway across her, with my head on her chest and her arms encircling me. The harder I tried to suck some air into my lungs, the more my throat closed up. I was going to die there on that cold floor.

Crying and gagging at the same time, I pushed Diane's hands off me and tried to pull away from her, but the harder I struggled, the harder she hung on. I heard screaming, realized it was me. I was powerless to stop the screams, which bounced off the walls and echoed in my head.

Up came the coffee and muffin, all over myself and Diane. She still wouldn't let me go. My head rested on her huge boobs, which smelled like warm vanilla cookies. Gary crouched in front of us, saying something I couldn't hear. As Diane rocked me back and forth in her arms, I wanted to struggle and take back control, but my mind and body wouldn't cooperate. I lay there, sobbing and screaming.

The screaming finally stopped, but I felt so cold, and

everyone's voices seemed to be coming from far away. Diane whispered, "Everything's going to be okay, Annie—you're safe now."

What a crock. I wanted to tell her I was never going to be okay, or safe, but when I tried to form the words, my lips froze. Then there was a new set of feet in front of me next to Gary's crouched figure. A voice said, "She's hyperventilating. Annie, my name is Dr. Berger. Try to take some deep breaths." But I couldn't. And I don't remember anything after that.

SESSION TWENTY-ONE

So I finally heard from Gary at last, Doc, but I'm not sure I feel any better. He didn't tell me where he'd been—I didn't ask and he didn't offer—which annoyed me a little. When I told him about the timing of the robberies and my new "freaky friend" theory, he said the kid could be changing his pattern to throw off the cops, or it could be a crime of opportunity—he might have just been walking by and seen me leave with Emma.

I was still mulling that over when he said, "These guys usually work alone." *Usually?* I asked him what the hell that meant, and he said he knew of a couple of cases where two guys worked together—one the finder and one the doer—but he doubted that was the case here because it didn't fit with The Freak's profile. Then he said, "And other than his comment about the cabin being hard to set up, he never did or said anything to make you think he had a partner, right?"

"Guess not. But he had an older picture of me, and that's weirding me out big time."

"What photo? You never mentioned a photo."

Then he started hitting me with the same questions I've been asking myself. Where could The Freak have gotten it from? Why would he have wanted that one in particular? And then he said something that still doesn't make sense. He said, "So anyone had easy access to the photo if it was at your office." His final question was, "Does anyone know you brought it back with you?" When I said no, he told me to keep it that way.

It was the first time I can remember feeling worse after talking with him. Put me in such a bad mood I took it out on Luke. I just don't know what's going on with us these days anyway. I figured our visit and honest talk would bring us closer, but when we've chatted lately there was a lot of dead air, and the last time he phoned I ended the call, told him I was heading to bed. I wasn't even tired.

I can't seem to let go of the fact that Luke was late that day. Was he being nice to some customer while I was being abducted? Why didn't he drive to the open house as soon as he realized I wasn't home? And why the hell didn't he call the cops the second he knew something was wrong? Calling Mom could have waited. It's horribly judgmental, because God only knows how I'd have handled things if I were in his shoes, but I keep thinking every second he delayed lessened any chance of my being found.

During our relationship I saw him as laid back but now I'm beginning to wonder if he's just passive. He'll complain about a waitress or one of his cooks, but he doesn't *do* anything about it.

The whole time Luke and I were together he was never anything but patient, loving, honest—just so *nice*. Sometimes, like right before I was abducted, I wondered if I should be wanting something more than nice, but on the mountain all I ever thought about him was how wonderful he was. Now he's still being patient, loving, and honest—he's the nicest man I know. So what the hell's wrong with me?

My first image on opening my eyes after my meltdown at the cop shop was of Mom and Gary standing at the foot of my hospital bed. There was no sign of Wayne. I didn't notice Diane sitting on a chair beside me until I heard her say, "Look who's up."

She gave me a kind smile and I remembered her rocking me, which made my cheeks burn. Then Mom realized I was awake and almost knocked the IV out of my arm as she crawled halfway on top of me, sobbing, "My baby, my poor Annie Bear."

Whatever shit they'd given me was starting to make me nauseous, so I said, "I'm going to be sick," then burst into tears. A doctor reached for my arm and I pushed him away. Then there were more hands holding me down and I was fighting all of them. I felt a prick in my arm. The next time I woke up, my stepdad was sitting beside me with his cowboy hat clutched in his hands. As soon as I opened my eyes he jumped out of the seat.

"I'll go get Lorraine—she just went to make a call."

"Let her finish," I whispered. My throat was sore from

screaming, and the drugs had dried it out. "Could you get me some water?"

He patted me on the shoulder and said, "I better find one of the nurses." With that he was out the door, but the drugs kicked in again and I was asleep by the time they came back.

Hospitals are strange places—doctors and nurses touch and prod your body in areas you would never let an ordinary stranger near, and I had at least two panic attacks that first day. They put me on something for the anxiety, then something at night that made me wake up feeling hung over, then something for the nausea. It was a small hospital, so I usually got the same nurse, and she always called me honey in the gentlest voice. It made me tear up every time and I wanted to tell her to stop, but in my shame I just turned my face away until she was done. Before she left the room she'd run her warm hand down my forearm and squeeze my fingers.

On my second day in the hospital, when I was a little calmer, Gary told me the Crown was reviewing all the information I'd given at the station, and they'd be deciding whether to charge me with anything.

"Charge *me*? For what?"

"There was a death, Annie. No matter what the circumstances we still have to go through the process."

"Are you arresting me?"

"I don't think the Crown will go in that direction, but I still have a duty to inform you of the situation." At first I was scared, and kicking myself for not getting a lawyer, but when I looked at Gary's flushed face I realized he was embarrassed as hell.

"Well, if the Crown does decide to charge me, they're going to look like a bunch of assholes."

Gary grinned and said, "You got that right."

He started asking me a couple of questions about The Freak, and when I reached up to scratch my neck, I realized I wasn't wearing the necklace anymore.

Gary said, "The doctors took it off when you were admitted. You'll get it back when you're released—it's with your personal effects."

"The necklace wasn't mine. He gave it to me—he said he'd bought it for another girl."

"What other girl? Why didn't you say anything about this before?"

Hurt by his abrupt tone, I said, "I got used to wearing it, so I forgot—maybe if you guys backed off on the questions once in a while I'd have had a chance to tell you. Besides, in case you haven't noticed, I've been a little distracted." I shook my arm with the IV in it at him.

In a calmer voice he said, "Sorry, you're right, Annie. We've been hitting you with some hard questions, but it's really important you tell us *everything.*"

Over the next couple of days I tried to fill him in on what I knew of The Freak's history—including his mother, his father, and the female helicopter pilot. Gary often stopped me with questions and sometimes his body was stiff with tension as he leaned toward me, but he was careful to keep a calm tone of voice and he let me get the story out at my own speed. If we talked about the rapes, or The Freak's schedule and system of punishments, his hand would tighten on the pen as he took notes, but he was good about keeping a neutral expression. Half the time I couldn't look at him. I'd stare at the wall, counting cracks, and recite my abuses like I was listing the ingredients to a recipe from hell.

Mom insisted on staying by my side when he talked to me and she usually sent my stepdad to get a coffee—I've never seen a guy look so relieved. If I hesitated for even one second when Gary asked me something, Mom jumped in saying I looked tired or pale and suggested we call one of the doctors, but I thought she was the one who looked pale, especially when I talked about the rapes. And she developed this habit of tucking the blanket tight around me. The harder the words, the tighter she tucked, like she was trying to contain them within me. I didn't appreciate the attention, but I knew she had to be feeling pretty helpless, listening to what I went through, and hell, if it made her feel better . . . Besides, I didn't have enough strength to fight her.

On my third day in the hospital, Gary told me that the cabin being so customized had helped convince them I was telling the truth, and he was pretty sure the Crown wasn't going to be putting forth any charges. Diane had stopped coming along by then, and Gary said she'd gone back to Clayton Falls to handle "other aspects of the investigation."

I tried to be patient when Gary asked me to describe the same things over and over again, because I knew they were having a hard time identifying The Freak. It didn't help that he didn't have any fingerprints. They extracted some DNA but Gary said that's only useful if they have something to compare it to, and there weren't any hits in their system. The Freak's face wasn't looking so good after he'd been left in a hot metal shed, so they took a photo and touched it up on the computer, but they weren't getting any workable leads. When I asked about dental records Gary said they weren't conclusive. Even the van wasn't helping them. It had been stolen, along with the plates from another van, from the parking lot of a local mall that didn't have a security camera.

"Do you think we'll ever find out who he was?" I said one day. "Or who the other girls he hurt were?"

"Anything you remember can help us."

I sat up so I could look him straight in the face. "Don't give me a line from a police training manual—I want to know what you think. What you *really* think."

"Honestly, I don't know, Annie, but I'm going to do everything in my power to get you an answer. You deserve that." There was an intent fervor in his eyes I hadn't seen before. "It would be a lot easier if your mom wasn't here when we're talking. You okay with that?"

"Yeah, it is pretty hard to talk about this in front of her."

When Mom came back in, reeking of cigarettes, Gary said, "I think it would be best if I did the interviews alone, Lorraine."

She held my hand and said, "Annie should have family with her."

"It upsets you too much, Mom." I gave her hand a squeeze. "I'll be okay."

She looked back and forth between Gary and me.

"If that's what you want, Annie Bear, but Wayne and I will be sitting right outside if you need us."

In between my getting interviewed by Gary and prodded by doctors, the next couple of days were a blur. It was bad enough I wasn't allowed to leave because I was dehydrated, among other things. After my meltdown at the police station and my reaction at the hospital, the doctors were concerned that I might be a danger to myself and wanted to keep me for observation. But then after a few raging nightmares and another panic attack, triggered by an interview with Gary, they started playing with my doses—up and down I went, and it was getting increasingly hard to separate my dreams from life. I'd hear a baby cry and think they'd found mine or I'd wake up with a doctor leaning over me, and in a panic, thinking it was The Freak, I'd push him away. I lived in terror all over again as my last bit of control slipped away to pharmaceuticals.

It was during that endless confusion of questions, an over-attentive mother, and drug-happy doctors that Luke and I had our awkward reunion. Christina was spared the same treatment since she was on a Mediterranean cruise at the time. Aunt Val also made the trip, delivering an enormous bouquet of flowers, but Mom allowed her only fifteen minutes of small talk before she told her I needed rest. I actually found Aunt Val more sensitive than usual, even asking if there was anything she could get me, "anything at all." She must have said something that pissed Mom off, because I didn't see her again until I got home.

I'd been there for about eight days when Mom and Wayne headed back to Clayton Falls—the hotel was too expensive for them. Once they were gone I realized I'd been letting Mom, the cops, and the doctors decide what was best for me. It was time I made a few of my own decisions.

The next morning, I stopped the nurse about to give me more drugs. The doctor who was called in said either I took them or I consented to see a shrink. I'd been refusing to see one up to that point, but by then I'd have agreed to anything just to get the hell out.

They were such a small hospital they didn't have a psych ward or a resident psychiatrist, so they brought in some kid who must have been straight from shrink school. Even though his questions were ridiculous, I made myself sound sane while still managing to shed enough tears so he wouldn't think I was handling things *too* well. I'd rather have walked over hot coals than tell that guy how I really felt.

The doctors wouldn't let me have any newspapers, and boredom was making me bitchy. Gary started to bring me fashion magazines, probably in self-defense, when he came to talk to me.

"Want me to cut out some photos of designer suits for you?" I said the first time he handed me one.

He grinned and tossed a couple of chocolate bars on the bed. "Here, maybe these will keep that smart mouth of yours busy."

He also started to bring me coffee laced with hot chocolate, and one time he brought some crossword puzzle books. I didn't mind the questions so much when he came bearing gifts. In fact, he was becoming the highlight of my day. It didn't hurt that his voice was so low and smooth. Sometimes I just closed my eyes, focusing in on his voice. He had to repeat a few of his questions more than once, but he never sounded annoyed—amused, but never annoyed.

When I asked him to explain about his job and rank, he told me he had a sergeant, two corporals, and a few constables working under him. So he *was* the top dog—not of the whole office, but of the Serious Crime Unit, and that was reassuring. He always clammed up when I asked him specific questions about the investigation, though, and said he'd tell me when they had "concrete information."

Once he came in during the tail end of one of my shrink sessions and turned to leave, but I asked him to stay. The shrink said, "Do you think you might have some anger towards the man who abducted you?" Gary raised an eyebrow at me behind his back, and I had to struggle not to laugh.

After about two weeks of doctors, hospital Jell-O, and pacing my room, the shrink gave me a final assessment and said he didn't see any reason why I couldn't go home, but the doctors had to review the assessment before I could be released. I didn't have any more freedom than I'd had on the mountain.

Apparently the shrink said my actions were "consistent" with the trauma I'd endured, and the Crown had officially decided not to put forth any charges. Guess the pipsqueak was good for something, after all. But still no word from the doctors about when I'd be released.

Gary told me the RCMP was paying close attention to my case because they needed to learn everything they could about The Freak, not only to help solve cold cases but for future investigations as well. Sometimes we took a break from talking about the mountain and instead he caught me up on world events, or we just sat and did crossword puzzles together. It had been days since the shrink's assessment.

"You have to get me out of here," I said when Gary waltzed in with two coffees one morning. "The shrink said I was fine to go home, the doctors are just dicking around, and I'm going *crazy*. I'm being treated like a goddamn prisoner. I'm supposed to be the victim here—this is bullshit."

He set the coffees down on the bedside table and with a decisive nod strolled back out the door. Within a half hour he was standing at the foot of my bed.

"You just have to hang on for one more night. You'll be out in the morning."

Pulling myself up into a sitting position, I said, "You didn't shoot someone, did you?"

"Nothing that drastic, I just lit a little fire under them."

Something told me there was more to it than that, but before I could press for details he picked up the crossword book from the bedside table, lowered himself into the chair, and said, "Hmmm. Maybe you're not so smart after all—couldn't finish this one, huh?"

"*Hey*, you came in and interrupted me, I was doing just fine."

As he stretched out his long legs in front of him and crossed them at the ankles, I caught a suppressed smile on his face and realized he'd just done a great job of changing the subject.

Mom told me in the hospital my house was rented out, and I was so glad to hear it wasn't sold I didn't think about having nowhere to live until Gary said I was getting released. I thought about asking Christina if I could stay at her place, but her ship still wasn't back in port, then Mom called and said they were coming back up to get me. I knew it would be a huge scene if I told her I didn't want to stay in the trailer, so I figured I'd just deal with it when I got home.

The morning of my release Gary warned us photographers were probably waiting outside and suggested we go out the back, but Wayne and Mom had come in the front and Mom didn't see any. Of course the second we left, a swarm descended upon us. Mom walked in front of me and pleaded with the media to "give us some time." But you could barely hear her as we fought our way through the surging crowd.

We pulled into a gas station just outside of Port Northfield, and Mom went inside to pay while Wayne pumped. I hid in the backseat. When Mom got back in the car she tossed a newspaper over the seat and, shaking her head, said, "Someone has a big mouth."

MISSING REALTOR RELEASED FROM HOSPITAL! Underneath the front-page headline was an old business photo of me. While Wayne pulled away from the gas station, I read on in shock. An "unidentified source" had informed them I was being released from the hospital today. According to Staff Sergeant Gary Kincade of Clayton Falls, I wasn't under investigation, I was a brave young woman, they were working hard on identifying the deceased perpetrator. . . .

I'd never told the cops my baby's name, but someone had told the newspapers I'd had one, because the article quoted a specialist's opinion on the effect my baby's death might have had on me. I chucked the newspaper onto the floor and ground my feet into it.

SESSION TWENTY-TWO

Good thing you were able to fit me in today, Doc. If I'd had to deal with this latest shitstorm by myself for much longer, you'd have been visiting me in the nuthouse. Then again, it's probably a hell of a lot safer in there. I'm sure you've seen me in the news again. Who the fuck hasn't?

A couple of nights ago I pulled out the older photo The Freak had of me. Didn't seem to be any tack marks and I still couldn't for the life of me think why I'd have had that one at my office. But no matter how much I've tried to focus on where else it might have come from, the only image that ever comes to mind is The Freak holding it up like a prize.

The next morning I headed out for a run. At the end of my driveway I turned right onto the road, and as I ran past a white van parked on the side I called to Emma, who was ahead of me, to wait before she crossed the next road.

Focused on making sure she'd stopped, I barely noticed the van's side door opening. As I passed by I caught a flash of a large body wearing black clothes and a ski mask lunging at me. My ankle twisted as I sidestepped and my foot came down on some loose gravel. I hit the sidewalk hard, biting my tongue as my chin connected and scraping my hands on the rough pavement.

As I struggled to get up, a hand grabbed my ankle and began to drag me back. I clawed at the pavement while trying to yank my leg free. For a moment I was let go and got to my knees, ready to run. Then a large hand slapped over my mouth and an arm circled around my rib cage, lifting me up and slamming me back against a solid torso. The hand over my mouth pressed my head into a shoulder while the arm squeezed the air out of my chest. The body began to move backward. My heels dragged on the pavement. Emma raced down the road barking.

I wanted to scream, wanted to fight, but I was paralyzed with fear. All I could see was The Freak smiling, all I could feel was his gun pressing into my back.

We were at the van. The man shifted his weight to one leg and gripped me tighter like he was about to step up. I remembered The Freak closing the door on me, crossing around the front, getting in—

Focus, dammit! You have seconds, only seconds. Don't let him get you into the van.

I bit the hand covering my mouth and kicked back with my legs. Heard a grunt. I jammed elbows in wherever I could, slammed up into what I thought was a chin. I was shoved so hard I sprawled and landed on the hard edge of the curb, hitting my temple. It hurt like hell, but I rolled onto my back. As the guy reached for me, I started screaming as loud as I could and managed to land a kick in his stomach. He groaned but kept trying to grab me.

I rolled from side to side, punching at his arms and yelling, "HELP! SOMEONE HELP!"

I heard growling and barking. The man stood back up.

Emma had hold of his leg, and he was kicking at her.

"YOU DON'T TOUCH MY DOG, MOTHER-FUCKER!"

Still on the ground, I braced with my elbows and kicked him hard in the groin. Doubled over, he stumbled backward, groaning and gasping for air, then fell to his knees.

On my left a woman screamed, "Leave her alone!"

The man staggered to his feet and tried to get past me to the van but Emma still had hold of his pants. I grabbed the other leg. He shook both of us free and climbed in. Emma narrowly got out of the way as it took off down the road, tires squealing. I tried to see its license plate, but my eyes wouldn't focus and it was moving fast.

My breath sounded like I was strangling. I eased up onto my knees and looked over my shoulder. I could just make out my neighbor from across the street running toward us with a phone in her hands. My vision blurred and I collapsed back to the sidewalk.

"Is she okay?"

"The police are on their way."

"Oh, my God, what happened?"

I wanted to answer the voices but my body was shaking uncontrollably, my breath came in quick hard pants, and I still couldn't see clearly. Emma's fur brushed against my cheek and her warm tongue licked my face. Someone pulled her away, then a woman's voice said, "Can you tell me your name?"

"Annie. My name's Annie."

"Okay, Annie, help is on the way, just hang in there."

Sirens. Uniforms. Somebody put a blanket over me. I answered questions in fragments.

"A man . . . black clothes . . . white van."

More sirens, then the uniforms changed.

"Where does it hurt, Annie?"

"Try to take some deep breaths."

"We're going to stabilize your neck."

"Can you tell us your birth date?"

Hands on my body. Fingers on my wrist. Numbers shouted out. As I was placed on a stretcher and strapped on, I recognized a voice.

"She's my niece, let me in." Then my aunt's concerned face looked down at me. I grabbed her hand and burst into tears.

Aunt Val rode with me to the hospital.

"Annie, you're going to be okay. Mark's calling your mom so she can meet us at the hospital—he's taking Emma to our house." I don't remember much after that, just the feeling of going fast and her hand in mine.

At the hospital I started hyperventilating again—too many people yelling, babies crying, bright lights, nurses asking questions—so they put me in an observation room to wait for the doctor, but I could still see cops talking to the nurses and my aunt in the hallway.

I started counting ceiling tiles. A nurse came in and made me squeeze her hand, then took my blood pressure and checked my pupils. I kept counting.

When the doctor finally arrived and asked all the same questions again, I still kept counting. When they took me for X-rays I counted the machines. When they brought me back to the room and the cops came in with their questions—what was the man wearing, how tall was he, what make was the van—I counted faster. But when a large male nurse came in and suddenly reached for my arm, I started screaming.

Everyone was told to leave the room. The doctor ordered a nurse to get the Crisis Response Team "down here right away." I closed my eyes and counted the beats of my racing heart while they talked over me. Someone gave me a shot. More talk, I didn't follow it. Fingers pressed to my wrist, counting my pulse. I counted along.

I heard heels running down the hall, then Mom's voice, but I checked out.

One, two, three . . .

When I opened my eyes, Mom and Aunt Val were at the window with their backs to me, talking low.

"Mark was driving me to get my lab tests and we saw the crowd. She was just lying there. . . ." My aunt shook her head. "I had to fight to get close to her. The press was there in minutes, must have followed the ambulance. Just look at them all out there now."

Mom said, "What did you tell them?"

"The press? I didn't tell them anything, I was more concerned about Annie, but Mark may have answered a few questions."

"Mark?" Mom sighed. "Val, you have to be careful what you say to those people. You never know how—"

I cleared my throat and they turned to look at me. I started crying.

Mom rushed over and put her arms around me. I sobbed into her shoulder.

"I was so scared, Mom, so scared."

By the time the doctor came back I'd calmed down. It helped to find out I didn't have any broken bones but did have assorted bruises, cuts, and scrapes, not to mention a killer headache. I'd gone into shock from a combination of pain and terror. No shit.

Their main concern was possible head injury from the blow to my temple, so they wanted to keep me overnight. The Crisis Response Team also wanted to assess me again in the morning. Through the night a nurse came in every couple of hours to wake me in case of concussion, but I was usually up anyway, tensing every time footsteps came down the hall, jerking at every loud noise. Sometimes I just stared at Mom's tiny sleeping form on the cot beside me and counted her breaths.

My last stint in the hospital taught me being difficult just earned you a longer stay, so I played along when the Crisis Response Team came in to assess my emotional stability the next morning. They mostly wanted to know what kind of support system I had waiting for me when I got out. I told them I was seeing a shrink regularly and they gave me some crisis hotline phone numbers and a list of support groups.

They decided I was stable enough to talk to the cops, so I filled them in as best as I could—no, I didn't see his face, no, I didn't get a license plate, no, I don't know why the fuck some asshole tried to grab me.

I'd thought they would set up some around-the-clock stake-outs, but the most they could promise was some drive-bys and a special alarm installed to ring direct to the station. They reminded me to take my cell phone everywhere, avoid parked vans—no shit!—and to be "aware of your surroundings" but try and keep living my life while they conducted their investigation. What life? This shit *is* my life.

The doctors said I was okay to go but should have someone keep an eye on me for the next twenty-four hours. Mom insisted I come home with her and I was still so freaked out, not to mention stiff and sore, I jumped at the idea. Mom spent the day watching TV on the couch with me, bringing me ice for my bruises and countless cups of tea. I didn't mind her fussing.

Later Uncle Mark brought Emma over and Mom even let her inside the house, telling her to "guard Annie." And guard she did. Even though Uncle Mark had kept her for the last day, she was skittish with him, barked at every noise, and talked trash to Mom whenever she came in the room. Wayne just stayed clear to give her time to settle down.

That night Mom slept in my bed with me just like when I was a kid, but she was the only one getting any rest. Hours later, when I still couldn't sleep, I crept to the hall closet with my cell in hand and Emma following close behind. Gary, the one cop I really wanted to talk to, was the only one who *didn't* show up the morning the guy grabbed me, or the next day. I'd asked for him in the hospital, but they said he was out of town again. Back in the closet, I tried to call him but his cell phone went straight to voice mail.

My body aching, I curled up in the closet, but this time I still didn't feel safe and all I could think was, *Am I ever going to feel safe again?* Eventually I fell asleep, the image of the white van chasing me into my nightmares.

When I first got home I often went into the cop shop in Clayton Falls to look through mug shots, but after months of examining photos of bad guys and never finding The Freak, I just got too discouraged. The cops' photo of The Freak has been all over the TV and papers, even on an RCMP Web site for unidentified bodies, but to me it just looks like a picture of a dead guy. Shit, even if it did look like him, The Freak was just too damn good at being invisible.

They know the cabin and surrounding property were bought and paid for in cash a couple of months before I was taken, but there's no evidence the guy who bought it exists—no credit card info, driver's license, or anything. The Freak must have had fake ID. He even set up a bank account under the fake name so property taxes could be paid, but nobody at the bank remembers him either.

The original owner never met the buyer because it was a private sale handled through lawyers in Clayton Falls. Only one signature was needed and the lawyer must have had his head stuck up his ass because he can't describe the buyer at all. His excuse is that he registered sixty titles that month, and I wondered if he even asked for ID.

Gary called me a couple of days after the guy grabbed me on the street—I was still at Mom's—to tell me the alarm was now installed and he was sorry he hadn't called sooner. He'd been working on a case in a fishing camp up north and only had radio access. We went over everything together, then he asked me about the damn photo again and when I told him it still hadn't come to me, he just grunted and moved on. He said that because The Freak had stalked me they originally thought he might be local, but now he figured the guy could have been staying in a hotel and driving to Clayton Falls.

"I've spent every weekend for the last month showing a photo of the body to every hotel or motel in a one-hour radius," Gary said. Clayton Falls is in the central part of the island, so that's a lot of area he's been covering.

"Why don't you just fax the hotels? And how come *you're* doing it? Don't you have constables you can send?"

"First off, if I fax it, odds are it'll just end up in the trash. Over the winter a lot of the staff gets laid off, but now that the tourist season is picking up, they're coming back, and I want to talk to them in person. Second, I don't send anyone else because most of them are working on active cases. I'm doing a lot of this on my own time, Annie."

Impressed and feeling sheepish that I was sitting in front of the TV every night while he was out there pounding the pavement, I wondered if that's why he wasn't married.

"Guess your girlfriend must really hate me," I said. He was quiet for a few beats, and as I felt my cheeks grow warm I was glad he couldn't see my face.

"I know you got frustrated with the process before, but now with this second abduction attempt, I think you should come down to the station and look through some more photos."

Still feeling like an idiot for my unanswered girlfriend question, I said, "So you think whoever grabbed me is connected to The Freak?"

"I think it's important we consider all possibilities."

"Meaning?"

"A couple of things about this case don't fit the typical profile, like your photo, for one—we still need to consider how he got it and why he needed it when he had so many he'd taken himself. If you can identify a suspect for us, the rest will hopefully fall into place."

I told him I'd do it the next day.

This one morning Gary came to visit me the first time I was in the hospital still stands out in my mind, Doc. He'd been out "in the field," whatever that means, and he was wearing jeans and a black Windbreaker with the RCMP logo on it. He even had a baseball cap on. I asked him if all his suits were at the dry cleaner's, but the truth is, I thought he looked tough. As much as I tease him about his fancy clothes, that guy has a serious don't-fuck-with-me vibe.

I stayed over again at Mom's last night, but after listening to her and Wayne fight all night—she's been drinking like a fish since my latest stay in the hospital—I had another nightmare about the white van, only this time the nightmare ended on a good note: a man was shielding me in his arms. When I woke up I realized the arms were Gary's. I felt guilty as hell. I mean, here's poor Luke who's tried so hard and been so patient, and I'm having dreams about the cop who put him through hell.

Sometimes I wish Gary could go everywhere with me, like a bodyguard. Then I mentally kick my ass, because I know that no one can make me feel safe all the time. It's funny, because I always thought I felt safe with Luke, but it was a different kind of safe—a calm, *simple* safe. Nothing about Gary feels simple.

After I got back to my house this morning, I did a perimeter patrol with Emma, jumping at every shadow, then checked the alarm a gazillion times. To distract myself I had another look at that brochure for the art school I told you about. It's in the Rocky Mountains and so beautiful—like how I always imagined Harvard would look. I even downloaded some forms from their Web site. God knows why.

Only damn thing I have left that I give a shit about is my house, and I may be crazy freaked out, but I'd have to be certifiable to sell it so I could pursue some adolescent dream. What if I tried, and I never got anywhere as an artist? Then what?

On that note, we better call this session quits, Doc. I still have to go down to the station on my way home to look through more photos. Least it's a good excuse to call Gary tonight.

SESSION TWENTY-THREE

Sorry about calling you on such short notice for this session, Doc, but so much shit happened in the last couple of days, I couldn't wait for our regular appointment to roll around.

After I left here last time I drove straight to the cop shop in Clayton Falls and spent an hour looking through photos. I was just about to quit because my back was killing me, and all the freaks were beginning to look the same, only one guy looked familiar but I remembered seeing his picture in the paper recently. Then I thought of Gary out there showing the sketch around and made myself keep going. I almost flipped past a picture of a guy with a shaved head and a full beard, but something about his guileless blue eyes, a contradiction to the rest of his face, made me look closer.

It was him.

My body broke out in a cold sweat and my vision blurred. To stop myself from passing out, I tore my gaze away and laid my forehead down on the table. Focusing in on my frantic heartbeat, I took a few deep breaths and chanted in step with the thuds, *He's dead . . . He's dead . . . He's dead.* When my vision cleared up and my heartbeat had slowed, I faced his image.

I motioned for one of the cops to come over, and when I told him what I'd found, he called Gary on his cell. None of the photos had names, and the cops wouldn't answer any of my questions, so I insisted on speaking to Gary.

"I don't understand why nobody will tell me who he is—he has a *record.* I've spent hours looking through these *fucking* photos, the least you can do is give me his name."

"It's great you've identified a picture, Annie, but first we have to verify the information. I don't want you getting all worked up over this and finding out it's the wrong guy—"

"It's him. I spent a *whole year* with him."

"I don't doubt you for a second, and I'll call you as soon as I have the full story on him. Meanwhile, just go home and try to get some rest, all right? And I need you to make me a list of anyone you think might want to harm you."

"There isn't *anyone,* I already did one for my shrink, listed every damn person I know. The Freak must have had a friend who—"

"And that's what I'm working on finding out. Now go home, send me the list you made, and we'll talk soon."

The next day I paced around my house waiting for Gary to call, which he didn't, nor did he answer his cell. I killed a couple of hours cleaning, then, curious about the guy whose picture at the cop shop had looked familiar, I went through all my recycled newspapers, page by page. In the very last one I spotted a headline about the "recently released felon wanted in connection with a convenience store robbery" and took a closer look at the article. As soon as I read the name I knew who he was. Mom's stepbrother. The date told me he'd been released a few weeks ago and I wondered if Mom knew, or if I should tell her. All afternoon I weighed the pros and cons of being the one to fill her in. By five I was like a squirrel on speed, so when my mom called and invited me over for pasta, I said yes.

Dinner wasn't so bad, but when we finished eating and I was still debating whether to tell her the news about her stepbrother, Mom started talking about a little girl who just went missing in Calgary. I told her I didn't want to hear it. She sailed on without skipping a beat about how the mother was pleading on TV for the daughter's return, but Mom didn't think she was handling the press right.

"She's rude to them—if she wants help getting her daughter back she better lose the attitude."

"Reporters can be pretty rough, Mom, you know that."

"The press is the least of her problems right now—the police are questioning the father, apparently he had a girlfriend on the side. A *pregnant* girlfriend."

"*Mom*, can we please drop it?"

She opened her mouth but before she could get going again, I blurted out, "I saw Dwight's photo in the paper."

She closed her mouth with a snap and stared at me.

"Your stepbrother? He's been released, Mom, but he's wanted for questioning in a robbery of a—"

"Did you want anything more to eat?" We held eyes for a moment.

"Sorry if I upset you, I just thought—"

"There's more sauce?" Her face revealed no emotion, but her hand twisting the napkin told me to back off.

"No, I'm done. My stomach's all messed up because I finally identified a photo at the cop shop today. Gary wouldn't give me his name yet, but he's looking into the guy's history—he said he'd have more information for me soon."

Mom paused for a second, nodded, then said, "Good. Maybe now you can put this behind you, Annie Bear." She patted my hand. Wayne got up and headed outside for a smoke.

After he left I said, "Well, not quite yet. Gary thinks the guy could've had a partner, that's who may have tried to grab me the other day."

Mom frowned. "Why on earth would Gary try to scare you like that?"

"He's not *trying* to scare me, it's because of this one photo The Freak had of me. I just figured he'd taken it from my office or something, but Gary's questioning why he'd want that one, you know? He even got me to fax him this list. . . ." Shit. In my zeal to defend Gary I'd not only told Mom about the photo, I was about to spill my very own personal shit list.

"What list?"

"Just this dumb thing my shrink suggested I do—it's nothing."

"If it's nothing, why did Gary want it? What was on the list?" Damn. She wasn't going to let it go.

"Just a few people from my past who might have a grudge or whatever."

"Like who?"

I sure as hell didn't want to tell her I put everyone close to me on it, so I said, "Just some exes and a couple of old clients. Oh, and the 'mystery' Realtor I was competing against."

"You mean Christina."

"No, the Realtor I was *competing* against in the beginning."

Her eyes narrowed. "She didn't tell you?"

"Who didn't tell me what?"

"I don't want to stir up trouble."

"Come on, Mom—what is it?"

"I suppose you should know." She took a deep breath. "You remember my friend Carol? Well, her daughter Andrea works in your office and she's friends with Christina's assistant. . . ."

"So?"

"So Christina was your competition for that project all along. She was the other Realtor."

"No way. Christina would've told me. The developer just picked her because I was gone."

She shrugged. "I thought the same as you, but then Andrea said Christina's assistant was working weekends to get the proposal done. She said she even saw some marketing Christina designed for the developer."

I shook my head. "Christina would never screw me over like that. Friends are way more important than money to her."

"Speaking of money, I heard her husband is having some financial problems. That house he bought her wasn't cheap, but she sure doesn't seem to be putting the brakes on her spending. He must be a very understanding man—Luke and her were awfully cozy while you were missing."

"They were trying to find me, of course they spent time

together. And Drew didn't buy the house *for* her, they bought it *together*. So she likes a nice life, what's wrong with that? Christina works hard for her money—"

"Why are you getting so defensive?"

"You just implied Christina and Luke were fooling around!"

"I never said any such thing—I was just telling you what I heard. She was at the restaurant night after night, a lot of times right until closing. Which reminds me, did you know things weren't going so good for the restaurant before you went missing? Wayne was talking to the bartender down at the pub just the other day, he knows Luke's head chef and he was saying there was even talk about the place maybe having to close, but then after you were missing he got all that news coverage and things picked right up. I guess something positive came out of all this."

The chicken Alfredo I'd enjoyed now sat like a lump in the pit of my stomach.

"I have to go to the bathroom."

For a minute I thought I might be sick, but I ran some cold water on my hands, splashed my face with it, and leaned my forehead on the vanity mirror until the feeling passed. My hair was hot and sweaty on the back of my neck, so I rummaged around in the drawer and used a pink hair elastic to pull it back. When I got out of the bathroom Mom was pouring another drink.

"I have to get going, Mom—thanks for dinner."

"Call me if you find out anything else." She rubbed her hand down my back and said, "I'm sure everything will work out."

By the time I got back home the sick feeling had turned into a restless energy, so I decided to go for a run. It wasn't that late yet, but I couldn't have gone to sleep even if it was bedtime—I was wired for sound. While my feet pounded the pavement, my thoughts ran wild.

Did something go on between Luke and Christina? I couldn't recall them ever being overly friendly when we were together in the past. Then again, I never picked up on the fact that she was my competition for the project. Had she known from the start? Was that what she was trying to tell me when I interrupted her? Or was she trying to tell me about her and Luke? And how come Luke never told me the restaurant was having troubles? Questions crashed around in my mind, smashed into each other, and splintered into more questions.

After a half hour's hard running I'd calmed down a lot, but a vague sense of unease followed me home and into the shower. If I just heard their voices all the crazy thoughts would go away. Still wrapped in my towel, I called Luke at the restaurant. He answered abruptly.

"Am I catching you at a bad time?" I said.

"I got a few."

"I just wanted to tell you I identified a photo of the guy down at the cop shop today. I don't have a name yet but Gary's going to fill me in as soon as he can."

"Hey! That's good news."

"I guess. I still need to know more."

"Keep me posted on what they find out, but I gotta go—I'm sorry, there's a lot going on around me, place is packed."

Still feeling unsettled, I almost told him I'd stop in for a drink so we could talk, but I hesitated too long and he was gone.

I called Christina on her cell, but she told me she'd have to call me back because they were doing the launch of the waterfront project that night and she was greeting people at the door. After we said good-bye, I stared at the phone in my hand. Emma, sitting at my feet, looked up at me with her big brown eyes.

"I'm being a dumbass, aren't I?" She wagged her tail furiously. I took that as a yes.

But then, on the way to my bedroom, I finally remembered where the photo came from.

It took Gary a while to answer the phone. I didn't realize I was holding my body rigid until I heard his calm voice, and the tension in my muscles eased a little.

"I've been trying to call you all afternoon," I said.

"Sorry about that, my phone battery died."

"I need to talk to you." I hated how desperate I sounded.

"I'm listening."

"I was just thinking about this little shelf cluttered with photo frames I used to have in the hall outside my bedroom, and—I remembered. There's this pewter frame I'd stuck in behind the rest because it had an older picture of me in it, the same picture The Freak—"

"The photo was from *inside* your house?"

The sick feeling was back.

"The Freak could never have gotten past Emma, so it has to have been when we were out on a walk. But why would he risk breaking in for that photo?"

"That's a good question. Did anyone have keys to your place?"

"I lost my set on a hike a few months before I was taken, so I had the locks changed—I hadn't given anyone a spare yet."

"So it was probably someone you let in, Annie. They gave him the photo—presumably as a way of identifying you."

My heart started to pound. "But why that one?"

"Might've thought it was one you wouldn't miss. Could be any number of reasons."

"And whoever tried to grab me—"

"Could be the same person who took the photo or someone they hired to finish the job."

"This doesn't make any sense. Why would someone want me abducted? There were never any ransom demands."

"We don't know that you were supposed to be *abducted*. It's possible he was hired for a different reason, then decided to keep you for his own purposes."

"You think he was actually supposed to *kill* me? Jesus Christ, Gary." My eyes went to the alarm.

"They're not going to try anything again this fast—there's too much attention on you right now—but I'll make sure the patrol cars are still driving by. And I'm going to need the names of anyone who had access to that photo."

"Lots of people have been in my house, I'd just had some work done on the furnace—"

"This is too complicated to be a crime of opportunity. It has to be someone with a personal motive."

"I already sent you the stupid list—"

"Don't just think in terms of who might have wanted to hurt you, think about who benefited the most from your disappearance."

My mind reeled. "I need . . . I need some time. To think."

Gary said, "Sleep on it, okay? I'll give you my motel number in Eagle Glen. If you come up with anything, call me right away." I was about to hang up when he said, "And, Annie. Just keep this to yourself for now."

I got dressed with shaky hands and Gary's words repeating in my head. *Who benefited the most?* I thought of Luke's busy restaurant. I thought of Christina getting a real estate project.

Then I remembered The Freak saying he chose me because "an opportunity arose," and it was odd that my normally punctual boyfriend was so late for dinner that day of all days. Also The Freak had said he saw Luke with a woman, but he liked tormenting me—wouldn't he have told me if it was Christina? Or was he saving that detail for a rainy day? But if there was something going on between Luke and Christina, why didn't they get together once I was out of the picture? And why would they give him that photo? They'd both had pictures of me. No, this was ridiculous. Christina and Luke loved me—they'd *never* hurt me.

Who benefited the most?

I stared at the spot in the hall where the shelf used to be. Someone stole a photo of me, someone I let in my home. I checked the alarm again, the locks on the door. Emma barked at a car driving by and I just about jumped out of my skin. I had to get out of there.

On the hour-long drive to Eagle Glen—Gary's motel's name, room number, and a Googled map on the seat next to me—I realized I hadn't asked him why he was there, but I assumed it was because of the case. I can't remember anything I passed that night, and I felt cold all over—in my haste I hadn't grabbed a coat and was just wearing a tank top and yoga pants, which didn't help. My hands shook on the steering wheel.

I had to wait a couple of minutes for Gary to answer my knock.

"Sorry, I was just getting out of the shower. What's going on? You okay?"

"Hey," I said. "I need to talk." He gestured for me to come in.

The air was still steamy and he was buttoning up the last few buttons of a white shirt. He took the towel from around his neck and rubbed it over his hair, which the water had turned steel-colored, and after he tossed the towel onto the back of a chair, he quickly smoothed his hands over his head.

It wasn't a very big room, just one bed, a phone desk, TV, and a bathroom, and it felt even smaller when I realized it was the first time we'd ever been alone together.

A half-empty bottle of red wine rested on the night table. He didn't strike me as the drinking type, but what the hell did I know? Without saying anything, he lifted up the bottle and raised his eyebrows. I nodded. He filled up one of the motel room glasses and handed it to me. Glad to have something in my hands, I took a big gulp and felt it hit my bloodstream instantly. My muscles uncoiled and a warm glow spread through me. I sat on the end of the bed.

Gary pulled a chair from the phone table and turned it to face me. He leaned forward with his elbows on his knees and his chin in his hands.

"So what's up?"

"This shit—it's making me *crazy*. You *have* to find the guy who grabbed me, Gary. Not knowing who may have done this is seriously screwing with my head—I'm doubting *everyone*. I even started wondering if it could be Christina and Luke just because of some crap my mom heard. How fucked is *that*?"

"What did your mom hear?"

"They didn't do it, Gary. It was just some stuff about that waterfront project I was supposed to get and that they were spending a lot of time together after I was gone. Apparently their finances were screwed up too, but that crap doesn't matter. My point is, this shit's making me *insane*."

Gary stood up and paced around the room, rubbing his chin with one hand. "What happened with that project again?"

I gave him the lowdown but ended with, "Christina wouldn't do this to me, Gary."

"If you want me to find who's responsible, I have to consider every scenario."

"Well, that's not one."

"How stable is her marriage?"

"It's fine, I think. . . . She doesn't say much about it, but that's probably just because of everything I'm going through."

"And she was seen at the restaurant with Luke a lot?"

"Yes, but they're *never* together now, they were just meeting because they were trying to find me."

Gary continued to pace.

"Why are you in Eagle Glen, by the way?" I said. "Are you showing the sketch around still?"

"I just got here this afternoon and talked with the night staff. Tomorrow I meet with the day shift."

"Do you have anything more on the guy? Was David his real name? You told me you'd fill me in as soon as you got his file, but you haven't called."

"I'm getting some information from another department faxed over tomorrow. That's all I can tell you at this point."

"I hate it when you use that cop talk. I'm shooting straight with you, it's the least you can do for me."

Frustration and wine combined to erode what remained of my self-control, and I burst into tears.

With my head down to hide my face, I got up off the bed and walked toward the door, but Gary grabbed my arm as I passed and spun me around. I shoved at his chest with my free hand, but he didn't budge. The tears were gone now.

"Let me go, Gary."

"Not until you calm down."

I slammed the heel of my hand into his chest, a quick blow. "Fuck you, Gary. I'm sick and tired of this bullshit. You cops sat there and did nothing the whole time I was gone and you're still giving me the runaround. I was raped almost every *fucking* night and you can't even give me a *name*? Don't you get it? Not only is my life *fucked*, but now I have to wonder if someone I know *wanted* it fucked. And you're going to stand there and tell me I don't have the right to know anything about the guy who did this?" This time I hit his shoulder. He didn't move. I hit him again.

He grabbed my wrist. "Stop it."

I glared at him. "Stop being a jerk."

"I'm telling you everything I can without compromising the case."

"That's all this is to you, isn't it? Just a case."

Now he looked angry. "Do you know how many people go missing every year? How many children? And most of them don't come back. My older sister disappeared when I was just a kid and we never found her. That's why I got into the force—I didn't want anyone to go through what my family did." He dropped my wrists. "My marriage broke up because of this case."

"I didn't know you were—"

"We were having some problems before you went missing, but we were trying to work them out. That's why I asked to be transferred here from the mainland. But not long after I got here you were abducted and I put so many hours on your case . . . She walked out a month before you came home." A rueful laugh. "She told me I was so busy looking for other people I don't see the ones standing right in front of me."

"I'm sorry, Gary, about everything. I know I'm being a bitch. But I'm just so fucked up. I don't know who to trust anymore. Someone wants me dead, and—" My voice broke and I started to cry.

Gary stepped forward and wrapped his arms around me. My face is about the same height as his chest, and his chin was on top of my head. The rumble of his voice moving up through his chest vibrated against my cheek.

"No one is going to hurt you, Annie. I won't let that happen, okay?"

I peeled my face off his chest and looked up at him. His eyes were dark and his arm around my back burned through my shirt. It felt good to lean into the power of his body and I wanted to absorb his strength and take it with me. Our eyes locked.

On my tiptoes, I stretched my body against him and pressed my lips to his. For a second his mouth didn't yield, and then he muttered, "Oh, shit."

With Luke everything was always sweet and soft, passionate but never intense. Gary and I kissed with quiet desperation. With both hands around my bottom, he lifted me up against him, then lowered me onto the bed. When he leaned over me with both arms braced on either side of my body, The Freak flashed before my eyes and I froze. Gary gave me a searching look and started to stand back up, but I pulled him down on the bed beside me, pushed him onto his back, crawled on top of him, and gripped the bedding on either side of his face. We lay like that for a second, my body aware of every inch of him and my heart thudding against his chest. His arms were rigid as they held me up slightly under my rib cage and his legs tensed as though he was about to lift me away from him.

With my cheek pressed to his, I whispered into his ear, "I have to . . . be in control. It's the only way I can . . ."

Relaxing his body, he cupped my face with one of his hands, then turned it toward him until I was forced to make eye contact. His voice ragged yet still gentle, he stroked his thumb against my cheekbone.

"Are you sure you want to do this, Annie? If this is as far as you want to go, I'm okay with that."

A shiver of fear slid through me, but I turned my face into his hand and bit down softly on the fleshy part of his thumb. Then I leaned down, my hair curtaining us, and pressed my lips to his.

But as soon as he began to kiss back harder, holding my butt and grinding my groin against his, panic rose in me, and I froze again. He sensed the change and started to say something, but I pinned his hands above his head and, my face burning in humiliation, murmured against his mouth.

"You can't touch me . . . you can't move."

I wasn't sure he understood, but his lips relaxed, and when I moved my mouth against his, he didn't kiss back. Pressing and pulling, tugging and nibbling, I worked his lips. Sliding my tongue into his mouth, I stroked and sucked until he moaned.

I took off our clothes until we were both in our underwear and kissed his chest, softly dragged my hair back and forth until his nipples hardened and his skin broke out into goose bumps. Straddling him, I held eye contact as I brought his hand to my breasts and stroked around my nipples with it, moving his hand down over my rib cage, and then, as I grew more comfortable, between my legs. I caressed myself with his hand—the first hand to touch there, including my own, since The Freak. When my body began to respond in a wave of pleasure I wasn't quite ready to surf, I moved his hand back to cup my breast. I kissed him again, hooked my toes into his boxers, and slid them down. Then, still kissing, I drew my panties down and kicked them off.

Holding his arms above his head, our foreheads touching, I lay still on top of him and rested my lips just slightly over his, feeling his hot breath moving in and out, mixing with my own. His skin was burning, feverish, and a fine sweat coated both our bodies. At first his breathing was ragged, but he smoothed it out, holding it in check, for me.

Lifting myself up onto my toes, I opened my legs, then shifted down, sliding myself onto him. He didn't enter me, I took him.

His breath caught in his throat, and I paused, heart fluttering, waiting for him to lose it, to flip me on my back and pound at me, to thrust up, to do *something*. But he didn't. And I wanted to cry. At his gift.

As I slid up and down on him, he never moved. Stroke after stroke, his breath was my only monitor of the fierce struggle going on within, and knowing I had this strong, confident man on his back made me move harder. Faster. Rougher. Daring him to try to touch me, I took my anger out on his body. Using my sex as a weapon. And when he came, his hips still didn't lift, didn't thrust, only his hands flexed in my own as his whole body tightened, and I felt exhilarated. Powerful. I continued to ride him until it must have been painful. But he still didn't touch me. Finally I stopped, turning my face to the side and releasing his wrists. Only then did he lift one hand to cup the back of my head as he rocked me slightly in his arms. And then I cried.

Afterward we lay side by side on our backs, staring at the ceiling while we tried to catch our breath. Neither of us said a word. It was so much the opposite of my experience with The Freak, total control versus no control, I'd actually been able to keep The Freak's memory out of the room, out of the bed, out of my body. But my haze began to lift as I sobered up and I thought about what was really going on in my life, and what I'd just done. Gary started to say something, but I interrupted him.

"This was the first time that I . . . did what we did since I came home. And I just want you to know I'm glad it was with you, but you don't have to worry—I don't have any expectations or anything. I hope this doesn't change things between us."

The rhythm of his breathing broke, paused, and resumed. He turned his face toward me, opened his mouth, but I cut him off again.

"Don't get me wrong, I don't have any regrets or anything, and I sure as hell hope you don't, but I don't want to have some big talk about it, okay? Let's just move on. . . . What's the next step in the investigation?"

I felt his eyes burning into my face but I kept my gaze focused on the ceiling. In a low voice he said, "After I question the hotel people tomorrow with the sketch and the mug shot that was faxed to me, I'll be heading to the next town. Kinsol." I had forgotten how close I was to Kinsol. It's not a big town—

probably only has one or two motels—and most of the population work at the prison.

I laughed and said, "You could've said hi to my uncle, but he was just released."

Gary propped himself on an elbow and looked down at me. "What uncle?"

I assumed he'd have known, but Mom and my uncle have a different last name, so maybe not.

"My mom's stepbrother, Dwight? He robbed a couple of banks. He was just in the paper—you guys want him for questioning in another robbery. But we don't have anything to do with him, so can't help you there."

Gary rolled onto his back and stared at the ceiling. I wanted to ask what he was thinking, but I'd learned that leaning on him didn't get me answers.

"Is there anything I can do to help my investigation?" I said.

"Just try to stay clear of everyone for now. I have to do some more digging but should have more information tomorrow, and I'll let you know how we're going to proceed from there. If you find out or remember anything that might help, call me right away. And you can call if you just need to talk too."

His voice was starting to drift and I knew he'd fall asleep soon, so I said, "I should get going. Emma's at home."

"I'd like it if you stayed."

"Thanks, but I can't leave her all night." Truth is, I didn't trust myself to lie quietly beside him with the bedding all tangled around us—would have been hard to explain why I was in the closet in the morning.

"I don't like the idea of you driving alone on the roads this late."

"I made it here, didn't I?"

In the dim room he raised an eyebrow at me, so I tucked my face into the warm groove between his shoulder and neck and said, "I'll have a shower, okay?"

After a quick shower, which I spent trying not to think about what I'd just done, I tiptoed by his sleeping form on the bed and slipped out. The streets were empty on my drive home and I was in my own little world. Had Emma been with me, I'd have just kept on going.

My mind floated back to my conversation with Gary, and I wished I hadn't told him what Mom heard about Christina and Luke. Cops look for ulterior motives in everything. Not that I wasn't just as guilty of that myself. But I knew those two wouldn't hurt me. Still, I felt like there was something I should be seeing but wasn't. My mind turned over everything I knew, but I just couldn't put my finger on the missing piece of the puzzle.

It was a long night. I slept in the closet but tossed and turned, as much as you can turn in a closet, and woke up early this morning. Groggy, I sat out on my back deck with the cordless near me, waiting for Gary to call and tell me what he'd found out.

I'd forgotten Luke was coming by to drop off receipts and some books he was lending me, so I was surprised when I heard a truck pull up. When I looked out and realized it was him, my legs turned to rubber. Pulling myself together, I opened the door. He tried to hug me but I barely hugged back.

"Everything okay?" he said.

"Sorry, I'm just tired—didn't sleep very well last night." I aimed for light and casual, but my voice sounded strained. I avoided his eyes.

"Find out anything more about that picture you identi-fied?"

I mumbled something about Gary looking into it. Then I dropped one of the books he'd brought over, and when I bent down to pick it up, we almost knocked heads. When I jumped back, he gave me a searching look, so I quickly offered him a cup of tea. Praying he'd drink his fast, I gulped mine back.

I've never felt like such a fraud as I did in that moment, talk-ing about our dogs and his work while I waited for the phone to ring and wondered what I would do if Gary called while Luke was still there.

Our conversation was riddled with pauses and he barely touched his tea before he said he had to go. When he gave me a hug at the door I forced myself to hug him back and won-dered if he could feel guilt through my skin.

"Annie, you sure you're all right?" I wanted to confess ev-erything. I couldn't confess anything.

"I'm just really bagged."

"Well, get some rest, okay? Doctor's orders." He smiled.

I forced a smile back. "Yes, sir."

After he left I knew I could never tell him what had hap-pened between Gary and me. I also knew I could never get back together with him now. Luke belonged to the woman who was abducted, not the one who came home.

An hour later the suspense was killing me, so I called Gary, but he didn't answer and his cell phone was off. It wasn't until later that afternoon that he finally called back. I wish he hadn't.

The Freak's real name was Simon Rousseau, and he'd have been forty-two at the time of his death. He grew up in a small town in Ontario, moved to Vancouver in his early twenties, but eventually settled on the island. The mug shot was taken when he was arrested at thirty-nine for beating a man so badly he was hospitalized for weeks. The Freak, who claimed the wife hired him to do it because her husband was cheating on her, cut a deal. A year later his conviction was overturned based on the RCMP having mishandled some evidence. Upon his release from Kinsol prison he moved back to the mainland and dropped off the police radar until I identified his mug shot.

Now that they had a name, they traced back trying to match his whereabouts with any unsolved crimes. They discovered his mother did die of cancer and his father indeed disappeared, and to this day the father's car and body have never shown up.

When they couldn't find any cold cases that fit, they reviewed some that were "solved" and came upon the case of a young woman named Lauren who was raped and beaten and left dead in the alley behind her house. A homeless man was caught with her bloody sweater and purse and tried for her murder. He died in prison a year later.

Simon Rousseau, who lived a few blocks down from Lauren, remained close to the family for years, even visiting Lauren's mom every Christmas up until her death five years ago. I was glad the mom would never have to know she welcomed her daughter's killer into her house every Christmas.

During his twenties Rousseau lived in Vancouver but worked in logging camps up north as a cook. And yes, a female helicopter pilot from one of the camps was found dead. But it was never investigated as a homicide. After her boyfriend got back to camp, he realized she was taking too long and went to find her. When he couldn't, a search party was sent out but it took them a month to find her body at the bottom of a gulley. She was fully dressed and her neck was broken. Because it had been dusk when she was heading back to the camp, they assumed she had lost her way and fallen over the cliff.

Rousseau's exact location and activities since he left prison were still unknown, and Gary said they might never know if he was responsible for any other crimes.

While Gary talked I'd been sitting on my couch fiddling with a loose thread on my throw. I'd just about unraveled the damn thing.

I said, "Are you back in Clayton Falls?"

"Still up in Eagle Glen."

"You said you were going to Kinsol today?"

"I was, but a staff member I need to talk to at this motel isn't coming in until tonight."

"Talk to about what? I thought you were just showing the picture around. Did someone recognize him?"

"I'm just making sure I follow up on every avenue, then I'll come back to Clayton Falls in the morning. Are we clear?"

"Yeah, clear as mud."

"Sorry, Annie, but I can't tell you anything more until all the facts are in. If we're wrong it could cause you a lot of unnecessary anguish—"

"What are you saying? Are you telling me you know who hired The Freak? You can at least tell me if it's someone I know, can't you?"

"Annie . . . a lot is at stake here."

"I'm perfectly aware a lot is at stake—it's my *life*, remember? Or did you forget about that part?" At the sound of my harsh tone Emma left the room.

"Look, all I can tell you at this point is that after you identified Rousseau we obtained his criminal record, and based on the record we had another look at his known associates—that's standard procedure in any investigation."

While he was waiting for that information, he met with a few of the maids from the day shift at the motel in Eagle Glen. One of them thought the drawing of The Freak looked familiar, but when he showed her the mug shot she didn't recognize him. But if it *was* the same guy in the sketch, she'd seen a woman wearing large sunglasses go into his room one morning and leave about fifteen minutes later. She didn't see the car, but she thought one of the other maids had been cleaning the rooms on the lower floor where the parking lot was. That's who Gary was waiting to speak with.

My head was spinning. What woman met with The Freak?

I said, "Sorry, I'm just trying to . . . It's a lot to take in all at once."

"I understand. But it's really important you don't—"

"Sorry, my mom's calling on the other line, I'll pick it up and get rid of her or she'll—"

"Don't answer it!"

"Okay, okay." But when the beeping finally stopped I said, "She's just going to call back."

"Have you talked to her about anything we discussed last night?" His voice was tight.

"Luke's the only one I spoke with today, but I never—"

"You can't discuss any of this with her, Annie." Something in his tone set off alarm bells.

"Gary, this is my *mom*. If you don't tell me what the fuck is going on right now, I'm going to call her and tell her every damn thing."

"Jesus." He was silent for a moment, then I heard him take a deep breath. "This is going to be hard for you to hear. . . ."

"Just say it."

"When you came up last night you mentioned your uncle was in Kinsol prison, so I checked if he and Simon Rousseau were there at the same time. They were. It's also been confirmed that your uncle was known to have photos of his nieces on his cell walls. So after the maid's description we faxed a request for a warrant to check your mother's bank records for any unusual transactions."

"I don't . . . Why the hell would you do that?"

"I still need to talk to the other maid, but, Annie . . ." His voice turned gentle. "It looks like your mother might be involved."

Oh, shit.

And that's all I know. Right after Gary dropped his bombshell he had to take another call. He made me promise not to talk to anyone and said he'd phone me later. So that's why I called you, Doc, and why I've been gripping this cell phone like my life depends on it, I had to get out of there, had to talk to somebody. I couldn't stand pacing around my house wondering what bullshit theory the cops are coming up with now. Some dingbat maid sees a woman at a motel and they decide it's my *mom*? Talk about grasping at straws.

I wonder if Gary left a message at my house or if he remembers my cell number—can't recall if I left it on his voice mail. Or even worse, what if he tried to call me on my drive here but I didn't have cell coverage? There are some dead spots on the highway. I've got to get out of here—I need to try him again.

SESSION TWENTY-FOUR

I know I look like shit today, but trust me, Doc, when you hear how my week went you'll understand, and you'll know why I asked for a longer session too.

On the drive home from our last appointment I passed a new billboard on the highway advertising the real estate project I was supposed to get. It was right near the turnoff to my aunt's house and I thought about how annoyed she used to get when Mom talked about that deal. Then I realized Aunt Val doesn't brag about how well Tamara's doing in real estate anymore.

As soon as I got home I checked out Tamara's Web site. She had a few nice listings but not nearly as many as she used to. Just for the heck of it I Googled her name and it came up on the Real Estate Council Web site—under disciplinary decisions. Turns out my perfect cousin was suspended last year for ninety days. She represented a numbered company buying a large piece of commercial land and never disclosed she was the owner of said company. Not smart.

Obviously Mom didn't know or I'd have heard by now, *everyone* would've heard. Aunt Val's lucky I went missing just before Tamara's suspension was announced in our monthly Report from Council. Then it came to me.

When Gary called a half hour later I jumped right in. "I know who could have met with The Freak."

Gary was quiet for a moment, then said, "Go ahead."

"I just found out my cousin lost her real estate license right after I was abducted, but she'd have known it was going to happen for a while and my aunt *never* mentioned it. My mom and her sister are supercompetitive, and I was supposed to be getting this big project—"

"Annie—"

"Just *listen*. You said it was a woman wearing big sunglasses, right?"

"Right, but—"

"My Aunt Val, she started wearing these big sunglasses right after my mom did." Mom wears them because she thinks they make her look like a Hollywood star, and man, was she pissed when Aunt Val showed up in a pair. "They look a lot alike, Aunt Val's a little taller but from a distance they could pass for the same person. And it's my aunt who used to go see my uncle—she could've brought him the pictures. When that guy grabbed me last week she was there in minutes and—"

"Our records show that your mother did visit your uncle, Annie."

"That's not possible—she won't even *talk* about him."

"Annie, we have video and her signature in the visitors' log."

"My aunt could've just dressed like her and forged her signature, Mom's writing looks like a kid's—"

Gary sighed. "We'll consider that possibility, okay? But I have to ask you some more questions. When you were at the cabin, was there ever anything that stuck out as not belonging? Anything at all, something like the photo?"

"The whole place was fucked up, what's that gotta do with this?"

"It might not have seemed relevant at the time, but he may have had an item that didn't seem to fit?"

"I've told you everything, Gary."

"Sometimes a shock can cause memories to resurface. Just go through the cabin in your mind."

"There's *nothing.*"

"Something in the shed maybe or the cellar . . . ?"

"How many times do we have to go over this? He had boxes, he had guns, he had my clothes, he had a wad of money with a—"

Pink, it was pink. I sucked in a lungful of air.

"Oh, shit." And then we were both quiet.

"You remembered something?" Gary said finally.

"The Freak had this wad of money. And it had a pink band around it, then when I was at my mom's the other day, she had the same kind of hair bands in her drawer, the same color, pink, in the bathroom, I used one in my hair. But my aunt—"

"Did you keep it?"

"Yes, but I told you—"

"We're going to need it for comparison."

I *had* to tell him about the stupid pink band. I wanted to be sick.

From a long way off I heard Gary say, "Is there anything else you can think of?"

"My mom's stepbrother, maybe he's involved somehow. I could try to talk to Wayne, find out if he knows anything. Mom might have told him why she hates—"

"That's the last thing I want you to do. Remember, we're not yet positive your mother's involved, and I hope for your sake she's not, but if she is, you could really damage the investigation. In fact, don't say *anything* to *anybody*, okay?" When I didn't answer right away, he said in his cop voice, "I'm serious."

"What are you going to do now?"

"We should have the warrant by the morning, but it will take a few days for the bank to actually get the records to us. Meanwhile, we gather as much evidence as we can. If we bring your mother in for questioning too soon there's always a chance she could destroy evidence or run."

"There's nothing to question her *about*—she didn't do anything."

He softened his voice and said, "Look, I know how confusing this must be, but I promise I'll call when we have anything more conclusive. Until then try to stay away from everybody. And I'm *really* sorry, Annie."

I put the phone back in the cradle, but it rang as I walked away. Thinking it was Gary again, I picked it up without looking at the call display.

"Thank *God*, I was *so* worried about you, Annie Bear. I left you a message *hours* ago and after what just happened recently—" Mom paused for breath and I tried to say something but my throat clamped shut.

"Are you there? Annie?"

"Sorry I didn't get back to you sooner."

I wanted to warn her that Gary was coming for her, but what could I say? Gary thinks you're involved in my abduction but I think it was your sister? No, Gary was probably wrong about the whole damn thing and it would fuck Mom right up. I had to keep my mouth shut. I clenched the phone till it hurt and, with my back against the wall, slid to the floor. Emma came out of hiding and pushed her face into my chest.

"So do the police have any more information on that terrible man?" Mom said.

Oh, yeah, they have a lot more information. More than I ever wanted to know.

"No new leads—the investigation seems to have dried up. You know what the cops around here are like, they couldn't find their own assholes if their life depended on it." I slumped to my side on the floor. My breath blew dog hair into tumbleweeds.

"It's probably for the best. You need to just concentrate on getting better. Maybe you should take a little holiday."

I squeezed my eyelids tight against the hot tears building there and bit my tongue, hard.

"That's a great idea. You know, I think I might take off and go camping with Emma for a few days."

"See, your mother knows what's best, but don't forget to check in and let us know you're okay. We worry about you, Annie Bear."

After I hung up the phone I looked around my house, and all I could see was dirt. I rearranged my books alphabetically and washed my walls with bleach and water. The rest of the night I scrubbed the floors on my hands and knees. Not one inch of my house was spared. While my body worked on cleaning, my mind worked to explain it all away.

Just because someone hired The Freak in the past didn't mean my situation wasn't random—maybe it was just a friend of his that stopped by the motel. Being in prison at the same time as my uncle didn't necessarily mean anything. A lot of prisoners were in there and they might never have even met. And if they did, that's probably how The Freak got this weird obsession about me—he saw all the pictures of my family. Aunt Val might not have mentioned Tamara's suspension because she was waiting for the council's final decision, then I disappeared and that overshadowed everything. Good thing they were looking into Mom's records, because when they didn't find anything they could concentrate on finding The Freak's real partner—if he even had one. It was going to be okay.

It wasn't until seven the next morning, when I finally stopped, that I realized I'd scrubbed my knuckles raw and hadn't eaten in more than a day. I managed to get down some tea and dry toast.

When Gary called later that afternoon to tell me he was coming by to pick up the elastic hair band and the photo I took from the cabin, I filled him in on my conversation with Mom, including my so-called camping trip. I explained I'd have to call her at least once or she might start wondering, and he said it was okay but to keep the calls brief.

He also suggested I tell Christina and Luke the same story so no one inadvertently screwed things up, and he wanted me to go stay in a motel, but I refused—this shit was bad enough without having to actually leave my home. We agreed I'd hide my car in the backyard and keep a low profile. Luke and Christina had been phoning every day since the second abduction attempt, and Christina offered in an I'm-trying-so-hard-not-to-be-pushy way for me to crash at her place for a while and accepted my "No, thanks" with a big pause, a deep breath, then an "Okay, whatever works for you." But I knew it was killing her and they'd worry if I just didn't answer, so I e-mailed them both that I needed to get out of town for a couple of days and hadn't phoned because I didn't want to talk to anyone right now—"Sorry, I'm just going through a rough patch."

No kidding.

For the last few days I've been hiding out in my house and using candlelight at night. The closet hasn't been an issue, because I haven't been sleeping. I haven't even gone for a walk—most of the time I cuddle with Emma and cry into her fur.

Once I got in my car, revved it up a few times, called my mom from my cell phone, and made a bunch of static noise. I told her I was okay but I was driving and my phone was cutting out so I couldn't talk. Least that part wasn't a lie—I was barely able to say hello without choking from the effort of keeping everything inside.

When I checked my e-mail, Christina had written that she hoped the time away helped and that I felt better when I came back. "I'll miss you," she wrote. She signed the message with xxx's, ooo's, and a little smiley face icon.

The next day I spotted her car heading down my driveway and wrapped my hand around Emma's muzzle before she could bark. Christina walked around outside for a couple of minutes, then drove away. When I looked out I realized she'd picked up all the newspapers that were cluttering the doorstep. I felt like such a jerk.

Gary called to tell me things were progressing and he appreciated my cooperation. I wondered if he was excited about closing in on the "bad guy." He's a cop for a reason.

I didn't tell him I was still planning on coming to my shrink appointment today—he would have just told me not to—and I was glad I hadn't canceled when he called around eight this morning to tell me they finally located the other maid at the hotel. And yes, she did remember the woman wearing sunglasses—the car was so big and the woman was so small, she had to struggle to push the car door open.

"I know what you're thinking, Gary, but there must be . . . Shit, just give me a minute here."

"I'm really sorry, Annie, but all the evidence is pointing to your mom. We're just waiting for her bank records before we bring her in for questioning. Meanwhile, we—"

"But you don't know for sure it was her at the hotel. So it was a small woman, that doesn't mean—"

"It was a small *blond* woman, Annie. The maid never got a license plate, but the car was bronze-colored, just like your stepfather's, and she identified a photo of your mother."

My blood roared in my ears.

"But I *told* you, my aunt looks like her and she drives a Lincoln, it's the same color as the Caddie. Maybe she's working with her stepbrother and that's who tried to grab me. He could be blackmailing her—fuck, I don't know. But he's still out there and if you just talk to Wayne, he'll tell you Mom had nothing to do with this."

"When we're ready, we'll bring Wayne in."

"When you're *ready*? What the hell are you waiting for, me to go missing again?"

"Annie, I understand you're frustrated—"

"I'm not fucking *frustrated*, I'm furious. You guys are totally off track. If you're not going to do anything, then I'm going to talk to Wayne and—"

"Get yourself hurt? That would really help, wouldn't it?"

"Wayne's not going to do anything to me, he's an idiot but he doesn't have a violent cell in his body. Wire me if you're so worried."

"This isn't a *Law and Order* episode, Annie, we don't wire civilians, and you're not trained for this—say one wrong thing and you screw up the case you're so anxious to solve."

"Please, Gary, for a whole year I couldn't do one damn thing up there to help myself. *I need to be a part of this.* I know Wayne. If Mom told him anything about her stepbrother, I can get it out of him."

"Sorry, not negotiable. You're just going to have to be patient. I have to head to court now, I'll call you later."

"Okay, *okay.*"

I glanced at my clock. Eight-fifteen A.M. In two hours Wayne would be sitting down alone at the diner he goes to every morning when he doesn't have a job, which is most mornings—Mom never goes because she's usually sleeping off her hangover. Yeah, sure, I'd be patient, for about an hour and forty-five minutes.

Most of the morning rush at the diner had cleared out, but the scent of bacon grease still hung in the air as I slid into a booth right in front of the window.

A waitress came over with a notepad and pencil. The pencil had teeth marks in it and her nails were chewed to the quick. Like mine. I wondered what made her nervous.

"What can I get you?"

"Just a coffee for now."

"Oh, I know you—you're Wayne's daughter, Annie, aren't you? How you doing, sweetie?"

The tape recorder burned in my pocket. What the hell was I doing here? What if Gary was right and I screwed everything up?

"I'm fine, thanks."

"Wayne should be in any minute. I'll tell him you're here, okay, hon?"

"That'd be great."

She brought the coffee, and no sooner had she left my table than I heard the door jingle. I couldn't see over the booth unless I stood up or peeked around the side, but I didn't need to do either.

"How's the best-looking waitress in town, Janie?"

"Just fine, handsome. Guess who beat you here."

My stepfather came around the corner of the booth.

"Holy crap, Annie—what are you doing here? Your mom said something about you going on a holiday."

The waitress came back with another coffee. Wayne sat down across from me.

I said, "I had to go talk to the cops again. That's why I came back early."

He nodded and stirred his coffee.

"They have some more information about the guy who abducted me." He lifted the spoon mid-stir.

"Yeah? What's that?"

"Maybe we should get some air," I said. "It's hot as hell in here—why don't we get coffees to go, then we can sit in the park?"

"I don't know, your mom's going to be up soon and I was supposed to bring her a pack of smokes."

"We don't have to be all day, I just don't want to go home yet. Got your cards with you?"

"You want to play?"

"Sure, but let's go to the park. I need to get out of here, smells like someone burned some toast."

I paid our tab, Janie got us a couple of fresh coffees to go, and we headed across the street to the park. I found us a picnic table in the shade, away from the other ones. Wayne shuffled the deck. I tried to remember our ever doing anything else together, alone.

"To be honest, Wayne, it wasn't an accident I ran into you." He paused with the deck in hand, about to deal. "I wanted to talk to you."

"Yeah?"

I kicked Gary out of my head and plunged. "The cops think Mom had something to do with me being abducted. Someone saw a car like your Caddy at a hotel where that guy was staying, but I think—"

"Lots of people have cars like mine."

"I know, but apparently the maid's description—"

"The cops have it wrong."

I stared at him. He stared at the cards.

"Look at me, Wayne."

"Thought you wanted to play—"

"Just look at me." He raised his head slowly and met my eyes.

"Do you know something?"

He shook his head.

"Wayne, they have a *warrant*, they're getting Mom's bank records."

His face paled.

My voice was calm but my ears were roaring again.

"Does Mom have something to do with this?"

For about five seconds he tried to keep eye contact. Then he put his head in his hands, and I saw them shaking.

"Wayne. You have to tell me what's going on."

"It's all fucked up, so fucked up." He was mumbling. "Shit, what a mess. . . ."

"WAYNE!"

Head still in his hands, he shook it back and forth.

"You tell me now, Wayne, or I call the cops and you tell them."

"I'm sorry, I'm so sorry, we didn't know he liked to hurt girls—I *swear*." He looked up at me with desperate eyes. "I would have stopped her anyway, I would have, but I didn't know."

"Know *what*?"

"You know, that your mom was going to have that guy . . . take you."

No, no, no, no.

Across the park a young mother pushed her toddler on a swing set. The little girl was squealing and giggling. The sound was muffled by the roaring in my ears. Wayne's lips were moving up and down, but all I caught were broken words, fragments of sentences. I tried to focus on what he was saying, but I couldn't stop thinking about the little wheels on the tape recorder going around and around.

He stared at my face. "Shit, Annie, you look like . . . I don't know."

I stared back at him, shaking my head slowly. "You guys. It *was* you guys. . . ."

He leaned in and started talking fast. "You've got to hear my side, Annie. It got all fucked up. But I didn't know, I *swear* I didn't know. When you first got taken, your mom seemed kind of calm about it all, you know? Wasn't like her, I thought she'd be going ape-shit. But after you'd been gone over a week she started pacing at night and going through booze like shit through a goose. The second week she went to see your uncle like three times, so I came right out and said, 'What kind of trouble you in, Lorraine?' All she keeps saying is, 'It's not my fault.' " He swallowed a couple of times and cleared his throat.

"*What* wasn't her fault? You still haven't told me exactly what it is she did!"

"You were just supposed to disappear for like a week or something, but it didn't go right."

It didn't go right. That's all, it just didn't go right. I didn't know whether to laugh or scream.

"No shit. Why the hell was I supposed to be abducted in the first place? Was The Freak blackmailing Dwight or something? Or was Dwight threatening Mom? Has she always visited him? What the fuck *happened*, Wayne?"

"I don't know what the deal is with Dwight—she gets all weird when I ask about him. But no, she saw a movie about some girl who got kidnapped for two days, and after the movie they did one of those interview things with the real family . . . you know, she gets these ideas and she's on them like a pit bull on a steak."

I connected the dots. "Mom got the idea to have me abducted from a *movie*?"

"Lorraine, she said you were way prettier, and if you were gone a whole week it would be worth more."

It took a moment for Wayne's words to sink in. "Worth more—are you fucking telling me she did this for *money*?"

"It started when she heard you might not get that project. Val was going to roast her over the coals when she found out—you know those two—but if you were famous? Val would have to eat shit for the rest of her life."

"And you had no idea what she was up to?"

"Shit, no! I swear I didn't know anything. She said your uncle knew a guy from jail who could do it, also he knew the loan shark who lent her the thirty-five grand—I didn't know nothing about that, either."

"*Thirty-five fucking grand?* That's how much it cost to ruin my life. Some goddamn family I have."

"Your mom didn't mean for you to get hurt. The man, he never called her when he was supposed to—that's why she was so upset after the first week. Your uncle put feelers out, but no one knew where the guy had taken you."

"But why didn't she call the cops when I didn't come home? Why didn't *you*? You guys just left me there. . . ." My voice broke.

"As soon as I found out what went down, I told her we should tell the cops right away, but the guy she borrowed money from said the cops would come looking for him if she opened her mouth, then he'd slash her face and break my legs. He said he could have Dwight killed in prison. We told him we'd say we paid with our own dough, but he still wanted his money back—he was never going to get it if your mom and I were in the slammer. And if we did go to jail, he said he'd just get us in there."

I realized this was probably the longest conversation I'd ever had with my stepdad, our first heart-to-heart, and we were talking about my mom having me kidnapped and raped.

"Weren't you worried that I was being *hurt*? That I might be *killed*?"

His face looked miserable. "Every damn day, but there was nothing I could do. If I tried to help you, Lorraine was going to get hurt. When you were missing she was buying time with the loan shark with the money she got from selling your stuff and trying to get someone to make a movie, but nothing was coming through. We were just about dry when you came home."

He took a deep breath. "After I saw you in the hospital I was messed right up, but Lorraine said we had to just move on and be strong for you. And we still had the loan shark breathing down our necks. Lorraine told him she'd get some money when you sold your story, but you kept shutting her down. She was trying like hell to make sure the media still gave a shit." I flashed to all the times the reporters seemed to know exactly where I was and how right from the beginning they knew inside information.

"Any money they gave us went on our debt. But a month or so ago the guy said we had to pay in full or he was coming for us."

"Wait a minute, the man who tried to grab me off the street. Was that the loan shark or Dwight?"

Wayne stared down at his feet.

"Did you guys hire someone to fucking abduct me *again*?"

"No." His voice was so low I could barely hear him. "It was me."

"*You*? Jesus Christ, Wayne, you scared the *shit* out of me, you *hurt* me."

He turned to face me and started talking fast. "I know, I know, I'm sorry. I didn't *want* to. You weren't supposed to fall—I didn't know you'd fight that hard. Your mom, she said the media was losing interest. We didn't have any other options, we were fucked, Annie."

"*You* were fucked? No, Wayne, *fucked* is being raped almost every night. Fucked is having to struggle and cry and *scream* because it got him off faster. Fucked is having to pee on a schedule. Do you know what he did when he caught me sneaking a pee? He forced me to drink water from the toilet bowl. From the *toilet bowl*, Wayne. People don't even let their dogs do that. *That's* fucked."

Tears in his eyes, Wayne just kept nodding.

"My daughter *died*, Wayne." I reached over, took one of his hands in mine, and flipped it over. "Her head wasn't even bigger than the palm of your hand, and she's *dead*. And you're telling me my *family* did this to me? You're the ones I'm supposed to be able to trust the most, and you—"

Then I heard myself, and it all hit.

Doubled over, I hugged my legs as an enormous pressure bore down on my chest and my head felt like it was being squeezed in a vise. I sucked in big gulps of air while Wayne patted my back and said over and over again how sorry he was. He sounded like he was crying. The edges of my vision darkened. I felt my body slide forward.

Wayne threw his arm around me and held me in place. "Oh, shit, Annie, don't pass out on me."

After a few minutes I got my breathing under control, but I still felt shaky and cold all over. I brought my head up and shrugged Wayne's arm off. I took another deep breath, then got to my feet and paced in front of the bench, hugging myself.

"Did you guys break into my house, too?"

"Yeah, your mom was going to come in right behind me and save you, but I got to your bedroom and you weren't there, the alarm was going off, and I bailed out the window. Then when your mom stayed the night at your house, you told her when you ran in the mornings. . . ." The night my mom brought me Annie Bear cookies and my photos. I sat back down.

For the longest time we just sat there looking at each other, not saying anything, understanding everything. At least I was. Finally I broke the silence.

"You know you're going to have to turn yourself in, right?"

"I figured."

We stared out at the playground. No children were in sight. The sun had disappeared behind a cloud and it was cool in the shade. A slight breeze moved the swings back and forth. The air was filled with the rhythmic squeaking of their chains and the scent of a storm coming.

"I really love your mom, you know?"

"I know."

He took a deep breath, then put the deck of cards back in their box. I wanted to stop him, wanted to say, *Let's just play one last game.* But it was too late. It was too late for everything.

"I'll walk into the station with you."

Gary had just gotten in from court and looked pissed off when he saw me with Wayne, but as soon as Wayne told him he wanted to make a confession, Gary pointed to me and said, "Don't go anywhere," then whisked Wayne away.

I spent the next couple of hours wandering around the station, flipping through magazines and staring at the walls—counting cracks, counting stains. The betrayal by my family had hurt more than anything The Freak ever did to me, and in a place he'd never been able to touch. I was running from that pain as fast as I could.

Finally Gary came out.

"You shouldn't have talked to him, Annie. If that had backfired—"

I handed him the tape. "But it didn't."

"We can't use this—"

"You don't need to, do you?" I said. No way was I apologizing.

He shook his head, then told me that Wayne, after speaking with a legal aide, had decided to give a full statement and testify against my mom in exchange for a lighter sentence. He was under arrest, charged with accessory to kidnapping, extortion, and criminal negligence. They'd be holding him until his bail hearing.

Gary said the bank records should come in later this afternoon or in the morning. They didn't actually need them to arrest Mom now, but he wanted to verify Wayne's statements before they interviewed her. They were also waiting to hear from the lab about the elastic hair bands but might not get that report until the morning. They didn't consider Mom a flight risk—she didn't even have a car—and she wasn't a threat to society, so unless something changed they'd pick her up in the morning.

They had Wayne call Mom and tell her he was going to check out a hot lead on a business for sale up-island. If it got too late to drive home he was just going to crash at a buddy's place. Then he mentioned running into me, in case somebody told her, and added that I was back in town but tired from driving and was heading home to get some rest. She bought it.

Afterward, Gary walked me out to my car.

He said, "Are you okay? It had to be hard to hear all that."

"I don't know what I am. It's all just . . . I don't know." I shook my head. "Have you ever heard of a mother doing something like this?"

"People do terrible things to people they love all the time. Just about every crime you can think of has been done at least once."

"Somehow I don't feel better."

"I'll try to call you as soon as we pick her up. Want to watch the interview?"

"God, I don't know if I'm up for that."

"I know she's your mom, and it must be really hard to understand what she's done, but I need you to be tough here. You can't talk to her until we do, okay?"

"I guess."

"I'm serious, Annie. I want you to go straight home. I shouldn't even be telling you everything I just did, but I didn't like keeping you in the dark before. You might be tempted to warn your mom, but I trust you to do the right thing. Don't prove me wrong. Just remember what she did to you."

Like I needed a reminder.

Well, I obeyed part of Gary's request—I did drive straight somewhere, but to your office, not home. I didn't even care if anyone saw me. Against all reason, I just keep hoping that somehow it's all a huge mistake.

SESSION TWENTY-FIVE

You've probably seen the papers—I'm hot news again. All the way home after our last session I kept thinking about Mom. She could be a right bitch at times, she's generally selfish, and sure she lives in the land of it's-all-about-me, but capable of something like *this*?

When I got home that night I had a message from Luke on my voice mail. Of course he's too nice to outright say, "Where the hell are you?" Instead it was something about letting him know when I'm home. I didn't call back—didn't know what to say.

That night in my closet, I thought about Mom—Gary hadn't called yet—and I imagined her sitting at home in front of the TV, smoking and drinking, with no idea the shit's hit the fan and she's standing downhill. As hurt and betrayed as I felt, I still hated knowing she had no clue what was going to happen.

Then I remembered her phoning me the day of the open house. She'd made me feel guilty about a *cappuccino* machine, knowing an ex-con was going to abduct me a few hours later. Not to mention how she'd taken care of me after the second abduction attempt—I felt *loved*, and she'd set the whole damn thing up. Right then I knew I had to watch the interview. Had to hear for myself why my mother did this to me.

Around ten the next day I got the call from Gary. They'd received all my mom's bank records early that morning, which matched up with Wayne's statement, and they'd confirmed the pink elastic bands were of the same dye lot. She'd been arrested—that must have sent the trailer park into a tizzy— and now they were letting her brew at the station until I got there. It didn't take me long, even though I wanted to turn around the whole way.

I hadn't realized I was shaking until I got to the cop shop and Gary offered me his coat. It was still warm and smelled like him. I wished I could cloak myself in it and disappear. In a small room off the one where they had my mom, I stared at her through a window I assumed was a mirror on the other side. A couple of cops were there with me, and when I made eye contact with one of them, he looked down at his shoes.

Mom was perched on the edge of the chair with her hands tucked under her thighs, her feet not quite touching the floor. Her makeup was faded and smeared, probably left over from yesterday, and her ponytail was crooked. Then I saw it. One eyelid drooped slightly lower than the other. She wasn't totally wasted but she'd definitely had some vodka with her orange juice that morning. Gary came in the room and stood beside me.

"You holding up okay?" He rested his hand on my shoulder. The weight of it felt solid and warm.

"What's the point of this? You have all the evidence."

"There's never enough evidence. I've seen a lot of cases we thought were a slam dunk go sideways down the road. It would be better if we can get her to admit some involvement."

"Who's going to interview her?"

"Me." His eyes glittered. If he were a horse, he'd have been chomping at the bit.

Mom brightened right up when Gary walked into the room. My stomach churned.

He started off by telling her she was being audio- and video-taped, which got a smile for the camera, and then he asked her to say her name, address, and the date out loud. He had to tell her the date.

Once all that was out of the way, he said, "The officers who brought you in today read you your Charter of Rights and warning, but I want to state again that you're entitled to legal counsel before you talk to us. You don't have to say anything to me, but anything you do say can be used in court."

Mom shook her head. "This is so silly—who am I supposed to have kidnapped?"

Gary raised an eyebrow. "Your daughter."

"Annie wasn't *kidnapped*. A man took her."

Apparently deciding that explaining the legal definition of kidnapping to her was pointless, and I had to agree with him there, Gary moved on.

"We have a signed statement from Wayne setting out exactly what transpired and both your parts in it." He opened a file on the table, laid out a statement, then pointed to an item on it. "We also have your Visa bill, which proves you rented a van from out of town the day before Annie was attacked. We have the invoice from the rental company for the *white* van with *your* signature. We have an eyewitness who can place you and Simon Rousseau at a motel in Eagle Glen. We've confirmed that an elastic hair band found amongst Simon Rousseau's belongings matches hair bands currently in your possession. We know you did it."

Mom's eyes were enormous as she tensed in her chair, but a second later she relaxed her body and rearranged her skirt hem. She then turned her attention to a fingernail.

With both hands on the table, Gary leaned forward.

"See, my superiors—they think you didn't just want Annie gone for a week. That's what you told Wayne, but they think you hired Simon Rousseau to kill her—Annie had a life insurance policy with her company, which I'm sure you knew you were the sole beneficiary of. Your plan went wrong, all right—Annie was never supposed to come home alive."

With every sentence Mom's body flinched and her eyes grew bigger. She began to stammer, "No . . . no . . . of course not . . . *kill* her? *No* . . . I'd never in a million years . . ."

"I don't think you understand me, Lorraine. They don't just *think* you hired Simon Rousseau to kill her, they *want* you to have hired him to kill her, because that will make a big difference in time served."

I watched Mom's face as she licked her lips a couple of times. To Gary it would look like nerves, but I knew my mom, and licking her lips was a sure sign she was trying to get her vodka-addled mind to focus.

"They want me to have done it?"

"A lot of time and a lot of money, *taxpayers'* money, went into this case. My superiors, well, they're none too happy about that. And the public? The public who spent their weekends searching the woods and putting up flyers while you knew what had happened to Annie the whole time? Well, they're crying out for blood. So they don't just want someone to pay for this, they *need* someone to pay for this."

"Well, it's good they want someone to pay. The person who did this *should* pay." Her eyes moistened. "When I think about what Annie went through . . ."

His voice gentle, Gary said, "Look, Lorraine, I'm on your side here. I'm trying to help you get out of this mess. They don't just want to convict you, Lorraine—they want to nail you to the wall. So unless you give me something to work with, you're going to go down for hiring someone to kill your own daughter, and I won't be able to stop it."

Both eyes drooped as she watched him warily. Not ready to walk into the trap and nibble the cheese, but sniffing the air. I watched the two of them—horrified, fascinated, yet somehow removed, as though this were someone else's mother, some other cop.

"I was in that hospital with you, Lorraine—I saw how hard it was on you. I know you really love your daughter—you'd do anything for her." She began to kick her feet in the air beneath the table. "But Annie, she can be pretty stubborn, I know, and no matter how good your advice is, she doesn't listen, does she?" Not sure I liked where he was going with this.

"No one listens to you, do they? Not your daughter, not Wayne. It can't be easy watching him blow chance after chance, nothing ever coming through for you."

"That man couldn't find his way out of a paper bag unless I was standing over him." With a toss of her ponytail, she shifted gears. "Some men just need an extra push to realize their potential."

Gary gave her a sad smile. "But you shouldn't have had to push him, Lorraine. If he'd been a better husband, a better provider, well, you wouldn't have had to do any of this, would you?" She started to shake her head in agreement but caught herself and became very still.

"And we both know Wayne should've straightened things out with the loan shark so you could save Annie. But he didn't, did he? Nope, he left it to you to try to fix. And now he's putting it *all* on you."

He leaned toward her until their noses were almost touching. She sucked on her lip like she was trying to get the last traces of alcohol out of it. She wanted to say it, wanted to tell him—she just needed a little push.

In a voice dripping sympathy, Gary said, "Wayne let you down, no doubt about it, but *we* can help you, Lorraine. *We* can make sure you're safe. It's not your fault things got so out of hand." And with that little nudge she tumbled over the edge, her face flushed and her eyes feverish.

"He was just supposed to keep her for a week. He told me the cabin was nice, he spent over a month getting it ready for her, but he wouldn't tell me where it was because he said I'd be more believable if I truly didn't know where to find her. He had a drug that would make her calm so she wouldn't be scared or anything—she'd mostly just sleep—and it was totally safe. At the end of the week he was going to leave her in the trunk of a car on a street, then phone and tell me where it was so I could make an anonymous call to the cops. But he *didn't call*, and the cell number he gave me didn't work anymore. And I couldn't do anything to save her. The loan shark said he'd cut my *face*." Her eyes wide, she touched both hands to her cheeks. "I sent Wayne to talk to him and he screwed it up so bad we owed *more*."

"Did you give this to Simon?" Gary slid the photo of me I'd found at the cabin across the table.

"It was the only decent photo I could find—she's always frowning in the pictures I take."

"So you thought it was important he find Annie attractive?"

"He'd seen photos of her in Dwight's cell from when she was young, he wanted to see how she'd grown up."

Gary, who had been taking a sip of coffee, choked and broke into a coughing fit. He took a few deep breaths and cleared his throat, but before he could say anything Mom launched into her closing argument.

"So, you see, it's *not* my fault—if he'd kept to *my* plan, she'd have been fine. But now that I've told you everything you can talk to your bosses for me and straighten it all out." She smiled prettily and reached over the table, placing her hand over his. "You always struck me as the kind of man who knew how to take care of a woman. I'd like to make you a nice dinner, show you my appreciation . . . ?" She tilted her head and gave him another smile.

Gary sipped the coffee for at least a minute, then set the cup down and drew his other hand out from beneath Mom's.

"Lorraine, you're under arrest. You won't be going anywhere for a very long time." She actually looked surprised. Then confused. Then hurt.

"But I thought you understood."

Gary straightened up. "I do understand, Lorraine. I understand that you committed a crime, you broke the law, several of them in fact, and did nothing to rectify the situation. I understand that you turned a *killer* loose on your *daughter*. I understand that the killer impregnated her, then killed her baby girl. That she was terrified, alone, beaten, raped, and brutalized—never knowing from one day to the next whether it was her last. Never knowing *why* this was happening to her. Now I can finally give her an answer, but I wish to hell it wasn't this one."

When Gary began to walk out of the room, she stood up and grabbed his arm as he tried to brush past her. Tears shimmering in her blue eyes, she pressed her breasts against his arm.

"But I didn't *know* he was a killer, I never wanted her hurt— I'm a good mother, don't you understand?" Her voice cracked on the last word.

Gary took her by the shoulders, gently moved her away from him, and continued toward the door.

"This isn't fair!"

At the door he turned and said, "What isn't fair is that Annie ended up with you for a mother."

He came into our little room and stood beside me. In silence, we watched Mom through the mirror. For a few moments after he left, her face was stamped with outrage, but her eyelids lifted as the last of her liquid courage left her and Gary's final words sank in. She paled and put both her hands over her mouth. No fake wails now. Her body began to jerk and shake violently as she sobbed. Her eyes cast wildly around the empty room. She stumbled backward and sat down hard on the chair, staring at the door, still sobbing.

"Do you want to go in and talk to her?" Gary said.

"I can't right now." I was shaking.

When I asked him what was going to happen next, he said Mom and Wayne would be held until the arraignment, then bail would be set. I hadn't even thought about the fact that there might be a trial. Surely Mom will take a plea bargain.

Even though I know I shouldn't care about what happens to her, I still wondered whether she'd get a lawyer and how they'd be able to afford one.

"What about the loan shark? Are they in danger?"

"We're going to be looking into that right away. But we'll make sure they're safe."

Neither of us said a word as Gary walked me out to his car—I sure didn't know the appropriate thing to say. *Thanks for arresting my mother and interrogating her so skillfully—you really know how to screw with her?*

As I turned to get into my car, he said, "I have something for you," then handed me a pack of playing cards. "Wayne had them in his pocket when we arrested him and he asked me to give them to you. He wanted you to know how sorry he is." He paused and looked at me intently. "I'm sorry too, Annie."

"You don't have to be sorry—it's your job, and you're really good at it." I knew I sounded bitter, and he looked miserable. "It would be even worse if she'd gotten away with it," I said, even though at that moment I had no idea whether it was true or not.

I needed to know that he was more than this man I had watched take down my mother.

"Tell me something no one knows about you."

"What?"

"Just tell me something—*anything*." We held eyes.

"Okay," he said finally. "Sometimes when I can't sleep, I get up and eat peanut butter straight out of the jar with a spoon."

"Peanut butter, huh? I'll have to try that someday."

"You should—it helps."

We looked at each other a moment longer, then I got in my car and drove away. In my rearview mirror I saw him watching me until a couple of cops came up to him, clapped him on the back, and shook his hand. Guess there was some celebrating at the cop shop that day. When I glanced over I saw the pack of cards on the passenger seat and realized I was still wearing Gary's coat.

The papers got wind of things faster than my mom can pour a drink, and my phone's been ringing off the hook. I busted a reporter sneaking up to my window yesterday—Emma chased him away. I'm not just that girl who went missing, now I'm the girl whose mother had her abducted. I don't know if I can handle all this shit again.

Yesterday I called Luke because I wanted to tell him what was up before he read about it. He was at home and for a second I thought I heard a girl's voice in the background, but it may have just been the TV.

I told him what Mom had done and that she'd been arrested.

At first he was horrified, kept asking if I was sure, but when I repeated her side of the story he just said, "Wow, she must be feeling pretty bad—sounds like it got totally out of control on her."

He felt sorry for *her*? *What* about some righteous indignation on my behalf? I wanted to tell him off. But it just didn't matter anymore.

After I hung up the phone I stared at a picture of us on my mantel. We looked so happy.

The next day I called Christina and told her. She inhaled sharply, then said, "Oh my *God*, Annie. Are you okay? No, how could you be? I'm coming right over. I'll bring a bottle of wine, is that enough? No, we need a case. Your *mom*? *Your* own *mother* did this?"

"Yeah, I'm still trying to wrap my head around it myself. Can we hold off on the wine? I just need . . . I just need a little time."

She paused, then said, "For sure, yes, of course, you call if you need me, though, okay? I'll drop everything and come right over."

"I will, and thanks."

I didn't tell Christina or Luke that I didn't really leave town, nor am I going to, and I'm sure not going to tell Christina my mom tried to incriminate her. For the last couple of days all I can hear is this constant keening sound in my mind. And I can't seem to stop crying.

SESSION TWENTY-SIX

Sorry I missed our last session, but I saw my mother and I needed some time to pick myself back up off the floor. You know, it's funny, but the night after I saw her I really wanted to sleep in the closet. I stood outside it for the longest time with my pillow in hand, but I knew opening that door would be going backward, so I lay back down on my bed and conjured up your office in my mind. I told myself I was resting on your couch and you were watching over me. That's how I fell asleep.

They brought Mom back into the same interrogation room and her eyes met mine briefly, then slid away as she sat down across from me. The sleeves and cuffs on the gray baggy coveralls she was wearing were rolled up and the color turned her skin to ash—it's been years since I've seen my mom with a bare face. Both corners of her mouth were drawn down, and without her bubble-gum-pink lip balm her lips were so pale they blended in with her skin.

My heart tap-danced in my chest while my mind wrestled with what to say—*Umm, gee, Mom, what's with having me abducted?*—and whether I wanted to hear her answer. But before I could ask anything she said, "What's Val been saying?"

Caught off guard I said, "She left a message but I haven't—"

"You can't tell her *anything.*"

"Excuse me?"

"Not until we figure out what we're going to do."

"*We?* You're on your own with this one, Mom. I'm just here so you can explain why you did this to me."

"Gary said you were told everything. You *have* to help, Annie, you're my only chance to—"

"Why the hell would I help *you*? You *paid* someone to abduct me, to *hurt* me, and then you—"

"NO! I didn't want you hurt—it just . . . everything, it went wrong, it's *all* wrong, and now . . ." She put her head in her hands.

"And now my life's fucked and you're in jail. Way to go, Mom."

She brought her head up and looked around the room with frantic eyes. "This isn't right, Annie. I can't be in here, I'll *die.*" She leaned across the table and gripped my hand. "But if you talk to the police, you can tell them you won't press charges, or explain that you understand why I had to—"

"I *don't* understand, Mom." I pulled my hand away.

"I didn't have any other choice—you were always coming in *second.*"

"It was *my* fault?"

"You saw how Val treated me. How she looked down at us."

"And I saw how you treated her, but she didn't have her daughter abducted, did she?"

Eyes filling with tears, she said, "You have no idea, Annie. *No* idea what I've been through—" She broke off.

"It has something to do with Dwight, doesn't it?"

Silence.

"If you don't tell me, I'm just going to ask Aunt Val."

Mom leaned on the table. "You CAN'T DO THAT TO ME, she'll just use it to—"

The door opened and a cop stuck his head in. "Everything okay in here?"

I said, "We're good." Mom nodded and the cop closed the door.

"You do realize the media is probably already talking to Aunt Val."

Mom's shoulders tensed.

"Reporters will want every detail about you, what you were like as a kid, what happened in your childhood to make you such a crappy mother."

"I'm a *great* mother, nothing like mine. And Val will never talk about our childhood. She doesn't want anyone in her perfect world finding out what she did." Her voice turned thoughtful. "She'd hate that. . . ." One fingernail started to tap.

My stomach filled with dread. "Mom, don't make this any worse than—"

She leaned across the table. "She was our father's favorite, you know, but she was our stepfather's *most* favorite." She gave a bitter smile. "When my mother realized her husband was sleeping with one of her daughters, Val told her it was me. Next thing you know, my stuff is on the front lawn and our stepfather left town. If it hadn't been for Dwight I'd have been living in a box."

"Dwight?"

"When I got kicked out, I moved in with him. I was wait-ressing and he was laying brick when we came up with the idea for that bank." Her eyes glistened. "After he got caught I was barely getting by working two shifts a day. Then Val came over with a guy she'd met, talking about how great his parents' house was, how successful their jewelry store was. . . ."

"Dad."

We were both quiet for a moment.

"When Dwight was released, we were going to be to-gether, we just needed money. But he got caught again, so I told him I had to move on and I did, I married Wayne. " She shook her head. "It wasn't until you were going to get the proj-ect that I thought things might get better for me. But then I heard Christina was who you had to go up against. She was a much better Realtor." Her breath hissed out between her teeth. "If you lost, Val was going to lord it over me for the rest of my *life*."

"So you decided to ruin mine instead?"

"My plan would've *helped* you—you would've been set for life. But nothing worked out right. Wayne was useless but Dwight at least tried to do something."

"Did he rob that store for you?"

She nodded. "I gave that movie producer your number, but you were wasting time and I needed a payment for the loan shark. I don't know where Dwight is now."

"Don't you care at all about what you put me through?"

"I hate what that man did to you, but you were only sup-posed to be gone for a *week*, Annie. What happened after was an accident."

"How the hell can you say this was an accident? You hired a man who raped me, who caused the death of my child!"

"It was like when you wanted ice cream, you asked your dad to go to the store."

It took a moment for her words to register, even longer for me to find my voice.

"You're talking about the accident."

She nodded. "You didn't *mean* for them to die."

All the breath left my body as my chest constricted. The pain was so intense I wondered for a moment if I was having a heart attack, then I broke out in a cold sweat and started shaking. I searched her face, hoping I'd misunderstood, but she looked satisfied—*vindicated*.

My eyes filled with tears as I choked out, "You—you do blame *me* for their deaths. That's what this was all really about, you—"

"Of course not."

"You do. You *always* have." I was crying now. "That's why you thought it was okay to—"

"You're not listening, Annie. I know you just wanted ice cream—you didn't plan for getting it to kill them. And I never meant for anything bad to happen to you, I just wanted Val to stop lording it over me."

I was still reeling from that when she said, "But she won't be for long. A lawyer is coming to talk to me tomorrow." She stood up and started pacing in front of the table. I noticed the color was back in her cheeks. "I'll tell him what it was like to grow up with Val as a sister, what she did with our stepfather, what my life was like after I got kicked out, how she's always put me down—that's verbal *abuse*." She stopped abruptly and turned to face me. "I wonder if she'll come to court. Then she'd have to sit there and watch while my lawyer—"

"Mom, if you take this to trial it's going to wreck my

whole life again. I'm going to have to talk about what happened. I'm going to have to *describe* how he raped me."

She kept pacing. "That's it! We have to get her on the stand so she has to describe what she did."

"*MOM.*" She stopped and looked at me.

I said, "Don't do this to me."

"This isn't about you, Annie."

I opened my mouth to argue, then froze as her words hit home. She was right. In the end it didn't matter whether she'd done it for the money, to get attention, or to beat her sister once and for all. None of it was about me. It had *never* been about me. Not with her or with The Freak. I didn't even know which one was more dangerous.

As I stood up and walked toward the door she said, "Where are you going?"

"Home." I kept walking.

"Annie, *stop.*"

I spun around, braced for the tears, the I'm-so-sorry's, the don't-leave-me-here's.

She said, "Don't say anything to anybody before I get a chance. It has to be handled just right or—"

"Holy shit, you really don't get it, do you?"

She stared at me blankly.

I shook my head. "And you're never fucking going to."

"When you come back, bring me a newspaper so I can—"

"I'm not coming back, Mom."

Her eyes were huge. "But I need you, Annie Bear."

I rapped on the door and said, "Oh, I think you'll be just fine," as the waiting cop opened it. While he locked Mom back in, I stumbled to a bench against the opposite wall. After he was done, he asked me if I was okay and did I want him to get Gary. I said I just needed a couple of minutes, and he left me alone.

I counted blocks on the wall until my pulse settled down, then walked out of the station.

The papers found out about my visit to the jail, and the next day's headlines screamed speculations. Christina left a message for me to call her day or night if I needed to talk. She tried to hide it, but I could tell from her tone she was hurt I hadn't told her myself I'd gone to see Mom. Aunt Val also left a hesitant-sounding message, making me wonder how much she knew. But I didn't call either of them back, I didn't call *any* of the people who left if-you-need-to-talk messages back. What was there to talk *about*? It was over. Mom did it—the end.

A couple of days later I put the brochure for the art school on my night table. When I saw it the next morning I thought, *Fuck it, if I'm going to follow my dream I need money,* so I caved and called that movie chick. We had a good talk. I was right, she did seem to have some sensitivity and it sounded like she would respect my wishes. Even though she's Hollywood, she talks like a normal person.

There's a part of me that still doesn't want a movie, but I know one will get made, and if anyone is going to benefit from a movie about my life, it might as well be me. Plus, it's not really about me, just the Hollywood version of me—by the time it hits the screen it'll just be a movie. Not my life.

I agreed to meet with the movie chick and her boss in a week. They're talking some big numbers, big enough that I should be able to live comfortably for the rest of my life.

As soon as I got off the phone, I called Christina. I knew she'd think I was calling to talk about Mom, so when I told her I was finally going away to art school, I took her silence for surprise. But when the silence continued, I said, "Remember? The one in the Rockies I was always talking about in high school?"

"I remember. I just don't know why you're going now."

Her tone was casual but I felt the undercurrent of disapproval. Even back then she never really encouraged my going away to school, but I thought it was just because she'd miss me. I didn't know what the reason was this time, but I knew I didn't want to hear it.

"Because I want to," I said. "And I'd really like it if you listed my house for me."

"Your house? You're selling your house already? Are you sure you don't want to just rent it for—"

"I'm sure. And I want to spend the next couple of weeks fixing it up, but I'd like to get the paperwork out of the way soon, so when can you come over?"

She was silent for a bit, then said, "I could probably swing by on the weekend."

The next Saturday morning she came over. While we filled out the forms, I told her about the school, how I couldn't wait to go, how I was going to drive there the next day to check it out, how nice it was going to be to leave all this shit behind. She didn't say anything negative, but her responses were subdued.

Business out of the way, we sat side by side on my front porch steps in the morning sun. There was something else I wanted to talk about.

I said, "I think I know what you were really trying to tell me that night you came over to make me paint." Her eyes widened and a flush rose in her cheeks. "You can just let go of it. I'm not mad at you—or Luke. Shit happens."

"It was just once, I swear," she said in a flustered voice. "We'd been drinking, it didn't mean anything. We were both so upset about you, and nobody else understood what we were feeling. . . ."

"It's okay. Honest. We all did stuff through this that we regret, but I don't even want you to *regret* this one. Maybe it needed to happen or something. But it doesn't matter anymore."

"Are you *sure*, because I feel so—"

"I'm over it, really. Now will you get over it, please?" I bumped her shoulder with mine and made a silly face. She made one back, then we lapsed into silence as we watched a young couple with a stroller pass the end of my driveway.

"I heard your mom has been telling people I was trying to beat you out of the project before you were abducted," she said after a while.

"Yeah, she said your assistant told a friend of hers or something that you were my competition all along, but I know it was probably just another of her lies."

"Actually, she got part of it right. They did ask me to put together a proposal for them and we met a couple of times. I knew they were talking to someone from another company, but I didn't know you were also going out for it until you mentioned it one day. I pulled out of the running right away and they didn't contact me again until after you were missing."

"You pulled out? Why?"

"There's business, and then there's good business. Your friendship was more important to me."

"I wish you'd told me, I'd have dropped out myself and let you go for it. You had way more experience and you'd waited longer for a deal like that."

Christina said, "That's why I didn't tell you—I knew we'd end up fighting over who was going to give it up!"

We broke out laughing, but then Christina grew quiet again as she surveyed my yard.

"This is such a great place." Shit, I knew where this was going.

"Yes, it is, and I'm sure someone's really going to love it."

"But *you* love it, Annie, and it just seems such a shame—"

"Christina, drop it."

She was quiet for a moment, her body stiff beside me. Then she shook her head.

"No. Not this time. I've respected your wishes these last couple of months, sat by in silence while you struggled with all of this on your own, but I'm not going to let you run away, Annie."

"Run away? Who the fuck said anything about running away? I'm finally getting my shit together, Christina. I thought you'd be happy."

"Selling the house you love? Going to an art school in the Rockies when one of the top schools is an hour from here? That's not getting your shit together. You said it yourself, you're just leaving it all behind."

"I've wanted to go to this school since I was a kid, and this house is a reminder of everything in my life, including my mom."

"Exactly, Annie. You've wanted to run away from your mom since you were a kid. Do you think that's going to make the pain go away? You can't just erase everything that's happened to you like that."

"Are you fucking kidding me? You think I'm trying to forget what happened to me?"

"Yeah, I think you are, but you can't. You think about it every day, don't you? And it kills me that you don't trust me enough to tell me about it. That you don't think I can handle it."

"This isn't about *you*, this is about me. *I* can't handle it. I can barely talk about it with my shrink. And to say it *out loud* to someone who knows me, to say what he did, what *I* did . . . to see in your eyes . . ."

"Are you ashamed? Is that it? This wasn't your fault, Annie."

"It is, don't you see? No, you wouldn't, you couldn't. Because you'd never let this happen to you."

"*That's* what you think? Jesus, Annie, you survived a year with a madman, you had to *kill* him to escape, and I can't even leave my marriage."

"Your marriage? What's wrong with your marriage?"

"Drew and I . . . it's not good. We're talking divorce."

"Oh, shit, you never said . . ."

"You wanted it light, remember? Not much light about a marriage falling apart." She shrugged. "We'd been having problems before you were taken, but in the last year it's gotten worse."

"Because of me?"

"Partly. I was just so consumed with trying to find you, but even before that . . . You know this business doesn't leave time for much else. I thought the new place might help, but . . ." She shrugged her shoulders again.

They'd bought a house a month before I was taken, and all she talked about was the new furniture they were shopping for together. I assumed they were doing great.

"So much has changed, Annie. After you disappeared I had nightmares every night for almost a month. I can't do any open houses. Last week a strange guy called to see a vacant home, and I referred him to a male Realtor.

"For a whole year everything was about trying to find you, then finally Drew talks me into taking that cruise and I wasn't here for you when you were in the hospital. Now that you're home, I still don't have you back—I miss you. And I can't avoid dealing with my marriage anymore. Drew wants to go to counseling, and I don't know what the *fuck* I want to do. . . ."

She started crying. I stared at the grass and blinked back my own tears.

"This *thing*, this *terrible* thing, didn't just happen to you. It happened to *everyone* who cared about you, but it didn't just stop there, it happened to the whole town—even women across the country. Lots of people's lives have been changed, not just yours."

I began counting blades of grass.

"*None* of this is your fault. I just wanted you to know you're not alone, other people are hurting too. That's why I understand why you want to run away, I want to run away myself, but you have to stand and face things. I love you, Annie, like a sister, but ever since I've known you, as much as you've let me in, you've kept me out. And now you're about to make that final cut altogether. You're giving up. Like he did. . . ."

"He who?"

"The guy."

"Holy shit, Christina, please tell me you aren't comparing me to that asshole."

"But it was all too much for him, right? Living among people? So he ran away—"

"I'm not *running away*, I'm moving on and building myself a new life. Don't *ever* compare that to what he did. This conversation is over."

She stared at me.

"In fact, I think you should leave."

"See? There you go, running away. I'm making you *feel* something, and you can't stand it, can't face it, so the only thing you can do is push me away."

I got up, walked into the house, and slammed the door behind me. A couple of minutes later I heard her car leave.

Gary called later that night to tell me they found the loan shark and are building a case against him. He also told me Mom's had a constant round of visitors and is giving interviews to just about anyone who asks.

"No surprise there," I said. "I've got one for you, though." I told him how I was finally going to pursue my dream.

"Good for you, Annie! Sounds like you're on the right track."

Glad he didn't see it Christina's way, I said, "I'm getting there. What about you?"

"Been doing some thinking myself. One of the guys who trained me is starting a consulting company and wants me as a partner. I could live anywhere, travel, give speeches, take time off whenever I need it."

"I thought you liked your job."

"Me too, but after we wrapped up your case, I started wondering. . . . And then with the divorce . . . I don't know, just seems like a good time to make some changes."

I laughed. "Yeah, I know exactly what you mean. I still have your coat, you know."

"I know. I'm in no rush. I just bought a new Yukon Denali—"

"Wow, you weren't kidding about making changes. Aren't guys who go through midlife crises supposed to buy sports cars?"

"Hey, once I decide on something, I don't mess around, but what I was getting to, smart-ass, is that I'm thinking about taking it for a road trip one of these weekends. If I make it up your way, or even when you're back here for the trial, I'd like to buy you a coffee or lunch or something?"

"I'm going to have a lot going on with school and all."

"Like I said, I'm in no rush."

"You bringing the peanut butter?"

"You know, I just might." He chuckled.

"Guess I could lay my hands on a couple of spoons."

The next morning I got up early and took a drive out to the school. Man, did it feel good to get away from this town, even if it was just for a couple of days. The Rockies are an amazing sight this time of year, and seeing those huge peaks stretching to the sky almost had me forgetting my fight with Christina. My window was rolled down the whole way so the clean pure scent of warm pine needles could fill my car. Emma was in the back with her head out the window—whenever she wasn't trying to lick my neck. Driving slowly up to the school, then seeing this beautiful Tudor-style building in front of me with the Rockies in the background, made me feel giddy. Things would be different there.

After I parked my car, Emma and I walked around the campus. As I strolled by a couple of girls sitting on the lawn sketching, one glanced up and we smiled at each other. I'd forgotten how nice it was to get a smile from a stranger. But then her glance turned to a stare and I knew she recognized me. I turned away just as she nudged her friend beside her. I put Emma back in the car and looked for the registration office.

I'm too late to apply for the September semester, so I filled out the application for January. I didn't have a portfolio with me but I'd thought to bring my sketch pad and I showed it to the guidance counselor. He said I shouldn't have a problem getting in and suggested which pieces to submit. I was disappointed I have to wait, but the counselor guy said I could take some evening classes on campus to prep myself.

On the way home I mentally made plans for the upcoming move, but as I neared Clayton Falls Christina's words, *You're running away*, haunted me. I still couldn't believe she had the nerve to say that. What the hell did she know? And telling me I wasn't alone? Of course I was alone. My daughter was dead, my dad was dead, my sister was dead, and my mother might as well be. Who the hell was Christina to judge me for anything I did?

You're running away.

Hours later I parked in Christina's driveway, stormed up to her door, and rapped hard.

"Annie!"

"Is Drew here?"

"No, he's staying at a friend's. What's going on?"

"Look, I appreciate you're going through a rough time, Christina, but that doesn't give you the bloody right to control my life. It's my life, *mine*. Not yours."

"Okay, Annie, I just—"

"Why can't you *just* leave me alone? You don't have a clue what I went through."

"No, I don't. Because you won't tell me."

"How could you say those things to me? My mother had me *abducted*, Christina."

"Yes, she did."

"She lied to me."

"She lied to everyone."

"She left me up there. Alone."

"Completely alone."

"My mother did it to me."

"Your *mother*, Annie."

"And now she's going to jail. I have no one left. No one."

"You have me."

And then I finally broke.

Christina didn't hold me while I cried. She sat beside me on the floor, shoulder to shoulder, as I sobbed out grievances against my mother. Every unjust action that had been committed on me by her since I was a child, every broken dream and unfulfilled wish. And after I got one out, Christina would nod and say, *Yes, she did that to you. And it was wrong. You were wronged.*

Eventually my sobs turned to the occasional sniffle, and an odd kind of calm settled over me.

Christina said, "Why don't you get Emma out of the car and I'll make us some tea."

We changed into pajamas—Christina lent me a pair of hers. "Silk," she said with a smile, earning an "Of course" and a shaky smile back. Then, with a full pot of tea in front of us, we sat at the kitchen table. I took a deep breath.

"My baby? Her name was Hope."

ACKNOWLEDGMENTS

Wow, do I ever owe a lot of people a debt of gratitude for their help with this novel! It's impossible for me to list them in order of importance as all of these wonderful people were essential to my journey, so I'm just going to start at the beginning—where all good stories start.

My aunt, Dorothy Hartshorne, because she read every draft, argued psychology with me, and always encouraged me to keep going. She also promises not to sell my first draft on eBay! My beta readers, Lori Hall, Tracy Taylor, Beth Helms, and Clare Henderson, who all took time out of their busy lives to read my book and share their thoughts. My amazing mentor, Renni Browne, for her astute insights and unwavering belief in this book. Peter Gelfan and Shannon Roberts also provided valuable feedback that helped me take *Still Missing* to the next level.

For sharing their professional knowledge, I'm grateful to Constable B. D. McPhail, Constable H. Carlson, Staff

Sergeant J. D. MacNeill, Constable J. Moffat, Dr. E. Weisenberger, Peter Gallacher, and Stephanie Witzaney. Any mistakes and embellishments are entirely my fault—I tend to get a little carried away while in the artistic throes!

Many thanks go out to my fantastic agent, Mel Berger, for answering all my questions with great patience and wisdom— and boy, do I have a lot of questions! An enormous thank-you to my wonderful editor, Jen Enderlin, who loved my book enough to take a chance on it, then worked with me to take it over the finish line. My gratitude to the rest of the team at St. Martin's Press who made this a great experience for me: Sally Richardson, George Witte, Matthew Shear, Matthew Baldacci, John Murphy, Dori Weintraub, Ann Day, Lisa Senz, Sarah Goldstein, Sara Goodman, Elizabeth Catalano, Nancy Trypuc, Kim Ludlam, Anne Marie Tallberg, the entire Broadway sales force, and the entire Fifth Avenue sales force. Last but not least, Tom Best, Lisa Mior, and all the great people at H. B. Fenn.

I'm also deeply grateful to Don Taylor and Lisa Gardner for their help in spreading the word.

On a personal front, I'd like to thank all the friends and family who believed in me—even when I was threatening to burn my manuscript. All my love to my husband, Connel, who brings food to my desk, hides the chocolate where I can still find it, and always makes me feel like I'm the luckiest woman in the world.

Finally, although Vancouver Island is a real place, all the towns on the island in the book, including Clayton Falls, are purely fictional.

1. How would you describe Annie's character...especially those qualities that enable her to survive her ordeal at the hands of The Freak? How well might you have fared?

2. At some point during captivity, Annie begins to almost like The Freak. She goes to far as to admit that "sometimes he's kinda sweet." Although identifying with a captor is a known phenomenon—referred to as the "Stockholm Syndrome" in psychiatric parlance—how do those feelings develop in Annie?

3. Are the early parts of the novel, the sex scenes, too lurid for your taste—do you consider them sensational? Or are they an integral part of the plot, necessary for us to grasp Annie's tormented state?

4. Is "The Freak" a good name for Annie's abductor? What would you have called him? Describe him.

5. Chevy Stevens has written her book as a flashback, the present peering back into the past. We know at the outset, therefore, that Annie escapes her ordeal. Why might the author have structured her book in such a way?

6. David-The-Freak tells Annie that she is perfectly safe with him. There's a degree of ironic truth in his statement. How so? (Consider what happens when she escapes to freedom.)

7. Describe what Annie finds once she returns home—starting with her mother and the accident that took her father's and siblings' lives. Then there's the old boyfriend, Luke, as well as her best friend.

8. What prompts Annie to realize that her captivity was intentionally set up by someone in her old life?

9. What is the significance of the title, *Still Missing*?

10. What was the most satisfying aspect of the book? Is there anything that you wish had turned out differently? Did you guess any of the plot twists?

*A
Reading
Group
Guide*

St. Martin's
Griffin

Turn the page for a sneak peek at
Chevy Stevens's new novel

NEVER KNOWING

Available July 2011

SESSION ONE

I thought I could handle it, Nadine. After all those years of seeing you, all those times I talked about whether I should look for my birth mother, I finally did it. I took that step. You were a part of it—I wanted to show you what an impact you had on my life, how much I've grown, how stable I am now, how balanced. That's what you always told me, "Balance is the key." But I forgot the other thing you used to say: "Slowly, Sara."

I've missed this, being here. Remember how uncomfortable I was when I first started seeing you? Especially when I told you why I needed help. But you were down-to-earth and funny—not at all how I imagined a psychiatrist would be. This office was so bright and pretty, that no matter what I was worried about, as soon as I walked in here, I felt better. Some days, especially in the beginning, I didn't want to leave.

You told me once that when you didn't hear from me you knew things were going well, that when I stopped coming altogether you'd know you did your job. And you did. The last couple of years have been the happiest of my life. That's why I thought it was the right time. I thought I could withstand anything that came my way. I was solid, grounded. *Nothing* could send me back to the nervous wreck I was when I first met you.

Then she lied to me—my birth mother—when I finally forced her to talk to me. She lied about my real father. It felt like when Ally used to kick my ribs when I was pregnant with her—a sudden blow from the inside that left me breathless. But it was my birth mother's fear that got me the most. She was *afraid* of me. I'm sure of it. What I don't know is why.

It started about six weeks ago, around the end of December, with an online article. I was up stupidly early this one Sunday—no need for a rooster when you have a six-year-old—and while I inhaled my first coffee I answered e-mails. I get requests to restore furniture from all over the island now. That morning I was trying to research a desk from the 1920s, when I wasn't laughing at Ally. She was supposed to be watching cartoons downstairs, but I could hear her scolding Moose, our brindle French bulldog, for molesting her stuffed rabbit. Suffice it to say, Moose has a weaning issue. No tail's safe.

Then somehow or another I got this pop-up advertising Viagra, which I finally got closed, only to accidentally click on this other link and find myself staring at a headline:

Adoption: The Other Side of the Story

I scrolled through letters people had sent in response to a *Globe and Mail* piece, read stories of birth parents who've been trying to find their children for years, birth parents who didn't want to be found. Adopted children growing up feeling they never belonged. Tragic tales of doors slammed in faces. Joyful stories of mothers and daughters, brothers and sisters reuniting and living happily ever after.

My head started to pound. What if I found my mother? Would we instantly connect? What if she wanted nothing to do with me? What if I found out she was dead? What if I had siblings who never knew about me?

I didn't realize Evan was up until he kissed the back of my neck and made a grunting noise—a sound we picked up from Moose and now use to signal everything from *I'm pissed off* to *You're hot!*

I closed down the screen and spun my chair around. Evan raised his eyebrows and smiled.

"Talking to your online boyfriend again?"

I smiled back. "Which one?"

Evan clutched at his chest, collapsed into his office chair, and sighed.

"Sure hope he has lots of clothes."

I laughed. I was forever raiding Evan's shirts, especially if he had to stay with a group at his wilderness lodge in Tofino— three hours from our house in Nanaimo and right smack on the west coast of Vancouver Island. Those weeks I often wore his shirts around the clock. I'd get caught up working on a new piece of furniture, and by the time he was home the shirt would be covered in stains and I'd be exchanging all sorts of favors for his forgiveness.

"Sorry to break it to you, honey, but you're the only man for me—no one else would put up with my craziness." I rested my foot on his lap. With his sable hair spiked in all directions and his usual outfit of cargo pants and polo shirt, he looked like a college student. A lot of people don't realize Evan actually owns the lodge.

He smiled. "Oh, I'm sure there's a doctor somewhere with a straitjacket who'd think you're cute."

I pretended to kick at him, then said, "I was reading an article," as I started to massage the throbbing pain on the left side of my head.

"Getting a migraine, baby?"

I dropped my hand down to my lap. "Just a little one, it'll go away."

He gave me a look.

"Okay, I forgot my pill yesterday." After years of trying various medications I was now on beta blockers and my migraines were finally under control. The trick was remembering to take them.

He shook his head. "So what was the article about?"

"Ontario's opening up their adoption records, and . . ." I groaned as Evan worked a pressure point on my foot. "There were all these letters from people who were adopted or who gave up their children." Downstairs, Ally's giggle rang out.

"Thinking about finding your birth mother?"

"Not exactly, it was just interesting." But I *was* thinking about finding her. I just wasn't sure if I was ready. I've always known I was adopted, but I didn't realize that meant I was different until Mom sat me down and told me they were having a baby. I was four at the time. As Mom grew bigger and Dad prouder, I started worrying they were going to give me back. I didn't know just how different I was until I saw the way my father looked at Lauren when they brought her home, then the way he looked at me when I asked to hold her. They had Melanie two years later. He didn't let me hold her either.

Evan, willing to drop things long before me, nodded.

"What time do you want to leave for brunch?"

"A quarter past never." I sighed. "Thank God Lauren and Greg are coming, because Melanie's bringing *Kyle*."

"Brave of her." As much as my father loves Evan—they'd probably spend the entire brunch planning their next fishing trip—he despises Kyle. I can't say I blame him. Kyle's a wannabe rock star, but as far as I'm concerned the only thing he's playing is my sister. Dad always hated our boyfriends, though. I'm still shocked he likes Evan. All it took was one trip to the lodge and he was talking about him like he was the son he never had. He's still bragging about the salmon they caught.

"It's like she thinks if they're around each other more Dad will see all his good qualities." I snorted.

"Be nice, Melanie loves him."

I gave a mock shudder. "Last week she told me I better start working on my tan if I didn't want to be the same color as my dress. Our wedding's nine months away!"

"She's just jealous—you can't take it personally."

"It sure feels personal."

Ally came barreling into the room with Moose in fast pursuit and threw herself into my arms.

"Mommy, Moose ate all my cereal!"

"Did you leave the bowl on the floor again, silly?"

She giggled against my neck and I inhaled her fresh scent as her hair tickled my nose. With her dark coloring and compact body, Ally looks more like Evan than me even though he's not her biological father, but she has my green eyes—cat's eyes, Evan calls them. And she got my curls, though at thirty-three mine have relaxed while Ally's are still tight ringlets.

Evan stood up and clapped his hands.

"Okay, family, time to get dressed."

A week later, just after New Year's, Evan headed back to his lodge for a few days. I'd read a few more adoption stories online, and the night before he left I told him I was considering looking for my birth mother while he was gone.

"Are you sure it's a good idea right now? You have so much going on with the wedding."

"But that's part of it—we're getting married and for all I know I was dropped here from outer space."

"You know, that might explain a few things. . . ."

"Ha, ha, very funny."

He smiled, then said, "Seriously, Sara, how are you going to feel if you can't find her? Or if she doesn't want to see you?"

How was I going to feel? I pushed the thought to the side and shrugged.

"I'll just have to accept it. Things don't get to me like they used to. But I really feel like I need to do this—especially if we're going to have kids." The entire time I was pregnant with Ally I was afraid of what I might be passing on to her. Thankfully she's healthy, but whenever Evan and I talk about having a child the fear starts up again.

I said, "I'm more worried about upsetting Mom and Dad."

"You don't have to tell them—it's your life. But I still don't think it's the best timing."

Maybe he was right. It was stressful enough trying to take care of Ally and run my business, let alone plan a wedding.

"I'll think about putting it off, okay?"

Evan smiled. "Riiight. I know you, baby—once your mind is made up you're full speed ahead."

I laughed. "I promise."

I did think about waiting, especially when I imagined my mom's face if she found out. Mom used to say being adopted meant I was special because they chose me. When I was twelve Melanie gave me her version. She said our parents adopted me because Mom couldn't have babies, but they didn't need me now. Mom found me in my room packing my clothes. When I told her I was going to find my "real" parents she started crying, then she said, "Your birth parents couldn't take care of you properly, but they wanted you to have the best home possible. So now we take care of you and we love you very much." I never forgot the hurt in her eyes, or how thin her body felt as she hugged me.

The next time I seriously thought about looking for my birth parents was when I graduated, then when I found out I was pregnant, and then seven months later when I held Ally for the first time. But I'd put myself in Mom's shoes and imagine what it would feel like if my child wanted to find her birth mother, how hurt and scared I'd be, and I could never go through with it. I might not have this time, either, if Dad hadn't phoned to ask Evan to go fishing.

"Sorry, Dad, he just left yesterday. Maybe you can take Greg?"

"Greg talks too much." I felt bad for Lauren's husband. Where Dad despised Kyle, he had no use for Greg. I'd seen him walk away when Greg was in midsentence.

"Are you guys going to be home for a while? I was just going to get Ally from school and come by for a visit."

"Not today. Your mom's trying to rest."

"Is her Crohn's flaring up again?"

"She's just tired."

"Okay, no problem. If you need help with anything, let me know."

Throughout our lives Mom's health had been up and down. For weeks she'd be doing fine, painting our rooms, sewing curtains, baking up a storm. Even Dad was almost happy during those times. I remember him lifting me onto his shoulders once, the view as heady as the rare attention. But Mom would always end up doing too much and within days she was sick again. She'd fade before our eyes as her body refused to hang on to any nutrients, even baby food sending her rushing for the bathroom.

When she was going through a bad spell Dad would come home and ask what I'd been doing all day, like he was trying to find something, or someone, to be pissed at. When I was nine he found me in front of the TV while Mom was sleeping. He dragged me to the kitchen by my wrist and pointed to the stack of dishes, calling me a lazy, ungrateful child. The next day it was the pile of laundry that set him off, and the next, Melanie's toys in the driveway. His big workingman's body would loom over me and his voice would vibrate with anger, but he never yelled, never did anything Mom could see or hear. He'd take me out to the garage and list my shortcomings while I stared at his feet, terrified he was going to say he didn't want me anymore. Then he'd barely speak to me for a week.

I started doing the household chores before Mom could get to them, staying home when my sisters were out with friends, cooking dinners that never got my father's approval but at least didn't earn his silence. I would do anything to avoid silence, anything to keep Mom from getting sick again. If she was healthy, I was safe.

When I phoned Lauren that night she told me she and the boys had just gotten home from dinner with our parents. Dad had invited them.

"So it was just my kid who wasn't allowed over."

"I'm sure it wasn't like that. Ally just has so much energy, and—"

"What does *that* mean?"

"It doesn't mean anything, she's adorable. But Dad probably thought three kids were too much." I knew Lauren was just trying to make me feel better before I went on a rant against Dad, which she hates, but it drives me nuts that she can never see how differently Dad treats me, or at least never acknowledges it. After we hung up I almost called Mom to check on her, but then I thought about Dad telling me to stay home, like a stray dog who's only allowed to sleep on the porch because she might mess in the house. I put the phone back on the charger.

The next day I filled out the form at Vital Statistics, paid my $50, and started waiting. I'd like to say patiently, but I practically tackled the mailman after the first week. A month later my Original Birth Registration, or OBR, as the woman at Vital Statistics called it, arrived in the mail. I stared at the envelope and realized my hand was shaking. Evan was at his lodge again and I wished he could be there when I opened it, but that was another *week*. Ally was at school and the house was quiet. I took a deep breath and ripped open the envelope.

My real mother's name was Julia Laroche and I was born in Victoria, BC. My father was listed as unknown. I read the OBR and the adoption certificate over and over, looking for answers, but I just kept hearing one question: *Why did you give me away?*

The next morning I woke early and went online while Ally was still sleeping. The first thing I checked was the Adoption Reunion Registry, but when I realized it could take another month to get an answer, I decided to look on my own first. After searching Web sites for twenty minutes, I found three Julia Laroches in

Quebec and four down in the States who seemed around the right age. Only two lived on the island, but when I saw they were both in Victoria my stomach flipped. Could she still be there after all this time? I quickly clicked on the first link, and let my breath out when I realized she was too young, judging by her article on a new mom's forum. The second link took me to a Web site for a real estate agent in Victoria. She had auburn hair like me and looked about the right age. I studied her face with a mixture of excitement and fear. Had I found my birth mother?

After I drove Ally to school, I sat at my desk and circled the phone number I'd jotted on a piece of paper. *I'll call in one minute. After another cup of coffee. After I read the paper. After I paint every toenail a different color.* Finally I forced myself to pick up the phone.

Brrring.

It might not even be her.

Brrring.

I should just hang up. This was a bad way to—

"Julia Laroche speaking."

I opened my mouth, but nothing came out.

"Hello?" she said.

"Hi, I'm calling . . . I'm calling because . . ." *Because I stupidly thought if I said something brilliant, you'd instantly regret giving me up, but now I can't even remember my own name.*

Her voice was impatient. "Are you looking to buy or sell a home?"

"No, I'm—" I took a deep breath and said it in a rush. "I might be your daughter."

"Is this some kind of joke? Who are you?"

"My name is Sara Gallagher. I was born in Victoria and given up for adoption. You have auburn hair and you're about the right age, so I thought—"

"Honey, there's no way you're my daughter. I can't have children."

My face burned. "God, I'm sorry. I just thought . . . well, I hoped."

The voice softened. "It's okay. Good luck with your search." I was about to hang up when she said, "There's a Julia Laroche who works at the university. I get calls for her sometimes."

"Thanks, I appreciate that."

My face was still hot as I dropped the phone onto my desk and headed out to my shop. I got most of my paintbrushes cleaned, then sat and stared at the wall, thinking about what the real estate woman had said. A few minutes later I was back at my computer. After a quick search the other Julia's name came up under a list of professors at the University of Victoria. She taught art history—was that where I got my love of all things old? I shook my head. Why was I letting myself get excited? It was just a name. I took a deep breath and called the university, surprised when they put me straight through to Julia Laroche's extension.

She answered, and this time I had my speech ready. "Hi, my name is Sara Gallagher and I'm trying to find my birth mother. Did you give a child up for adoption thirty-three years ago?"

A sharp intake of breath. Then silence.

"Hello?"

"Don't call here again." She hung up.

I cried. For hours. Which kicked off a migraine so bad Lauren had to take Ally and Moose for me. Thankfully, Lauren's two boys are around Ally's age and Ally loves going over there. I hated being away from my daughter for even one night, but all I could do was lie in a dark room with a cold compress on my head and wait for it to pass. Evan phoned and I told him what had happened, speaking slowly because of the pain. By the next afternoon I'd stopped seeing auras around everything, so Ally and Moose came home. Evan phoned again that night.

"Feeling better, baby?"

"The migraine's gone—it's my own stupid fault for forgetting to take my pill again. Now I'm behind on that desk and I wanted to call some photographers this week and—"

"Sara, you don't have to do everything right away. Leave the photographers for when I get back."

"It's fine, I'll take care of it." I admired Evan's laid-back personality in many ways, but in the two years we've been together I've learned "we can do it later" usually translates into me rushing around like a crazy woman to get something done at the last minute.

I said, "I've been thinking about what happened with my birth mother. . . ."

"Yeah?"

"I was wondering about writing her a letter. Her address is unlisted, but I can just leave it at the university."

Evan was silent for a moment. "Sara . . . I'm not sure that's a good idea."

"So she doesn't want to get to know me, fine, but I think the least she could do is give me my medical history. What about Ally? Doesn't she have a right to know? There could be health issues, like . . . like high blood pressure, or diabetes, or *cancer*—"

"Baby." Evan's voice was calm but firm. "Take it easy. Why are you letting her get to you like this?"

"I'm not like you, okay? I can't just brush things off."

"Listen, cranky-pants, I'm on your side here."

I was silent, my eyes closed, trying to breathe, reminding myself it wasn't Evan I was angry at.

"Sara, do what you have to do. You know I'll support you no matter what. But I think you should just leave it alone."

As I made the hour-and-a-half trip down-island the next day I felt calm and centered, confident I was doing the right thing. There's something about the island highway that always soothes me: the quaint towns and valleys, the farmland, the glimpses of ocean and coastal mountain ranges. When I got closer to Victoria and drove through the old-growth forest at Goldstream Park, I thought about the time Dad had taken us there to watch the salmon spawning in the river. Lauren was terrified of all the seagulls feasting on the dead salmon. I hated the scent of death in the air, how it clung to your clothes and nostrils. Hated how Dad explained everything to my sisters but ignored my questions—ignored me.

Evan and I talked about opening a second whale-watching business in Victoria one day—Ally loves the museum and the street performers in the inner harbor, I love all the old buildings. But for now Nanaimo suits us. Even though it's the second largest city on the island, it still has that small-town feel. You can be walking on the seawall in the harbor, shopping in the old city quarter, or hiking up a mountain with an amazing view of the gulf islands all on the same day. Whenever we want to get away, we just take the ferry to the mainland or drive down to Victoria to do some shopping. But if things didn't go well in Victoria this trip, it was going to be a long drive home.

My plan was to drop off the letter requesting information at Julia's office. But when the woman at the front desk told me Professor Laroche was teaching a class in the next building, I had to see what she looked like. She wouldn't even know I was there. Then I'd leave the letter at the front desk.

I slowly opened the door to the auditorium-style classroom and crept in with my face turned away from the podium. I found a seat in the back, scrunched down—feeling like a stalker—and took a look at my mother.

"As you can see, architecture of the Islamic world varied . . ."

In my daydreams she was always an older version of me, but where my hair is auburn, falling in unruly waves down my back, her black hair was cut in a sleek bob. I couldn't see her eye color, but her face was round, with delicate bone structure. My cheekbones are high and my features Nordic. The lines of her black wrap dress revealed a slight boyish frame and small wrists. My build is athletic. She was probably a couple of inches over five feet and I'm almost five-nine. The way she pointed out images on the projector's screen was elegant and unhurried. I talk with my hands so much I'm always knocking something over. If her reaction on the phone wasn't still haunting me I'd think I had the wrong woman.

As I half listened to her lecture, I fantasized about what my childhood might've been like with her as my mother. We'd have discussed art at dinner, which we'd eat off beautiful plates and sometimes light the candles in silver candlesticks. On summer holidays we'd have explored museums in foreign countries and had deep intellectual talks over cappuccinos in Italian cafés. On weekends we'd have browsed bookstores together—

A wave of guilt swamped me. *I have a mother.* I thought of the sweet woman who raised me, the woman who made cabbage-leaf compresses for my headaches even when she wasn't feeling well herself, the woman who didn't know I'd found my birth mother.

After the class ended I walked down to the stairs toward the side door. As I passed near Julia she smiled, but with a questioning look, like she was trying to place me. When a student stopped to ask her something, I bolted for the door. At the last second, I glanced over my shoulder. Her eyes were brown.

I went straight back to my car. I was still sitting there, my heart going nuts inside my chest, when I saw her leave the building. She walked toward the faculty parking lot. I inched my car in that direction and watched her get into a white classic Jaguar. When she pulled out, I followed.

Stop. Think about what you're doing. Pull over.

Like that was going to happen.

As we drove down Dallas Road, one of the more upscale areas in Victoria along the waterfront, I kept back. After about ten minutes Julia turned into the circular driveway of a large Tudor house on the ocean. I pulled over and got out a map. She parked in front of the marble steps, followed a path around the corner of the house, then disappeared through a side door.

She didn't knock. She lived there.

So what did I do now? Drive off and forget about the whole thing? Drop the letter in her mailbox at the end of the driveway and risk someone else finding it? Give it to her in person?

But once I reached the big mahogany front door I stood there like an idiot, frozen, torn between tucking the letter into the door and just sprinting back down the driveway. I didn't knock, I didn't ring the doorbell, but the door *opened.* I was face-to-face with my mother. And she didn't look happy to see me.

"Hello?"

My face was burning.

"Hi . . . I . . . I saw your class."

Her eyes narrowed. She looked at the envelope clutched in my hand.

"I wrote you a letter." My voice sounded breathless. "I wanted to ask you some things—we talked the other day. . . ."

She stared at me.

"I'm your daughter."

Her eyes widened. "You have to leave." She moved to shut the door. I put my foot on the jamb.

"*Wait*. I don't want to upset you—I just have some questions, it's for my daughter." I dug into my wallet and pulled out a photo. "Her name's Ally—she's only six."

Julia wouldn't look at the photo. When she spoke her voice was high, strained.

"It's not a good time. I can't—I just *can't*."

"Five minutes. That's all I need, then I'll leave you alone."

She looked over her shoulder at a phone on a hall table.

"Please. I promise I won't come back."

She led me into a side room with a mahogany desk and floor-to-ceiling bookshelves. Moved a cat off an antique brown leather high-backed chair.

I sat down and tried to smile. "Himalayans are beautiful." She didn't smile back. She perched on the edge of her seat. Hands gripping each other in her lap, knuckles white.

I said, "This chair is gorgeous—I refinish furniture for a living, but this is pristine. I love antiques. Anything vintage, really, cars, clothes . . ." My hand brushed the fitted black velvet jacket I'd paired with jeans.

She stared at the floor. Her hands started to shake.

I took a deep breath and went for it.

"I just want to know why you gave me away. I'm not angry, I have a good life. I just . . . I just want to know. I *need* to know."

"I was young." Now her voice was reedy, flat. "It was an accident. I didn't want children."

"Why did you have me, then?"

"I was Catholic." Was?

"What about your family, are they—"

"My parents died in an accident—*after* you were born." The last part came out in a rush. I waited for her to say more. The cat brushed against her legs, she didn't touch it. I noticed a pulse beating fast at the base of her throat.

"I'm very sorry. Was the accident on the island?"

"We—they—lived in Williams Lake." Her face flushed.

"Your name, Laroche. What does that mean? It's French, right? Do you know from what part of—"

"I've never looked it up."

"My father?"

"It was at a party and I don't remember anything. I don't know where he is now."

I stared at this elegant woman. Not one thing about her fit with a drunken one-night stand. She was lying. I was sure of it. I willed her to meet my eyes. She stared at the cat. I had an insane urge to pick it up and throw it at her.

"Was he tall? Do I look like him, or—"

She stood up. "I told you I don't remember. I think you'd better go."

"But—" A door slammed at the back of the house.

Julia's hand flew up to cover her mouth. An older woman with curly blond hair and a pink scarf draped around her thin shoulders came around the corner.

"Julia! I'm glad you're home, we should—" She stopped when she saw me and her face broke into a smile. "Oh, hello, I didn't realize Julia had a student over."

I stood up and held out a hand. "I'm Sara. Professor Laroche was kind enough to go over my paper with me, but I should be off."

She took my hand. "Katharine. I'm Julia's . . ." Her voice trailed off as she searched Julia's face.

I jumped into the awkward silence. "It was nice to meet you."

I turned to Julia. "Thanks again for your help." She managed a smile and a nod.

At my car I glanced over my shoulder. They were still standing in the open doorway. Katharine smiled and waved, but Julia just stared at me.

So you understand why I had to talk to you. I feel like I'm standing on ice and it's cracking all around me, but I don't know which way to move. Do I try to find out why my birth mother lied or heed Evan's advice to just leave it alone? I know you're going to tell me I'm the only one who can make that decision, but I need your help.

I keep thinking about Moose. When he was a puppy we left him in the laundry room one cold Saturday when we went out, because he wasn't housebroken—little guy piddled so much Ally tried to put her doll's diapers on him. We had this beautiful bright-colored rope rug we'd brought back from a trip to Saltspring Island, and he must've started nibbling one corner, then just kept pulling and pulling. By the time we got home the rug was destroyed. My life is like that beautiful colored rug—it took *years* to sew it together. Now I'm afraid if I keep pulling on this one corner it's all going to unravel.

But I'm not sure I can stop.